THE PROMISE OF HAPPINESS

Erin Kaye was born in 1966 in Larne, Co Antrim to a Polish-American father and an Anglo-Irish mother. She pursued a successful career in finance before becoming a writer. Her previous bestselling novels include *Mothers and Daughters, Choices, Second Chances, Closer to Home* and *My Husband's Lover*. She lives in North Berwick on the east coast of Scotland with her husband Mervyn, her two young sons and Murphy the dog.

By the same author

The Art of Friendship

ERIN KAYE

The Promise of Happiness

AVON

AVON

A division of HarperCollins*Publishers*
77–85 Fulham Palace Road,
London W6 8JB

www.harpercollins.co.uk

A Paperback original 2011
1

A catalogue record for this book is
available from the British Library

ISBN 978-1-84756-201-2

Set in Minion by Palimpsest Book Production Limited,
Falkirk, Stirlingshire

Printed and bound in Great Britain by
Clays Ltd, St Ives plc

Mixed Sources
Product group from well-managed
forests and other controlled sources
www.fsc.org Cert no. SW-COC-001806
© 1996 Forest Stewardship Council
FSC

FSC is a non-profit international organisation established
to promote the responsible management of the world's forests.
Products carrying the FSC label are independently certified
to assure consumers that they come from forests that are managed
to meet the social, economic and ecological needs
of present and future generations.

Find out more about HarperCollins and the environment at
www.harpercollins.co.uk/green

To Mary Clare, my eldest sister

Chapter One

'Nearly there, Oli!' said Louise McNeill brightly to her three-year-old son, Oliver James.

Somewhere in the bowels of the ferry the engine growled and a shudder ran through the ship. Louise put her hand on her belly and her stomach lurched – though not with nausea. She'd spent her youth sailing on these waters – in the sheltered safety of Ballyfergus Lough or, sometimes, venturing out into the choppy waters of the Irish Sea – and not once had she been seasick. And she wasn't pregnant. No, her nausea was caused by nerves. Louise took a deep breath, glanced at Oli and wondered – panicked suddenly – if she was doing the right thing by coming home.

Oli, restless, banged the fleshy pads of his palms against the sloping window, leaving smudges on it. 'Now, now,' said Louise, fretting that he might pick up germs from the glass. Instinctively, she reached out and caught one of his hands in her own. Oli's olive skin tone came from his father's side – it certainly hadn't been inherited from the pale, Celtic-skinned and fair-haired McNeills. She touched a dimple on the back of his hand with her thumb – he was losing his baby fat rapidly, moving on to another stage of development.

Oli was a constant source of fascination to Louise – every

new word was an achievement, every task accomplished a source of wonder. Each step along the long, slow road to independence seemed like a miracle. And it was a miracle – rather *he* was a miracle. Her baby. Hers alone. The child she had thought she would never have. Love and pride swelled in equal measure, threatening to choke her.

'Are we nearly there yet?' said Oli, in the high-pitched monotone common among children of his age. Louise found listening to other people's children grating, but never Oli. He let out a long sigh, having long ago lost interest in the view of the calm, glittering sea, pale blue sky and swooping gulls. Louise put her arm around his waist where he stood on the blue leatherette bench beside her. She pressed her face into the small of his back and inhaled, knowing that if they were ever separated she could recognise him by smell alone.

The boat swung slowly round on its axis and hot July sunshine flooded through the glass. She squinted as the land mass of East Antrim, and the town of Ballyfergus, came slowly into view.

The town was just as Louise had remembered it. The shoreline was dominated by the big working port with its hulking cranes and drab, pre-fabricated buildings. A docked P&O ferry discharged its cargo, an endless stream of lollipop-coloured container lorries, onto the shimmering black asphalt of the quay. Further inland, arcs of slate-roofed white houses, none more than two storeys high, inched up the hills like cake mixture on the side of a bowl. And beyond that the gentle rounded green hills.

'Look,' she said and pointed through the window. 'That's Ballyfergus. Where Nana and Papa live. That's where we're going to live too.' The idea of this, of bringing Oli home to his grandparents, to be amongst his own, filled her with pleasure. And the feeling of doing something right by her child momentarily displaced the gnawing doubt that she had failed him.

'Where? Where are we going to live?' persisted the child. His dark brows came together in a frown and he glared mistrustfully at the lush green hills overlooking Ballyfergus Lough, oblivious, it seemed, to the breathtaking beauty surrounding them.

'There,' said Louise pointing at the town, which had served as a port and gateway to the rest of the province for over one thousand years. She remembered that Oli had last visited when he was two and would not recall the trip. 'See those houses there. Not up on the hill. Down there.' She pointed at the sprawling cluster of grey and brown buildings on the flat plain. 'They look really tiny, don't they?'

Oli nodded.

'That's because we're so far away. We're going to live in a house down there.' She pointed roughly in the direction of the indoor swimming pool, a grey block of a building, which sat only metres from the shore.

'With Nana and Papa?'

'No, Oli,' said Louise and he plopped down suddenly onto his bottom. 'Just you and me. Like always,' she added, careful to deliver this news in a neutral tone and eradicate any hint of disappointment or anxiety from her voice. She brushed his straight brown fringe, so different from her fine fair hair, off his forehead. He swatted her hand away absent-mindedly.

'Why?' said Oli.

'Oh,' said Louise, not expecting this question, not here, not now. 'Well,' she said carefully and took a deep breath.

3

'Because your daddy doesn't live with us, does he? He lives in Scotland. But of course it might not always be just the two of us. One day Mummy might meet a nice man and . . .'

Suddenly, Oli slid onto the floor and disappeared under the table. Mischievous brown eyes, the same colour as his father's, stared up at her. 'But why can't we live with Nana and Papa?'

Louise put a hand over her heart and let out a silent sigh of relief. In her zeal to ensure Oli understood, she had yet again answered the question she *thought* Oli had asked, rather than the one he actually had. It was a fundamental pitfall she'd read about more than once in the library of parenting books that now lay in storage, boxed up in some Edinburgh warehouse.

'Come on out of there, Oli,' she said, pulling him gently out from under the table. 'You don't know what's on that floor.'

Louise extracted a bottle of antibacterial gel from her bag. 'We can't live with Nana and Papa because they haven't got enough room for us. Their house is very small.'

But Oli was now more interested in the gel than pursuing this topic of conversation. Louise held his hand by the wrist and squeezed a translucent green blob onto the centre of his palm. 'This'll kill all the nasty germs. Now, rub your hands together like this,' she said, squirting some of the gel onto her own palm and rubbing her hands briskly together.

Oli held his hand inches from his face, stared at the gel and said, 'It's got bubbles in it, Mummy.'

'Yes, I know, darling.'

'Why?'

'It just has.'

He extended his hand towards her face, his chubby fingers

spread like the fat arms of the starfish that Cameron, her former husband, had once fished out of Tayvallich Bay on the west coast of Scotland. Together they'd knelt on the pebbly beach and wondered at its pale lilac beauty, heads bent together like children. Oli smeared a blob of gel, wet and surprisingly cold, on Louise's nose. She blinked, surprised, and he let out a squeal of delight.

She laughed then, coming back to the moment, to her perfect boy, and he said, 'I love you, Mummy.'

She swallowed, fought back the tears of joy. 'I love you too, my sweet angel.' She beamed at him and added, 'Now, hurry up. It goes runny if you don't do it quickly.'

'Okay, Mummy.' Oli slapped his hands together, sending splatters across the Formica table. He let out a cry and looked up at her, slightly shocked-looking, for reassurance.

Louise smiled. 'That's it. Now rub them together,' she said and Oli complied.

She loved the unquestioning trust her son placed in her. She was the epicentre of his world, his everything. And he was hers – she craved his neediness and the fulfilment it gave her as a mother. And for the last three years – no, from the moment of his conception – he had been her obsession.

Her decision to relocate from Edinburgh to Ballyfergus had been taken entirely with Oli's welfare at the forefront of her mind. Though it was also true that, after many years in Edinburgh, she now primarily associated the city with disappointment and heartache. She had been glad to leave. Her only regret was leaving her best friend, Cindy, behind. But this, she told herself bravely, was a new chapter for her and Oli, though coming back to the town of her birth induced an odd feeling. It *was* a fresh start but it also felt like she was returning to an old, familiar life. A life she had carelessly left behind as an eighteen-year-old without so much as a backwards glance.

A voice over the tannoy told them to return to their car and Louise gathered up their possessions – colouring books and crayons, books, snacks, a copy of *Marie Claire* magazine (an optimistic purchase from the shop on the ferry) and her mobile phone. She stuffed them into the stylish, capacious patent leather bag that had become her constant companion since Oli's birth. Not that she cared much for fashion – not any more. She liked to look her best, of course, and she had not, like some other mums she knew, let herself 'go'.

Louise descended the first lethal flight down to the car deck, gripping Oli's hand like a vice. Twice he slipped on the steep metal steps and she hauled him back to his feet. Her left shoulder ached with the weight of the bag and her heartbeat accelerated, her brow beaded with sweat. Her stomach flipped with nerves and excitement. She squeezed Oli's hand even tighter. He glanced up at her.

'Watch where you're going, pet!' she said, as his foot slipped again and he almost landed on his bottom on the ribbed metal floor at the foot of the stairs. Doors led off from this landing to the top level car deck.

A portly middle-aged man, a member of the ship's crew, stood on the landing dressed in a short-sleeved pale blue shirt and navy polyester trousers with a perma-press crease down the front of each leg. 'Do you want a hand, love?' he said, in the hard-edged, down-to-earth accent of North-East Antrim, and stepped forward with one hand outstretched. 'If you carry the wee man, I'll help with your bag.'

'No, thanks. I'm fine,' bristled Louise automatically. She missed no opportunity to demonstrate to the world in general that she could cope alone. 'I can manage.'

The pleasant smile fell from the man's face. He said nothing more, stepped back and adopted his guard-like stance once again, hands behind his back, and nodded in a tight-lipped manner to the person behind Louise. Realising how rude she had sounded, Louise ducked her head and proceeded quickly to the top of the next flight of stairs, her face flaming with embarrassment.

She told herself she was tired and emotional. The drive across Scotland to the port of Cairnryan had taken the best part of four hours, including a stop for lunch. And she'd not slept well the night before, her sleep disturbed by dreams of Cameron. In the dream she was following him in a storm along a narrow cliff pathway on the southern side of the Firth of Forth – a path they had once walked together in happier times. He wore a bright red jacket, his dark hair plastered to his scalp by the driving rain, his face dripping with water. It was high tide and she could hear the ferocious crash of waves on the treacherous rocks below. She stopped and called out to him that it was too dangerous, that they should turn back. And then, right at that moment, without any warning at all, the coastal path crumbled and Cameron plunged over the edge of the cliff, lost to her forever.

They had been divorced for three years – she had not seen him in as long. Why was she still haunted by dreams of him? Perhaps it was understandable – after living with someone for fifteen years you couldn't expunge all the memories of your life together from your consciousness. And she didn't want to. For some of the happiest times of her life had been spent with Cameron. She had given up so much in leaving him. It had taken such courage. And such bravery to build the independent life she now enjoyed.

Why was she thinking of him now, on this day? Annoyed with herself, she tossed her head, shaking off thoughts of him like raindrops, and brought her analysis to bear on the present.

'There you go again,' she mumbled under her breath as she and Oli picked their way carefully down the next flight of narrow metal steps into the gloomy bowels of the great ship, 'pushing people away to prove your independence.' She hadn't always been like this – only since Oli. She wanted to run back up the steps and apologise to the man but it was too late. Instead she resolved to stop interpreting kindly offers of help as assaults on her independence.

'Not long now, honey!' she said, doing up Oli's seatbelt. She jumped into the driver's seat, clapped her hands together and rolled her shoulders in an attempt to ease some of the tension that had built up between her shoulder blades. She imagined her parents, and her older sister Joanne and her three children, all squeezed into the modest home on Churchill Road watching and waiting eagerly for their arrival. It was going to be all right, she told herself.

Once she'd negotiated the tricky ferry ramp, she set off along Coastguard Road, the old route into Ballyfergus, avoiding the harbour bypass. She passed landmarks as familiar as the back of her hands.

'Look,' she cried, slowing the car down to a crawl, and staring out the passenger window at a nineteen-sixties concrete block fronted by a big, unimaginative rectangle of dusty tarmac. 'That's where I went to school, Oli. That's where you'll go to school too when you're a big boy.' In the rear-view mirror she saw Oli straining for a better view, his eyes wide with curiosity.

A car behind tooted. She waved good-naturedly and accelerated away. 'And look, there's the fish and chip shop,' she said, as they passed a cluster of small businesses on Upper Cross Street. But on closer inspection she saw that the fish and chip shop was gone, replaced by a plumbing suppliers. 'Oh, it's not there any more. But look, there's the library. I used to go there every week with my mum, and we will too, Oli. Would you like that?' She kept up this bright trail of chatter, seeking out familiar, reassuring places and noticing changes too, changes that reminded her how Ballyfergus had moved on.

Then, at last, she turned into Churchill Road, where children played in the blazing sun just as she had done as a child. Her hands began to tremble and the perspiration on the palms of her hands made it difficult to grasp the steering wheel. She pulled up outside her parents' semi-detached house and took a deep breath to calm herself. She smiled to reassure Oli, who was looking at her with his thumb stuck in his mouth, then cut the engine. She stepped out of the car into the sunshine and a warm westerly breeze rolling off the Sallagh Braes, a ring of dramatic rounded cliffs overlooking Ballyfergus. Today the hills were framed by a cloudless cobalt sky, the brilliant shades of green softened by a heat haze rising from the black tarmac.

Louise tucked a stray strand of hair behind her ear and remembered the first time she'd brought Cameron home and they'd parked in the very same spot. He'd been driving then – he always did. He'd looked at the modest house and said, 'Is this it then?' and she'd felt herself blush, embarrassed for the first time by her humble origins.

Cameron had been to Watson's, a private school in Edinburgh and studied English Literature at Edinburgh

University. Although only a few years older than Louise he had lived in Paris for a year and spoke fluent French. He seemed so sophisticated and experienced. His worldliness contrasted with her sheltered, mundane upbringing. She realised she had so much to learn about everything and she was his willing pupil. The tone of their relationship was set from the outset. He was the leader, the decision maker – she was the follower, happily compliant. She allowed him to educate her, coach her, mould her. She had told him once that she would follow him to the ends of the earth and she'd meant it.

And here she was all these years later, back it seemed, to where she had started.

Joanne ran out of the house and Louise took a few steps towards her. They briefly embraced and cried, 'Look at you!' in unison.

Joanne gave an impression of girlishness despite her forty-five years with her tight-waisted, delicate frame and long wavy blonde locks. The illusion was further reinforced by a knee-length floral printed dress, flat ballerina pumps and a cropped cerise cotton cardigan.

Joanne's olive-green eyes gleamed with emotion. 'Welcome home!' she cried and they hugged again. Louise put her hand on Joanne's back and was surprised to feel a hard and bony frame under the thin layers of clothing. She realised now how much weight her sister had lost.

'It's good to be back,' she choked, her eyes filling up.

And then the neat, small figure of their mother appeared at the doorway to the house, her hand raised feebly in greeting. And behind her was their dad, with his hand on their mother's right shoulder. Quite unexpectedly, and uncharacteristically, Louise couldn't control her tears.

*   *   *

Later, after they'd eaten a lasagne made by Joanne, and Oli was happily watching TV in the little room at the back of the house with his cousins, the women – Louise, Joanne and their mother – sat in the lounge, around the coffee table, chatting. Louise's dad was in the kitchen with Frankie Cahoon, a neighbour from two doors down, drinking whiskey and talking about their days in the GEC factory. Louise looked down at the dainty china cup and saucer balanced precariously on her knee. It was her mother's best china – a wedding present from her parents – adorned with delicate red roses and rimmed in gold leaf. If only her cosmopolitan friends could see her now, thought Louise, with a deliciously wry sense of humour.

'What are you smiling at?' said Christine McNeill, pale blue eyes, the colour of washed denim, staring at her daughter from behind steel-rimmed glasses. At seventy-three, she had lost none of her perceptiveness. Her gnarled hands rested on the arms of an upright Parker Knoll chair.

'Oh, I was just thinking how the house hasn't changed at all,' said Louise, casting her gaze around the cluttered room. The big flowery paper pressed in on every side, so loud it almost screamed, and the nineteen-fifties walnut cabinet was stuffed to bursting with all manner of trinkets and old-fashioned ornaments.

Her mother followed her gaze and said, a little defensively, 'Well, I like it. I don't like all this modern design. Bare walls and hardly any furniture. I like a place to feel homely.' Her nod was like a full stop at the end of a sentence. 'Now, would you like some tea?' Without waiting for an answer she leant forward and gripped the handle of the china teapot with her right hand.

'Why don't you let me—' began Joanne.

'Ouch!' cried her mother and she let go of the pot

immediately. It wobbled uncertainly for a few moments. A little spurt of brown liquid slopped onto the pristine tray cloth and spread like a bloodstain.

'Did you burn yourself?' cried Louise, already out of her seat and by her mother's side.

'It's her arthritis,' said Joanne flatly.

'It's all right,' said Christine, and she held her hand protectively to her chest. 'It'll pass in a minute.'

Joanne sighed loudly. 'I wish you wouldn't do that. You know you can't lift heavy things.'

Louise sat down again and Joanne poured the tea.

'A teapot isn't heavy,' said Christine, glaring at the pot, her lips pressed together in a thin line.

'It's too heavy for you. You know that.' Joanne sounded cross and harsh. She passed round the milk.

'Joanne,' said Louise warningly and glared at her sister.

'What?' Joanne's eyes flashed defiantly. She set the milk jug down on the tray, avoiding eye contact.

'Don't . . .' Louise lowered her voice. 'Don't talk to Mum like that.'

'She's only got herself to blame.'

'What? For her arthritis?'

'No, of course not. But she's always doing things the doctor's told her she mustn't.'

Their mother blinked and said, as though she'd not heard this last exchange, 'It's so frustrating not being able to do all the things I used to take for granted.' She looked at her hand, the thumb joint red and swollen, and suddenly Louise was struck by how much her mother had aged since she'd last seen her. Now that she looked more closely she noticed how grey her mother's hair had become and how lined her face was. Sitting perched on the chair she seemed shrunken somehow, as though she was slowly disappearing.

'I know, Mum,' said Joanne, her voice softening. 'But it's best not to try. You only end up hurting yourself.'

Louise swallowed the shock like a dry, hard crust. Up until now she had clung to an image of her mother as she had always been – capable, reserved, self-effacing. The constant, steady backdrop to a happy childhood. Louise remembered sleeves rolled up on wash day revealing taut arms stronger than they appeared; slender pink hands, slimy with sudsy water, hauling clothes out of the twin tub, the water grey from previous washes. She remembered a slim, resolute woman who moved through her narrow life with purpose and busyness, ever watchful for extravagant waste and moral laxness.

She recalled the relentless, tight-fisted management of household finances so that there was always just enough money for Christmas and a week-long summer holiday in a grotty boarding house in Ballycastle. And the going without on her mother's part that this rigorous budgeting required.

Her mother shifted in her seat, and winced. She flexed the fingers on her right hand and looked at the deformed knuckles with a scowl on her face. 'The doctor's put me on a new drug but he says it'll take weeks, months even, before I notice any difference. Maybe I need another one of those injections . . .'

'I'm sorry, Mum,' said Louise, feeling a sudden rush of compassion for her mother – and a creeping sense of guilt. Balancing the cup and saucer on her knee, she reached over and patted her mother's knee. 'I'll be able to help out more now.' Why hadn't Joanne, or Sian, warned her that her mother's health had deteriorated so?

Thinking of their younger sister, Louise said, 'Where's Sian and Andy tonight?'

13

Joanne replied, 'Oh, she and Andy had to go to some meeting about that eco-development at Loughanlea.' Joanne fiddled with the tiny shell buttons on her cardigan, her small feet neatly tucked together under her knees. She seemed restless, on edge and she radiated what Louise could only describe as ill-will. 'As Chair of Friends of Ballyfergus Lough, Sian said it was really important that she was there for tonight's meeting,' she went on, and then added rather formally, 'She sends her apologies.'

'That's okay. I'll see her tomorrow.' Louise held her breath while her mother shakily lifted the cup to her lips, its dainty handle sandwiched awkwardly between her forefinger and swollen thumb. She managed to take a sip and return the cup to its place on the saucer without a spillage. Louise relaxed while Joanne, still on edge, let out air like steam.

'She ought to have been here to welcome you. But you know Sian. Saving the world comes before her own family.'

'Oh, Joanne,' said Louise, scolding gently, 'I'm sure she would've been here if she could. And I don't mind. It's better for Oli this way. Meeting too many people all at once would just overwhelm him.'

Joanne raised her eyebrows and looked out the window, unconvinced. Louise, wanting to avoid further discord, ploughed on with a change of subject, 'Anyway, how's the redevelopment of the old quarry at Loughanlea coming on? It must be nearly finished.' The disused cement works, located just a few miles outside Ballyfergus on the western shore of the Lough, had blighted the landscape for over two hundred years. Four years ago ambitious plans for its regeneration had finally received the green light from the authorities.

'According to Sian,' said Joanne, 'most of the major

construction work's completed. As well as the mountain bike centre, they're building a scuba diving centre, a bird watching centre, a heritage railway centre and God knows what all else. And when it's finished, the eco-village will have over four hundred homes. It'll cover the northern part of the peninsula.' She was referring to a wing-shaped spit of land formed from basalt excavated from the quarry and dumped into the Lough.

'And when's Sian and Andy's house going to be ready?'

'September, I think. Theirs is going to be one of the first to be completed.'

Louise nodded thoughtfully. She'd been so wrapped up in her own plans she'd almost forgotten that Sian was about to move home too, albeit not halfway across the UK.

Her mother tutted loudly, shook her head and set the cup and saucer down noisily on the table. 'I don't know what Sian's thinking about, buying a house with a man she's not even married to. Don't get me wrong, your father and I are very fond of Andy.' She folded her arms across her chest. 'But we don't approve of this living together business.'

Louise rolled her eyes at Joanne who said, 'Everyone lives together before getting married nowadays, Mum.'

'You didn't,' she snapped.

Joanne thought for a moment. 'Well, maybe I should have. You can't really know someone until you live with them.'

'And a fat lot of good it did me,' said Louise, looking into her cup. She sighed, took a sip of tea and added, 'Mind you, I imagine an eco-village, whatever that is, will be right up Sian and Andy's street.'

'Oh, you should hear the two of them banging on about it,' said Joanne, diving back into the conversation with sudden

15

energy. 'They're like religious zealots. What they don't know about sustainable living isn't worth knowing.'

'They're always on at your dad and I to grow our own food,' interjected her mother, nodding, 'and make compost out of our used tea bags.' She snorted. 'I think they forget that your father and I are in our seventies.'

Her mother's uncharacteristic ridicule took Louise slightly by surprise. 'Well, the whole project sounds very exciting,' she said feebly, feeling a little guilty at her participation in the mean-spirited mockery, albeit gentle, of Sian and her fiancé. 'And it's good that Sian and Andy are involved. You need passionate people to get something like that off the ground.'

Joanne pulled the edges of her cardigan together. 'Hmm . . . I'm just glad she found someone like Andy who shares her views, that's all.' But she said it like she was affronted, rather than pleased.

'Andy's lovely,' said Louise. 'He really is.'

Her mother nodded. 'Yes, he is a decent fella.' A pause. 'In spite of his . . . ideas.'

'Well,' said Louise, 'there's nothing wrong with being concerned about the environment.'

Joanne snorted dismissively like Louise didn't know what she was talking about. She folded her legs and said, snippily, 'It's not what they do that bothers me. It's going round telling the rest of us how to live that grates. It drives Phil nuts.'

Joanne had been married to handsome Phil Montgomery for fifteen years. A little flash of envy pricked Louise. She wished she had a husband and everything that went with it – the sharing of worry and responsibility, the freedom to have as many kids as they pleased, the security of two incomes, the social inclusion. But envy was a destructive emotion – she tried to put these thoughts out of her mind.

'Wait till Sian starts on you,' said Joanne, raising her eyebrows and running the flat of her palm down a smooth tanned leg. 'You'll know all about it then.' She stood up suddenly, while Louise was still formulating a reply and slung her bag over her shoulder. 'Well, I suppose I'd better take my lot home and give you a chance to get Oli to bed. Oh, how could I forget? The keys to your flat!' She pulled a yellow plastic key fob from the bag and passed it to Louise. 'It was the best one I could find. Furnished flats are a bit thin on the ground in Ballyfergus.'

'Thanks.' Louise nodded, staring at the two shiny Yale keys, the passport to her new life, and rubbed one of them between her finger and thumb. 'You know it's really weird moving in somewhere I haven't seen, even if it is only rented. The pictures on the internet looked nice.'

'I think you'll like it,' said Joanne and frowned. 'Though it's not as big as you're used to.'

'I'm sure it'll be just fine. Thanks for sorting it out for me.'

'Now's the time to buy, you know,' said Joanne, dusting something imaginary off the front of her cardigan.

'And I will,' said Louise, 'just as soon as I get my place in Edinburgh sold.'

'Are you moving in straight away?' said Mum.

'Tomorrow. The removal van's due at eight-thirty but most of my stuff's staying in storage until I buy a place.'

'I'll meet you there at nine to give you a hand,' said Joanne. 'Phil can look after the girls for a change!' She laughed humourlessly, then marched purposefully out of the room. Moments later howls of protest echoed up the hall.

Her father's voice bellowed from the kitchen, not sounding nearly as scary as he intended. 'Will you wee 'ans keep the noise down in there? We're trying to talk.'

'I'd better go and see what your dad's up to,' said her mother, hauling herself to a standing position and hobbling painfully out of the room.

Louise went and stood at the door to the TV room which seemed so much smaller than she remembered it. She slipped her hands into the back pockets of her jeans, and leant against the door frame. The two younger children – seven-year-old Abbey and Oli – were seated cross-legged on the floor in front of the TV. Abbey wore a grubby candy pink T-shirt and mismatched fuchsia-coloured shorts. She insisted on choosing her outfits herself – and it showed. Ten-year-old Holly, thin-faced, with long brown hair and pale blue eyes, was draped over the sofa.

Maddy, womanly at fourteen, was perched on the arm of the sofa, texting furiously with the thumbs of both hands. She possessed a full chest, brown eyes and shoulder-length, dark brown hair streaked with blonde. She wore a short denim skirt over bare orange-brown legs and, even though it was summer and warm outside, a pair of fake Ugg boots. A fringed black and white Palestine scarf was draped around her neck – a fashion, rather than a political, statement.

'I said it's time to go,' said Joanne, authoritatively. She picked up the remote, switched the TV off and threw the control on the sofa with some force. Instantly the air was thick with tension. Holly glanced at Maddy. Louise bit her lip, sensing a confrontation, afraid to watch, afraid to look away. Abbey leapt instantly to her feet, placed her hands on the place where she would one day have hips and stared at her mother, her face hard with anger.

'Put it back on! I hadn't finished watching,' she demanded. Blonde hair, tied up in two pigtails, stuck out either side of her head. Her freckled cheeks were pink with indignation and her entire body shook with rage. Oli's cherubic mouth fell open in amazement.

The muscles on Joanne's jaw flexed. 'I said it was time to go, Abbey.'

'But you don't understand. It's not finished yet, Mum!' wailed the child, arms held out to convey her frustration at her mother's ignorance.

Oli stood up, a toy car dangling from his right hand, his mouth still gaping open, utterly transfixed by his cousin.

'Mum, there's only a few minutes left to go,' ventured Maddy, looking up momentarily from her texting. 'Why don't you—'

'That's enough,' snapped Joanne, pushing her hair back. 'I don't know why you lot can't just do what you're asked. Just once.' Her voice rose to a shriek. 'Would that be too much to ask? I work my fingers to the bone for this family and I ask you to do one thing. One thing! And you can't do it.'

Maddy sighed loudly and turned away, her features hidden by a curtain of hair. Joanne put her hands over her face, stood like that for a few moments and then removed them. 'You can finish watching the programme another day, Abbey,' she said, her calm voice barely disguising hysteria. She gave Holly a poke in the leg with her finger. 'Now come on all of you. It's time to go. Oli needs to go to bed.'

'It's not even dark yet,' said Holly huffily from her slouched position on the sofa, arms folded across her chest. Her skinny legs stretched out Bambi-like from beneath a flowered skirt.

Maddy looked up and said, 'Holly, can we just, like, go please?'

But Abbey would not give up. 'It's not a DVD, Mum!' she

screeched. 'Don't you understand? It's on TV. I'll never, ever get to see it again. You're . . . you're . . .' She bubbled with rage. '. . . so stupid.'

'Don't you dare speak to me like that young lady!' snapped Joanne, and she reached forward and swiped ineffectually at Abbey's legs – the child, too quick for her mother, side-stepped nimbly out of harm's way.

Louise bit her lip and winced. Oli ran over to her and peered out from behind her legs, no doubt keen to see, as Louise was, how this fracas would play itself out.

Maddy groaned quietly, rolled her eyes at Louise and returned to her texting. Common wisdom dictated that an only child was harder work than a bigger family, the idea being that an only child, with no sibling to play with, always looked to the parents, or in Louise's case parent, for enter-tainment. Louise wasn't so sure that the theory held. She'd never attempted to hit her child like Joanne had just done. Louise wondered what was going on with her sister. She seemed to be on the verge of losing it.

Abbey looked about feverishly, spied the remote and dived for it, just as Holly scooped it off the couch and clutched it to her chest. 'Mum said the TV was to stay OFF, Abbey,' she said sternly, and gave her sister a devilish smirk.

It had the desired effect. Abbey pounced on her sister screaming and both rolled on the couch wrestling with the device.

'Mum, get her off me!' yelled Holly. 'She pulled my hair.'

'Give me that,' hollered Abbey, throwing her head back to reveal a face red with exertion and two missing front teeth. 'Give me that now!'

'That's enough both of you!' screamed Joanne, her eyes bulging with rage, her face puce.

Immediately the children went silent – even Maddy paused in her texting – and stared at their mother. Joanne closed her eyes and sliced the air horizontally with a slow cutting motion, like a conductor silencing the orchestra. She lowered her voice until it was full of menace and barely audible. 'I have had enough,' she said, pronouncing each word like an elocution teacher.

Frankie Cahoon shouted a goodbye from the other end of the hall and the front door slammed.

'What's going on in here?' came her father's genial voice over Louise's shoulder. He smelled of whiskey and aftershave. What remained of his hair was grey and short and his bald patch, browned by the sun, shone like a polished bowling ball. His jaw was slack with age but his brown eyes twinkled with the same good temper Louise remembered from his youth.

'World War Three,' said Louise without humour and she cast a worried glance over her shoulder. Her father chuckled, his whiskery cheeks crumpling into a smile. He rocked a little in his slippers, his hands deep in the pockets of his navy slacks.

'Let me guess – Abbey?' he said.

'Yep.'

'Grandpa,' cried Holly, as soon as she saw him. 'Abbey pulled my—'

'She wouldn't let me have the—' interrupted Abbey.

'Enough,' commanded Joanne in a loud, forceful voice and Abbey, now seated on the floor, started to cry.

When it came to tears, their father was a pushover. 'There, there now, pet,' he said, shuffling past Louise into the room. He sat on the sofa, pulled the crying child onto his knees and stroked her hair. Abbey's sobs, instead of abating, intensified.

'She started it,' said Joanne, clearly not impressed by this intervention. She folded her arms across her chest and glared at Abbey.

'Now that's not very nice, is it, Abbey?' asked her father and Abbey, glancing furtively at Joanne, sniffed and shook her head.

'But she wouldn't give me the remote,' protested Abbey.

Holly retaliated quickly. 'She wanted to turn the TV on and Mum said—'

'I want you both to say sorry to each other,' said their grandfather, cutting Holly short. After a brief exchange of petulant glares, amazingly, both girls complied. Under their grandfather's direction, they even embraced and in moments all was forgotten.

Then suddenly Joanne grabbed Abbey by the arm and pulled her off her grandfather's lap. 'We're going now. Come on. Bye, Dad.' She marched Abbey out of the room brushing past Louise, Maddy and Holly trailing in her wake. 'You three go on out to the car. I'll be out in a minute,' she instructed, giving Abbey a rather forceful shove out the door.

Joanne said a brief goodbye to her parents and Louise followed her out to the car. As soon as the front door closed behind them, Louise said, 'Are you okay?'

'Of course I'm okay. Why shouldn't I be?'

'It's just that . . . well, don't you think you went a bit over the top in there with the girls?'

'No,' said Joanne irritably.

Had Joanne lost all sense of perspective? In Louise's book, physical punishment was the last resort of out-of-control parents. 'You tried to hit Abbey, Joanne. And if she hadn't jumped out of your way, you would have.'

Joanne stopped and turned to face Louise. 'She deserved it. They all did. They didn't do what they were asked.'

'Show me a kid who does?' said Louise with a laugh, trying to inject some humour into the situation. But her sister remained stony-faced. 'She's only seven, Joanne,' said Louise softly. 'You have to remember that.'

'Seven,' said Joanne, unmoved, 'is the age of reason. Abbey is old enough to know the difference between right and wrong.'

There was a long pause and, sensing that it would be fruitless to pursue this subject any further, Louise said, 'Mum and Dad have aged terribly, haven't they? Mum especially.'

'Yes, they have,' sighed Joanne and she rubbed the back of her neck. 'At least you'll be able to help out a bit now. It's been quite a strain on me – what with work and the girls as well. Sian's only interested in the common good – not helping her own family.'

'Of course I'll help out. As for Sian, well, she is working full-time,' said Louise in her younger sister's defence.

'And you think I have more spare time than she does?' Joanne shook her head. 'I might work part-time at the pharmacy, Louise, but believe me, running a home and looking after a family as well is more than equivalent to a full-time job. Sian has no idea.' With that, Joanne got in the car, waved goodbye tersely and drove away.

Later, when Oli had finally fallen asleep, Louise crept up to the bedroom and knelt on the floor and watched him. His chest moved with the gentle rhythm of his breath, his eyelids fluttered in his sleep. Damp curls clung to his sweaty face, and he stirred, throwing a chubby arm up over his head. Louise sat back on her heels and thought about the day's events. She had done the right thing in coming back, hadn't she? Oli should know his grandparents and his family. This was the right place for him – and her. And it looked like she had come back at just the right time. For Joanne, it seemed, was barely holding it together.

Chapter Two

With Joanne's help it didn't take Louise long to organise the small, two-bedroom flat on Tower Road. Joanne had chosen well. On the first floor in a modern two-storey building, it was bright and functional with pale cream carpet and walls, a brand new blonde wood kitchen and a pristine white bathroom. The bay window in the small, narrow lounge overlooked a pleasant residential street and the flat was only a few minutes' walk from the seafront. Once Joanne had helped her unpack Oli's toys, and her own familiar belongings, it started to feel like home.

In Oli's bedroom, after Joanne had gone, Louise wrestled with a Thomas the Tank duvet cover while Oli played happily with his rediscovered Brio train set.

'It's nice here, isn't it? Do you like it?' said Louise happily, shaking the cover like a sail in the wind. If everything else went as well as today, their new life would work out just fine.

He shrugged without looking up. 'It's okay. Look. Choo-choo. The train's coming into the station.' He pushed a red engine along a wooden track. 'When can we go home?'

The smile fell from her lips. She sank down dejectedly on the tangle of bedcovers and sighed. 'This is home, Oli. For the time being anyway.'

'But I want my old room. And I want to see Elliott,' he said, referring to his best friend at nursery. He stuck out his bottom lip.

'Oh, darling,' said Louise, momentarily stuck for the reassuring platitudes that usually sprung so readily to her lips.

He got up then and ran to her and buried his face in her lap. She smoothed the fine soft hairs at the nape of his neck, closed her eyes, and prayed to God that he would settle down.

A few days later, she visited her parents and found her mother in the kitchen drying dishes from the evening meal with a red and white checked tea towel. Mindful of the signs of stress she'd detected in Joanne, Louise was trying to do her bit to support her parents.

She heaved a canvas shopping bag onto the kitchen table. 'I made a big stew last night,' she said lifting three foil containers out of the bag and setting them on the table. 'I thought some would be handy for you and Dad. It'll do for when you don't have time to cook.'

Of course this wasn't true. Her mother had all the time in the world – she was just no longer capable of running a house and putting a square meal on the table every night.

'Well, thanks, love,' said her mother, graciously. 'That is very kind of you.'

'It's no bother. I get Oli to help me. It passes the time.'

'How's he settling in?'

Louise sighed. 'He's been having bad dreams. He's had me up nearly every night this week.' She yawned. 'It's like having a baby again.'

'It must be terribly unsettling for him.'

Louise nodded. 'I've tried my best to explain what it means to move house, but I'm not sure how much he understands. He keeps asking me when he can see his friends. I feel awful.'

'Never mind, love,' said her mother, with an encouraging smile. 'He'll soon make new friends.'

'Perhaps you're right,' said Louise hopefully.

Her mother examined the packages on the table and shook her head. 'I don't know where you get the time.'

Louise smiled in acknowledgement. 'Well, I'm not working and I only have Oli to look after. Not like Joanne.'

She watched her mother dry the bottom of a china dinner plate, then the top. She was so painfully slow. Louise resisted the urge to intervene, placing the portions of stew in the freezer instead. 'Do you think Joanne's all right?' she said casually, closing the freezer door.

'What do you mean? Like not well?' Her mother set the plate on the counter and picked up another one.

'No, she just seems a bit stressed to me.'

Her mother rubbed the tea towel on the surface of the wet plate in a languid circular motion. 'She probably is. Those girls can be a bit of a handful. And Phil's not around much to help.'

Louise paused, considering the wisdom of sharing any more of her concerns with her mother. She looked at her gnarled hands, decided against it and said instead, 'I suppose it's hard when there's three of them.'

'What?' asked her mother distractedly, stacking the plates.

'It's so much easier with just one child.'

'Easier, maybe,' her mother replied and left the sentence unfinished – like an old plaster partially hanging off a wound.

'Go on.'

Her mother sighed, shuffled over to a chair, sat down and regarded Louise thoughtfully. 'It might be easier for you. But it might not be best for Oli. It's not healthy him being with just you all the time.'

'He's not with me all the time,' said Louise evenly. 'He

sees other people – adults and kids – regularly. And that's one of the reasons I moved back, isn't it? So he could be closer to his family and cousins and grow up knowing them.'

Her mother shrugged her shoulders and Louise found herself compelled to pursue this topic, realising as she spoke that it was essential to her that her mother endorse her lifestyle.

'Oli has a very happy life, Mum. He wants for nothing.'

'Except a father.'

Louise bit her lip, anger bubbling up like boiling fudge in a pan. 'There's nothing like stating the obvious, is there?' she said. 'Why do you have to focus on the one thing he doesn't have instead of all the things he does? Like a mother who adores him and gave up her job to look after him?'

'I know just how much you love him, Louise,' her mother acknowledged, her voice softening. 'It's just, well . . . you know.'

The unsaid words hung between them, fuelling Louise's anger. A father was the one thing she could not give her son. The only thing. The single, glaring flaw in the almost-perfect life she had so carefully carved out of the wreckage of her marriage. And she tried not to be bitter about the past. She ought to be applauded for what she had done, not derided.

Louise's chest was so tight, she could hardly breathe. She fought against it for a few moments and managed to say, 'It's not how I would have wanted it either, Mum. Not in an ideal world. You know that. But do you have to go rubbing salt into the wound? What I need is support – not people, not my own mother, criticising me.'

Her mother let out a long weary sigh. 'I'm sorry. I didn't mean to upset you.'

'You didn't mean to upset me?' cried Louise. 'That's a good one.'

Her mother glared at her then, her eyes flinty and full of rare anger. 'You can't expect your father and I to approve of something that goes against our values. And people won't understand.'

'So that's what this is about, is it? What other people think? Do you care more about that than your own daughter's happiness?'

'No,' said her mother with a steely gaze. 'You might not care what people think, Louise. But you ought to. For Oli's sake. If I was you I wouldn't go round blabbing your story to people. I'm not sure Ballyfergus is ready to hear it. You don't want Oli singled out for being different.'

'He's no different than any other child from a single-parent family.'

'Most people don't set out to be a single parent, Louise.'

Louise took several deep breaths and fought to retain her composure. 'I know you don't approve but get over it,' she hissed. 'Oli's here now. Why can't you just get on with the business of grandmothering him and stop finding fault with us both?'

'I'd never find fault with Oli,' said her mother quickly. 'He's perfect.'

So the fault lay with Louise, did it? Louise blinked, tried to ignore the tightness in her throat and hold the tears at bay. Why did her mother have to be so judgemental? Why couldn't she give Louise the unqualified, wholehearted support that she so desperately craved?

Her father padded into the kitchen just then, breaking the tension. He rubbed his hands together briskly. Whiskey had lent his eyes a rheumy quality. 'Anyone for a wee drink?'

Louise shook her head. 'Not for me.' Since she'd had Oli she rarely drank alcohol – and she'd no stomach for it today, not after that horrible, hurtful exchange with her mother.

'You've had quite enough already, Billy,' said her mother sharply. 'Why don't you make us all a cup of tea instead?' She folded the tea towel and draped it over the radiator to dry.

Her father gave Louise a mournful look and she forced the corners of her mouth up in a smile. He filled the kettle noisily.

Louise glanced at the clock on the wall and said, 'It's time I took Oli home. He needs an early night.'

Her father switched the kettle on. 'Sit down and have a cup of tea. A few more minutes of TV won't do him any harm.'

Louise whipped her head around and said sharply, 'What's he watching at this time of night?'

'Oh relax, Louise,' said her father, taking mugs out of the cupboard. 'It's one of those children's channels. It'll not do him a bit of harm.'

'I don't like him watching TV this late. Not just before bedtime. It over-stimulates his brain.'

Her father rolled his eyes. 'You fuss too much, Louise. Let the child be.'

'I think I know what's best for my own son,' said Louise, tears pricking the back of her eyes. 'I am his mother after all.' And with that, she huffed into the TV room, grabbed Oli and stormed out of the house.

'That smells fantastic. What is it?' Gemma Mooney lifted the lid on a pot bubbling away on the stove in Joanne's kitchen on Walnut Grove. She bent her long elegant neck over the pot and peered inside, her chunky metal bracelet clanging against the lid.

'Black Bean Chilli,' said Joanne, smiling with satisfaction. She was no match in the looks department for Gemma – with

30

her long legs, angular athletic frame and those bright cat-green eyes – but at least Joanne could cook. While she often joked about Gemma's domestic incompetency, it made Joanne feel secretly superior to her friend.

'Hey, Gemma,' she grinned. 'What's in your fridge?'

Gemma shook her head of thick black curls. Not many women could wear their hair as short as she did and get away with it. 'Oh you know me. A lemon, a few mouldy spuds, some ice and a bottle of wine.'

Joanne laughed and wiped her hands on the front of her apron, acutely aware of her insubstantial, scrawny frame. She loved Gemma to bits but she always felt a little inadequate, a little child-like, in her presence. Still, today she'd made the best of what she had with high heels for extra height, a full skirt to fill out the hips she didn't possess, and a knitted cardigan to create the illusion of a chest.

'What about the kids? What do you feed them?'

'Oh, they're used to fending for themselves. Roz can rustle up a pretty mean pasta and tomato sauce.' Gemma replaced the lid on the pot. 'This'll be delicious,' she said and gave Joanne a brief squeeze across the shoulders. 'Everything you make is. You're such a good cook. Not like me – I'm hopeless.'

'You could cook, if you tried,' said Joanne but she couldn't resist a satisfied sigh as she looked around the kitchen. The table was laid with plates and dishes of food covered in cling film and cutlery rolled up in napkins. Heidi, the family's black, two-year-old Flat Coated Retriever, lay on her bed in the corner, watching them with soulful dark amber eyes, her ears flattened against her smooth bullet-shaped head.

Everything, from the home-made vol-au-vents to the fresh strawberry tart, looked good. So why did Joanne still have a niggling sense of dissatisfaction at the back of her mind?

Heidi lifted her head and let out a long low heartfelt whine, a protest at being surrounded by food yet not allowed to touch any of it. Roughly, she grabbed the dog's collar.

'Here, you'd better go in the utility room or you'll eat everything like you did last Friday. Did I tell you about that, Gemma? She ate an entire cream cake I'd bought for the kids as a special treat.'

'Yeah, you told me.'

The dog's claws scraped the floor as she was dragged away and she whined pathetically as the utility room door shut on her. Turning, Joanne caught a flicker of something in her best friend's eyes. She felt ashamed for taking out her feelings on the dog. What was wrong with her?

'Oh, we'll save the leftovers for her,' she said brightly.

'Of course,' said Gemma smoothly.

Joanne peered wistfully out the patio doors at a dull grey sky. 'Do you think it's going to rain? At least the garden's looking good.'

She'd made the most of the tight space, and the borders, still wet from the last shower, were brimming with summer flowers – pink and white foxgloves, frothy white gypsophila and pale purple lavender.

'Great in the kitchen – green fingers too. Your husband's spoiled,' Gemma said lightly and Joanne's chest swelled with pride.

She blushed and said, 'Have I invited too many people? I'd kind of banked on good weather and now, if it rains, everyone'll have to squeeze inside.'

The house was detached and had four bedrooms but everything about it was compact, a fact that constantly irked, like an itchy label on the back of a sweater. Considering she and Phil both had professional jobs, they really ought to be living in a bigger, better house. But that wasn't going to happen anytime soon – not with Phil squandering every spare penny . . . no, she mustn't go there, not today, not at Louise's homecoming party.

'It'll be fine,' said Gemma airily, 'And I'm sure Louise'll appreciate it.' She leant against the counter, her skinny black jeans and black boat-necked jersey top emphasising her sexy contours. Joanne, in her pretty, flared skirt and delicate high heels felt suddenly in danger of appearing frumpy in comparison. And once again, she found herself wondering why Gemma was still alone. Surely there must be a man out there for her?

'Do you think I've put on weight?' said Gemma suddenly, sucking her already flat belly in so that it was concave.

'Don't be ridiculous!' said Joanne loyally. 'You look fantastic. Like you always do.'

Roz, Gemma's daughter, popped her head through the kitchen door. 'Can me and Maddy go down the shop for some magazines?' It was Roz and Maddy who'd brought Gemma and Joanne together. They'd met at a mother and baby coffee morning when the girls were little.

Gemma looked at Joanne and shrugged her smooth right shoulder indifferently.

'Why not?' said Joanne as Maddy followed Roz into the room.

Gemma reached for her purse, found a fiver and handed it to her daughter. Joanne did the same with Maddy adding, as she handed over the money, 'Just don't be too long. Everyone'll be arriving soon.'

The girls, over-made-up and dressed like twins in leggings, ankle boots and baggy tops with a slightly disconcerting eighties look about them, had only just left the room when Abbey came running in, dressed in clothes of her own choosing – red leggings which bagged at the knees and clashed with her orange T-shirt. Her straight, fine hair was carelessly pinned to one side with a diamante barrette with half the stones missing.

'I want to go to the shop too,' announced Abbey breathlessly.

Joanne smiled patiently. 'You can't, darling. You're too young.'

'I'm not too young to go with Maddy and Roz! They can take me, can't they, Mum? Can't they, Auntie Gemma?' she pleaded, the hope in her voice slipping into desperation as the two women exchanged glances. 'Make them take me, Mum!'

'No, Abbey. I'm sorry, the answer's no.' Joanne paused and then added brightly, 'Anyway, I need a big girl to help me.'

Abbey folded her arms across her chest defiantly and Joanne pressed on, 'See all these crisps and nibbles. Can you put them in these bowls for me, please? The rest of our guests will be arriving soon.'

'That's not fair. I have to do all the work and *they* get to go to the shop.' Abbey glowered. 'I bet you a million pounds they're buying sweets.'

'They are not buying sweets, I can assure you,' said Joanne, losing patience. She moved towards Abbey, wafting a tea towel at her like a Spanish bullfighter. 'If you're not going to help, you can get out of my kitchen. Go on, out!'

'I'm not helping you ever again,' shouted Abbey and she ran out of the room and slammed the door behind her.

Both women burst out laughing.

'Why is Abbey so much work? If only I had a boy, like you, instead of all girls,' said Joanne. In addition to Roz, Gemma had a twelve-year-old son, Jack.

Gemma raised her eyebrows. 'Jack has his moments too, you know. But any problems and I just call his dad.' She

34

sighed. 'Having said that, Abbey's the feistiest little girl I've ever met. Do you remember that year on holiday in Spain when she was only four and we lost her at the pool?'

'I'll never forget it,' said Joanne, recalling the feeling of heart-stopping panic.

'And we found her a full twenty minutes later, sitting at the bar drinking orange juice, chatting away to the barman with her handbag on the seat beside her!'

Joanne shook her head, laughing at the memory of her fearless daughter though, at the time, it hadn't been at all funny.

'Oh my goodness. Would you look at the time? Gemma, love, you wouldn't do me a favour would you and put out the nibbles? And I wonder what's keeping Phil?' Joanne added. 'He knows everyone's due at five.' She slid on a pair of oven gloves, opened the oven door and waved away a bellow of steam.

Gemma sauntered slowly over to the island unit, ripped open a packet of crisps and ate one.

Peering inside the oven, Joanne said, 'The chicken's just about done. I'd better turn it off.'

'Wasn't he playing golf today?' said Gemma, tipping crisps into a ceramic bowl.

Joanne turned the gas off under the chilli. 'Yes, but he promised me he'd come straight home to give me a hand.' She stood up and made a sweeping gesture with her left hand around the kitchen. 'And of course everything's done and there's no sign of him. Typical.'

'He must've got held up,' said Gemma reassuringly. 'Have you tried calling him on his mobile?'

'I did. It just tripped to voicemail.' Joanne took off the oven gloves and placed them on top of the cooker. She shook her head. 'Sometimes I wonder, Gemma,' she said and paused.

'Wonder what?'

'If life wouldn't be easier on my own.'

Gemma looked at her sharply. 'Do you mean that?'

Joanne reddened, her bluff called. 'No, of course not. That was a stupid thing to say, wasn't it?'

Gemma said sadly, 'There's nothing easy about raising a family on your own.'

'Oh, of course, I'm sorry, Gemma,' said Joanne. 'That was thoughtless of me.'

'I tell you, what I longed for most after Jimmy left was another adult just being there so that I wasn't responsible for absolutely everything. I couldn't even go out for an evening walk around the block without getting a babysitter.' Gemma paused and looked out the window, then added quite brightly, tipping salt and vinegar crisps into a bowl, 'Those days are behind me now, of course. They're both pretty independent and Roz is old enough to mind Jack for a few hours.'

'And they stay with their dad every Tuesday night and every other weekend,' Joanne reminded her friend. 'You know sometimes I envy you those times – when you've no children or husband to worry about. When you can do things that *you* want to do and you don't have to be accountable to anybody else.'

Gemma gave Joanne a puzzled look and scrunched an empty crisp bag up in her hand. 'It can be lonely too though, Joanne. And it's not through choice. I'd love to be happily married like you.'

'And you will be,' said Joanne positively. The idea that Gemma envied her sent a little thrill of pleasure through her. She lifted a ripe avocado out of the fruit bowl and pierced the rough, mottled skin with a sharp knife. 'You just haven't met the right man yet.' She didn't add that, even surrounded by her family, she sometimes felt lonely too. Phil usually played squash on Friday night and then went to the pub with his pals. He regularly disappeared off golfing at lunchtime on a Saturday and sometimes didn't come home till midnight. She thought she'd married a home-loving man like her father – how wrong she had been . . .

Just then the mobile phone rang. Joanne wiped her hands quickly on a tea towel and answered it. It was Phil and he sounded drunk. The call was brief and contained no surprises. When it was over, Joanne set the phone down carefully on the counter, the feeling of disappointment as familiar as the simmering rage.

'Well?' said Gemma.

'You know what?' said Joanne, by way of reply. She did not wait for a response from Gemma. 'I seem to spend my life being let down by Phil. He's always promising the earth and never delivers.'

Gemma threw a clutch of crisp bags in the bin and licked the tips of her fingers. 'Where is he?'

Joanne let out a puff of air and shook her head. 'Right now he's in the bar at the golf club. They've just ordered food even though he knows there's food here. He says he'll be home after that.'

'Oh,' said Gemma. She rubbed at an old paint spot on the limestone floor with the tip of her open-toed sandal.

Joanne cut around the middle of the avocado and twisted it to separate the two halves. She prised out the stone, which skittered across the counter. 'Last week he promised Abbey he'd take her swimming on Sunday morning and he was too hung-over. He forgot about Maddy's parents' night at the school in spite of me reminding him three times and sending him a text.' She paused, held the knife in the air and went on, 'Two weeks ago we were supposed to be going round to

37

the Dohertys' for dinner and he came home pissed from the golf club at eight o'clock. You remember that? We had to call it off in the end. I had to pretend I had a migraine. And I really wanted to go.'

'I know. You got that new dress out of Menary's specially.'

Joanne viciously diced the avocado flesh and tossed it in a bowl. She lifted a lime from the fruit bowl and held it in the air between her index finger and thumb. 'And the week before that I opened a red credit card bill he'd not bothered to pay. Do you want me to go on?'

Gemma bit her lip. 'I get the picture.'

Joanne hacked a lime in two. 'There's always something. He's just so . . . so irresponsible, Gemma. It's like having a fourth child these days. No, it's worse because I've absolutely no control over what he does. I never relax. I never know what disaster's coming next.'

'Well, you know what I think,' said Gemma and she raised her eyebrows and gave Joanne a hard stare. She knew all about Phil's gambling, his drinking, his extravagant spending, his unreliability.

Joanne set the knife down on the chopping board and sighed, her anger spent. 'I know, I know. I should stop complaining and do something about it.'

'It's just that, honestly, Joanne, you should hear yourself,' said Gemma, sounding a little exasperated. 'I can't remember the last time I heard you say a good word about Phil.'

'That's because there isn't a good word to say.' She held half a lime over the bowl and rammed a wooden reamer into the flesh. Juice squirted out, stinging a nick on the back of her hand.

'You sound so cynical,' said Gemma sadly.

Joanne threw the squeezed lime in the bin and rinsed her hands. 'That's because I am.'

'Leave him then.'

Joanne looked out the window and sighed. 'You know I wouldn't do that to the children.' She dried her hands and fixed her friend with a steady stare. Didn't Gemma realise that she just wanted to let off steam, not be told what to do?

'Well,' said Gemma, looking away and speaking slowly, as if choosing her words very carefully. 'There's a lot worse things can happen to children than divorce. Living in an unhappy home can be just as damaging.'

'You didn't say that when Jimmy left. And I remember it, Gemma. I remember how awful it was for the kids. And for you.'

Gemma folded her arms. She tipped her chin upwards and said, 'They got over it. We all did. And Jimmy and I get on okay now. I mean we're civil to each other and we both put the children first.'

Aware she had touched a raw spot, Joanne rushed to bolster Gemma's confidence. 'I think you've done just great since the divorce, Gemma. I really admire you for how you've managed everything. The kids are happy and well-balanced. And I know how hard it was for you when he moved in with Sarah.'

Gemma suddenly smiled brightly. 'No, it's all right, really. It was a long time ago.' She paused and then added, 'Look, I was just playing devil's advocate there. You don't really want to leave Phil – or have him leave you – do you?'

Joanne stared at her open-mouthed. 'Phil wouldn't leave me. I—' She felt her heart begin to race.

'Oh, Joanne, I'm so sorry. I didn't mean to panic you. It was just a "for instance" – I was just thinking of me and Jimmy.'

'I – no, Phil won't leave me. I keep the house nice, the food . . .' She gestured helplessly. 'I really don't know what

I'd do without him.' Recovering her composure, she added, 'Look, I'm sorry to bang on about Phil all the time, especially when I don't take your advice.'

'I'm not trying to tell you what to do, Joanne,' said Gemma looking directly into her eyes. 'It's just that I care for you and I want you to be happy.'

Joanne smiled. 'I know that, love. And I guess I just want someone to listen.'

'That's what friends are for.'

Joanne went over and gave Gemma a hug and said, simply, 'Thanks.' It fell far short of conveying the gratitude she felt towards Gemma for her friendship and support over the years.

Then the doorbell went and the two women separated.

Joanne straightened her skirt and clapped her hands together. 'Right, party time!'

Chapter Three

Sian stood on the step at the back of Joanne's house, holding a glass of wine and looking out at the garden, relieved at being forgiven for being so late. Thankfully Joanne understood that they had to bike all the way from the other side of town – though she and Andy owned an old second-hand car, they rarely used it.

It had been nearly twenty years since she'd visited North Africa in her second year of a Geography degree course at uni and seen first-hand the effects of over-population on a fragile ecosystem – dried-up riverbeds caused by over-farming, starving livestock, ruined crops. She'd seen with her own horrified eyes what poverty looked like – children maimed at birth so they could 'earn' a living as beggars, others labouring like ants in a leather tanning factory from dawn till dusk, and stinking, reeking, overcrowded living conditions. She'd come home humbled – and thankful that she'd been born in a first world country where a full belly and medical care were taken for granted. And long before the phrase carbon footprint was coined, she'd devoted her life to minimising her impact on the earth. She fervently believed that, by example, she might persuade others to do the same.

She sipped the wine and looked up at the sky heavy with

clouds – so far the rain had held off. The patio doors that led into the lounge were open and behind her an assortment of aunts and uncles and cousins were sitting about chatting and eating. Younger members of the family ran in and out of the room until someone hollered at them to 'cut it out'. She eyed Joanne's flowers – one day she'd persuade her to put in veggies too. Everyone had to do their bit. She and Andy were in total agreement on that.

She looked over at Andy, tall and slim and fit, standing on the small square of grass in the centre of the garden. A worn grey T-shirt hung on his well-defined frame and he wore an old pair of shorts over shapely legs, browned from the sun. His short sun-streaked blond hair stood up in messy tufts. She remembered the day she'd first set eyes on him. She'd attended her very first meeting of Friends of Ballyfergus Lough nearly five years ago. And there he was in shorts and a torn T-shirt looking much the same as he did today. She'd fallen in love with him immediately and they'd moved in together within six weeks.

Sian sighed and ran a hand through her tightly cropped fair hair. Not only was he the sexiest man she had ever seen, she loved the languid fluidity of his movements, his relaxed smile, his easygoing nature. In these respects he was the very opposite of her – and maybe that was why their relationship worked. He shared her passion for saving the earth but didn't take himself, or the cause, quite as seriously as she did. He helped her to maintain perspective and, in the face of near apathy from ninety-nine per cent of the population, retain her sense of humour.

She could still hardly believe this gorgeous sexy man and she were getting married next year. Sometimes she couldn't believe her good fortune – both her sisters' marriages confirmed what she suspected. Not everyone found their soulmate. She and Andy were the lucky ones. And together they were invincible. Nothing could come between them, not now, not ever. They shared the same values – they both wanted the same things out of life.

Oli stood just a few metres away from Andy. The child wore clothes that looked like they'd never seen a spot of mud in their life – even his trainers were sparkling white. Sian was filled with dismay. Children should be grubby and messy and muddy, not clean and pristine like they'd just come out of a washing machine. But that was Louise all over. Joanne had proudly shown her the expensive wine and chocolates Louise had brought – whereas she and Andy had contributed organic vegetables from their allotment.

Andy smiled at the boy and the corners of his dark eyes crinkled up, his skin leathery from all the time spent outdoors. His smile was wide and genuine, and his gaze was focused on Oli as though he was the only thing of importance at that moment. Sian understood only too well why clients of the outdoor centre in Cushendall where he worked, loved him. Kids, especially, adored him.

Very gently, Andy tapped a football with the side of his trainer and it came to rest just in front of Oli.

The expression on the toddler's face as he squared up to kick the ball was fierce – his brows knit together, his tongue protruding slightly from the left side of his mouth. Sian smiled. She had seen that expression of quiet determination before – on her sister Louise's face. She'd always been single-minded and competitive. He took aim, swung his leg – and missed the ball.

The swinging action made him lose his balance, his foot gave way beneath him on the wet grass and he landed suddenly on his bottom. Unperturbed, he immediately rolled onto his knees and stood up, using his hands to lever himself onto his feet. Sian noted with satisfaction the grass stains on his knees and on the seat of his jeans. Oli wiped his muddy hands down the front of his shirt and Sian smiled.

The little boy stared at the ball wide-eyed and disbelieving as if some sinister trick was at work.

'You missed the ball,' called out Andy. 'It's okay. Have another go, big man.'

Oli screwed his face up in concentration, took another short run at the ball, swung his leg and this time made contact. The ball skidded across the grass and rolled slowly between Andy's legs. He made no attempt to stop it.

'Goal! Goal!' shouted Oli, punching the air with fisted hands.

Andy cheered and the boy ran to him and Andy scooped him up and swung him around in the air. Then he put him under his right arm, like a package, ruffled his hair with his left and deposited the boy back on the ground.

'Again! Again!' he squealed, jumping up and down. Just then Abbey and Holly came hurtling across the garden and threw themselves at Andy. He fell backwards onto the grass and the girls jumped on top of him, screaming with delight. Sian threw her head back and laughed.

'What's so funny?' asked Joanne, coming to stand beside her. She held a half-full bottle of white wine by the neck in her right hand, a wine glass in her left.

'Oh, it's Andy and the kids,' Sian smiled. 'They're having a great time. Look at them.'

'Poor Andy,' said Joanne with a wry smile as Oli threw himself on top of the heap of legs and arms, squealing with delight.

'Sure Andy loves it,' said Sian.

'He must do,' said Joanne watching as Andy scrambled to his feet, laughing, the back of his T-shirt soiled with stains.

Within seconds he'd organised a two-a-side football game. 'You know he's absolutely great with kids. Look at little Oli. He just adores Andy.'

Sian beamed with pride. The children made no secret of the fact that their (almost) Uncle Andy was their favourite male relative.

'I suppose that's what Oli's crying out for,' Joanne went on. 'A bit of male rough and tumble.'

'I guess so,' said Sian and this innocuous comment seemed to open the floodgates for Joanne.

'I feel awful saying this,' she confided, 'but I think Louise should've given more thought to what it would be like for Oli without a dad.' She leant forward conspiratorially and whispered darkly, 'I think it's already affected him, you know.'

'Surely not!' said Sian, glancing over at the happy, smiling child. 'He's little more than a baby.'

'Louise spoils him. Did you see his trainers? Dolce and Gabbana. I think she spoils him to make up for the fact that he doesn't have a father, but money can't make up for that, can it?' Joanne tutted her disapproval, which sounded more like jealousy to Sian, and went on, 'And he's far too clingy. He sleeps in Louise's bed every night, you know.' She nodded her head firmly as if she had just divulged a shocking secret, filled her glass to the brim, topped up Sian's, and set the empty bottle on the step.

'What's so wrong with that? Lots of parents let their kids sleep with them, don't they?'

Joanne laughed cynically. 'Only those that don't have a life.'

'Well, how she raises Oli is Louise's business,' said Sian. 'What I object to is the fact that she had him in the first place.'

'Because she's a single mum?' said Joanne incredulously. 'I wouldn't have put you down for a traditionalist.'

Sian shook her head. 'I couldn't care less whether she's married or not. What I care about is the fact that she had him at all. There are enough kids in the world without adding to the problem.'

Joanne rolled her eyes. 'Here we go again.'

Anger flared up inside Sian. As a child Joanne had never taken her seriously and she still treated Sian like the younger sister she was, putting her down, dismissing her at every opportunity. But this was a subject about which Sian knew far more than her sister. She *would* make her listen. 'The biggest problem facing mankind is over-population. There are too many people competing for scarce resources – land, water, food. And competition ultimately leads to war. Over-population is the primary cause of most of the world's ills. And it's forced us to embrace dangerous technologies like nuclear power. No, there are simply too many of us – way too many.'

'Not in the UK there aren't,' argued Joanne. 'Our problem is a falling birth rate. In a few years' time there won't be enough young people to support our ageing population. It's the people in the third world having ten, twelve babies that are the problem. Not us in the West.'

Sian sighed and said patiently, 'I'm talking on a global scale, Joanne. We all have to take some responsibility for the problem. People in the West don't realise that their luxurious lifestyles are effectively subsidised by the rest of the world. The earth simply doesn't possess the resources to enable everyone to live the way we do.'

Joanne folded her arms, her glass balanced in one hand, and narrowed her eyes. 'So are you saying that I shouldn't have had three children?'

Sian broke eye contact. 'I just wish more people were prepared to take action on a personal level,' she said, evasively. 'Procreating isn't the be all and end all. Louise's mistake was in believing that motherhood was the only route to personal fulfilment. But there are many ways to happiness.'

And Sian knew what she was talking about. She ran Earth Matters, the Fairtrade shop in Ballyfergus. She sold jewellery from co-operatives in Africa, toys made from recycled tin cans and bags fashioned from recycled rice sacks. She stocked organic clothing, Ecover home care products, washable nappies and Fairtrade rice, sugar and coffee from the third world. She worked hard in the business and nothing gave her more pleasure than the knowledge that, small as it was, she was making a difference.

Joanne stared at her and said, 'Well, I think it's a subject we should agree to disagree on, Sian. Anyway, now's not really the time, or the place, to discuss it.'

'Whatever,' said Sian pleased that she had rattled Joanne's cage.

Joanne cleared her throat and said, 'Thanks for the potatoes and carrots by the way. They look lovely.'

'Andy picked them this morning. First of the season,' said Sian. 'And all organic of course.'

'I'd be disappointed if they weren't,' said Joanne, poking a little of what she no doubt thought was good-natured fun at her sister.

Sian decided to let it pass. 'You know, our allotment is a fraction of the size of this garden and look at the amount of food we produce – more than the two of us can eat at the height of the season. Have you ever thought of growing your own food?'

The corners of Joanne's mouth turned downwards, a bemused expression on her face. 'Where would I find the time to do that, Sian? I do all the work in the garden as it is.'

'Oh, it's not too bad once you get it established. I would help you.'

'But the garden isn't big enough to have a vegetable plot, Sian.'

'Sure it is. You've loads of room. Just do away with that border for a start,' said Sian, pointing to a peony rose in full, pale pink flower. 'It's not doing anything.'

'For your information it's providing colour and interest,' said Joanne. 'And I like having cut flowers for the house.'

'You'd still have a good-sized lawn and border on the other side,' went on Sian, ignoring this observation and the sarcasm. 'And the girls would absolutely love it. Look how excited they get when they come down to help me on the allotment. Well, Holly and Abbey anyway,' she added, remembering that the last time Maddy had come she'd spent the whole time sitting on an upturned crate texting her mates. 'Just think how thrilled they'd be about growing food for the table in their own backyard! And it makes sound economic sense too, not to mention it'd all be organic and so much better for you than the stuff you buy in the supermarket.'

Sian paused for breath and Joanne said, rather sharply, 'Tell you what. The day that Phil starts helping in the garden, that'll be the day I plant a vegetable plot.'

Sian frowned and looked over her shoulder into the lounge. Everyone had finished eating and a bottle of Baileys had appeared. Even their mother had a glass. Phil was nowhere to be seen. 'Where is he anyway? I haven't seen him since we got here.'

'That's because he isn't here, Sian. He's at the golf club. Phoned me just before people were due to arrive to say that he was in the clubhouse with his mates and they'd all ordered food.'

'But what about all the food here?' blurted out Sian. 'You've enough to feed half of Africa.'

'Don't get me started,' warned Joanne, waving the glass in her hand so violently that a little wine spilled out onto the concrete step, narrowly missing the toe of her jewelled, high-heeled sandal. Sian looked down at her Merrill hiking sandals and smiled – Joanne's heels would be no use riding a bicycle. 'I swear to God,' went on Joanne, her voice shrill and taut, 'if I start, I'll never stop.'

Louise appeared suddenly beside them, face flushed, holding a glass of wine in her hand. 'Oh, is Andy playing football with Oli?' she smiled. 'Oh, he is. Oh, look!' she cried and she placed a hand on her throat and swallowed.

Just then Oli spied his mother and came barrelling across the grass. He threw his arms around her legs and cried, 'I scored a goal, Mummy!'

Louise scooped him into her arms and kissed him on the nose. 'That's fantastic, Oli. What a clever boy,' she grinned and Oli leant over and pressed his soft, rose-red lips to his mother's. Sian felt a stab of sudden sadness. She would never know such intimacy with a child of her own. She swallowed the lump in her throat and looked away.

'Mummy?' said Oli, all of a sudden. 'Can Andy be my daddy?'

Louise's face fell momentarily and Joanne, standing behind her, inhaled sharply. But Louise recovered quickly and smiled, 'No, darling. Andy can't be your daddy because he lives with Auntie Sian. But we'll see him all the time and you can play with him lots.'

Oli nodded, content with this reply, and wriggled free of his mother's embrace. He ran over to Andy, who was now being attacked by all the children, leaving Louise with a smear of mud on her white T-shirt.

Joanne tutted and shook her head. 'The poor child.'

'He's not a poor child,' snapped Louise. 'As far as he's concerned a daddy is just someone you play football with and rough and tumble. And if he has someone to do that with – like Andy – he's happy.'

'I don't know about that. I think he's old enough to know what he's missing out on.'

'Did you get the box I sent over?' said Sian, desperate to change the subject and avoid an argument between her sisters.

Louise scowled at Joanne and then, turning to Sian said, 'Yeah, thanks a million. The goodies will come in really handy.'

'One of my customers lives round the corner from you,' explained Sian. 'He was going that way anyway so I just asked him to drop it off. One car journey instead of two.'

'Resourceful,' said Louise and Sian smiled, pleased with herself. There were so many ways to avoid unnecessary car journeys. You just had to be imaginative.

'Goodies?' said Joanne.

'Ecover products,' explained Sian. 'Biodegradable laundry liquid, fabric conditioner, cleaning products, washing-up liquid.'

'Oh,' said Joanne, her eyes glazing over with indifference.

'You can get refills for everything from the shop,' she added, hopeful that where she had failed with Joanne she would succeed with Louise.

'Oh, really. What a brilliant idea.' Louise's response was enthusiastic and genuine. Unlike Joanne, she treated Sian like an equal.

Sian laughed. 'I have to confess to an ulterior motive. I'm hoping to make you into a long-term customer.'

'I'd be that anyway with or without the gift. But thank you so very much.' Louise gave her a hug. 'And thanks for finding the flat, Joanne. It's great,' she added, by way of reconciliation.

Joanne beamed, pleased, and the atmosphere returned to normal.

'Joanne rejected my offers of help, you know,' said Sian and ran her tongue around the inside of her mouth.

Joanne blushed. 'It was a simple enough task. There was no need for both of us to get involved.'

'Oh, it's all right,' ribbed Sian gently. 'I'm only teasing. You can tell the truth. You just like being in control and doing things your way. You always have done.'

Joanne shrugged and made no attempt to deny it. 'Is that so awful?'

Louise laughed. 'No, not at all. You've been the boss in our family for as long as I can remember. Do you remember the rotas you used to write out for all the household chores? And you were only eight or nine.'

'I think it's because I'm the eldest.'

'Mmm,' said Sian, 'I'm not so sure about that. I think you'd be just as bossy even if you'd been the youngest.'

'Cheeky cow!' Joanne gave her a playful thump on the arm and they all laughed. There was a short pause while they watched Andy run around the garden, the children in hot pursuit.

'Andy'll make a great dad,' observed Joanne.

The assumption behind the question needled Sian. With her wedding pencilled in for next year she thought it best to put Joanne straight. 'Andy doesn't want to be a dad.'

Joanne tucked her chin in and frowned. 'Has he said that?'

'Yes. We've talked about it at length.'

'But you're getting married.' Joanne brought her perplexed gaze to bear on Sian.

'So?' Sian returned a hard stare.

'But . . . but the whole point of getting married is to have a family, or at least try for one. Isn't it, Louise?'

A twisted smile passed fleetingly across Louise's lips. 'You're asking the wrong person, Joanne,' she said, grimly.

'Well, you know what I mean,' said Joanne, with a dismissive wave of her hand and a faint blush on her cheek. She quickly brought her gaze back to Sian and ploughed on as though she had not touched a raw nerve with Louise. 'That's one of the reasons most people get married anyway.'

Sian smiled patiently. 'We're not like most people, Joanne. You know that.'

'But what about you, Sian? Don't you want children?' said Louise with a look of curiosity on her face.

As though she was the one who was utterly mad, thought Sian, and not the rest of the world. She took a drink of wine and collected her thoughts, remembering the way Oli had looked so lovingly at his mother.

'I don't need children to make me happy. Not my own anyway. I have my nieces and nephew, don't I?'

Joanne shot Louise an appalled look and Sian went on, 'Don't act so surprised. Sure you both know I've never wanted children.'

'But that was before you met Andy.' Joanne's voice was full of dismay.

They all looked out across the garden at Andy who was crouched down, talking to Oli.

'And,' said Louise, who had been quiet for some moments, 'you used to want children. When you were a little girl you played with your dolls all the time.'

52

Sian sighed. 'That was before I knew what . . . what I know now.'

Joanne shot Louise a cautious glance. 'What do you mean by that?'

'There are simply too many people on the planet. And I for one would rather reduce the human population with voluntary birth control than war and famine.'

Joanne rolled her eyes at Louise, then buried her expression in a big glassful of wine.

Sian sighed, feeling belittled by her older sister yet again. 'Anyway,' she went on, doing her best to ignore Joanne. 'I couldn't possibly run the shop and look after a baby at the same time. Plus The Friends of Ballyfergus Lough takes up almost all my spare time. And I don't see the point of having a child if you pay other people to look after it all day. Do you?'

'Some people don't have any choice,' said Louise.

Sian's reply was swift. 'But they do, you see. They have the choice not to have the child in the first place.'

Louise shrugged, indicating that she wasn't going to take the discussion any further. She knitted her brows together, pulled her thin beige cardigan tightly around her body and asked, 'But don't you have any . . . any maternal feelings?'

'Nope.' Sian shook her head.

Louise persisted. 'No desire, no urge, to give birth to your own child?'

Sian shivered involuntarily – the very idea making her break out in a cold sweat. 'No.' She had meant what she said about the need to curb the growth of the human population, but that wasn't the only reason why she would never have a child of her own.

'I imagine seeing Abbey born put you right off,' said Joanne flippantly.

Sian tried to laugh in response but it came out off key.

'It was very special being there,' she said blandly, not wanting to hurt Joanne's feelings, and added, 'Though I have to admit it was a bit scary.'

'Well, I think you might be making a mistake,' said Louise, staring at her son. 'Having Oli is the best thing that's ever happened to me.'

'Is that why you had him? For you to feel happy?' The words, judgemental and accusing, slipped out before Sian could stop them.

Louise looked at her younger sister with steely blue eyes and her voice in response, though defensive, had a well-practised air about it. 'Yes, one of the reasons I had Oli was because I felt something was lacking in my life.' A pause to let this sink in. 'I've thought harder about this than most people, Sian, and you're right, choosing to have a child *is* an entirely selfish act. But I'm no different from anyone else in that respect, married or single.'

'I don't know about that,' snorted Joanne. 'I'm never done doing things for my three. I can't remember when I last put myself first.'

'I'm not disputing that,' said Sian. 'As a mother you do selfless things every day but the *decision* to have a child in the first place is self-centred. That child doesn't exist unless you create it. It's not asking to be born. It doesn't *need* to be born. You have it to enhance your life and make you feel fulfilled in many different ways.'

Joanne shrugged and pulled a face. 'People usually say the opposite – those that choose not to have children are the selfish ones.' She flashed a quick glance at Sian who opened her mouth to respond but before she could do so, Joanne turned her attention back to Louise. 'But it's an interesting point. I guess I haven't ever really considered my motivation for having children.'

'You haven't had to. No one's ever accused you of being selfish just because you're a mother, Joanne,' said Louise, effectively bringing to an end this particular thread of the conversation.

She turned her gaze, softened now, to Sian. 'All I'm saying is don't make any hasty decisions, Sian, and don't leave it too late either. You might regret it.'

Sian sighed and tried to smile. The decision was far from a hasty one. In fact she was quite sure that she'd put more thought into the implications of *not* having a child than Joanne ever put into having hers – and at least as much as Louise. She'd come to terms with the idea that she would never be a mother and she was certain that her decision was the right one for her – and Andy. It frustrated her no end that her sisters treated her like she didn't know her own mind. In fact, while paying lip-service to the idea of sustainable living, they treated everything she felt passionate about as though it was all some big joke. Just like they'd always done. Perhaps it was time to prove to them that she was serious.

She had tried to get her doctor to sterilise her when she was in her early twenties and again when she was thirty, but he had refused. But she was older now and about to be married to a man who felt the same as she did about having children. No doctor would refuse her now, surely?

'Right! Time out!' called Andy and he formed his hands, like a basketball coach, into the internationally recognised 't' signal. He loped across the grass towards the women in a few athletic strides, his face beaming. He came to a halt in front of Sian and ran his hand through his hair. 'That lot are absolutely crazy,' he said rubbing his right elbow, and then the small of his back. There were smears of mud and grass down the front of his T-shirt. Sian put out a hand and touched his arm, muscled and brown where it appeared beneath his short sleeve. 'I feel like I've just gone ten rounds with Mike Tyson,' he went on.

Joanne laughed heartily. 'You look like you have too! But I bet ten rounds with Tyson would be a walk in the park compared to wrestling three hyper kids!' Everyone laughed and she added, 'You look like you could use a beer.'

'Please,' he gasped, resting his hands on his thighs.

'I'll get it. Here, give me your glass too, Sian, and I'll top it up when I'm in the kitchen.' Joanne picked up the empty wine bottle and tucked it under her arm.

Sian finished what was left in the bottom of the glass and handed it over. 'Thanks.'

Just then Heidi, a flash of black, streaked across the grass and ran three times around the garden barking manically, her tail wagging.

'For heaven's sake! Somebody's let her out of the utility room!' cried Joanne and she marched off into the house mumbling to herself. A moment later she appeared on the kitchen doorstep, waving a piece of beef jerky, Heidi's favourite snack, in her hand. She called Heidi's name and the dog raced over, gulped down the treat and disappeared inside the house. The door slammed shut behind her.

'I wonder if Joanne has any idea what her family's carbon footprint is,' observed Sian.

'What?' said Louise.

'I was thinking about the dog. Recent research estimates that the ecological impact of a large one like Heidi is the same as driving a 4.6-litre four-wheel-drive vehicle twelve-thousand miles a year.'

Louise filled her cheeks with air and blew out noisily. 'I'm sure Joanne's not given it much thought, Sian. She seems to have other things on her mind lately.'

'It's up to Joanne how she lives her life, Sian,' interjected Andy with a gentle smile. He grinned at Louise and said, 'Who knows, if we set a good enough example, some of it might rub off on others.'

Louise smiled and looked out across the grass at Oli, who was now happily playing chase with Abbey, their shrieks of laughter filling the air like sirens. 'Oli seems to be enjoying himself.'

'He's a natural with the ball,' said Andy and gave Sian a wink. She grinned back, marvelling at the fact that she had found him, that he was hers. 'He'll be keeping you in your old age, Louise.'

Louise, straight-faced, glanced across at Oli once more and said anxiously, 'I saw a poster at the library for a class called Enjoy-a-Ball. They teach basic ball handling skills to young children. Do you think I should sign him up for that?' She frowned and shook her head, clearly annoyed with herself. 'Why didn't I think of that before?'

Andy threw his head back and laughed, his Adam's apple like a knot in a rope. 'There's plenty of time for that sort of thing when he's older, Louise. He's still a baby. Anyway, kids come to things when they're ready. You can't force it.'

Louise smiled tightly. 'I guess you're, right. I just want to do what's right, you know. What's best for Oli.'

'Well by the looks of it you're doing a grand job, Louise,' said Andy kindly and Louise visibly relaxed.

'Do you think so?'

'You're giving him the best start in life,' said Sian, seeing suddenly how much her sister needed reassurance. 'Not many people have the luxury of being a full-time mum, especially single ones.' Sian's gaze was drawn momentarily to Gemma who was standing on the far side of the garden with a plate in one hand and a fork in the other, talking to her eldest child. She'd gone back to work as a legal secretary soon after her marriage broke up and her son was only four – a tough decision, Joanne had told her at the time, motivated by necessity rather than choice.

Louise cleared her throat, drawing Sian's attention, and let out a long heartfelt sigh. 'That might have to change,' she said flatly, toying with a lock of fair hair by her left ear, the way she used to as a child when she was bothered by something.

'What do you mean?'

'I mean I'm going to have to return to work sooner than I'd planned.'

'But I thought you said you wouldn't go back to work until Oli went to school.'

Louise looked at the ground and bit her lip. 'That was the plan, but I'm not sure I can afford to now. I put cash away for the first three years and the plan after that was to cash in shares. But they've fallen so much, I'm not sure that's a sensible thing to do right now. I'd be better off waiting until they recover some of their value, otherwise I'll be eating into Oli's university fund. I still have to sell the Edinburgh flat and buy a place here and that'll involve legal fees and stamp duty.' She shook her head resignedly. 'I can't see any way round it. I think I'm going to have to go out to work and full-time at that.'

Sian, surprised by this news, was momentarily at a loss for words. Louise had prepared so carefully for Oli's birth and childhood, both practically and financially. Being at home for him, in his early years at least, had been one of the cornerstones of her dream. It was disconcerting to hear that these plans had gone awry. Sian glanced across the garden at Oli, now sitting on the grass making daisy chains under the guidance of Abbey. He would have to go into full-time childcare of some sort – a very different proposition from the one morning a week he'd done in Edinburgh and the very last thing Louise had wanted for her son.

'Would you be looking for something in your old line of work?' said Andy, breaking the silence.

Louise's last job – before she'd resigned six weeks before Oli was born – had been as Tourism Marketing Director for Historic Scotland with responsibility for Edinburgh Castle, the city's most visited tourist attraction.

Louise scratched her head. 'Ideally, but realistically, I might have to cast my net a bit wider. There aren't many senior jobs in tourism marketing in Northern Ireland and with this recession I doubt if there'll be much recruiting in the field at the moment.'

Sian, suddenly inspired, said sharply, 'Aren't they looking for a Tourism Marketing Manager out at Loughanlea, Andy?'

'Yeah,' said Andy vaguely, rubbing his chin, 'it was mentioned at the meeting last week. I got the impression they wanted the vacancy filled by the autumn. It's going to be a world class venue, so I imagine they'll be looking for someone with your level of experience, Louise.'

Louise put a hand to her breast. 'It sounds too good to be true – a marketing job like that right on my doorstep.'

Sian nodded. 'It sounds as though it might be perfect for you, Louise. You should give it some serious thought.'

Louise nodded. 'I'll do that.'

'I wonder where Joanne's got to with that beer,' said Andy, craning his neck to peer into the lounge. 'She's been gone ages and I'm gasping.'

'I'll go and look,' said Sian.

'I'll come with you,' said Louise and they started off in the direction of the kitchen door. Just as they got there the sound of raised voices, a man's and a woman's, drifted into the garden through the open kitchen window. Sian held her breath and stared at Louise.

'Does that,' she said, pulling a face, 'mean that Phil's home?'

The two sisters stepped quietly into the kitchen and closed the back door. Joanne, standing behind the breakfast bar, barely glanced at them. It was strewn with dirty plates, scrunched-up napkins and used cutlery. Her chest, under folded arms, felt tight and her breath was shallow. Her cheeks burned hot. She stared at Phil, sprawled in a chair in front of the crumbled remains of the chocolate welcome home cake she'd baked, and she blinked to hold back the tears of frustration.

'Okay, so you couldn't be arsed coming home in time to help me. Nothing new in that. You'd think I would be used to that by now, wouldn't you? But to turn up now – when the party's almost over. And drunk.' Her voice rose against her will to a high-pitched shriek. 'That's . . . that's . . . un-forgivable,' she hissed, finishing the sentence. 'You always put yourself before everyone else. You don't give a shit about anyone but Phil Montgomery, do you?'

Phil closed his eyes and raised his face to the ceiling, an infuriating smirk fixed in place. He was incredibly handsome – dark-haired, brown eyes framed by long black lashes, a strong square jaw and tanned muscular frame under his golfing polo shirt and pale pink sleeveless sweater. Usually his physical presence was enough to mollify her, but today Joanne barely registered these physical details. She forgave him so often because her physical attraction to him was still, at times, overwhelming.

But today, something had changed. She felt sudden, cold clammy fear. She recognised something underneath his looks and what she saw, she did not like. She shivered suddenly and rubbed her upper arms roughly. Phil brought his cold gaze to bear on her, his eyes red-rimmed with drink, his stare arrogant.

'Do you?' shrieked Joanne.

'Shush,' said Louise, putting a finger to her lips. 'People will hear. Can't you . . . discuss this another time?'

'I don't care who hears,' said Joanne, defiantly, not really meaning it. She covered up for Phil all the time. It was what she did.

Heidi, confined once more to the utility room, started scratching at the door and whimpering.

Sian said, 'Mum and Dad'll hear you if you don't stop shouting. You don't want to upset them, do you? You know how Mum's been looking forward to this afternoon.'

Joanne let out a long slow breath. 'No, of course not,' she said, lowering her voice. 'But will you look at the state of him!' she hissed pointing at her husband, the corners of her mouth turned down in disgust. She grabbed a used napkin and threw it at him – with no weight behind it, it fell pathetically short. Phil did not even notice.

'Bla . . . de . . . bla . . . de . . . bla,' he said, his face raised to the ceiling. He brought his head down suddenly and glared at Joanne. 'It's your frigging family, Joanne. Not mine. I told you I was playing golf today weeks ago and you still persisted in having people over. And then you go about like a martyr accusing me of being in the wrong.'

'You didn't have to stay for a meal at the clubhouse. You could've come home after the game.' And then – because there was a grain of truth in what Phil said which frustrated her even more – Joanne burst into tears. Immediately her sisters ran over and stood on either side. Each placed a hand on her shoulder.

61

'Phil,' pleaded Sian, 'can't you just leave it?'

'I can. She won't,' he growled.

'Please, Phil,' said Louise. 'She's upset.'

Joanne wiped away the tears, black with mascara, with the back of her hand. 'I'm okay,' she sniffed. 'I'm used to this.'

'Pah,' spat out Phil. 'Look at you. The three bloody degrees. Telling me what to do in my own home.'

'But Phil—' began Louise's reasonable voice.

Joanne cut across her. 'Don't you talk to my sisters like that,' she snapped. 'Don't you dare.'

'I pay for this house, slave all hours to keep a roof over our heads and food on the table. I'll do whatever I bloody well like in my own home.'

'That,' said Joanne with a dramatic pause, 'is exactly your problem.'

The back door burst open all of a sudden and Andy came in, his T-shirt spotted with dark splats of rain.

'Not now, Andy,' snapped Sian but he was pushed further into the room by a horde of giggling children, trailing muddy slicks across the clean kitchen floor.

'Sorry,' said Andy with a quick glance at the glum faces in the room and a shrug of his shoulders. 'The rain's really chucking it down, man. Hi, Phil.'

Phil nodded in acknowledgement. 'Andy.'

'Dad,' cried Holly, running over to her father and throwing her arms around his neck. Maddy gave him a wary look and shot a searching glance at her mother. Abbey ran over to the table, grabbed a chocolate muffin and stuffed as much of it as she could into her mouth, moist crumbs falling to the floor. Oli followed suit. Nobody chided them.

Heidi, on hearing the commotion, started howling and Abbey cried, 'Heidi's locked in the utility room!' She paused momentarily to put her hands on her hips. 'Mum,' she scolded, 'did you lock Heidi in the utility room, *again*? She doesn't like it, Mum. She gets scared.'

When Joanne did not reply Abbey ran over to the utility room door, opened it and the dog bounded into the room. She made straight for the table, put her front paws up on it and wolfed down a muffin, paper case and all. Then, before anyone could stop her, she grabbed another one in her long snout. 'No, Heidi. Bad girl!' cried the children in unison and the dog, duly chastised, shot out the back door like a black bullet with her tail between her legs and the muffin lodged firmly in her mouth.

'Wow!' said Oli and the children and Andy laughed.

'That, Abbey,' said Louise wryly, 'is why I think your mum keeps Heidi in the utility room when there's food about.'

Abbey shrugged her shoulders nonchalantly and said, 'Heidi likes chocolate muffins.'

'But they're not very good for her, are they?' said Louise.

'Well, looks to me like this party's well and truly over,' said Phil, disentangling himself from Holly. He stood up, his tall, athletic frame wavering slightly as if in a breeze, and left the room.

Joanne turned her back to everyone and cleaned up her face as best she could by wiping under her eyes with a napkin. Then she busied herself at the cooker, scraping the remains of the chilli into a bowl. She did not want the girls to see she had been crying – she did not want them to know she and Phil had been fighting yet again. But who was she kidding? In a house with walls as thin as paper, of course the girls overheard every argument, every bitter word between them. What was all this fighting doing to them, her precious daughters? How could she get it to stop?

'Right you lot,' said Sian with spirit. 'Out of the kitchen now. Or you'll get a job to do. Who wants to help with the washing up?'

She held out a tea towel, eliciting a shriek of horror from the children and they ran, en masse, out of the room.

'Okay,' said Sian when the children were gone, their peals of laughter echoing down the hall, 'I'll stack the dishwasher.'

'I'll clear the table,' said Louise quietly.

Andy got himself a beer from the fridge and, sensing the strained atmosphere, quietly disappeared.

When the door shut behind him, Joanne said, 'I'm sorry about that. For what he said about you.'

'It was nothing,' said Sian. 'It doesn't matter.'

'I'm sure he didn't mean it,' said Louise.

Their readiness to dismiss Phil's rudeness touched Joanne deeply. They did it, of course, not for him but for her.

The women worked without talking then, the silence broken only by the clank of dishes, the scraping of plates and the rattle of cutlery, while Joanne gradually pulled herself together.

'I'm sorry,' she said when she was composed once more. 'I just wanted today to be perfect for you, Louise.'

'You don't need to apologise,' said Louise, as she stretched a piece of cling film over the remains of the cake. 'It was Phil's fault. Getting pissed and talking to you like that.'

'Maybe I provoked him,' she said quietly.

'What?' cried Sian. She paused by the door of the dish-washer with a clutch of dirty cutlery in her fist. 'Don't be ridiculous, Joanne. And stop apologising for him. You're always doing that.'

Louise glanced sharply at Sian. How long had things between Joanne and Phil been this bad? What had been going on in her absence?

'No, you don't understand,' said Joanne, who looked completely wrung out. 'I was just as much at fault as he was. He's right. He did say weeks ago that the date clashed with his tournament but I went ahead and organised the party anyway. I guess I wanted him to put me first for a change.' She let out a hollow, sour laugh. 'But that backfired, didn't it?'

Tears came again and she put her hand over her face.

Louise, filled with sudden compassion, went over and put her arms around her sister. 'I remember having fights like that with Cameron,' she said and painful memories came flooding back. The fights had started when she, who had given so much in their marriage, asked for something back. 'About different things, of course. But I know how awful it feels. I was so angry with him.'

Joanne looked up, her face tear-stained and said, 'Bet Cameron never spoke to you like that.'

'Oh, he did, believe me,' said Louise, letting go of Joanne. 'Towards the end when our marriage was on the rocks.'

She remembered his exact words and they cut her to the core still.

'If you think having a baby is more important than our marriage, then just go, Louise. I'm sick to death listening to you banging on about it.' He'd thrown a book across the room in frustration. 'Is that the only bloody thing you care about, for God's sake?'

But she'd said awful things too, things she shouldn't have – they'd both been angry.

And now she felt awful that her welcome party had led to this row, yet Sian's comment seemed to indicate that things had not been right between Joanne and Phil for some time.

'Time I was off, Joanne,' said a cheery female voice and they all looked up to find a grey head poking around the kitchen door. It was Aunt Philomena, their mother's sister, whom Louise had not seen since before Oli was born. 'Youse are awful busy in here,' she observed. 'Men left you to it, have they?'

'Funny that,' said Joanne, with forced jocularity. 'When there's work to be done in the kitchen, men disappear like snow off a dyke!'

'Some things never change,' said Aunt Philomena with a hearty chuckle. 'Thanks for a lovely afternoon, Joanne. It was smashing. Louise,' she said, 'I never got to speak to you all afternoon. Come on, love. Walk me to the door.'

In the hall, her tipsy aunt, smelling of Baileys and Imperial Leather soap, pulled Louise to her ample breast – an embrace that required some contortion on Louise's part given that Aunt Philomena, even in heels, was only five foot three. Oli came tottering up the hall, his face smeared with chocolate frosting, and Auntie P's eye fell on him. She leant conspiratorially towards Louise and said, 'Oh, love, I know you did the right thing not getting rid of the adorable wee thing. Your mum told me all about how the father let you down. But that's men for you, isn't it?'

And then she staggered out the front door leaving Louise utterly dumbfounded. She turned to find Joanne and Sian standing in the kitchen doorway. One look at their faces told her all she needed to know.

'Wait. Wait just a minute.' Louise unfolded her arms as realisation hit home. She raised her index finger in the air in a Eureka moment. 'You two knew, didn't you? You knew about this already?'

Sian straightened up. 'What Aunt Philomena said . . . that's pretty much what Mum and Dad told everyone. They said you'd been seeing this guy for a while, got pregnant and then he left you.'

'We only found out afterwards,' added Joanne quickly, looking at Sian.

'And you didn't think to correct these . . . these lies?' demanded Louise. How could her sisters let her down like that? How could they not defend her and Oli?

Joanne shrugged. 'At the time we didn't think it mattered. You were in Edinburgh. Correcting the story would've embarrassed Mum and Dad—'

'Embarrassed Mum and Dad!' repeated Louise. 'What about embarrassing me?'

Joanne wiped her brow with the back of her hand. With much of her make-up rubbed off, she looked pale and tired. 'Look Louise, they didn't mean any harm. And to be honest I kind of agree with them. A lot of people wouldn't understand why you chose to be a single mum – or approve of the way you went about it. A lot of people would think it just plain wrong.'

Louise took a deep breath. 'Let me get this straight. You think it's better that people think Oli was an accident rather than a much-wanted, planned-for child? Not to mention the fact that this ludicrous story paints me as a naïve idiot who got herself knocked up and then dumped.'

Joanne blushed and looked at Sian who said quietly, 'I guess Mum and Dad thought they were acting in Oli's best interests, Louise. And yours. And anyway, what does it matter how he got here?'

'The truth always matters,' said Louise, choked with anger. Her disappointment in her sisters cut deep. Since she'd had Oli, Louise tended to categorise people into one of two camps – either they were on her side or they weren't. She had always thought she could count on her sisters. Now she wasn't so sure. 'You don't know how I agonised about telling Oli who he is and where he came from. How I worried

67

about explaining it to him in ways he could understand. I made the decision from the outset to tell him the truth, no matter how difficult it was. And now I find out that you lot have been spreading all these lies. Lies I'm going to have to undo.'

'We didn't tell any lies,' said Sian boldly.

'You acquiesced. It amounts to the same thing.'

Her sisters glanced at each other again – but this time sheepishly. Louise waited for an apology but none was forthcoming.

'You've let me down,' she said, her bottom lip starting to tremble. 'Both of you.' She felt the tears prick her eyes and bit her lip, the pain a momentary distraction from her distress. It helped her to focus her mind – and retain her dignity.

'I'm going to take Oli home now,' she said, walking over to the table and unhooking her bag from the back of a chair where she'd hung it earlier. The strap got tangled and caught between the bars on the back. Viciously, she yanked it free.

When she turned to leave, Sian blocked her way but Joanne stopped her.

'I think we all need to cool off – let her go.'

Louise found Oli in the playroom with Abbey and Holly, all three quietly watching a DVD of *The Incredibles*. He was lying on a beanbag, his eyelids fluttering like moth's wings, with his thumb wedged in his mouth. Overcome with a sudden fierce love for her child, Louise knelt on the floor beside the beanbag and planted a gentle kiss on his smooth brow and on his round, red cheek, so soft and hot. He was as pure and innocent as an angel – *her* angel, her gift from God, sent from heaven. Oblivious to just how much he had been wanted and how much she loved him.

She thought of the conversation with her aunt and anger

coursed through her veins once more at the thought of how her parents had denied his origins. And in their denial they had made Oli's story a shameful one, something to be hushed up, avoided, condemned and criticised. Louise looked into the face of her child and determined not to let him be affected by such prejudice. Not her darling boy.

Chapter Four

A week later and Louise surveyed the table in front of her, littered with bank statements and an opened laptop displaying a spreadsheet. She ran her hand through hair she should've washed that morning and sighed. No matter which way she looked at the figures in front of her, it seemed she had no choice.

She glanced at Oli sitting too close to the TV on the cream carpet watching cartoons. Her gut tightened. She hated the fact that the decision to return to work was, for financial reasons, being forced on her. She began to prowl through the small neat flat, straightening the cushions on the sofa, picking Oli's toys off the floor. This wasn't how it was supposed to be. Looking after a pre-schooler single-handedly was hard enough without the pressure of having to earn a living. Before Oli, when she'd worked full-time she had only herself to take care of – and Cameron. But he looked after her too.

She sat down on the sofa, hugged the cushion to her chest and remembered how Cameron used to meet her after work and take her to dinner. Once, for no particular reason, he'd turned up with a bunch of forty red roses in his arms. He had been romantic and fun – they'd had great times together. She smiled and imagined him turning up on her doorstep now with flowers in his hands, like he did that day, grinning from ear to ear. She glanced at Oli and thought that if only Cameron could see him, he would love him as much as she did . . . But that was a fantasy, of course. And the life she'd lived before felt as though it had belonged to someone else entirely . . .

Oli had changed everything. Her circle of friends had changed. More and more she found herself socialising with other mothers, women she doubted she would have bothered with if it hadn't been for the fact that they had children the same age. Amongst the people she regarded as her true friends, like Cindy and Max, whom she had known for the longest time, she had begun to feel boring, out-of-touch, uptight and out of date. They didn't want to listen to stories of Oli's latest accomplishment or how long he'd slept the night before. And she hated it when she caught herself indulging in obsessive mum-speak or spent the end of an evening glancing at her watch, worrying about getting home in time for the babysitter.

They listened politely, of course, too kind to tell her to shut up, but she could see the way their eyes glazed over while their minds drifted off. At the end of the day, she had realised, nobody was as interested in Oli as she was. Not even Max, despite his promises and good intentions. Because in the end he'd let her and Oli down, and she really wasn't sure if she could ever forgive him.

But, Louise had told herself, the sacrifices would all be worth it in the end. She had prided herself on the fact that her child would never be shoved into a crèche or raised by strangers – bar the few hours a week in Edinburgh that she had felt essential for her sanity. And now, because of events beyond her control, that was precisely what she would have to do. Anxiety tightened around her neck like a noose.

She took a deep breath and told herself to keep things in perspective. Most mothers worked, single or not, and their children grew up into perfectly well-rounded, happy, successful adults. Look at Joanne's family – the girls hadn't suffered from their mother going out to work, albeit it was part-time and she was always there for them when they got home from school . . . A very different proposition, thought Louise with an anxious glance at Oli, from going out to work full-time. But, Louise reminded herself, being at home with Oli had been a luxury, an indulgence, a privilege. She had lived an inward-looking, self-contained life for the last three years – it was time to join the real world once again.

She googled Loughanlea and spent half an hour bringing herself up to date with the extraordinary project. The scale and scope of it was impressive, and the objective, visionary – it had taken over ten years of dreaming and planning to reach the stage it was at today. The old abandoned cement works – a fifteen-acre site of the most unprepossessing land imaginable on the fringes of Ballyfergus Lough – was in the process of being transformed into a major, ultra-green, recreational and leisure centre. The development would create four hundred permanent jobs – and hundreds more in the construction phase – and bring millions pouring into the local economy. Northern Ireland had never seen anything quite like it. Something in the pioneering spirit behind the project, the idea that someone had dreamt this and then made it a reality, moved Louise. And made her want to be part of it.

Louise looked at the number scribbled on the piece of paper that Sian had pressed into her hand at Joanne's party. It belonged to one of Andy's close friends who, as well as being a site architect for Loughanlea, was also a member of the board. With one last glance at Oli, she steeled herself, picked up the phone and dialled. 'Hi,' she said. 'I'm Louise McNeill, Sian's sister. She gave me your number . . .'

The voice that replied was as rich and velvety as that of the Jamaican continuity announcer Neil Nunes on Radio 4 – though the accent was all Ballyfergus. 'Hi. I'm Kevin Quinn.'

'I was wondering if you could spare a few moments to talk about Loughanlea?' said Louise.

'So you're Sian's sister,' said the voice like melted chocolate. 'She said you might call. It's great to hear from you. How are you settling in? Sian tells me you've just moved into a new flat on Tower Road.'

The personal nature of these questions threw Louise for a moment. 'Why, yes, that's right. I moved in a couple of weeks ago.'

'Good. Good,' he said, his bass voice like an instrument. 'And how are you finding Ballyfergus?'

Louise felt herself go weak at the knees and then caught herself. She cleared her throat. 'Not much changed to be honest, Kevin,' she smiled into the phone.

He chuckled. 'Well, that just about sums up Ballyfergus, Louise. You're not in the big smoke now. Things move more slowly here, though Loughanlea might be the exception. I think it might just put Ballyfergus on the map.'

She could've listened to his voice all day but, realising this was her cue to get the conversation on track, she said, 'Yes, tell me about the marketing job. It sounds interesting.'

'Well, from what I understand, Louise, they're looking for someone with the experience and drive to market a world-class venue. Do you think you're up to the job?'

She gave him a brief résumé of her skills and qualifications and he gave a long low whistle through his teeth.

'That sounds pretty impressive to me, especially what you did at Edinburgh Castle, not that I'm an expert. The Belfast office of the Hays Recruitment Agency will be handling the recruitment process on behalf of Loughanlea and your timing couldn't be better.'

Louise's heart started to race. 'How's that?'

'An advert's going to run in the quality papers next week. If I was you, Louise, I'd get an application in pretty sharp.'

'Well, thanks, Kevin. Thanks so much – for your time and for the advice.'

'Anytime. I hope we meet one day very soon.'

'Me too.'

'Good luck, Louise,' he added and the phone went dead.

Louise put down the mobile and wiped her sweaty palms on the fabric of her trousers. This was a once-in-a-lifetime opportunity to get involved in something really exciting right from the outset. The only way to make Loughanlea into a world-class attraction was through professional, modern marketing techniques – the post of Tourism Marketing Manager was pivotal to its success. Louise suddenly realised, guiltily, how much she wanted the job.

'That sounded very promising, Oli. And what I need to do next,' she said, opening a file on the computer, 'is to brush up this CV of mine.'

There was no response. She glanced at Oli. He was sitting on his bottom, his legs sticking out in front of him and his eyes glued to the screen. She loved him to bits, but sometimes, just sometimes, it would be nice to have another adult to talk to. She liked the sound of Kevin Quinn's voice on the phone – warm and friendly. And she found herself wondering idly if he had a wife – or partner. Almost certainly yes. All the good men, it seemed, were taken.

Oh, what was she thinking! Maybe she had never given up hope of meeting someone, not like some other single mums who more or less resigned themselves to celibacy.

But she had to sort herself out first. She needed a job and a permanent home.

Louise turned her attention back to the computer. She only had a week – there was a lot to be done. Things were moving faster than she liked, but when would another opportunity like this present itself? If she didn't go for it, she could end up unemployed for months. And that was completely out of the question.

The doorbell rang and Louise glanced at her watch. She couldn't believe that three-quarters of an hour had passed or that Oli had managed to leave her alone undisturbed for that length of time. She glanced up – he was playing on the floor with his Planet Protectors from the Early Learning Centre – Max had bought him the entire collection for Christmas. An expensive gift to salve his guilty conscience.

Louise walked to the end of the hall, opened the door and frowned. It was her father, dressed in pressed slacks and an unzipped khaki blouson jacket with a crisp white shirt underneath. He had sunglasses on and sweat beaded his brow. The top of his balding head was sunburnt – it looked painful. He smiled widely, exuding a roguish, even boyish, charm with which he thought he could inveigle himself anywhere. 'Can I come in?'

Louise said, unsmiling, 'If you like.' He hesitated just a moment at this frosty reception, then, when she turned and walked inside, followed her. He called for Oli and he came and stood at his bedroom door. Her father pulled a big family bag of Maltesers out of his pocket and Louise gasped. 'You're not giving him all those are you?'

Her father chuckled. 'Sure I am. If his Papa can't spoil him, who can?'

'There's more sugar in there than he normally gets in a month,' said Louise sullenly.

Ignoring Louise, her father held the bag out to Oli. 'There you go, son.'

Oli, who had never before received such a quantity of sweets all at once, opened his eyes wide in astonishment, then grabbed the bag out of his grandfather's hands and held it protectively to his chest.

'Here, let me open it for you,' said her father. Oli handed it over.

'Not so fast,' said Louise. She snatched the bag and went into the kitchen followed by a whining Oli.

'They're my sweets. Give them back!'

'Just a minute, Oli. I'm just going to—'

He stamped his foot on the floor and pouted his full, delicious lips. 'Give them back!' he screamed.

Something inside Louise snapped. 'How dare you be so rude, Oli! Demanding sweets like that. Stop that at once! Do you hear me?' She glared at Oli who lowered his head like a bull about to charge, folded his arms across his chest and glowered at her.

'Don't be so hard on him, Louise. He's only a baby.'

'Babies can't talk and walk and demand sweets. He's a toddler, Dad, and he has to learn what's acceptable behaviour and what's not.' She took a deep breath, pulled a small green plastic bowl out of the cupboard and, addressing Oli, said, 'I was going to say that I'm going to put some of the sweets in a bowl for you. And I'll put away the rest for later. Okay?' This was a lie – the rest would be binned. All that sugar and fat wasn't good for anyone, let alone a tiny three-year-old. By tomorrow Oli would've forgotten all about them.

Oli nodded reluctantly.

Her parents had no sense – they always plied her son with excessive quantities of sweets. It hadn't been a problem when they only saw him a couple of times a year. But if this was going to be a regular occurrence, she really would have to lay down a few ground rules. She held the bowl out to Oli, he grasped it and a short tug-of-war ensued until Louise commanded, 'Say thank you.'

Oli complied and Louise released the bowl. He ran off into the bedroom clutching it in both hands.

'What's eating you?' asked her father, who'd followed her into the kitchen.

'Nothing,' said Louise and she slipped past him into the lounge and went over to the table. She turned the papers she'd been working on face down and folded her arms defensively.

'You and Oli shouldn't be stuck inside on a glorious day like this,' said her father, with a glance out at the cobalt blue sky. He acted as though he had not noticed her non-verbal signals, which only a blind man could've failed to see. 'Why don't we take a walk down to the front?'

Louise looked out the window, noticing properly for the first time what a beautiful day it was. On the other side of the street the grey-harled terraced houses, much older than the nearly new block she lived in, shimmered in the heat of the afternoon sun. Down on the street two small girls in vest tops and leggings played hopscotch on the pavement, their shrill voices rising like hot air. It was nearly two and she and Oli hadn't set a foot out the door all day. It wasn't, she realised, fair on the boy. 'Okay. I'll get him ready.'

Louise marched at a brisk pace down Tower Road. As they approached the promenade a light breeze, laden with the smell of seaweed and salt, played with her hair and clothes as she thrust the buggy forward like a weapon. Her father walked at her side, struggling to keep up. 'Hey, what's the hurry?' he said, with irritation in his voice. 'It's supposed to be a walk, Louise, not a frog march.'

She sighed loudly and slowed down and they were both silent until they came to the promenade at the end of the road. Behind them lay the hulking grey building that had started life in the seventies as Ballyfergus Swimming Pool. With the more recent addition of a gym and two sports halls, it had been renamed Ballyfergus Leisure Centre. And straight ahead lay the Irish Sea, calm and inky blue, the surface of the water like ruffled lace in the breeze. On the other side of this sea, beyond her vision, lay Scotland – and Cameron. She wondered momentarily what he was doing now.

To their right lay the mouth of the harbour where a small sailing craft was making its way slowly into Ballyfergus Lough. And almost directly ahead was a long, straight path which led to a memorial tower erected some hundred metres offshore in memory of some long-dead merchant from Ballyfergus's past.

The tide was out, revealing a shoreline of black, wet rocks rounded into orbs and strewn with flotsam and jetsam thrown up by the sea – uprooted seaweed, segments of brightly coloured plastic, a tangle of blue nylon rope, a smashed-up lobster pot, a brown leather safety boot. The stench of decaying seaweed was almost overpowering. It had always characterised this part of the town, Louise remembered. But the smell whilst unpleasant was also reassuring, timeless – a reminder that some things never change. Like her parents' attitudes.

Her father leant on the blue railing, crusty with layers of flaking paint, a futile attempt to keep the rust at bay. The vertical posts were streaked with ochre red, like dried blood. He removed his sunglasses, narrowed his eyes and stared out to sea. 'That'll be the Cairnryan ferry,' he said and she followed his eyes to the misty, hulking shape of a vessel some miles out to sea. Uninterested, she looked away.

'You haven't returned any of our messages. We haven't heard a peep from you since the party. Your mother was worried.'

No answer.

'Did you get the messages?' he persisted.

'Oh, I got them all right.'

He turned his head towards her, one foot on the lower rung of the railing, the stance of a much younger man. 'Are you upset about something, Louise?'

Louise secured a stray lock of hair, blown about in the wind, behind her ear. 'Why did you tell Auntie P that I'd got pregnant by some bloke who subsequently left me?' she asked, locking eyes with him.

'Ah, that,' he said softly and looked away.

Louise crouched down in front of the buggy and unbuckled Oli. 'Come on out, darling. Time for a little walk.' Oli tumbled out of the buggy, picked up a stick and started whacking the metal railing with it. It made a tinny sound that was evidently satisfying to his ear. He whacked it again and again. To her father she said, 'Yes, that.'

'We didn't tell her anything much. She came to her own conclusions.'

'Delusions more like. And knowing Auntie P she'll have gone about telling half of Ballyfergus. Why didn't you tell her the truth?'

Dad sighed again and rubbed his forehead with his right hand. 'We didn't think it was anybody's business to know how Oli came into this world. People think what they want to think.'

'Rubbish,' said Louise and her father baulked slightly.

'People think what you let them think, what you *lead* them to think. And you were quite happy for her to assume that about me, weren't you? You'd actually rather she thought that than knew the truth.'

Her father turned to face her then and regarded her thoughtfully as though deciding on something. 'Yes,' he said at last. 'We did think it was for the best.'

Louise's head filled with fury. 'You're ashamed of me and Oli, aren't you? Admit it,' she demanded, her voice high like the wind.

'Calm down, Louise,' he said, not refuting her accusation. 'Surely you acknowledge that what you did is . . . is un-conventional to say the least.'

'So was marrying a Catholic fifty years ago, Billy,' she snapped and glared at him.

He shot her a warning look. A woman passed by with a Golden Labrador on a lead. It looked harmless enough but frothed at the mouth, its breathing laboured. Oli, cautious, scampered back to his mother's side. She placed a hand on his head.

'This isn't about your mother and me, Louise.'

'Well I see quite a few parallels myself,' said Louise, who had given the subject considerable thought. 'Mixed marriages are two a penny these days but back then you broke a taboo. In your own way, you were trailblazers.'

'Don't exaggerate, Louise. There were other mixed marriages.'

'Not among any of the kids I went to school with, there weren't.'

Dad sighed. 'I don't see what that has got to do with this discussion.'

Oli ran along the promenade, hitting the railing rhythmi-cally with the stick like a drum. They started after him, but slowly. The road was a long way away and he was in no immediate danger. 'Well, I would've thought that you of all people would be open minded, having experienced prejudice yourself. In a few years' time what I did won't be so exceptional. Lots of single women will have babies the way I did and raise them alone.'

'I sincerely hope not,' said her father glumly.

'Pahhh,' cried Louise in exasperation. 'You will insist on seeing this in a negative light. And I absolutely refuse to. Look, it's not how I wanted my life to turn out either. I wanted to have children with Cameron. But he didn't and I've had to deal with that,' she went on, her voice breaking. She paused to regain control and continued. 'But having Oli is the most positive, the most empowering thing I've ever done. And I won't let you take that away from me.'

'No one's trying to take anything away from you, Louise. But you can't ignore the fact that the God-fearing people of Ballyfergus might find it unusual . . . hard to understand. We didn't want people judging you, talking about you behind your back. We didn't want Oli to be thought of as . . . different.'

'He's no different than any other child from a single-parent home with no contact with his father.'

'Well I beg to differ, Louise. He is different. His story makes him unique – in Ballyfergus anyway.'

'And that's a bad thing?' she said, almost choking on the words.

Her father fixed his gaze out to sea once more in the direction of the three small rocky islands called The Maidens. He squinted and sighed loudly. 'There's something . . . something unnatural about the way he was conceived. Children should be born out of love between a man and a woman.'

Louise gasped and the back of her throat swelled up until she could hardly breathe. Tears pricked her eyes but she would not let them fall. Her anger held them in check. She swallowed. 'Oli *was* born out of love. No one could love him more than I do.'

There was a long pause and when he spoke again her father's voice was quiet and sad. 'I know you love him, Louise,' he said, looking at his hands, 'but a child needs two parents. No matter how much you love Oli you can never make up for that. There it is. I've said it. And I'm sorry if it hurts you.'

The words stung her like hard rain in a storm. She had wrestled with this belief herself over many months and eventually put it to rest – or so she thought. Now, it was being thrown in her face, like a bucket of icy water. Maybe it was true – maybe her attempt to raise Oli single-handedly, no matter how dedicated, no matter how well-intentioned, could never compensate for this fundamental handicap. It was her greatest fear. But even as these doubts crossed her mind she said stoutly, 'You're wrong. I don't agree with you.'

He made a little tut-tutting sound and shook his head.

'I've made a terrible mistake,' she said, staring at the back of Oli's head. She gripped the handles of the buggy so hard it hurt. 'I never should've come back. I thought I could count on your support and Mum's and everybody else's. But you're all judging me, even Sian and Joanne.'

'Don't be ridiculous. Of course you can rely on us, Louise. And on your sisters. We'd do anything to help you. We all love you. And Oli. And by the way, what Auntie P and everyone else thinks has nothing to do with your sisters. It was our doing – your mother's and mine. We thought we were doing the right thing. And we didn't think it really mattered – you'd been away for so long we didn't expect you to ever come home. Look,' he said and paused. 'If we've upset you, then I'm truly sorry.'

Louise hardly registered the apology. 'I've never been ashamed of what I did and I won't let you make me ashamed now.' She turned her back to her father and pulled a hankie from her pocket. She dabbed at her eyes – tears had fallen in spite of her resolve – and tried to compose herself. Her father continued.

'Look, I can't lie to you about how your mother and I feel about what you did. You knew what we thought from the outset. You can't *make* us approve, Louise. But we can accept. And we do. Look, perhaps it's best if we just move on from here. Put all this behind us and concentrate on doing the best for Oli from now on.'

But that wasn't enough, not for Louise. By sheer force of willpower and reasoned argument she had thought she could blast her way through every objection, every taboo and force her family to come round to her way of thinking. Now she realised that what she craved most was the one thing she would never get – her parents' wholehearted approval.

'Try to put yourself in my shoes, Dad,' she said quietly. 'What would you have done if your husband didn't want children and time was running out? What if you knew you'd never meet another guy in time to have his kids? What would you have done if you'd been me?'

But there was no answer. She felt a hand on her shoulder, a gesture of reconciliation. But she did not want it, not without the approval that she so desperately sought. She dipped her shoulder – and the hand slipped away.

That night she dreamt of Cameron once more and in this dream he was on a small fishing boat with Oli out on the Firth of Forth, teaching him to fish for mackerel. The two of them wore matching yellow oilskins, Oli a mini-me version of Cameron. She was on the boat watching and yet she wasn't – for they could neither see her nor hear her. She smiled at the tenderness with which Cameron positioned Oli's hands and the patience with which he listened to the child's disjointed chatter. And when she woke up – before she remembered that it had only been a dream – she was happy.

Chapter Five

It was early, but the day was already hot and sticky. In the kitchen, Joanne, in a thin silk dressing gown, wiped perspiration from her brow. She collected together the things for making sandwiches – bread, butter, ham, cheese and shop-bought egg mayonnaise. Heidi settled on the floor at her feet, nostrils flaring in the vain hope that a morsel of food might fall into her jaws. Two weeks had passed since the party and Joanne still couldn't look back on the events of the day without flinching in embarrassment. She hoped no one outside the kitchen had heard her argument with Phil.

She laid six slices of wholegrain bread on the chopping board and buttered them haphazardly. She was still furious with her husband for coming home late and drunk that day and she was just as mad with herself for rising to the bait. She should've simply ignored him when he came in – she ought to have challenged him after everyone had gone. Not that the outcome would've been any different, she thought bitterly. He never took responsibility for his own behaviour. She put ham in the sandwiches, stacked them and cut them with a knife. Heidi made a pathetic whimpering sound and rested her head on her paws, her dark eyes staring up at Joanne like oiled chestnuts.

She sighed. Why couldn't she and Phil get on these days? Why was it such mixed messages with him? He loved her food, wanted her home and yet, and yet . . . he didn't see her as a person. Was that the problem between them? Because there was a problem, that much she had acknowledged to herself. The question was – was she at fault in some way? Was she bossy and controlling, like Louise and Sian said she was? Did that make her hard to live with? And, more importantly, what could be done to put things right between them?

It hadn't always been like this. Once they'd worked together as a team, curled up together on the sofa at night with a glass of wine each, talking about their day, making plans together. She'd been warm and loving towards him, he'd been gentle and kind. But somewhere, in the hubbub of family life, that easy intimacy had been lost. If only he would spend more time at home, if they both made the effort, maybe they could find a way to reconnect.

Heidi licked the top of her foot making Joanne laugh – with no one about to observe the breaking of house rules, she tossed the dog a slice of ham. Heidi gobbled it up and slobbered over Joanne's foot some more by way of thanks.

Holly shuffled sleepily into the room just then with her pink dressing gown hanging open and huge furry slippers in the shape of bunny rabbits on her feet. 'What're you doing, Mum?'

'Making sandwiches for our picnic.'

'Picnic?' said Holly sleepily.

'Yeah. Don't you remember? We're going to the beach today with Auntie Louise and Oli.'

'Oh yeah. I forgot!' said Holly, her eyes lighting up and a big smile spreading across the broad face she had inherited from her father. 'Can I help?'

Joanne smiled. Holly was such a good-natured child – in marked contrast to her resentful little sister who walked around as though a black cloud hung over her. 'I'm okay here. But I'll tell you what you could do for me.'

'What?'

'Go and get dressed and tell Abbey to get dressed too. And while you're upstairs tell Maddy it's time to get up. In fact, go in and open her curtains. That should do the trick.'

Holly dashed out of the room. 'Abbey,' she shouted, 'we're going to the beach!'

Minutes later Abbey was in the room, her face contorted with rage. 'I can't go to the beach,' she said. 'Me and Katie-May are going to make a shop today.'

Joanne rolled her eyes, put a round of sandwiches in a sandwich bag and sealed it shut. 'Look,' she said, taking a bunch of grapes out of the fridge and rinsing them under the cold tap. 'You can play shops with Katie-May any day of the week. We've never been to the beach before with Auntie Louise and Oli. Won't it be fun? You can show Oli where the crabs hide.'

'I don't want to.'

Joanne turned off the tap, set the grapes on the draining board and turned to face Abbey. If her youngest daughter thought there was any mileage in putting up a fight, Joanne was determined to deal that misconception a fast and decisive blow. 'You are going to the beach,' she said with dark menace, enunciating each word like a child in the early stages of learning to read. 'You are going to enjoy it,' she said, her pace picking up to a canter, 'and you will not spoil today for me or Auntie Louise. Now go upstairs, get dressed and pack your things.'

She turned back to the sink and, when she looked a

minute later, the child was gone. She hoped Abbey wasn't going to be this difficult all summer long. Joanne enjoyed fantastic school holiday arrangements from her job at the pharmacy – her employers were exceptionally generous in permitting her to take eight weeks off and she was grateful. But, still, she missed the work and her colleagues. She would be ready to go back when the holidays were over. But not yet – the prospect of a day at the beach filled her with excitement.

Louise had taken some persuading – she was apparently still annoyed with Joanne for not correcting the stories their mother and father had circulated about her. But the fact that she had agreed to come in the end was a sign that she was prepared to forgive – albeit probably for Oli's sake.

An hour and a half later, dressed in a knee-length denim skirt, lace-up red plimsolls and a blue and white striped T-shirt, Joanne herded everyone, including Heidi, into her silver Volkswagen Touran. Naturally an argument ensued between Holly and Abbey about who would get to sit in the third-row seat. This was a coveted position because the fold-down seats in the boot were rarely used and therefore somewhat of a novelty. Abbey, the loser, after the argument was settled with the toss of a coin, sat fuming in the middle seat of the second row, her arms folded across her chest and a look on her face that said she would happily throttle anyone who came within a foot of her. She ignored Oli, strapped in beside her, who seemed to be the only one as excited as Joanne. Poor Heidi was curled up uncomfortably on the floor of the middle row along with an assortment of beach bags, buckets and spades.

Louise sat beside Joanne in the passenger seat dressed in khaki knee-length shorts and a bright multi-coloured stripy T-shirt with large red buttons on the shoulder. Joanne knew it was from Boden – she'd seen it in the catalogue. She couldn't afford to buy from there – her top came from George at Asda. Joanne gave her head a little shake, resolving to banish such destructive, jealous thoughts from her mind.

She reversed the car out of the drive singing the first few lines of 'Summer Holiday'. She glanced in the rear-view mirror – Maddy grimaced and put her head in her hands. Joanne smiled and carried on singing even louder than before and after a while, her reserve cracking, so did Louise. No one, Joanne decided, was going to put a dampener on this day.

There were beaches close to Ballyfergus – the rather unattractively named Drains Bay and Ballygally to the north and, to the south, Brown's Bay on Islandmagee. These were well-known to Joanne and Louise but today they were going farther afield – to Whitepark Bay, which lay between picturesque Ballintoy harbour and the tiny fishing village of Portbraddon on the north-east coast of Antrim. The drive took an hour and a half and it was almost lunchtime when they finally pulled into the car park. Outside the Youth Hostel, two female cyclists wearing full-face helmets fiddled with luggage on the back of their bikes. A couple of backpackers ate sandwiches at a picnic bench, huge rucksacks leaning against the end of the table.

Everyone tumbled out of the car, stretched and looked down at the swathe of golden sand below, great waves breaking white and frothy on the beach. Heidi barked at the sea then belted off down the long path towards the beach. Joanne perched her sunglasses on top of her head and squinted down at the breathtaking view, equalled perhaps, but not surpassed in the whole of Ireland.

'Heidi! Heidi!' called Louise frantically.

Joanne put her hands on her hips and smiled at the now-distant streak of black as the dog disappeared into the sand dunes. The sun was high in the sky, hot and fierce – the light north-easterly breeze a welcome, cool caress.

'It's okay, leave her be. She'll not go far.' Heidi was a terrible scavenger – all she seemed to think about was food – but not, thank goodness, a wanderer.

Even Abbey who had resolutely maintained a stubborn silence throughout most of the car journey, suddenly came to life, energised by the sight of the ocean.

'I'm going swimming,' she cried, her mood entirely shifted.

'I forgot how beautiful it was,' said Joanne. 'And how empty.' The wide sands, lapped by wave after wave of frothing sea, were virtually deserted. A few surfers in wetsuits, black and leggy like spiders, rode the waves. On the beach, a flock of grey-white sheep wandered from the dunes onto the sand.

'Mum would love this,' said Louise, conjuring up memories of happy days spent on this beach as a child.

'I know, she used to love coming here,' said Joanne, a little sadly. She pointed at the long flight of steep steps that led down to the strand. 'But she couldn't have managed those steps or stayed very long. We'll take her to Portstewart next week. She'll be able to manage the promenade there much better.'

'Yes, that'd be nice,' agreed Louise and then added doubt-fully, 'You know, I forgot how long the walk was from the car park.' She cast a worried glance at Oli who was examining the small stones on the ground by the car.

Joanne laughed, took the sunglasses off her head and put them on her face. 'He'll be fine, Louise. A bit of a walk won't hurt him. Didn't we do it when we were his age?'

'I suppose so.'

'Well, then,' said Joanne, unwilling to let anything get in the way of her good mood. 'Let's go. If everyone takes a bag each, we should manage it all.' She paused, aware that, despite congenial conversation in the car on the way up, things weren't quite right between her and Louise. She lowered her voice so that Maddy, hovering only a few feet away, would not hear. 'But before we do that, I wanted to say that I'm sorry about not speaking up about you and Oli. For not telling everyone the truth. I'm so glad you returned my call and agreed to come today.'

Louise shrugged. 'It's okay. Though I'm still cross with Mum and Dad.'

Joanne smiled gently. 'Try not to be, Louise. Annoying though it is, they did do it out of love, for all the right reasons.'

Louise nodded and said tightly, 'I know. They'll never approve of what I did but I guess I just have to accept that.'

Joanne nodded thoughtfully and then she cocked her head to one side and gave Louise a broad smile. 'Are we friends again?'

Louise's face broke into a grin. 'Of course we are, you daft brush,' she said and gave Joanne a brief hug. She let her go and hauled the picnic hamper out of the boot. 'We'd better get a move on before I die of hunger and one of these kids,' she said, with a nod over her shoulder in the direction of Oli, Abbey and Holly, who were playing tig, 'gets run over by a car!'

They made camp in a sheltered spot close to the dunes, the fine gold sand dotted with black sheep droppings. Largely untouched for thousands of years, and now protected by the National Trust, the bay teemed with wildlife. A blue butterfly skittered briefly around Joanne's head and disappeared. The cry of Fulmars and other birds Joanne didn't recognise filled the sky as they swooped and glided overhead. Small Ringed Plovers, with their distinctive black-and-white head markings, and the larger Oystercatchers with their bright orange-red bills, patrolled the shoreline. Oli shrieked with delight, clapped his hands at the birds and sent them skywards like a cloud of dust.

After their picnic, the children in wetsuits (Maddy excepted) played in the surf with Heidi, the birds scattering like confetti. Joanne hovered by the water's edge warning them not to go in below waist level – the waters here could be treacherous. Oli wore an old wetsuit Abbey had outgrown, itself a hand-me-down from her older sisters, flashes of bright pink neoprene on the arms and legs. Later they built a dam to divert the course of one of the many trickling streams that traversed the dunes and journeyed to the sea and finally, with the afternoon sun casting long shadows on the beach and everyone happily tired, they climbed back up to the car park, Oli clinging to Louise's back like a monkey.

On the way home they took the scenic road that cut across Ballypatrick Forest, dropped dramatically into Cushendall and hugged the coast all the way down to Ballyfergus. Oli and Heidi, both done in, fell asleep as soon as the car pulled out of the car park. Oli woke in time for fish and chips in Carnlough and they ate them and traditional dulse – dried, salty seaweed – on the limestone harbour wall. By the time they got back to Ballyfergus it was seven-thirty and everyone's cheeks were flushed with the happy afterglow of a day spent in the sun.

Joanne dropped Louise and Oli off first and then drove the short distance home to Walnut Grove. She had disliked the street name from the start – why were new developments given such daft names? What had walnuts got to do with Ballyfergus? It sounded like a street from a soap on the telly. As soon as the car pulled into the driveway, Holly and Abbey ran off to play with the other girls in the street. Abbey really ought to be getting ready for bed but how could the child be expected to sleep when it was broad daylight outside? Heidi hopped out of the back of the car and sniffed happily in the borders, squatting by the pampas grass to relieve herself, before trotting round to the back of the house. Maddy got out of the car, earphones still plugged in, and stretched. In her right hand she clutched her mobile like a talisman.

'Mum, can I go round to Charlotte's just now? She texted to say she's been shopping in Belfast and has some really fab new clothes to show me.'

'Sure you can,' said Joanne indulgently. 'Just don't be any later than ten-thirty, okay?'

The back door was locked and there was no sign of Phil. She resolved to put the past behind her and make an effort tonight – she would get tidied up quickly and perhaps they could open a bottle of wine and sit down and chat properly like they used to. Tired but happy, she staggered into the kitchen laden with bags, in the process almost tripping over Heidi who, despite a small fortune spent on dog-training classes, had never learnt to wait at a door until called in. Joanne dumped the bags in the kitchen and, in the hall, found the wooden floor littered with mail.

Joanne sighed, picked it up and was just about to throw the bundle on the hall table when something caught her eye. 'LAST REMINDER' screamed the block capitals in red on the front of a white, windowed business envelope. Her heart began to pound. She picked up the envelope, turned it over and examined the address on the back – it was from Phil's credit card company, or rather one of them.

All the energy drained out of her at once, the warm, happy glow of the day put out like a fire in a downpour. She sank down on the bottom stair, feeling like a puppet whose master has just let go of the strings. She set the envelope on her knees and wiped the sweaty palms of her hands on her thighs.

The envelope was addressed to Phil. She had no right to open it. But hell, who was she kidding? She had been opening his mail for years. And she did so for very good reason. She saw this not as an invasion of his privacy but as a means of protection for herself, the kids and, ultimately, Phil himself. This was not the first such letter she had seen over the years – nor, she supposed, would it be the last. Overdue bills, parking tickets, even a court summons once for dangerous driving – she had seen them all.

But she knew that when a last reminder was issued, things were very far down the line indeed. Many warnings would've preceded this one. Phil had managed, somehow, to hide them from her. No wait, that wasn't true. There had been a similar envelope a month or so back with something written on it in red, along the lines of 'Urgent! This requires your immediate attention. This is not a circular!'

That day, Phil had been at home and snatched it out of her hand at the breakfast table. 'That's for me,' he'd said, without glancing at the envelope, and stuffed it into his jacket pocket.

'Phil, that'd better not be a red bill.'

Silence.

'Is that a red bill?'

'Just leave it, Joanne,' he'd warned.

'It's not a parking ticket, is it? Not again.'

'I said, will you leave it alone?' And with that he grabbed his jacket off the back of the chair and left the room.

She'd got up from the table and followed him up the hall. 'Whatever that is, Phil, you'd better sort it out. Do you hear me?'

He shrugged his jacket on and opened the front door. 'For the last time, Joanne.' He paused, exasperated. 'It's my business. Not yours. I'll take care of it.'

And really, she could say no more for it was true – it was *his* business. They had always kept separate credit cards and bank accounts. During the short period in her marriage when she was working full-time and before Maddy came along, the idea of keeping their money separate had appealed to her fledgling feminist instincts. Everything was paid for on a fifty-fifty split – furniture, the mortgage, insurance, holidays, food bills. At the time, it had given her a sense of independence. She had liked the idea that she contributed exactly the same as Phil and what was left over at the end of the month was hers. It had worked well enough while they were both earning roughly the same salary.

Now, she realised with sudden clarity, it didn't seem like such a good idea. Now it seemed as though Phil used this financial ring-fencing as a mechanism to avoid fully committing to family life and to his marriage. Why had she ever agreed to such an arrangement? Looking back, the idea of separate finances had been largely Phil's idea though she'd not put up any resistance – she'd been too much in love, too starry-eyed back then to care. Or to stop and consider that maybe, for a newly married couple, this was an odd arrangement. It smacked of mistrust on his part though the irony was that it was *he* who couldn't be trusted with money – not the other way round. She looked at the envelope once more and suddenly, despite her earlier resolution to work at her marriage, it seemed like the last straw.

She was married to an irresponsible spendthrift. In the garage was a sporty blood red Buell motorbike he hadn't ridden in over a year. His biking leathers alone had cost over a thousand pounds. He drove a brand new BMW, wore expensive suits, clocked up speeding fines like she did Tesco Clubcard points, and gambled. He was like a kid, always buying himself new toys. To her knowledge they had no savings between them. Every penny she earned was spent on the kids. Meanwhile, Phil was living like some carefree bachelor. If she ever challenged him about his spending he simply said, 'I can afford it.' Clearly, she thought looking down at the envelope, that wasn't true.

There was nothing wrong with pursuing one's dreams and interests – indeed she'd initially encouraged Phil in his pursuits. But now she begrudged the money he spent because it came at the expense of the family. Sure, the girls were fed and clothed and given cash for all life's little necessities. But they did none of the things Joanne wanted – annual skiing holidays in the Alps, beach holidays in the Med, trips to second homes on the north coast. All the things Joanne thought they ought to be able to afford, if only Phil wasn't such a squanderer. And now he was in trouble yet again.

And the worst of it was that she knew, in her heart, that he was beyond redemption. Hadn't she tried before? How many times had he promised to be more prudent, less impulsive? How many times had he broken his vows?

A cold chill ran down Joanne's spine and she stared at the envelope knowing that he had lied to her yet again. She turned the envelope over. Her fingers were shaking, her stomach knotted like a wet rag. Her heart pounded with fear, while anger towards him for putting her through this torture, surged up inside her like a wave. She prised open a small hole in the corner of the envelope, inserted her pinkie and ripped it open. Inside was a folded piece of typed, official-looking paper. She skim read it, gasped, and let it fall to the floor.

It was from one of the credit card companies. Phil owed them nearly five thousand pounds. If he didn't pay it in seven days, they were threatening to take him to court. The blood drained from her face and she let out a soft, wounded moan. Hearing the sound, Heidi appeared. She sat down and licked the back of Joanne's hand.

Five thousand pounds! What the hell had he spent five thousand pounds on? Nothing that she or the girls had seen, that was for sure. This time he had gone too far. Where on earth was he going to get the money to repay the debt?

She spent the next hour in a daze, her heart racing with panic, her skin damp with a cold, clammy sweat. On auto-pilot, she made a supper of beans on toast which she could not bring herself to eat, supervised Holly and Abbey in the shower, put a load of dirty towels in the machine and went out and watered the plants. And all the while she could think of nothing but Phil and the five thousand pounds. How could he do this to her – and the girls? She resolved not to shout, not to become hysterical. She would remain calm and rational – this had to be dealt with. Right now she had to focus on finding a solution, not solving the underlying problem of Phil and his errant lifestyle.

Later, when Phil walked through the door, the girls were safely tucked up in bed and Joanne, worn out with nervous energy, was sitting on the bottom stair with Heidi's head in her lap. As soon as the dog heard him come in, almost as if she could sense that *he* was the cause of Joanne's upset, Heidi lifted her head and padded back into the kitchen.

'Hi Joanne,' said Phil without looking at her. He emptied his pockets into the top drawer of a small chest that stood against the wall. He took off his sports jacket and hung it on the newel post. There were sweat patches under the arms on his white shirt, stains that would be hard to get out. 'What're you doing sitting there?'

'Reading this.' She handed the letter to him and watched as his eyes scanned the letter and his expression darkened.

'Been opening my post again, I see. Little Miss Detective.' He crumpled the letter into a ball.

Joanne wasn't intimidated. He was annoyed that she had found him out, that was all. 'Just as well, isn't it?'

'It's none of your business.'

Joanne leapt to her feet, her voice raised, her resolve to remain calm forgotten. 'How can you say that? Of course it's my business. It affects all of us.'

'It's my money.'

'That's not money, Phil,' she said, pointing at the scrunched-up piece of paper in his hand. 'That's debt. A lot of debt. Debt that can get you – and us – into serious trouble. You could end up in prison, for God's sake!'

He let out a long, infuriated sigh and hurled the ball of paper at the wall. It bounced off and landed, boomerang-like, at his feet.

'This isn't going to go away, Phil.'

'Stop talking to me like I'm a child, Joanne. I know that. Of course, I bloody know that.' He marched into the lounge and threw himself onto the sofa. He placed his thumb and forefinger on the place between his eyes.

'Then why are you acting like it is?' she said, following

98

him into the lounge. 'Why did you ignore the warnings? There were other letters, weren't there?'

He stared sullenly at the empty fireplace and did not answer. At the far end of the room, the last golden rays of the evening sun streamed into the stuffy room through the closed patio doors. The air was thick and heavy, like her fury.

'And how did you rack up a debt like that in the first place? What on earth did you spend it on?'

He shrugged. He would never submit to her questioning. He hid behind the fallacy that their finances were separate. He convinced himself that he somehow stood apart, independent, unaccountable. And utterly unrepentant.

She continued coolly. 'Have you got the money to pay off the card?' She hated having to take charge like this. Stepping into a role she never imagined would be foisted upon her by Phil's incompetency, taken aback that she wasn't as usual, a shouting, weeping wreck.

He hesitated for a moment, then said quietly, 'No. Not straight away.'

'Right, you need to contact the credit card company immediately, and arrange a monthly repayment schedule. It doesn't have to be much. If you can get them to agree to an arrangement, they'll not take any legal action.'

Phil let out a small, derisive snort. 'What are you? A financial and legal expert rolled into one?'

Joanne took a deep breath and counted to ten. 'If you read the advice column in any paper or magazine that's what they advise people in debt to do. Face up to the problem. Take ownership of it.' The idea of Phil taking ownership of anything, of him taking responsibility, was so ludicrous, she paused for a moment. 'If you show a willingness to repay, even if it takes a long time, the company will usually accept that. They won't want to go to court. It only costs them more money in the long term.'

'I was going to do that.'

Liar, she thought. She blinked at him, holding back the rage like a dam. She knew if she let it burst forth, it would be indescribable, hideous. It would end everything. Her chest was tight with it, her head pounded with it, but now was not the time. She needed to be certain that he was going to take the necessary action to resolve this crisis. She needed to know that her family would be protected.

'Good,' she said. 'So you'll phone in the morning, first thing?'

He nodded and she waited. He cleared his throat and turned his head away from her and said no more. Joanne turned on her heel and marched into the hall, no idea where she was going – and almost collided with Abbey just outside the door to the lounge. She was clutching her favourite teddy bear, his left ear stuffed into her mouth. Her eyes were wide with anxiety.

'What's a "debt", Mum?'

Joanne felt herself blush. She had thought the girls fast asleep. How much had Abbey heard? 'Oh, nothing that you need to worry about, Abbey. It's a grown-up thing.'

'Dad has one, hasn't he?'

'As I said, Abbey,' said Joanne, trying to summon up a reassuring smile, 'it's not anything to worry about.'

'Then why are you cross with Dad?'

'I'm not cross,' she lied. 'I'm just a . . . a little tired, that's all. And we all get a little cranky when we're tired, don't we?' Without a pause for breath, or to give Abbey a chance to reply, she carried on, 'Speaking of which, it's time you got back to bed. It's late.' She put a hand on Abbey's bony little shoulder and guided her, unresisting for once, towards the stairs.

They climbed them together and, when they reached the landing at the top, Abbey stopped and looked at her mother. Her cheeks were flamed by a day in the sun, the freckles even darker and more numerous than before. Tears suddenly appeared in her pale blue eyes.

Alarmed, Joanne knelt on the floor and grasped her daughter's thin upper arms. 'What's wrong, Abbey?'

The child broke eye contact. Joanne's level of concern rose a notch and her heartbeat quickened. 'What is it, Abbey? Has something happened?'

Abbey's face was solemn, hurt-looking, wary. She looked like . . . like Joanne had never seen her before. Her heart constricted a little more. She took a deep breath and, suppressing the hysteria she felt rising within her, managed to say smoothly and evenly, 'You can tell me, Abbey. Whatever it is, you can tell me.'

Abbey nodded. 'Okay.'

Joanne held her breath. Waited.

'Is Dad going to prison?'

Joanne let out a strangled sound, her emotions a tumultuous mix of relief and horror. She pulled the child to her bosom and pressed her face into her neck. Then she pulled away again and looked Abbey straight in the eye. 'No,' she said firmly. 'Your father is not going to prison. Do you hear me? That is not going to happen.'

She pulled the child to her breast again, her heart pounding against her ribs. And, for the first time, she wondered if Abbey's difficult nature wasn't the result of her genetic make-up, after all, but her parents' dysfunctional marriage. Suddenly she was deeply envious of Louise and her simple family structure – just her and Oli. For all the drawbacks of single motherhood, it had advantages and one of them was that Louise, and Louise alone, was in charge.

There were no compromises to make, no arguments, no stress – just a mother and her child living in harmony.

Joanne had resisted the emotion from the day Oli was born but the truth was, she was jealous of Louise. For Joanne's dream of family life – the dream she had fought so hard all these years to hold together – had turned into a nightmare.

Chapter Six

Louise was looking forward to the night out with Joanne, Sian and Gemma. Oli had been packed off to his grand-parents', bless them. Louise's feelings towards them had mellowed. She understood why they wanted to hide the truth of Oli's origins and she pitied them for it – their minds circumscribed by social mores and outdated morals that nobody cared about any more. But what if people here did care – enough to ostracise Oli, to make him feel odd, different, ashamed?

Louise shook her head crossly and resolved to stop torturing herself. Tonight she would not think of herself as a mother. She would think of herself as a single woman – a carefree girl out for a laugh and some innocent fun. There was always the outside, tantalising chance that she might meet someone, but she knew from Gemma and her sisters that the pickings in Ballyfergus were slim. Who would be interested in her anyway – a single mum with a toddler in tow? She had not dated anyone since she fell pregnant with Oli. The idea that she might, suddenly seemed so prepos-terous that she laughed out loud. Her happiness, she had decided after Cameron broke her heart, would never again depend on a man.

She examined her legs – last shaved a week ago – and the

dirt under her fingernails from picking daisies in the park, and frowned. She had her work cut out if she was to transform herself from frumpy mum to glamorous goddess. Time to get cracking.

Later, just before she left the house, Louise examined herself in the long mirror. The simple, wrap-over jersey dress the colour of pulped tomatoes, did much to create the illusion of a bust, and the short sleeves and above-the-knee hemline felt right for a summer's night. On her feet were fine gold sandals and under her arm a matching gold clutch-bag from Monsoon. Her blonde hair, her best asset, was gleaming and carefully-applied make-up disguised the deficiencies in her features – her rather large nose and small eyes. Her tummy protruded more than she would've liked – she stood up straighter and pulled it in. But, overall, she was pleased with the result. The doorbell went – Louise smiled and blew herself a kiss.

They had dinner at Osteria, the up-market Italian on the High Street where, Louise remembered, Lennan's fruit and veg shop used to be. Joanne wore one of her trademark pretty floral skirts and a buttoned-up pale green cardigan which complimented the green of her eyes. Sian, though casual, had made an effort in beige linen trousers and a surprisingly pretty printed cotton blouse in blue, the colour of her eyes. Gemma was chic in tight black trousers and an off-the-shoulder black jersey top. Effortlessly glamorous, she wore no jewellery save for sparkling studs in her ears.

The restaurant was small and intimate with the tables close together, soft lighting and neutral, understated décor. Most of the tables were taken – it being a Saturday night – and the room was filled with the quiet buzz of conversation punctuated by laughter. Once the food had been ordered and everyone had a glass of wine in front of them, the conversation turned to the latest trend in luxe sportswear as sported by Cheryl Cole. The general consensus was that it could only work on the young or the very slim and was thus best avoided. Then they moved on to a discussion about the best – and worst – hairdresser in Ballyfergus.

Louise noticed that Sian was quiet. She just wasn't interested in the things that the others wanted to talk about – girlie stuff like clothes and shoes, haircare and make-up. But being multi-faceted was part of the joy of being a woman, capable of an informed debate about the economic downturn one minute, say, and appreciating the sensuous pleasures of a well-made shoe on the other. All of the women around the table were educated – only Sian wore her seriousness on her sleeve like a badge. The waiter served the starters and Sian only came to life when Gemma asked about her new home at Loughanlea.

'We're moving in on the first of September,' she said, laying down her soup spoon. 'I'm so excited. I can't believe it's really happening after all this time.'

Gemma, who was seated opposite Sian at the square table, pushed the penne pasta around her plate. 'September's not far away. It'll come round quickly.'

'It will. But we haven't much to do. We don't have a lot of stuff and the place comes with flooring, blinds and all appliances. All we have to do, really, is move in.' Sian took a spoonful of bright green pea soup.

'What about getting to work? Will you still be able to cycle?' asked Joanne.

Sian swallowed. 'Absolutely. It's only a few miles outside Ballyfergus and the train service is very good. We shouldn't need to rely on the car any more than we do now. Our house is right behind the shops at the village so all the basics will be within a few minutes' walk.'

'Sounds fabulous,' said Louise, and she popped a spoonful of butternut risotto in her mouth.

'I think it is. There's nothing like it anywhere in the UK on this scale, you know, not at the moment anyway.'

Gemma frowned and rested her elbow on the table, her fork in her hand. 'They're calling it an eco-village, aren't they?'

Sian paused with her spoon suspended in the air above the soup bowl. Her face became suddenly animated. 'That's right. It's at the forefront of eco-friendly design, using all the latest technologies to build the most carbon-efficient, affordable housing available in the UK today. Have you been down to see it?'

'No.' Gemma laughed, rather dismissively, and knocked back the rest of the wine in her glass. 'So are they going to be like those pod things I saw on TV? You know, one-room, dome-shaped things.' She drew a picture in the air, her long slender fingers like a pianist's. 'They were like mini Teletubby houses,' she giggled. 'Imagine living in that!'

'No, they're nothing like that,' said Sian without a smile. She laid down her soup spoon and folded her arms. 'They look pretty much like any other new house. They're not gimmicks, you know, Gemma, they're real homes for real people to live in. Much of the technology integral to their construction is hidden from view.'

'This risotto is absolutely delicious,' said Louise hastily, in an effort to divert the conversation. Sian could be very forthright in her views and had a sharp tongue, though thankfully Gemma, topping up the wine glasses, seemed oblivious to the coldness in Sian's voice.

'So is my pasta,' said Joanne. She called the waiter over and asked for more bread.

'I don't know where you put it, Joanne,' said Gemma, spearing an olive with her fork. 'If I ate like you do, I'd be the size of a house.'

Joanne shrugged. 'Must be my genes.'

There was an awkward silence broken by the waiter bearing a basket of bread. Gemma asked for more wine and Louise, pairing the cutlery on her empty plate, seized the opportunity to change the subject. 'I got an interview for the marketing job at Loughanlea.'

'Good!' smiled Sian. 'I knew you would.'

'That's brilliant!' squealed Joanne, lathering a slice of bread with butter, under Gemma's watchful and, so it seemed to Louise, envious eye.

Sian reached out and touched Louise lightly on the shoulder. 'Well done. When's the interview?'

'Two weeks on Wednesday.' Louise swallowed, nerves suddenly getting the better of her. Up until now she had been confident of her qualifications and ability – if anything she was overqualified for the job. But suddenly it hit home – she had not worked in three years. Would she be in with any chance at all? And if she got the job, would she be able to cope? Would she be able to juggle work with raising Oli? Would he suffer because of it? Of course he would. She bit her lip.

'What is it?' asked Joanne gently.

'Oh, I guess I'm nervous about going back to work. And worried about Oli. About putting him in a nursery full-time.'

'Oh, don't look so glum, Louise,' said Joanne. 'It'll be fine, you'll see.'

'What about a nanny?' said Gemma, playing self-consciously with one of the diamond studs in her ear.

Louise took a slug of wine. 'I'd much prefer that.

Full-time nursery settings aren't ideal for young children. But a nanny would be more expensive than a nursery. I couldn't afford it.'

'I know!' cried Joanne, suddenly, laying down her knife and waving her hands excitedly. 'How about a job-share nanny? Oli could go to nursery half the week, a nanny the rest. And I know just the person. Do you remember me talking about Emma, the other part-time pharmacist? Her Polish nanny's looking for more work.'

Louise's spirits lifted. 'That could work. I'd have to meet her of course. I'd have to be sure she was right for Oli.'

'Klaudia's lovely. You'll like her. And so will Oli. I promise. I'll give Emma a ring and get Klaudia's number tomorrow.'

'I haven't got the job yet,' laughed Louise.

'But you will,' said Sian confidently. 'Kevin Quinn seems to think you're in with a good chance.'

'How do you know that?' said Louise, more than a little surprised.

Sian leant forward conspiratorially and rested her browned, well-defined arms on the table. She glanced around the room, lowered her voice and said, 'He told Andy. They go hill-walking together.'

Louise nodded, remembering her conversation with Kevin and the warm feeling she'd been left with after talking to him. 'I liked the sound of him on the phone.'

'And he liked the sound of you,' said Sian.

Louise twiddled with the stem of her wine glass. 'He said that?'

Sian smiled mischievously. 'Uh-huh.'

'Is he married?'

'Divorced. His kids are in their late teens, maybe even early twenties by now. A boy and a girl.'

'Hey, you're not interested in him, are you?' said Joanne,

forgetting her manners and speaking with a mouth half-full of chewed bread.

Louise shook her head. 'How could I be? I've never even met the man.' But she very much wanted to.

Then the main courses came and, to Louise's relief, the topic was dropped.

Later they went for a drink to No. 11, Ballyfergus's only wine bar cum café cum bistro. The evening was pleasant and mild and some of the tables outside on the pavement were taken by young women in short skirts and tight tops and men in hooded sweatshirts, legs splayed, smoking cigarettes. Inside a more mature clientele was clustered around the bar. The room was rather more chic and sophisticated than Louise had expected – the last time she'd visited the chintzy décor had been tired and in need of an update. Now it was all dark wood and sage green walls with arty monochrome photographs of local scenes arranged about the room.

They managed to find a free table and when they'd all got a drink and settled down in the comfortable brown leather chairs Gemma asked, 'So, if you don't mind me asking, Louise, why did you leave Edinburgh?'

'Lots of reasons,' said Louise and she paused, thinking, staring at the ochre shade on the stylish standard lamp made of black wood. The yellow light pooled on the worn wooden floorboards. She shifted her gaze back to Gemma. 'Well, first there was Cameron obviously.'

Gemma nodded. 'He turned out to be a bit of a shit in the end, didn't he?'

Louise broke eye contact and felt her cheeks redden. An image came to mind of her and Cameron in their early days together painting their first flat during a long, hot Edinburgh summer. They'd worked all day and collapsed at night on beanbags in front of the TV and eaten carry-out pizzas and drunk cold beer. It was the happiest time of her life, setting out on their path together, pursuing what she thought back then were shared goals. She swallowed. His loss was such a blow, she could not bring herself to talk about it even now. 'And of course the flat was broken into.'

'That really shook you up, didn't it?' said Joanne. She put her glass to her lips.

Louise shivered involuntarily. 'The worst thing was that it happened when we were actually in the house,' she said to Gemma, whom she presumed had heard about the break-in but perhaps didn't know all the details. 'It happened during the night, Gemma, when Oli and I were fast asleep. They got in from the back garden through a small window. Thank God Oli was in bed with me and the bedroom door was closed.'

Gemma tutted in sympathy and shook her head. She laid a hand on her heart. 'My God, that's awful. What did they take?'

'My purse and phone, iPod, the flat screen TV. Nothing that couldn't be replaced.'

'They're only things,' said Sian. 'They don't matter.'

And though Louise nodded in agreement, her heartbeat had increased. She knew what Sian said was true but it did nothing to lessen the trauma of the break-in. Even now, nine months later, thinking about it induced the same feeling of panic and fear she had experienced that morning. She wiped her sweaty palms on the back of her arms – and then took a long drink of cold white wine. Her nerves settled a little. 'They didn't even wreck the place. And it wasn't what they took that bothered me. It was what *might* have happened had I disturbed them. After that, I knew I couldn't stay there.' Louise paused recalling how the incident had shaken her confidence and coloured her view of her adopted city. Before, she'd felt invincible. Crime was something that happened to other, less vigilant people. After, she'd felt like a victim and she'd hated it. 'And the final straw was Max.'

Gemma looked up. 'What about him?' Louise remembered that Gemma had met Max once when she'd visited Edinburgh with Joanne.

Louise let out a long sigh. 'I thought I could count on him. I had long conversations with him about how important it was for Oli to have a male role model and he agreed to take on the responsibility before I even got pregnant. He was there throughout the pregnancy, offering advice, helping, as excited as if the baby were his. He was my best friend. That's why I asked him to become Oli's godfather.'

'He's gay, isn't he?' blurted out Gemma.

'Yes he is,' said Louise evenly, and she paused, eyeballing Gemma.

If Gemma had anything to say on the subject, it died in her throat. She shrugged her shoulders and Louise carried on. 'He more or less promised to be a pseudo dad to Oli and then he met Graham and before I knew what was happening he'd moved down to London to live with him. He's only seen Oli once since he left Edinburgh.'

'That's terrible,' said Gemma.

Louise nodded, acknowledging the truth of this statement. 'I know. That's when I realised that the only people I could rely on when it came to Oli were family.'

She looked at her sisters and smiled, feeling suddenly, irrationally, close to tears. She put it down to the drink – at nearly a bottle each, they had all had far too much.

'Oh, sweetheart,' said Joanne and she reached out and patted the back of Louise's hand where it lay on the table. 'Of course you can rely on us. But I'm sure other people care too.'

'What about Cindy?' said Sian.

Louise smiled. 'I love Cindy to bits but she lives the life of a single girl. She's good to Oli but, well, you know, she's got her own life to live. He's never going to be at the centre of her world.'

She paused momentarily to consider these past disappointments that had culminated in her decision to return to Ballyfergus. 'I came home,' she said at last, rubbing the back of her neck, 'because I thought it would be better for Oli to grow up here knowing his family, especially his male relatives.'

'I'm sure you've done the right thing, Louise,' said Gemma, but she looked at her hands as she said it. Her nails, perfectly manicured, were long and red. 'It'll all work out in the end.'

There was a silence then and everyone looked a little despondent. Sian set her glass down carefully. Then she leant forward and said, thoughtfully, 'I can't speak for Andy, but I'm sure he'd be happy to be more involved with Oli, if you wanted him to that is. Why don't you ask him, Louise?'

'I will. Thank you,' said Louise, delighted by the idea. She couldn't think of anyone better to mentor her son. 'That'd be fantastic. Andy's brilliant with kids and Oli needs all the male role models he can get.' She paused then and, not wanting to snub Joanne's husband, said, 'What about Phil, Joanne? Do you think he might be interested in playing a fuller role as Oli's uncle, especially as he doesn't have a son?'

Joanne threw her head back and let out a loud guffaw and her expression when she looked at Louise was one of cold bemusement. 'My dear Louise, I wish he would but the chances of Phil making time for Oli are next to zero. He can't even make time to spend with his own children, never mind a nephew.'

The harsh, bitter comment, even though not directed at

Louise, cut deep. Lost for words, she looked away. There was a football match on the TV and all the men at the bar had turned towards the screen like plants to light, beer glasses in their hands like trophies.

Joanne must've noticed the change in her sister's demeanour for she added quickly, 'I'm only telling it like it is, Louise. Trust me, based on Phil's previous form, you don't want him involved in Oli's life. He'll only end up letting him down.'

Louise opened her mouth to speak, but Gemma, who had been quiet for some time, beat her to it.

'Joanne,' she said sharply, arresting everyone's attention. 'Don't you think that's rather harsh – and more than a bit unfair?'

There was a long, shocked silence and then Joanne gave a hollow laugh and tucked her chin against her chest. She gripped the arms of her chair. 'I don't think so. I think it's perfectly fair and accurate. And if anyone should know, it's me.' She glanced at her sisters, looking for support. Louise shifted uncomfortably in her seat. Sian raised her eyebrows at Louise, then looked at the floor.

'The girls adore Phil,' Gemma continued, tapping the tabletop with the edge of a beermat.

'Of course they love him. He's their father. But that doesn't mean he's a good one.'

'Oh come on, Joanne,' said Gemma, without taking her eyes off the beermat. 'What has Phil ever done to you or the girls that's so bad?'

Joanne blushed and her grip on the chair tightened. Her knuckles went white. 'Drinking, gambling, over-spending, telling the girls that he's going to be at their parents' night, or school concert, or whatever and then not turning up. And he forgot our last wedding anniversary.'

Gemma made a sort of dismissive tutting sound, and

folded her arms on the table. She lifted one sharp, elegant shoulder and looked at Joanne from under slightly hooded eyelids. 'A lot of men are like that, Joanne. Especially ones in professional jobs like Phil. You can't expect him to be there for every play, concert, ballet show and God knows what all else. He does have a job to hold down.'

Joanne, open-mouthed, stared at her for some moments. Louise looked from one woman to the other, horribly transfixed by the exchange between these closest of friends. What was Gemma playing at? She had broken a cardinal rule – whatever tale of woe a friend related, you always sympathised, always took her side. Louise sought desperately for something to say – some way of defusing the situation. Then Joanne's expression hardened. 'So tell me, Gemma, when did you become Phil's defender?'

Gemma ignored the question. Her voice when she spoke was filled with passion. 'You're never done moaning about Phil, Joanne. If you hate him so much and he's such a useless husband and father – not to mention uncle – why don't you just leave him and be done with it? And spare the rest of us having to listen to you banging on all the time.'

Louise held her breath. There was silence for what seemed like a long time and then Joanne spoke, her voice low and even. 'You know why. Because of the children.'

Louise stared at Joanne and suddenly realised that her sister's marriage was in worse trouble than she'd imagined.

Gemma stood up abruptly and the chair legs screeched across the floor, drawing glances from people at the nearby tables. She looked around, her bag clutched to her chest, as if suddenly realising where she was. 'Well, I'm sorry. I'm sorry that you feel that way.' She looked at Louise and Sian and said in a wavering voice, 'I shouldn't have said that. I think I've had too much to drink.'

She made a little gasping sound that might have been a sob, put a hand to her mouth and ran out of the bar, leaving everyone in shock, and Louise wondering if, though she shouldn't have said it, Gemma had a point.

Chapter Seven

Sian, who had been awake since dawn, stood looking out the bedroom window of her new home wrapped in nothing but an old dressing gown. She pressed her hands together and took a long deep breath and smiled. On this overcast September morning the sea was the colour of steel and still as a pond. A bank of fog lay just beyond the mouth of the Lough – on the other side of Islandmagee the fog horn sounded like a dirge. But she could still see across the beautiful Lough to Ballyfergus and the grey ruins of Coraine Castle, a thirteenth-century tower house. It stood on the end of a sickle-shaped spit of land that jutted out into the Lough, on the fringes of the province's busiest ferry port. An incongruous juxtaposition of the ancient and the modern. Right now a huge white ferry was docked, cars crawling from inside its belly onto the quay like colourful ants in a slow, purposeful convoy.

On her right, to the south, the mudflats at the uppermost reaches of the estuary were exposed by a low tide and populated by feeding waterfowl – ducks and waders, herons, swans and Roseate terns, one of Europe's rarest seabirds, along with their less stellar cousins the Common and Sandwich tern. In the winter the Roseates would head for West Africa and be replaced by light-bellied Brent geese fleeing the brutal

Canadian winter for the relative balm of a wet, warm Ireland. One hundred and thirty-seven species of birds had been identified on Islandmagee. The Lough itself was designated as an area of Special Scientific Interest and a Ramsar site, an internationally important wetland. Swan Island, in the middle of the Lough – the only site in Northern Ireland for Roseate terns – was classed as a Special Protection Area. The Friends of Ballyfergus existed to ensure that this status quo remained and to balance the needs of the various users and businesses with an interest in the Lough. Sian considered the success of The Friends in meeting these competing demands and protecting this unique area to be the biggest achievement of her life.

Happiness bubbled up inside her. She placed her hand on the quadruple glazed window, the glass cold to the touch, as if she could not believe the house she stood in was real or that it was hers. Her palm when she removed it left a mark, like the stamp she and Andy would put on this bare shell of a home to make it their own. The terraced house was well-designed and compact but bigger than the one-bedroom flat they'd had before. Upstairs were two bedrooms of equal size – one soon to become a study – with built-in wardrobes and a bathroom sandwiched between them.

Downstairs was open-plan, the living and dining area leading into a small kitchen at the back of the house and a sizeable walk-in cupboard housing all the equipment for the energy and heating systems. She could hear the quiet hum of something – the pump for the hot water system, probably – in the background. She had yet to get used to the sounds of this new home. Outside there was no garage, only a bike shed in the back garden which they'd already decided to turn over to food production. The house was partly clad in planking giving it an American colonial look – the wood was painted the colour of faded blue nylon rope.

She loved it already. She loved the rainwater harvesting system for flushing the toilet, the water-saving taps, the low-energy lights, the freezer from Denmark that ran on the same amount of energy it took to power a light bulb. She loved the choice of materials – the carpet underlay made from recycled car tyres and the low-VOC paints, which ensured the house was odourless. Last night had been their first night here, and they'd slept on the futon they'd brought from the flat in a friend's Transit van. But already the house felt familiar – Sian's soul was calmed by the simple knowledge that living here meant that the imprint she would leave on the earth was smaller than before. At last, she would be able to live as ecological a life as she thought possible and practical in the modern Western world.

The shop was doing well as more and more people became interested in the ethics behind the production of the things they consumed. It provided a decent livelihood and that was all Sian asked of it. Wealth held no attraction for her – she had everything she wanted. Only one thing was missing. And once that was in place everything would be perfect, like a completed jigsaw.

Andy came into the room with a towel wrapped around his waist. His face was red and his chest pink. A bank of humid, damp air wafted in from the landing. 'The plumbing works anyway. And the water's hotter than yesterday. Wanna take a shower and try it out for yourself?'

He threw the towel on the futon, where they had lain together only twenty minutes before. Naked, his body was slim and brown with well-defined muscles on his chest and stomach. A body any man would be proud of, never mind someone on the cusp of turning forty.

'I'll get one in a minute,' said Sian, dreamily, averting her eyes. She did not want him to think she eyed him hungrily – her appetite had already been satisfied.

'You'd better get a move on,' he said, glancing at her, 'or you'll be late.'

She smiled. 'I can open up late for once. It's not every day you move into a new house, is it?'

He came up behind her then, put his arm around her waist and pulled her to him. She put her hand on his forearm, hard and sinewy, and bent her head to the left – he pressed his lips into her neck. 'Or,' he said huskily, 'christen a master bedroom in such style.'

She laughed, then wriggled out of his embrace. 'Oh, Andy. Isn't it just wonderful? Look, I can see all the way across to Islandmagee and Ballyfergus.'

'Yeah, it's great.' He walked over to the wardrobe and pulled out a bag containing his clothes – they hadn't had time to unpack yet. He extracted from it a crumpled pair of boarding shorts and a worn green Billabong T-shirt, for though it was dull outside it was not cold. He pulled on boxers, then the shorts. 'I forgot to tell you. I saw Phil yesterday.'

'Oh?'

'He was coming out of the bookies on Point Street. He tried to pretend he hadn't seen me.'

Sian's heart sank as she remembered the embarrassing scene in No. 11 only a few weeks ago. In the course of the conversation that night, Joanne had mentioned gambling in the same breath as Phil's drinking and unreliability. Phil had always enjoyed a flutter, but was it more than that? Had it become an addiction with worrying consequences for Joanne and the girls? 'He's been gambling again, then.'

'Looks like it,' said Andy.

Sian sat down on the edge of the futon, her legs splayed

out in front of her, and folded her arms. She watched Andy pull his T-shirt over his head and said, 'Do you think Joanne should leave him?'

Andy took a step back and raised his hands in the air like he was surrendering. 'Whoa! That's a big question, Sian. What do I know about their marriage? What do any of us know?'

He picked up the towel and rubbed his hair vigorously.

Sian paused to consider this and folded the dressing gown over her knees. 'I know she's not happy. I can tell you that much. Sometimes, from the things she says, you'd think she hated him. And it can't be healthy, staying with someone you hate, can it?'

Still holding the towel to his head, he looked at her. 'I guess not. Have you talked to Joanne about it?'

'She'll never give me a straight answer. She complains about him, but when I suggest doing something about it, she just shrugs her shoulders and won't discuss it any further.'

Andy cocked his head to one side, considering this and ran his hand through his hair. 'Well, maybe she is happy in her own way. Happy being miserable, if you know what I mean?'

'No,' said Sian and she examined her fingernails and waited. Andy had an uncanny knack for being able to see people and relationships with great clarity and understanding. He said he inherited this ability from his mother, a shrewd judge of character – between them they jokingly called her the 'white witch'.

'Some relationships are like that, Sian. They call it co-dependency. Joanne gives the impression that she's miserable. We certainly know that she and Phil argue a lot. But yet she's not prepared to do anything about it. He keeps doing the same old things and she keeps reacting in the same old way.

120

It's like the needle in an old record player, stuck in the same spot, repeating over and over again. I'm afraid that until Joanne decides to change something – or Phil does – nothing's going to happen.'

'But why would she choose to live like that, Andy? Why would she settle for so little?'

'I don't know. Maybe Phil's a habit that she doesn't know how to break. Or maybe she stays because of the children. It's a big decision breaking up a home when there are children involved.'

'Another reason not to have them,' said Sian darkly.

'I can't believe you said that, Sian.'

His voice was a reprimand – he sounded disappointed in her. 'Especially about your nieces.'

She couldn't bear for him to think badly of her. She let out a long, heartfelt sigh and lay down on her side, her head resting on her hands. 'I'm sorry. I didn't really mean it. I just wish she and Phil could be happy like us.'

Andy lay down on the futon beside her and stared into her eyes. 'I wish she was too. But we can't make her happy and worrying about it doesn't change anything. Be there for her, but don't let it make you sad.' He stroked her cheek with the back of his hand. 'What could you think about instead that would make you happy?'

Sian pressed her lips into a thin line and frowned. 'Louise getting the marketing job at Loughanlea?'

'That's the spirit.'

Sian's smile felt like it filled her whole face, and not just because she was delighted for Louise. Her happiness was due to the way Andy cared for her – she wanted it to be like this between them always and forever. Their life together was perfect – she didn't want anything to spoil it. After a few moments had passed in silence she said, 'You know what I was thinking?'

121

'What?' he said distractedly, staring out the window at the dull sky.

'I should get sterilised.'

Andy jolted like he'd had an electric shock, pulled his face away and focused on her face. 'What?'

'Don't look so surprised. You know it's something I've considered before.'

'But not since we met.'

'I know. But I've been thinking and it doesn't make sense to have to carry on with contraception when we don't have to, does it?'

'But it's a major procedure, Sian. Let's . . . er . . . let's not make any hasty decisions.'

'You sound like my sisters, Andy,' she said darkly, and then added, frowning, 'Though I can see your point about possible risks. Would you have a vasectomy instead?'

'A vasectomy?' he said, with a look of horror on his face.

She laughed. 'Don't be such a wimp, Andy. It's over and done with in an hour or less.'

He looked away and said, 'It . . . it just seems so . . . so final.'

'That's the idea, silly. Anyway, we don't have to make any decisions just yet. Though it might be an idea to do it before the wedding. You know I've been thinking, we should set a date.'

Though they had talked about getting married the following year, they had not in fact settled on a date or indeed finalised any other details. Their wedding would not be the usual extravagant white dress and church ceremony, of course, but Sian held conventional views about love and commitment. Her love for Andy was so strong it almost overwhelmed her sometimes. Life without him was utterly inconceivable and she was gripped by the need to declare that love, to bind herself to him forever. And she needed proof that he felt the same.

He got up suddenly and pulled a pair of socks from the bag. 'What's the rush?'

Sian propped herself up on her elbow and put the other hand to her heart. The throwaway comment hurt. But he would not have wounded her intentionally. He just didn't appreciate how much this mattered to her. He didn't fully recognise the need in her for a public expression of his devotion. And though she tried not to be influenced by them, her family were starting to ask when the Big Day was.

'No, there's no rush,' she said evenly. 'It's just that we've been so preoccupied with the house that everything else has had to go on the back burner for a while. But now that we've moved in, I thought we should make the wedding our priority.'

He blew air out through his nose and examined a hole in one of his socks. 'It'll only be more expense, Sian. And funds are low after buying this place. I'm not sure the time's right for blowing money on a wedding.' He looked about the room with a perplexed expression on his face, as though confused by something, then threw the sock to one side. He pulled another, mismatching one from the bag.

'It doesn't have to be,' she said carefully, 'it doesn't have to cost very much at all. We could have a simple service in a registry office followed by an exchange of vows, perhaps at home, in front of close friends and family. Or maybe a barbecue on the beach at Ballygally.' This was where they'd first talked about getting married on a long summer's night, sitting shoulder to shoulder on the slipway. 'The sort of wedding we talked about will hardly make a dent in our finances, Andy, let alone blow a hole in them.' She paused and added, even though it seemed highly unlikely, 'Unless you've changed your mind. Unless you want something more elaborate.' She frowned at him and asked again, 'Do you?'

He pulled the socks on then stood up, put his hands on his hips and went over to the window. He looked out, let out a long sigh, and said, 'Oh, I don't know.'

Sian's heart stood still. She took a deep breath and hauled herself into a kneeling position on the bed, legs bent underneath, and sat on her heels. What did he mean? He'd never cared, or worried, about money before – it was one of the things she loved about him, his utter lack of materialism. So why start now? Had he really changed his mind about the sort of wedding they should have? Or had he changed his mind about getting married?

'Andy?' she croaked, her voice tight with fear.

He ran his hands over his face as if rubbing away the troubling thoughts she saw etched in his features. He did not answer.

'Andy. This isn't just about money, is it?'

He looked at her, held out both hands, palms upwards. 'No.'

Her heart pounded in her chest. Of course it wasn't about money – her instincts had told her that. But she could think of only one other reason why he would not want to go through with the marriage. Did he no longer love her? She opened her mouth but no words came out.

'It's just,' he said, and he paused as if struggling to find the words, '. . . well, what do we need to get married for? Sure we've been living together happily for nearly five years. What difference will a marriage certificate, a piece of paper, make to our relationship?'

Sian sat perfectly motionless struggling to breathe. Andy had never spoken like this before. It was he who had asked her to marry him and now he was belittling the idea. She got to her feet unsteadily and pulled the dressing gown around her, feeling suddenly vulnerable – and unwanted. He did not want to get married – he was looking for excuses.

'Seriously Sian,' he went on, in the face of her silence, 'what difference will it make?'

The muscles in her jaw were tight and her words, when she uttered them, were dripping with disappointment. 'But I thought you wanted to get married. And it's not about a piece of paper. It's about us declaring our commitment to each other. About telling everyone that we love one another.'

He sighed and smiled but his eyes were sad. 'But we already know how we feel about each other, Sian. We don't need to get married to prove that. And it's not as if we're going to have children, is it? I could see the logic, the necessity, then.'

She shook her head, confused by his argument. What had children got to do with this discussion? 'Don't you love me, Andy?' she said at last, voicing her deepest fear.

He came over then and took her hand and held it between his own. 'Of course I love you, Sian,' he said, 'more than you will ever know.'

She shook her head, not understanding. If he loved her, what was the problem? 'Then let's get married,' she said simply.

His gaze slid away onto the floor and when he brought it back again something had altered. His expression was guarded and the smile he gave her was a painful one. He let go of her hand gently, reluctantly it seemed, and it fell lifelessly to her side. 'I'd better get going. I don't want to miss my train. Connor's picking me up at the station.' Connor was one of Andy's work colleagues – they shared a lift from Ballyfergus to the outdoor centre at Cushendall.

Fear gripped her heart. He couldn't go, not yet. She needed to remind him how much marriage meant to her – though how, she thought with a frown, could he have forgotten? For they shared everything, from the banal to the profound. Well, almost everything. There were things she kept from him of course. Like the real reason why she didn't want children.

But for the first time, she felt that Andy was keeping something from her. And she had the most awful feeling that if she let him go now, with things unsaid between them, their relationship would be forever altered. She reached out and touched his shoulder. 'Stay with me. Please.'

'I can't. You know I can't,' he said, running a hand through his still wet hair. 'I haven't even got time for breakfast and I can't afford to be late today. I've got a packed day ahead of me. We've a big crowd of kids coming down from Belfast. It's one of these cross-community initiatives and you know what some of those kids are like. They can be a handful. I can't let the rest of the team down.'

She took a step backwards, away from him. He wouldn't let his workmates down or a gang of troublesome kids he'd never even met before. But he thought nothing of letting her down. Of shattering her dreams. 'Of course,' she said, surprised that her voice sounded so normal, when her heart ached with anguish.

'Come here, you.' He pulled her to him in an awkward embrace. She did not respond. He acted as though he hadn't noticed and placed a kiss on her forehead. 'You'd better get a move on too. Bernie'll be waiting for you.' Bernie was the young woman who helped out at the shop a few days a week.

She couldn't give a toss about the shop. All she cared about was Andy and the fact that she knew, instinctively, that something was seriously wrong. Because she didn't buy his glib reasons for not wanting to get married – they sounded hollow and too well rehearsed. No, for what she believed to be the first time ever, he was holding out on her. But by the time she opened her mouth to tell him this, he had already left the room. Seconds later she heard the front door shut.

She crawled back into bed and lay on her side and looked at a small picture in a papier mâché frame sitting on the floor – the first thing she had unpacked. It was of her and Andy standing on the marshy shore of Upper Lough Erne, tanned and smiling, in shorts and T-shirts. It had been their first holiday together, a five-day kayak trip on the Lakes of Fermanagh. She smiled, remembering the thrill of setting out in the morning, the mist rising from the water, Andy beside her in his kayak. The rhythmic, synchronised beat of their paddles was the only sound to be heard, bar the call of great-crested grebes and the whoosh of wings as grey herons, startled by their approach, took to the wing. And she had marvelled then, as she did now, at her good fortune in meeting a man who shared her passions.

She pulled the bed covers, still smelling of Andy, up to her chin. An overwhelming sense of hurt and disappointment threatened to reduce her to tears. Her head was swimming, Andy's words ricocheting around like ping-pong balls. She blinked hard, trying not to cry, but there was no denying her feelings as she lay there alone on the unmade bed and stared out at the grey sky. Unable to stop them, hot tears slid out of the outermost corners of her eyes and down her temples, seeping into her hair like blood from a wound.

He had said he loved her. But if he loved her, truly loved her, he would not hurt her so. He understood damn well what marriage meant to her. Hadn't they talked about it often enough? Hadn't they both said that they wanted to commit to each other? That they would grow old together, loving each other till the last.

Unless . . . unless he no longer wanted to make such a commitment. But why? What had changed? She swallowed and the most treacherous of thoughts crept into her consciousness. Had the unthinkable happened? Had he met someone else? No, never, that could not happen. To other people who didn't love each other so much, yes, but not to them. Not to her. Never.

She rolled onto her stomach, pressed her cheek against the sheet and pulled the pillow over the back of her head, as if she could block out this idea with a physical barrier.

Love and peace, she said to herself. Love and peace.

It was the mantra she used when she meditated. She tried to focus on it, to let this destructive notion slip by like a passing train, observing, but not reacting to it.

Love and peace.

But what other explanation could there be? She recalled Andy's shifting gaze, the uncertain logic of his arguments. The awful suspicion – rapidly turning into a conviction – that he had lied to her.

Love and peace.

If she tried very hard, and concentrated, she could rid her mind of this destructive thought. She knew she could.

Love and peace.

There could be many other perfectly plausible explanations for Andy's behaviour. He could be going through some sort of personal crisis. He was thirty-nine, just one year shy of the Big Four-O, the age at which, in theory anyway, many men began to question their lives. He could be worried about work, about losing his job. He had said that bookings from corporate clients were down due to the recession. But why not tell her? Why lie?

Love and peace.

Her mind, restless and searching, came back inexorably to the same explanation, drawn to it like a wasp to ice cream. Infidelity – either in thought or deed.

Love and peace.

She gritted her teeth. Then she got onto her knees and, mad with exasperation, held the pillow above her head, then thwacked it on the bed.

Love and peace.

She formed her right fist into a tight ball, the thumb curled across the index and middle finger, her knuckles white with tension. Then she brought it down with force into the centre of the pillow, as if this inanimate object were responsible for her heartache. And she pummelled it until her brow was beaded with sweat and her arm weak with exhaustion.

Love and peace.

With the onset of the new school term looming, Joanne had spent the last few days of August frantically clearing out wardrobes, sorting through hand-me-down uniforms for Holly and Abbey and making a shopping list of all the things the girls would need. In a short while, they would need winter coats and boots as well. Raising children, she thought with a shake of her head as she stuffed Abbey's too-small uniform from last year into a bag for the Oxfam shop, was an expensive business.

On the last Tuesday of the holidays they went shopping in Belfast, Holly and Abbey giddy with excitement in the back seat of the car – and Maddy in the front, doing her best to maintain a nonchalant air. It was an airless day, humid and sticky. Grey clouds, the sort that would not produce rain, stretched across the sky like a thick mass of dusty grey cobwebs. In the car, while Holly and Abbey sang along to Girls Aloud, Maddy stared out of the window at the rolling hills patchworked with fields, playing with her hair, her eye-wateringly short skirt nearly up to her crotch. Joanne looked away, bit her tongue, and thought about her marriage.

After Gemma's outburst in No. 11 some weeks ago, she had taken a long, hard look at her attitude to Phil and she had found herself wanting. Gemma's observations had been uncomfortable, painful even, and Joanne's immediate reaction had been one of indignation that her friend had criticised her in such a public way. And though she forgave Gemma immediately when she phoned the very next day to apologise, it had taken her a few weeks to fully digest what had happened that night. Eventually she saw that her friend had been right. She had said what needed to be said, even at the risk of alienating Joanne, and that was a mark of true friendship.

She had become trapped in a vicious cycle of recrimination and reproach as far as Phil was concerned. In her defence, he had driven her to distraction over the years, but he did have redeeming qualities. He worked hard as regional sales manager for a pharmaceutical company, loved his daughters, kept a roof over their heads and food on the table. He could be spontaneous and generous, when the mood took him, and he loved her. Her mistake had been to try and change him, to iron out the flaws in his character, to make him into something he wasn't.

That was where she had gone wrong. She had entered into marriage, knowing full well that he liked a drink, that he had a dangerous, reckless side that did not like to be contained. Wasn't that what had attracted her to him in the first place? Wasn't that what made him devilish and irresistible? Phil hadn't changed, the circumstances in which he found himself had. Because the problem was that these characteristics were incompatible with the responsibilities of married life. But, as she had explained to a reticent Gemma only the other night, if she wasn't prepared to leave Phil – and she wasn't – then she had to find a way to make it work.

She loved Phil and did not want to be alone. She did not want to be like Gemma, whom she admired and pitied in equal measure. She thought she did not have the independent spirit necessary to survive as a single parent. And, for all Phil's faults, she didn't want to.

She might be lonely in her marriage sometimes, but she'd be a damn sight lonelier without it. Her role as a wife was as much a part of her identity as being a mother, pharmacist, daughter, sister. It was integral to how she viewed herself and her place in society. She had always seen coupledom as some sort of nirvana. Even now with all its ugly flaws she thought, slipping into fifth gear, she would still choose her marriage over single motherhood.

She had to rediscover her love for the man she had married, accept his failings and make her marriage a success. And if that meant shouldering responsibilities that she felt were rightly his, expecting less of him and not despising him for it, then she must do that and do it gracefully.

And that is what she had tried to do these last few days. She reminded herself that she'd forgotten what it was like to work full-time in a high-pressure job. She had tried hard to put herself in Phil's shoes, to appreciate the burden of responsibility he must feel towards her and the kids, and the pressures he worked under. All that travelling and those long hours – it couldn't be much fun – and neither could coming home to a nagging wife every night. She even tried to look at his extravagances in a different light. Perhaps they were his way of reminding himself that he was still hip and cool and had an identity other than husband and dad. Perhaps if she stopped trying to hold on so hard, he might stop pulling away.

She was determined to change. They reached Belfast and, as she navigated through the busy city streets, she reflected on the very great debt she owed Gemma – for opening her eyes to the fact that she had been very close to destroying her marriage.

In a funky shop filled with too-loud music on the first floor of Castle Court shopping centre, Maddy picked up a trainer and examined it.

'We just haven't got the money for those,' Joanne whispered into Maddy's ear. Outside the shop Holly and Abbey, bored already, were playing hopscotch on the smooth marble floor.

Maddy let out a long, ill-tempered sigh. 'We never have enough money for anything,' she said loud enough for the shop assistant, a skeletal creature dressed all in black, to hear despite the background racket, drawing red blushes to Joanne's cheeks. 'How come Charlotte and Roz can have whatever they want and I never can?' She threw the shoe down and marched out of the shop.

Joanne picked the trainer up and looked at the price tag – seventy quid. She sucked in her cheeks. Out of the question. She set it gently back on the display stand with a humble, apologetic nod at the sales assistant. Outside, she found Maddy leaning over the balcony looking down at the shoppers on the level below. Abbey was sitting on a nearby bench playing with her pink Nintendo DS, Holly hanging over her shoulder watching. Joanne stood beside Maddy in silence for some moments, not willing to admit that she didn't understand it either. Did other people manage their money better as she suspected? Or did they go into debt to spoil their children?

'I'm sorry, Mum,' said Maddy suddenly and she looked rather embarrassed. 'I know it's not your fault.'

Joanne smiled and thought about Phil, at whose door she firmly laid the blame. She was quite sure that if she had the job of managing the family's finances she'd make a much better job of it. Perhaps this was something, in her new-found conciliatory spirit, they could address together. 'You don't need them for school, anyway. Sure you don't?'

'I guess not.'

'Well then,' said Joanne, using brusqueness to deflect Maddy's disappointment – and hide her own. Immediately she thought of her husband's reckless spending and her heartbeat increased. She took a long deep breath and closed her eyes. She had promised herself she would not go down that route again. It was so easy to latch on to the negative and to blame Phil for everything that was wrong. She must focus on the positive, like the fact that she was spending the afternoon with her three gorgeous daughters. She opened her eyes and focused on an ice-cream stand on the floor below. She might not be able to afford designer trainers but she could buy the girls a Ben and Jerry ice cream. 'Come on, girls. Let's go get a treat.'

They shopped wisely and Joanne managed to kit out all three girls for school, within budget. By the time Joanne finally managed to drag Maddy out of Zara and they fought their way through the commuter traffic, it was late and everyone was hungry. When Joanne pulled into the driveway just after six Phil's car was, unusually, already in the drive.

Laden with bags from New Look, Primark, H&M, Mango and Zara they all stumbled into the house. Heidi came bounding through from the kitchen, jumped up on Joanne and slobbered on her right cheek. 'Get off, you daft thing,' she scolded but her voice was soft with laughter and the dog paid little attention. Maddy went straight upstairs with her purchases, while Holly and Abbey burst into the kitchen clutching plastic bags. Joanne and Heidi followed in their wake. Phil sat at the table reading the paper with a mug by his right arm. The smell of freshly brewed coffee filled the room. His jacket was slung over the back of the chair, the top two buttons of his shirt undone, his red and white striped tie askew.

'Dad,' shouted Abbey, commanding his attention immediately. She pulled something out of a bag. 'Dad! Look! I got this for school.' She held up a red scallop-edged cardigan from Primark. 'Dad, you're not looking!'

Phil, finally tearing his eyes away from the sports page, glanced up and smiled wearily. 'That's nice.'

'Hi, Phil,' said Joanne, bustling over to the table with a bag of groceries in her arms. He didn't reply.

'And look what I got,' said Holly, elbowing in front of Abbey with a *High School Musical* lunchbox in her hand. She held it up, inches from Phil's face and said, 'It's for my lunch.'

'Mum,' hollered Abbey. 'She just pushed in front of me!'

'Very nice, Holly,' said Phil and he glared at Abbey. 'Now both of you hop it. I'm trying to read the paper.'

The girls, immediately silenced in a way Joanne had never been able to achieve, ran out of the room jostling competitively with each other. Joanne set the plastic bag, full to bursting, on the table and looked at Phil. He turned a page of the broadsheet.

'Did you finish early today then?' she asked brightly.

'That's right,' he said without taking his eye off the paper.

She took a deep breath. If things were to improve between them, she couldn't do it alone. It was going to take effort on Phil's part, as well as hers.

'Well, it's nice to see you home early for once,' she said pleasantly and he grunted.

Joanne gritted her teeth and, determined not to be deflected from her new approach, started taking ready meals out of the bag. Heidi, who would've made an excellent sniffer dog, came and stood between two chairs, her snout resting on the edge of the table. Her nose was wet and her nostrils quivered in anticipation.

'There's nothing here for you, Heidi,' said Joanne as she set a packet of breaded fish on the table, and said to Phil, 'I bought a Marks and Spencers' pasta bake for our dinner tonight and fish and chips for the kids. A bit of a treat, I know. But I didn't think I'd have time to cook. Anyway,' she added, when this chatter produced only indifferent silence, 'how was your day?'

Phil folded the paper, leant back in the chair and stuck his legs out, crossed at the ankles. Even at forty-six he still had a toned, flat stomach. He looked at her oddly as if seeing her properly for the first time since she'd come into the room. 'You really want to know?'

Joanne pulled out a chair and sat down. 'Yes. Yes, I do.' She folded her hands in her lap and felt that she was waiting for something more than just an explanation of how Phil's day had gone.

A ghost of a smile passed across his face. And though his skin was still tanned from the summer sun, he looked tired, haggard even. He frowned, causing his eyes to narrow like a sleepy cat's. 'Why are you being so . . . so nice?'

She shrugged, looked away and said a little awkwardly, 'Am I?'

He nodded and in a slightly scathing tone said, 'Very different from the usual . . . you.'

She coloured out of embarrassment – was she habitually horrible to him? – and said, 'Well, I guess I . . . I'm trying to make things better. Between us I mean.'

'I see,' he said slowly, and he rubbed his chin, the frown deepening until his eyes all but disappeared under his black eyebrows. He drained the contents of the mug and set it down on the table. He hadn't thought to use a coaster and had already left a wet ring mark on the wood. Joanne tried not to let this annoy her.

She twisted her hands together in the folds of her skirt and said, stopping short of an apology, 'I thought that maybe we could try to work together instead of working against each other all the time. And maybe be more open with each other, especially when it comes to financial matters. I—'

'Oh, so this is about money, is it?' he said sceptically, cutting her off.

She shook her head, angry that his instinctive interpretation of her good intentions was negative. 'No, it's not about money,' she said, pushing thoughts of the red credit card bill to the back of her mind. She still didn't know whether he'd paid it or not . . . he'd better have. 'It's about us working together as a team, instead of working against each other. Sometimes we don't look like a married couple – we look like . . .' She glanced around the room, grasping for an analogy but settled for '. . . like two independent people sharing a house.' And sometimes also like two people who don't like each other very much, she thought, but refrained from sharing this opinion.

Phil shrugged. 'You lead your life, I lead mine. What's wrong with that?'

'I just think that maybe we should . . . try a little harder. Spend more time together as a couple – and a family.'

Phil snorted. 'Joanne, with the hours I work and the travelling I do there's not much time left for anything else. That's why you work part-time – so that you can be here for the kids. Because I can't.'

'What about the weekends?'

'You're not asking me to give up golf, are you?' He sounded horrified.

'No, but do you have to play every single weekend? And do all the social stuff afterwards?'

'Golf and going for a pint with the lads is the only relaxation I get. I'm not giving it up,' he said stubbornly.

'I'm not saying you should,' said Joanne levelly, the tension gathering between her shoulder blades. 'Only that maybe we should . . . try and change things a little.'

'I can't see how, Joanne. This family depends on my salary. I think you forget that sometimes.'

Joanne let out a long sigh. This wasn't going as well as she'd hoped. 'Can we not have a sensible conversation without you going on the offensive, Phil?' she said irritably and added quickly in a more conciliatory tone, 'I'm just saying that we could be so much better together. You must agree. We argue over things we shouldn't be arguing about. Like money.'

He rolled his eyes. 'Here we go again.'

'No, wait. Don't be like that,' she said and paused. She held a motionless hand in the air as if to still him. 'Though I do think that if we managed our money together, we'd make a better job of it. If we made joint decisions about spending – and saving – I'd feel so much more involved and less like the little woman sitting at home. And I do contribute, albeit not to the same extent as you.'

He stared at her with his lips pressed together, like a dam holding back water. When he finally spoke, he stunned Joanne into momentary silence. 'I could leave if you like,' he said quietly. 'Move out.'

Joanne's hand fell into her lap. Her mouth went suddenly dry. She swallowed, and finding her voice again, said angrily, 'Where did that come from? I'm trying to have a civilised conversation about our family,' she added, 'and you come off with something like that!' She would not entertain the idea that he was serious. It was typical of Phil to come off with something stupid to throw her off track, to try to win the upper hand in an argument.

Phil leant forward in the chair, his elbows resting on his knees. 'Joanne, all I ever get from you is complaints. I play too much golf,' he said calmly, counting off infringements on the fingers of his left hand, 'I don't spend enough time with the girls. I don't spend enough time with you. I go out too much. I drink too much. You don't like my friends.'

'That's not true,' she lied. She hardly knew them but she held them responsible for leading her husband astray. They were all drinkers and gamblers – and two of them, Mark and Craig, she knew for a fact had left broken marriages in the wake of their good-time living.

Well, Joanne didn't intend to be another victim. She had resolved not to try and change Phil. But unless he changed a little, unless there was give and take on both sides, how could she make their marriage work?

'Are you saying you're happy, Phil?' she said bravely, at last. 'Are you saying that you're happy with our life together? With this marriage and family the way it is?'

He looked quickly away, cleared his throat. 'It seems to me that this is the reality of family life, Joanne.' He looked around the compact kitchen that reflected how she felt about her life – so much smaller than she had hoped for. He folded his arms across his chest. 'And it's no better or worse than anyone else's marriage. Life's never perfect, is it? It's just a question of . . . of living with it.' He looked as if he was going to say more, then closed his mouth.

A question of living with it? Was that how Phil really saw his life, his marriage? If he did, it was beyond depressing – and grossly unfair. Yes, he worked full-time and brought in the main salary, but she was the one who did everything else to make this home run smoothly. Phil had never planned a kid's birthday party, ironed so much as a shirt, cleaned, cut the grass, made a packed lunch or cooked a meal. 'A question of living with it?' she said. 'What? Like living with a chronic illness?'

He brought his gaze to bear on her once more. 'Let me ask you the same question you just asked me. Are you happy?'

Joanne paused, sensing a hidden agenda behind the question. 'I could be,' she said cautiously.

'If what?'

'If—' she began but he did not let her finish.

He sat suddenly upright in the chair. 'If I changed into some sort of lily-livered lapdog who was at your beck and call twenty-four seven,' he said, raising his voice and tapping the table with his index finger. 'If I gave up golf and seeing my pals and spent my weekends doing DIY and gardening like Tommy along the road.' Tommy Gillespie, a teacher at St Pat's, lived two doors down. A homebody, he rarely went out and gave the impression of being devoted to his wife and two children. Once, when it was his wife Gaynor's birthday, he left a brand new car in the drive for her tied up with the biggest red ribbon Joanne had ever seen. It had created great excitement in the street – and jealousy in Joanne's heart. 'Well?' he demanded when she did not answer. 'That's what you want, isn't it?'

'Are you two arguing again?' said Maddy's world-weary voice from behind Joanne's head. She looked round to find her daughter lounging against the door frame.

'Can't your father and I have a conversation without one of you girls butting in?' said Joanne crossly, her face flushed with all the things she wanted to say to Phil but now couldn't. She glared at him.

'Didn't sound like talking to me,' said Maddy, playing with

139

the fringe of her scarf, the one she had worn all summer and hardly taken off. 'Because if you were just talking and not arguing, you would've noticed.' She stared at the food on the table and raised her right eyebrow.

Joanne snapped her head around to look in the direction of Maddy's gaze. She surveyed the table, seeing nothing amiss. 'Noticed what?'

'Heidi.'

Joanne looked under the table but the dog was nowhere to be seen. She heard the sound of plastic being gnawed and her heart fell. Heidi was in her bed in the corner chewing happily on a clear plastic container, the sort that Marks and Spencers used for their breaded fish products.

Joanne jumped up and ran over and snatched the box from Heidi's jaws. The dog immediately put her head on the edge of her bed and her ears flattened like closed mail flaps.

'That was the fish for tea! Oh, Heidi, you bad girl,' screamed Joanne with real venom in her voice, startling the animal who wasn't used to hearing her mistress scold her so thoroughly. Heidi scrambled out of her bed and made for the door into the hall, her claws scrabbling for purchase on the laminate flooring. Maddy stepped aside to let her pass.

'Why didn't you stop her eating it, Maddy?' cried Joanne. 'Instead of just standing there?'

'Don't shout at me. She'd already eaten the fish when I came in.'

'Wait till I get my hands on you, Heidi!' Joanne shouted after the dog and she threw the container on the dog's bed in frustration. She ran her hands through her hair and sighed heavily. 'So much for an easy tea,' she said, folding her arms and staring down at the box, empty but for a few bright orange crumbs. 'Now I'll have to cook something from scratch. And that'll probably make her sick.'

'There's one box left, Mum,' said Maddy. 'On the table. Look.'

'It won't be enough,' snapped Joanne, without turning round. 'Not for the three of you. You eat as much as an adult now, Maddy.'

'Bloody dog,' said Phil, under his breath.

Joanne went over to the peg by the door and grabbed her pinny. She pulled it over her head, trying to remember what she had in the house that could be transformed into a meal in a matter of minutes. She opened the fridge door and took out a box of eggs. 'The girls can have the fish. I'll make you an omelette.'

'Omelette!' cried Maddy. 'You know I hate omelette.'

'Well tough,' said Joanne irritably, turning on the oven and tipping the remaining piece of fish and some chips onto a tray.

'That's not fair,' grumbled Maddy.

Joanne slapped a frying pan onto the top of the cooker with a satisfying clang and sloshed some sunflower oil into it. She whacked the heat up underneath the pan and felt her own temper rising. 'Life isn't fair, Maddy. And unless you want to take over responsibility for the planning and production of meals in this house,' she said in a too-loud voice, cracking an egg violently on the edge of a scratched Pyrex bowl, 'I'd suggest you just eat what you're given and be grateful for it.'

Maddy's face coloured and she blinked back angry tears.

'I'm sorry,' said Joanne, chucking the eggshells in the bin. She rubbed the back of a hand across her brow. Her head had begun to ache. 'It's not fair of me to take it out on you. It's Heidi's fault, not yours.'

'Damn right,' said Maddy.

'Language,' said Joanne, cracking another egg into the bowl.

'The kids can have my food, if it helps,' said Phil and Joanne looked at him in astonishment, empty pieces of eggshell still in her hands. He closed the paper, folded it in half. Was he offering to do without for his children's sake? It was certainly not a gesture he was apt to make often or one that came naturally to him. Or was he trying to help her, realising she was at the end of her tether? Perhaps both. Either way, she blushed with embarrassment at her display of ill temper, made all the worse in the light of his generosity.

'Thanks,' she said and smiled gratefully. She threw the eggshell away and wiped her hands down the front of her apron. 'I'll make our dinner later,' she said, her anger subsiding. 'Maybe we could open a bottle of wine for a change.' And perhaps they could finish the conversation they had so abruptly aborted when Maddy came in – without snapping each other's heads off.

Phil stood up, peeled his suit jacket off the back of the chair and swung it over his shoulder. 'It's all right. I'll get something when I'm out.' He nodded at the clock on the wall. 'I need to get going.'

'Get going? But where?' cried Joanne. Her shoulders slumped as her vision of family time, followed by a heart-to-heart with Phil, evaporated.

'It's Tuesday, Joanne. Had you forgotten? I play golf on a Tuesday.'

Joanne followed his gaze. The hands on the clock showed six-twenty. 'But what about something to eat?'

'I'll get something at the golf club.'

'But what about Heidi?' said Joanne looking at the dog who had snuck back into the kitchen. At the mention of her name Heidi sat up eagerly, her black tail sweeping across the floor like a brush, and stared at Joanne. 'She hasn't had a proper walk today. I only had time to take her out for twenty minutes this morning. I can't do everything, Phil. I spent most of the day getting the girls kitted out for the new school term.'

'Can't Maddy walk her?'

'No. I'm going over to Charlotte's straight after tea,' said Maddy, quick as a flash, and she disappeared from the doorway as quickly as she had appeared. Heidi belonged to everyone in the family but the children had quickly learnt, like their father, to avoid the chore of dog-walking.

'How was I supposed to walk her, Joanne?' said Phil, 'I've been at work all day.' When she did not answer he added, with a shrug, 'She'll just have to do without for once.' Heidi cocked her head to one side and gave Joanne a soulful look as though she fully understood the exchange between her owners. Joanne felt her heart fill with anger. Phil never put anyone before himself and certainly not a dog. Food and walks were all Heidi lived for – it was cruel and negligent to deprive her of either.

Joanne felt the emotion well up. 'That's not fair on Heidi, Phil.'

'She's only a dog, Joanne,' he said, without looking at Heidi. He made for the door and stepped into the hallway.

'Exactly, Phil. She's a dumb animal. And it's our responsibility to care for her properly,' she said, her voice rising with every step Phil took away from her, 'and to make sure she gets proper exercise.'

He tossed a comment over his shoulder, like a coin. 'Oh, for God's sake, Joanne. Just this once isn't going to do her any harm.'

'And what about the conversation we were having before, Phil?' said Joanne, pursuing him into the hallway. 'Before Maddy came in.'

He turned to face her then – they stood feet apart at the bottom of the stairs. 'What about it?' His face was blank and closed to her.

'We can't just leave it like that, can we?'

He broke eye contact and looked past her at something on the wall. 'I don't want to talk about it any more, Joanne.'

'I knew you'd say that!' she retaliated, cross but strangely satisfied that she had, as usual, been able to second guess him. He thought that he could just walk away from their problems. He was too much of a coward to face up to the fact that he needed to change.

He put his hand on the newel post at the bottom of the stairs. 'Look, Joanne, I'm going to play a game of golf and have a pint with my mates. I don't have time for this.' And with that he stepped lightly onto the second step and ascended the stairs athletically, two at a time.

Joanne stood in astonishment and watched him go, realising that her husband was a stranger to her. She couldn't remember the last time they had talked on a deep, meaningful level, the way they used to. All their conversations were superficial, revolving around practical, everyday issues and generally witnessed by one of the children. If Phil wasn't out for an evening, he was preoccupied and distant. He always found something 'fascinating' or 'unmissable' to watch on TV from sport to late-night chat shows. In practice this often meant that, by the time he came to bed, she was already fast asleep.

She had assumed that closeness between them was simply a casualty of busy family life, just one of the many sacrifices made for the children. But now she saw that this wasn't true. Phil had no particular desire to rekindle their former intimacy. She had offered an olive branch and it pained her that he had rejected it.

'Is everything all right, Mum?' said Holly anxiously, coming into the hall. 'Is everything going to be okay?' Joanne turned around and tried to smile. But she could not, in truth, think of an answer to her daughter's question. Because she honestly did not know if everything was going to be okay or not. She and Phil were like mismatched pieces of crockery. They didn't seem to fit together any more – and she didn't know what to do about it.

Chapter Eight

'Bye, Oli. Mummy's going to work now,' said Louise, standing in her lounge dressed in a tailored navy suit and a crisp white cotton shirt all ready for her first day as Marketing Manager for Loughanlea. Her hair was swept up in a tight chignon at the back of her head and she wore full make-up. It had been more than three years since she'd last dressed like this and she knew from surveying her image in the mirror that, on the outside, she looked like a competent, in-control professional. But inside, she was a bundle of nerves. The surprise and euphoria of securing the job had rapidly been replaced by a list of anxieties as long as her arm, chief of which was leaving Oli.

On the plus side he was more settled. He wasn't nearly as clingy and he slept more soundly at night; the nightmares had all but ceased. But she did not want to entrust his care to others. Oli, who appeared not to have heard her speak, sat at the table by the window with Klaudia beside him, watching him colour in. They were framed by the roofs of the buildings opposite and above the roofline, a clear blue September sky.

Klaudia leant towards Oli, her hand on the back of his chair, stroking him with soft, heavily-accented words of encouragement. She was dark and pretty with straight long hair tied back in a ponytail, smooth unblemished skin, olive-coloured eyes and a full, sensual mouth. Slim and hipless she wore a pair of faded low-slung jeans, a red T-shirt and a pair of fake Ugg boots. She was personable, bright, warm but most of all, she was kind, loving even, towards Oli. He'd taken to her straight away on their first meeting and today, pausing only briefly to acknowledge Louise, she'd engaged him in a game of hide-and-seek almost as soon as she'd stepped over the threshold. She had only just turned twenty and had yet to lose entirely all the traces of childishness with which Oli so clearly identified.

Louise had secured a place for Oli at Wee Stars nursery for half the week, the other half he would spend with Klaudia. She had come with a glowing reference from Joanne's colleague, Emma, and a childcare qualification – Louise had seen the paperwork herself when she'd subjected Klaudia to an exhaustive two-hour-long interview.

This way, Oli got the best of both worlds, she told herself, biting her bottom lip – the chance to socialise with other children and the benefits of one-to-one care from a loving adult. Louise just wished that adult could be her and not Klaudia. She'd already taught Oli two nursery rhymes in her mother tongue – making Louise both happy and jealous.

Suddenly she was seized by panic. What if she couldn't do the job? What if she wasn't able to deliver what was expected and put Loughanlea on the map? She fretted that she simply wouldn't be able to keep it all together – and that she was failing Oli.

But then she remembered the long hours she'd spent convincing herself, and others, that she was ready for any challenge motherhood might throw at her, that she would overcome every obstacle. Now it was time to prove it. She stood up tall, tipped her chin up resolutely and forced her lips into a smile.

'You look very well,' said Klaudia, raising her head and giving Louise a firm nod. 'Very smart and what do you say? Like business.'

'Businesslike.'

'That's it,' said Klaudia with an endearing clap of her small hands. 'Businesslike.'

'Thank you, Klaudia.' Louise took a deep breath and put a hand on her aching stomach. Nerves had prevented her from eating breakfast.

'He will be absolutely fine. You wait and see. And don't worry. Please. There is no need.' She gave Louise a small, encouraging smile. 'You can go now,' she added with a happy nod, not realising how much her kindly meant comment sounded like a dismissal.

But Louise could not go without one last kiss, one last touch of Oli. She went over to him and hunkered down to his level, the straight, tight skirt straining on her hips. She kissed him on the cheek and ran her hands through his hair – he carried on scribbling with a pale blue crayon, one chubby hand laid flat on the paper to hold it in place.

'Goodbye darling,' she said with a smile like a shield.

Oli paused momentarily to look into her eyes. 'Bye, Mummy,' he said, with a small, sweet smile. 'I'm doing this picture for you.' He threw his arms around her neck then and held her tightly, fiercely for a long time. She swallowed, committing the smell of him to memory, then gently prised his arms from around her neck.

'Don't go, Mummy,' he said softly and she, unable to speak for the lump in her throat, placed her hand on the crown of his head and then slipped from the room.

Outside, the mobile phone vibrated in her bag, indicating

receipt of a text message. Was it Klaudia? Had something gone wrong at home already? Resisting the temptation to open the door and go straight back inside, she fished the mobile out of her bag, read the message and relaxed. It was from Sian wishing her good luck. And there was another earlier one, from Joanne, with a similar message. She smiled, chucked the phone back in her bag and tried not to think about Oli.

At Loughanlea not much had changed since her last visit a month ago. Mountain bike tracks had been hewn out of the steep sides of the abandoned quarry and the main buildings at the mountain biking centre, the diving centre and the museum were nearing completion. The eco-village nestled on the edge of the Lough like a bright jewel, the first, waterfront stage of the development complete.

The main road into the site had been tarmaced but the road to the management offices was still a mud track. Louise pulled up outside the cluster of one-storey red-brick buildings hidden from public view by a copse of trees. The small office assigned to her was functional and pleasant with a view out onto the trees outside.

She spent a little time getting to know her new assistants – cool, funky Steve, straight out of uni with ideas as shiny as his new degree in tourism marketing, and Amanda, a petite woman with dark cropped hair and elfin features about her own age and with many years' track record in various tourism marketing jobs. It struck Louise that between them they were a great team – Steve's youthful enthusiasm was tempered by Amanda's wise experience.

The rest of the morning Louise spent with the Director of Loughanlea, Agnes Ritchie, to whom she would report. Agnes was middle-aged with steel grey hair the same colour as her glasses. She was dressed formidably in a tweed suit and silk blouse and smelt of Chanel No. 5. But her formal appearance belied a warm, friendly personality.

'Sorry about the road,' she said as soon as Louise sat down. 'It was supposed to be finished last week.' Agnes served coffee, they exchanged pleasantries for a while and then she got down to business. 'Things have been a bit stagnant here since your predecessor resigned, I'm afraid. He devised the marketing strategy for Loughanlea.'

'Yes,' said Louise, holding up the document in her hand. She had read it the night before. 'There are one or two improvements that could be made,' she continued, understating the case. She thought the report shallow and unimaginative. She'd got no sense of commitment or enthusiasm from its author.

'Such as?' said Agnes, listening carefully with her head cocked to one side. She twirled a red pencil between both hands. Her nails were short and tidy and bare – no nonsense like the rest of her.

'Well, I had a look at the website and I think there's a lot more we could be doing with that. And whilst the strategy has detailed plans for attracting overseas visitors – and that's fantastic – I think we need to be careful we're not neglecting the local market here in Northern Ireland and the South. And—' Louise stopped herself, aware that she sounded heavily critical. 'Well, maybe I've said enough for now.'

'No, please, go on,' said Agnes, an enigmatic smile on lips thinned with age.

Louise took a deep breath. 'Well, I was going to say that all the emphasis is on the mountain biking centre. We must be careful not to overlook the other attractions, like the diving centre and the industrial heritage museum. They'll attract a completely different type of tourist.'

Agnes nodded thoughtfully. 'That's exactly the kind of challenging thinking I'm looking for, Louise. Without throwing the baby out with the bath water,' she said, holding up a copy of the old marketing strategy and dropping it again, 'I'd like you to write me a report with your recommendations. Once I have the board's approval, you'll have the freedom to implement it. What do you say?'

'How soon do you need it?' said Louise with a big grin, her confidence reignited.

'Let's say three weeks. That time enough?'

'Plenty,' she lied. There was a lot of research to be done. She would have to work nights but she had already decided she was not going to let Agnes down. She regarded the other woman thoughtfully for a few moments, debating with herself whether she ought to speak up. And, in the end, she did. 'You're aware of my personal circumstances, aren't you, Agnes? The fact that I have a young son.'

Agnes nodded, her pale blue eyes kind behind her glasses. 'Yes.'

'I'm a single mum.'

'You don't have to tell—'

'I want to though,' said Louise, cutting Agnes off. 'I want you to know that I will work all hours God sends to make Loughanlea a success. If there's work to be done outside of nine to five, I'll do it at home and willingly. But I have to leave here every night at five on the button.'

Agnes smiled and put down the pencil. She took her glasses off and blinked. 'I understand. And for the record, I'm not a fan of presenteeism either. So long as the job is done and done well, Louise – and I've every confidence it will be – you can do it your way, where and when you like, within reason, of course.'

Louise smiled and decided there and then that she and Agnes were going to get on just fine.

A few days later, she was alone in her office poring over

the visitor projections Steve had compiled. Her suit jacket hung on a hook on the back of the door and a notebook lay on the desk by her right elbow. Every now and then she would jot down thoughts as they came to mind. Her head was buzzing with ideas and she was so engrossed in what she was doing, that she did not notice anyone come into the room.

'How's the new job going?' said a familiar voice, and even though it was smooth like liquid caramel, it startled her. She dropped her pen on the table and looked up.

A man of average height in his mid-forties stood in front of the desk. He wore a light-coloured jacket and tie, and his right hand was shoved into the pocket of lived-in navy trousers. In his other hand, he held a yellow hard hat. Tanned and fit looking, he had straight brown hair, thick and short, greying slightly at the temples. His green eyes were staring at her intently, and his smile was so full and warm his whole face creased up with it. She felt compelled to return the smile, her face colouring a little as she did so.

She stood up and boldly held out her hand across the desk, trying to quell her inexplicable nerves. 'Hi. I'm Louise McNeill.'

He took a step forward and set the hat on the corner of the desk. He took her hand firmly in his, placed his other hand on her forearm and held her in this peculiar embrace for a few moments longer than was necessary. 'Good to meet you. Kevin Quinn,' he smiled into her face, the corners of his eyes creased with good humour. 'And I know who you are. You look just like your sister, Sian.' He let go of her, leaving her palm pulsing with heat and a hot patch on her forearm under her shirt.

'I do?' Though she and Sian shared the same high cheek-bones and slightly pointed chin they'd inherited from their mother, Louise had always considered herself the prettier of the two. But this perception, she had to admit, was largely due to the fact that she did everything to enhance her natural gifts, while Sian did absolutely nothing.

'How are you settling in?' he went on, with a glance about the room.

She shrugged, stroking the place on her arm where he'd touched her. 'It's early days. But I think I'm going to like it here.'

'Good.' He glanced at the mound of paperwork on her desk. 'I see they're keeping you busy.'

Louise laughed. 'That's the way I like it.' She paused, then added, with a glance at the hard hat, 'Are you working on site?'

He looked at the hat on the table as if noticing it properly for the first time, and picked it up. 'My firm, Mulholland, McMaster and Quinn, designed the eco-village and all the architecture on site. I'm here most days.'

'Impressive. Sian didn't mention you were involved in the eco-village. She and Andy are absolutely thrilled with their new house.' Nerves made her gabble on, but she was powerless to stop. 'I went to see it the other day. I have to confess, I didn't know what to expect from an eco-house but it's absolutely gorgeous. I wouldn't mind living in one myself!' she added, finally bringing her monologue to a halt. She hadn't actually considered the possibility of living in the eco-village until this very moment. Suddenly it made perfect sense. She knew from Sian that the village had already been nominated for an award for sustainable development.

'You could do worse,' he said modestly.

There was a short, awkward silence. He stared at her for a few moments, his eyes squinting slightly as if trying to focus on her properly. 'Why don't we do lunch tomorrow?'

'Oh,' said Louise and looked at the papers on the desk, not sure how to respond. Her confusion arose from the fact that she did not know if the offer arose from mere professional courtesy, his friendship with her soon to be brother-in-law, or a more personal interest. She felt her cheeks colour. 'I don't know. I have a lot to do,' she said feebly and immediately she could've kicked herself.

'All work and no play makes Jack a dull boy,' parried Kevin, the corner of his mouth turned up in a wry smile. 'Or Louise in your case.'

She bit her lip, unsure how to respond to this gentle teasing. 'Okay then,' she heard herself say. 'You're on.'

He nodded as though he was used to getting his way, and slipped his hand back in his pocket. 'Great. I'll call here about one.' Then he turned and walked away, his jacket swinging from broad shoulders. Just as he was going through the door he called over his shoulder, 'And bring a pair of flat shoes – and a fleece.'

She opened her mouth to ask what she would need them for, but he was already gone. Realising she was standing there like a goldfish, Louise closed her mouth and sat down abruptly. Outside her room, she could hear the sound of Amanda on the phone and the click-click-click of Steve's keyboard.

She was out of practice, there was no doubt about that. Kevin Quinn was the first man she'd met in years that she really liked and she'd very nearly rejected his invitation to lunch. His offer might be nothing more than a friendly gesture, of course, but she very much hoped it was more. For, she suddenly realised, she was finally ready to let someone into her life.

The next day was dry and breezy with white clouds scuttling across the sky, and Louise's head was still full of

Kevin Quinn when she bundled Oli into the car to take him to nursery. When they arrived, she hung his things on a little duck-shaped peg labelled with his name and kissed him on the lips. He clung to her for several minutes while she tried unsuccessfully to engage him in a puzzle, then in a box of bright plastic building blocks. Time was ticking by and her anxiety levels were starting to rise when one of the staff, a young girl with a smiley face and sing-song voice, approached. She led Oli outside to the sandpit where he was soon helping another little boy fill a bucket with golden sand. Louise, watching through the window, breathed a sigh of relief that a scene had been avoided.

Kevin turned up at her office bang on time, casually dressed in brown chinos and an open-necked sky blue shirt. She found herself staring at the dark hairs peeking out of the top of his shirt, imagining what the rest of his chest looked like. She blushed and looked away, nervously smoothing her skirt over her hips. She had worn a simple black skirt and fuchsia pink blouse but felt over-dressed in comparison to his smart-casual chic.

'Ready?' he asked, grinning from ear to ear like a Cheshire cat.

'Yes, but where are we going?'

'You'll see. Now did you bring flat shoes?' he said, rubbing his hands together and staring at her feet.

She nodded, pulled a pair of black ballet pumps out from under her desk, kicked off her heels and slipped into the cool leather shoes.

'Maybe you could leave that here,' he said, looking at the substantial handbag on her shoulder. 'We're not going far.' Observing her hesitation, he added, 'Come on. It's a surprise. You'll love it. And bring that fleece.'

She placed the bag in a drawer, locked it and picked up

the fleece draped over the back of her chair, wondering why she was blindly following the instructions of a man she hardly knew. And when she walked through the outer office and caught Amanda winking knowingly at Steve, she wished she had never agreed to this in the first place.

'Where are we going?' she asked again as they joined the main road leading towards the eco-village. Louise was so used to being in control, she did not take readily to being led. She remembered that there was a café restaurant called The Creel at the waterfront near Sian and Andy's new home. When Kevin did not immediately reply, she added, 'Are we going to The Creel?'

He stopped walking and turned to face her, his hands deep in his pockets. She hooked a lock of stray hair, dislodged by the breeze, behind her ear and looked up at him. Just then the sun came out from behind a cloud and she tried not to squint – it accentuated the deep frown line between her eyebrows.

'No. We're going to the marina,' he said, evenly. 'To have a picnic.'

Her mood instantly brightened. 'A picnic! That sounds like fun!'

'I think so. Come on, it's not far.'

They walked together along the pretty cobbled promenade while Kevin told her about the plans to build a boat club and small hotel in the next stage of development. They passed The Creel and a cluster of small shops on their right, most of which were still empty – a painter on a ladder was carefully applying undercoat to raw wooden window frames. Everything, from the bright white balustrade to the steel lampposts (designed to echo the shape of lighthouses) had a brand new sheen to it.

'It's beautiful here,' said Louise. 'You've done a fantastic job designing the village.'

He looked around him. 'Yes, the team did really well. It's one of the best projects we've ever worked on,' he said, conveying his obvious pride, while taking no personal credit for the project's success.

After a very short time, they came to the easterly-facing marina, enclosed on three sides by a substantial-looking concrete harbour wall. It was only half-full with crafts ranging from small dinghies to larger yachts nearer the mouth of the marina. The breeze picked up, filling the air with the sound of wires clinking against metal masts, and the slap of gentle waves against hulls. Louise shivered.

'Here, let me help you,' said Kevin. He took the fleece and stood behind holding it while she slipped her arms into the sleeves. She shrugged it onto her shoulders and, fleetingly, he placed a hand on her upper right arm.

'Thanks,' she said and zipped up the fleece. He came and stood beside her and she focused on the swirling seagulls and the view across the Lough, choppy with white-frothed waves. She found she was unable to meet him in the eye.

'She's right over there,' said Kevin, pointing at a handsome, old-fashioned sloop.

'What? That boat right at the end?' said Louise.

'Yes. *Jenny-B*. That's what I wanted to show you. Come on.'

He led her over to the quayside where Louise stared down at a long, graceful white wooden yacht with a varnished cabin and a weathered teak deck. Her sails were furled but the cabin was open – a wicker picnic basket sat on one of the slatted wooden benches.

'Did you name her after your wife?' Louise watched for his reaction.

He chuckled. 'No, that's her original name. My wife and I parted ways just before I bought this boat. I guess restoring

157

her was my way of getting over the divorce. It certainly kept me busy anyway.'

Louise nodded, understanding only too well. Feverish with hurt and disappointment, she had thrown herself into work after leaving Cameron. He would've adored this boat, even though he sailed only dinghies himself. That was one of the things she had loved about him – his enthusiasm for so many things in life and a genuine appreciation of beauty and craftsmanship.

'Well, she's a beautiful boat,' said Louise, casting out thoughts of Cameron with determination. She had to accept that he was no longer a part of her life.

'She's a twenty-five-foot Buchanan sloop. Built by Shuttlewood of Essex in nineteen fifty. It was a small yard known for high-quality work. She's planked in one-inch mahogany on steamed rock elm timbers.'

Louise, who had no idea what this last comment meant said, 'She doesn't look nearly sixty years old.' She pointed at the cabin, fitted with two small portholes on the starboard side. 'The wood – it's all in perfect condition.'

'It is now. But when I bought her she was in a sorry state. I spent the last six years restoring her – this was her first season on the water. And she's proved herself to be a fine yacht. Come on, let's climb aboard.'

He gave her an enthusiastic tour of the cramped but pristine living quarters – a small kitchen area, two bench seats with a folding table between them anchored to the floor and, forwards, a two-berth cabin. The interior was fitted out in wood and cream leather, many of the fittings obviously new but many original, so retaining the unique character of the vessel.

When the short tour was complete they sat on the deck in the sun, while the wind whipped around their heads, and ate a picnic of salmon sandwiches and fruit with hot tea. They talked about her job and the eco-village and he told her all about *Jenny-B*'s restoration.

Then Louise, with a cup of tea in her hands, closed her eyes and listened to the sound of the creaking timbers and the gulls screeching overhead, wondering what this boat would be like on open water. As if reading her thoughts, Kevin asked, 'Do you sail?'

She opened her eyes. 'I used to.' She looked out across the Lough to Islandmagee. 'Right out there in fact.'

He followed her gaze across the sea. 'Really?' He sounded delighted.

'Where did you learn?'

'Carrickfergus, where I grew up.' He leant towards her, his shirt straining across his broad back and his hands clasped between his legs. 'Would you like to sail *Jenny-B*? With me? We could take her up the coast. Have you ever sailed round Rathlin Island?'

She shook her head. 'I loved to sail. But it was a long time ago, Kevin.' She shrugged and went on, 'I don't really know why I never kept it up. And I only ever sailed small dinghies. Nothing as big as this.'

He touched her lightly on the knee, bare but for a pair of sheer tights. She caught her breath, looked down at the back of his weather-beaten hand, and smiled. Somehow his touch felt right – and electrifying.

'I'll teach you,' he said, his voice earnest. 'If you'll let me.'

The sun beat down on her face and her spirit soared like the gulls above their heads. Something inside her that had been dormant for a long time, woke up.

'I'd like that,' she said, staring straight into those sea-green eyes. 'I'd like that very much.'

When she got back to the office, her head swimming with

excitement, there was a message from her Edinburgh solicitor. Ring back as soon as possible, the message said and she wondered what could be so urgent.

'I'm delighted to tell you that we have received an offer on your flat,' said the solicitor as soon as he came on the phone. 'It's five thousand less than you wanted but it's a cash buyer and, in the current climate, it's a very fair offer, Louise.'

'Oh, that's the most wonderful news,' she said, feeling a tremendous weight lift from her shoulders. 'Tell them, I accept.'

Now, suddenly, everything seemed to be conspiring in her favour. Yes, she'd had to go back to work, but that would've been the case had she stayed in Scotland too. Oli seemed happy and content, she had a great job, the Edinburgh flat had finally been sold, meaning she could buy a place of her own – and she'd met Kevin. She looked out the office window at the tops of the trees swaying in the breeze and sighed happily. Only a few weeks ago she'd thought she'd made a terrible mistake. Today things looked very different – coming to Ballyfergus might turn out to be the best move she'd ever made . . .

'I'm really pleased for you,' said Sian a little distractedly, after Louise had told her the good news about selling her flat that very evening.

It was six o'clock and Louise, in jeans and a T-shirt she'd brought with her to change into, was standing in Sian's new kitchen. Sian, wearing a pair of raggedy olive green corduroy shorts, was sitting cross-legged and barefoot on the floor a few feet from Oli. They were taking turns to push little wooden cars, which Sian had just given Oli, to one another across the smooth tiles.

'Look, Auntie Sian! Watch this one. Look how fast it can go!'

Sian shrieking with laughter said, 'Not as fast as this one!' and sent a green vehicle hurtling across the floor like a mouse. It crashed into the skirting board and overturned.

'Pow!' cried Oli in delight.

Sian sprang lightly to her feet and ruffled Oli's hair, oblivious to the hole in the right thigh of her shorts. 'I have to do the dinner now, wee man. Play with me later, eh?'

'No.' His bottom lip went out and he folded his arms.

Sian came down to his level, nodded thoughtfully, and said, 'Tell you what. How about after dinner we make a spaceship? I've got lots of boxes I saved from the shop. Deal?' She held the palm of her hand out to Oli.

'Deal!' he cried happily and slapped his aunt's palm with his own small one.

'Good man.' Sian went over to the cooker. She wore a faded pink T-shirt with 'O'Neill' written across the front in black. There were splatters of mud up her brown calves, the result no doubt of cycling in the rain that had closed in that afternoon. She looked inside the two saucepans on the stove, a large one with penne pasta in it and another, smaller one, containing sauce.

'I'm going to start looking for somewhere to buy,' Louise went on, her head spinning with plans. 'I've only a few months left on the lease at Tower Road.'

Sian picked up a wooden spoon and stirred the sauce. 'What're you looking for?'

Louise gazed around Sian's kitchen, with its clean, simple lines, white walls and full-length patio doors leading out to a small garden. She ran a hand along the pale wood of a kitchen cupboard and thought of Kevin. 'Something like this.'

Sian stopped stirring and held the spoon, blood-red with sauce, suspended in mid-air. 'Are you serious? You mean you would consider moving out here?'

'Why not? It's as convenient for work and the nursery as anywhere.'

Sian set down the spoon and smiled. 'That'd be great, Lou,' she said, using her elder sister's childhood pet name. 'We'd be neighbours.'

'I know! Wouldn't it be fab? I picked up one of the brochures at the show house today.' She got her bag, pulled out a large glossy leaflet and flicked through it. 'There's four of these houses available. Though I'm a bit concerned about Oli – you know, being so close to the water.'

'Go for it. Oli will be fine. The fresh sea air'll do him good. You worry too much.'

Louise decided to ignore the last comment. Sian was always implying that she was over-protective but she would not let anything spoil her good mood. Changing the subject she said, 'Guess who I had lunch with today? On his yacht.'

Sian lifted the lid off the pasta and scalding steam billowed out like a cloud. She turned off the flame under the pot and said, distractedly, 'What?'

Louise set the brochure down on the table and repeated herself.

'Really?' said Sian. 'You couldn't pass me that colander there, could you?'

'You're not listening, Sian, are you?' said Louise as she handed the colander to her sister. 'This is potentially the most important thing to have happened to me in absolutely ages and you're not listening.'

'Just a minute.' Sian tipped the contents of the large saucepan into the colander over the sink, returned the pasta to the pan and chucked in a knob of butter. She wiped her hands on the front of her T-shirt and said, 'I'm sorry. I'm a bit preoccupied, that's all. Tell me all about it.'

'Kevin Quinn took me for lunch today.'

Sian took cutlery from a drawer and managed a tired smile. 'I'm not surprised. I thought you two might get along.' She moved over to the table and started laying out the forks and spoons.

Louise pulled out a chair and sat down at the table. 'He'd made a picnic and we sat and ate it on his boat. Have you seen it?'

Sian nodded.

'It's gorgeous,' Louise rattled on excitedly, 'He restored it himself. He told me all about it. He says he's going to take me sailing. And he's asked me out for dinner next Saturday night.' She clasped her hands together and held them to her chest. 'I'm so excited. I haven't had a date in years, Sian, not with someone I really like. I went through a phase of dating men after Cameron but all I was doing, I realise now, was looking for a man to father a child. Once I'd given up on that idea, I lost interest.'

'And you feel ready to date now?' Sian walked over to a cupboard and took out some chunky green glasses made from recycled beer bottles that she sold in her shop.

'I feel ready to date Kevin Quinn. We just seemed to hit it off. Tell me something, does he know about Oli?'

'He knows you're a single mum.'

'It's funny, he never mentioned Oli.'

'Does that worry you?'

Louise paused to consider this, then said, 'No, not at all. It was nice to have a conversation about other things, for a change. We just chatted away about things we were interested in. I loved talking to him. It made me feel like . . . like years melted away. Like I was twenty again. He has such a zest for life.'

'You sound like you've got it bad,' said Sian with a wry smile. She set the glasses down on the table. 'But for what it's worth Andy has a lot of time for Kevin. He's a good guy.'

Louise nodded happily, looked at the table and noticed that it was only laid for three. 'Where's Andy? Isn't he having tea with us?'

Sian shook her head. 'He's going straight over to Donegal with two pals after work tonight. They want to squeeze in a last surfing trip before the weather changes. He'll be back Sunday night.' She let out a long sigh and went over to the patio doors and stared out at the wet mud that had yet to be transformed into a vegetable patch. 'I envy you, you know.' The dreamy smile fell at once from Louise's lips and Sian went on, 'Everything seems to be coming together for you. While everything in my life's falling apart.'

Louise had a terrible sinking feeling, like she had suddenly been dropped from a height. 'What do you mean?'

Sian sighed again and touched the string of ethnic, multi-coloured birds that hung from a drawing pin pressed into the wooden door frame. They were made from scraps of fabric that might possibly have been left over from someone's quilt-making efforts. Sian turned to look at Louise with a morose expression on her face. Her hair, Louise suddenly noticed, needed to be washed and there were dark rings under her eyes.

Ashamed that she'd been too wrapped up in her own world to notice her sister's distress, Louise got up quickly and went over to her. The two women stood facing each other, equal in height and build. 'Sian,' she said, placing a hand on her sister's shoulder, 'what do you mean – every-thing's falling apart? Is there something wrong with the house?' she asked with a glance round the room, taking Sian's comment literally.

Sian attempted a smile and looked at the floor. 'I wish it was – that would be easy to fix. And not everything's wrong. That's a bit of an exaggeration.' She paused, raised her eyes to meet Louise's concerned gaze and said, 'But there's something wrong with the person who matters most to me.'

'Andy? What about him?' said Louise as possibilities flashed through her mind. Was he ill? Had he lost his job?

'There's something . . . something's not right between us. I can't put my finger on it exactly.'

'But you and Andy are like this,' said Louise, crossing her fingers and holding them up. She felt like smiling – the idea of disharmony between Andy and Sian seemed so unlikely – but the wretched expression on her sister's face held her back. 'What makes you think there's something wrong?'

'He doesn't want to get married, Louise.'

Louise removed her hand from Sian's shoulder and said, 'Of course he does.'

Sian shook her head miserably. 'No, he doesn't. Every time I try to talk about it, he changes the subject. First he said it was going to be too expensive – on top of buying the house. And then—' She broke off, a sob strangled in her throat, 'Then he said that we didn't need a marriage licence to prove that we love each other.'

'And have you told him how you feel?'

'He knows, Louise. He knows how much it means to me. And now he avoids talking about it altogether.'

'Well, maybe he's just changed his views on marriage,' said Louise feebly, desperate to give her sister some crumb of comfort.

Sian shook her head vehemently. 'No, he's holding something back from me, Louise. I *know* him. He's not telling me the truth.'

Louise bit her lip. 'What do you think might be wrong?'

Sian walked away from the window. 'I don't know. Maybe he's seeing someone else,' she said without conviction.

'No!'

Sian raised a ghost of a smile. 'I don't really believe that either. He still says he loves me. But I can't, for the life of me, think what could be wrong. It's making me ill with worry.' She put her thumb in her mouth and gnawed on the nail.

'Maybe it's got nothing to do with you, Sian. Maybe he's under pressure at work – or something – that's affecting the way he feels right now. Maybe,' said Louise, grasping at straws, 'with taking on the house, he feels under pressure financially.'

Sian shook her head. 'Then why not tell me?'

Louise pressed her lips together and was silent, unable to conjure up a convincing explanation. The picture Sian painted of Andy – taciturn and withdrawn – simply didn't fit with the man she knew.

'I haven't slept properly in days. This is driving a horrible wedge between us. I don't know him any more.' Sian put her hands over her face and her voice when she spoke again was thick and muffled. 'I fear I might lose him, Louise.' Immediately, Louise went to her sister and put her arms around her, rubbing her back in a circular motion with the flat of her hand, the room silent save for the sound of Oli's self-absorbed chatter, the muffled sound of cars scooting across the cork-tiled floor – and Sian's quiet sobs.

'You're not going to lose him, sweetheart,' Louise whispered into Sian's ear. 'That just isn't going to happen. Please don't cry. It's going to be all right. Do you hear me? Everything's going to be okay.'

Louise held Sian tighter and squeezed her eyes shut, the sound of her sister's sorrow cutting through her like a knife. 'There's going to be a perfectly simple explanation for all of this, you wait and see. And you and Andy will be back to the way you were before.'

And she prayed with all her heart that this might be so. Louise knew what it meant to have your heart broken, your dreams shattered. And she couldn't bear to see that happen to her little sister. 'Yes, everything's going to be all right. You just wait and see,' she whispered, as much to calm herself as Sian. As if, by repeating it, she could make it true.

Memories of her own heartbreak came flooding back, filling her head with a thousand images and her heart with an ocean of pain. She remembered with clarity the day she'd moved out of the flat they'd shared together and into her new one. She'd sat on the floor of the lounge that night with the lights switched off and a bottle of red wine for company. The curtains were open, the street lamp outside filling the room with an eerie orange glow. She'd listened to the sound of cars driving by and the happy chatter of couples passing by on the pavement outside, and sobbed herself dry. Letting Cameron go was the hardest thing she'd ever done.

When she opened her eyes and stared out into Sian's garden, she could not tell if the blurred image she saw was the result of her own tears or the rain on the window.

Chapter Nine

'If you don't hurry up, Holly, I'm going to be late for work and you're going to be late for school,' Joanne hollered up the stairs.

She could hear Holly scampering across the floor of the room that she shared with Abbey, as she assembled her PE kit. Behind the closed kitchen door, Heidi scratched and whimpered to be let out.

Joanne stood in the hall by the open front door dressed for work in a knee-length red skirt, white blouse, and sensible shoes for standing in all day. She held a clutch of keys in her hand.

Maddy had already left for school on foot despite the mizzling rain and Abbey was waiting in the car. The schools had been back for just four weeks and, if there was one thing she missed about the summer holidays, it was time. Back then it was there to be squandered. Now there wasn't enough of it to go around.

She checked her wristwatch yet again.

'If you'd got your bag ready last night like I told you, Holly,' she shouted, 'we wouldn't be in this position this morning. It's not fair, you know, keeping everyone else waiting. I got up at six-thirty to walk Heidi, made breakfast for everyone and all you—'

Her monologue was cut short as Holly came shooting down the stairs, her hair pulled back in a ponytail, her face flushed with panic. She had a rucksack on her back and a purple sports bag, almost as big as she was, over her shoulder. She ran past her mother and out the front door without a word and hopped in the car. Joanne rolled her eyes, locked up the house and got in the car.

'Don't do that again, please,' she said, once they were on their way, eyeing Holly in the rear-view mirror.

Holly let out a sigh. 'Sorry, Mum.'

Joanne drove the rest of the way in silence, running through a mental checklist of all the things she had to remember that day, while the girls bickered in the back seat. As they approached the school, Joanne said, 'Now listen, I'll come and collect you both after school. If I'm not in the playground when you come out just wait for me there in case I'm a bit late. Okay?'

'Okay,' the girls muttered in unison.

'And don't forget the most important thing of all.'

Holly, thinking, screwed up her face.

'Dinner money?' said Abbey.

Joanne, laughing, joined the queue of traffic snaking its way into the school car park. She sneaked a peek over her shoulder at her daughters. 'No, the most important thing is that I love you more than any other wee girls in the whole world are loved.'

'I know,' said Holly seriously and Abbey beamed, reminding Joanne that they were the reason she did it all.

She pulled into a parking space. The girls jumped out and she watched them run into the playground, Abbey's hair flowing wildly behind her, Holly dwarfed by her bags.

She put their happiness above her own. That was one of the reasons she stayed with Phil. That and the fact that, in spite of everything, she loved him still. And part of her could see no viable alternative to the life she had created for herself, warts and all.

But it wasn't altogether bad, she told herself. It was . . . better than tolerable. She'd not talked with Phil in any meaningful way since their last confrontation, it was true, but they weren't at each other's throats either. Her words must've had some effect for she had noticed a change in Phil since the day she'd taken the girls shopping in Belfast. He was more helpful and considerate around the house, noticing that the kitchen bin needed to be emptied rather than having to be asked, clearing up after a meal – that sort of thing. He was not the world's greatest conversationalist but, Joanne decided, actions spoke louder than words. And she, for her part, was trying very hard not to be a nag. As a result the atmosphere in the house had improved and everyone's mood had lifted.

She reversed out of the parking place and drove the short distance to work, reflecting on the fact that the calm at home had brought with it a sense of relative peace. For the first time in months, possibly years, she felt that her relationship with Phil was on more solid ground, though she had no hard facts on which to base this assumption – they had, for example, made no progress in amalgamating their financial resources. But, as far as she knew, there were no unpaid bills floating about and no final demands for payment about to wing their way through the letterbox. No, her contentment had more to do with her outlook than any material change in their circumstances.

And it filled Joanne with happiness to know that things were finally coming together for Louise. A new job, a new man on the horizon and now she was house-hunting. She did not envy Louise her life as a single mum but she admired her. When the going got tough Louise had got going – she'd recently gone from being a full-time mum to full-time marketing manager. And so far, fingers crossed, through grit and hard work she seemed to be holding it all together. Joanne wasn't sure she could've coped as well under the same circumstances. She wondered if Louise's relationship with Kevin Quinn would work out – and allowed herself the fleeting, pleasing fantasy of a wedding with little Oli as pageboy and Abbey and Holly as flowergirls.

The subject of weddings brought Sian to mind and Joanne frowned. It troubled her to think that while everyone else was enjoying this period of harmony, Sian's life had apparently run aground. Sian had told her about the coolness between herself and Andy, the result of his refusal to commit to the wedding. Lots of guys got pre-wedding nerves, Joanne had pointed out. She had actually tried to speak to Andy about it, believing that a good heart-to-heart would sort it all out. But he had steadfastly refused to talk to her, telling her politely, but rightly, that his relationship with Sian was really none of her business. She still felt inclined to dismiss Sian's concerns as nothing more than a storm in a teacup – if she had someone like Phil to deal with she'd know all about it – but it bothered her nonetheless to see her younger sister upset. She comforted herself with the knowledge that Sian and Andy were made for each other – everyone could see that plain as day. Surely, whatever it was that was bothering Andy would soon blow over?

At work, Joanne put on her white coat, fastened the press studs down the front, put on reading glasses and emptied her mind of all these thoughts. Her job as a pharmacist came with great responsibility – a mistake could cost someone their life – and she needed to be focused and clear-headed. That was why she loved her job. It was the only time she completely switched off from being a wife and mother and became someone else altogether – a competent professional.

She liked the calm, orderly atmosphere in the pharmacy, the methodical ways of working, checking and double-checking. She loved the way time flew when she was busy and the buzz she got from stretching her mental capabilities in a way she never did at any other time. And, off duty, she enjoyed the chat in the staff room. In short, she felt fulfilled both professionally and socially in her work.

She was good at her job. She was not afraid to challenge a prescription she considered ill-advised and once, she had saved a woman's life by noticing that old Doctor Doyle, since retired, had prescribed a hundred milligrams of morphine sulphate instead of ten for back pain. Had she not picked up the error, the woman would have died. The incident led to an internal inquiry and hastened poor Doctor Doyle's early retirement – not before time many people said. Joanne felt it was her finest hour. That one moment was what she had spent years studying and training for.

In the dispensing room in the back of the pharmacy Emma looked up when Joanne came in and smiled. Small and dark, she still carried the baby weight she'd put on during her second pregnancy three years ago. Her pretty face was heavily made up and she too was dressed in a white coat and low-heeled shoes.

Emma tossed a completed prescription in the basket on the bench before addressing Joanne. 'How's Louise getting on with Klaudia?'

Joanne popped a black pen in the top right-hand pocket of her coat. 'Good, thanks. Oli loves her.'

Derek Carmichael, one of the partners, came through from the front of the shop. He was tall and bald and under his white coat, straining at the buttons, he wore a pale green shirt and brown patterned tie. He looked at Joanne over the top of his steel-rimmed spectacles. 'Joanne, can you get cracking on these repeat prescriptions please? They're needed by lunchtime.'

'Sure thing.' She took the thick batch of papers and rolled her eyes at Emma. 'No rest for the wicked, eh?'

They worked wordlessly and companionably then, but not in silence. From the front of the shop they could hear the muffled murmur of conversation, and the air was filled with the soothing sounds of medicines being dispensed – the rattle of tablets in plastic bottles, the hum and pitter-patter of the automatic pill-counting machine, the glug of liquid medicine being decanted into brown glass bottles and the rustle of paper bags in which all the prescriptions and medicines were discreetly packaged and the tops stapled with a satisfying clunk-clink.

Joanne worked until ten-thirty then took off her glasses and rubbed between her eyes. 'Okay if I take my coffee break now?' she said to Emma.

'Yep. I'll go when you come back.'

After Joanne had a cup of coffee and signed up for a girls' night out to see *The Sound of Music* at the Opera House in Belfast, she swapped places with Emma. Alone in the back room, she tossed a paper bag in the basket and picked up the next prescription.

The name on it was Gemma Mooney. Joanne did a double take and checked the address. Yes, it was definitely her best friend Gemma. As a rule she did not fill scripts for people she knew very well, particularly close family. And Gemma was as close as family.

She had made the mistake once of reading a prescription for Uncle Seamus, married to her mother's sister, only to discover that it was for a beta blocker, used in the treatment of heart failure. She knew for a fact that his wife knew nothing of his heart complaint – if she had, the entire family would've heard about it ad nauseam – and could only assume that Uncle Seamus didn't want to worry his wife. She'd felt awful keeping a secret from her aunt and she'd worried terribly about her uncle. But, bound by the pharmacists' code of confidentiality, she had to respect his privacy.

So experience ought to have told her to put the prescription to one side for Emma to fill. She ought not to have looked at it at all. But she was only human and curiosity got the better of her. She read it.

She put her hand over her mouth and sat down abruptly on a nearby stool, shocked.

It was for three months' supply of Cerazette, a progesterone-only mini-pill, the sensible, safe choice for women over the age of thirty-five. Gemma was on a contraceptive pill. Gemma was having sex – regular sex.

Joanne's initial reaction, after the shock, was disappointment that her best friend had not seen fit to confide in her. She fought against these feelings of hurt, telling herself that Gemma was under no obligation to tell her about her sex life. After a few moments, considering the implications of this discovery, a smile came to her lips. Good on her! Gemma was single, free and entitled to have sex with whoever she wanted. She'd had a pretty miserable time since her divorce and if she'd found someone to have a bit of fun with, well good for her.

But this was a repeat prescription, not a new one. Joanne checked her watch. Emma would be back shortly. Quickly she went over to the computer in the corner of the room and called up Gemma's prescription records. She had first been prescribed at the beginning of July. Unless she was having sex with multiple partners, which Joanne deemed unlikely, she calculated that Gemma had been in a steady relationship for at least three months.

But why hadn't Gemma told her? And why not go to another pharmacy? She must've known, after all, that there was a chance Joanne would see the prescription – though it was possible the thought hadn't occurred to her. Joanne shared everything with Gemma – and thought that her friend did the same with her. Perhaps she was seeing someone she thought Joanne would disapprove of or perhaps the relationship was simply about sex. Maybe Gemma was ashamed – or maybe, thought Joanne, it was none of her damn business. She bit her lip, desperate to know who the mystery man was. But she knew she would have to bide her time, even though the suspense was absolutely killing her . . .

Louise had arranged to see Kevin on Saturday night in The Creel. The café was decked out like the inside of a boathouse in tongue-and-groove panelling, painted cream, and festooned with seafaring memorabilia – sailing flags in primary colours, battered oars and porthole mirrors lined the walls and lobster pots tumbled over each other in the corner by the window. The wooden floor was varnished like the deck of a yacht and the place was busy with couples and groups of friends. Although only recently opened, the restaurant was beginning to get a reputation for good food in a relaxed atmosphere.

As dusk fell, they took a seat by the window overlooking the twinkling lights of the marina and indulged in chit-chat while they ordered food and wine. Over starters of smoked mackerel he told her about his grown-up children, Aline and Gavin, and when he was finished, he pushed the bowl away.

'So,' he said, resting his elbows on the table and his chin on his closed fists. 'Tell me all about Oli.'

Louise, stalling, put the wine glass to her lips and took a drink of the inky Chianti, surprised to find that the question made her nervous. She cared for Kevin and she wanted him to think highly of her – and Oli. If she told him the truth, would he judge her harshly?

But she also believed in being honest. Her first marriage had failed because of the lack of honesty between her and Cameron. And she would never deny Oli the truth of his origins – and that meant being truthful with everyone else.

Thus resolved, she took a deep breath and said, 'How much do you want to know?'

'Everything,' he said without a smile.

Louise took a deep breath. 'You know I'm a single mum.'

He nodded.

She cleared her throat. 'Well, I'm also what people call an SMC, a Single Mother by Choice.'

His frown prompted her to explain. 'It's an American term for educated, professional, financially-independent women, usually in their late thirties. Women who choose – that is, consciously set out – to become single mothers and raise a child without any involvement from the father. Quite often the father and child never meet.'

His frown deepened. 'So Oli isn't your ex-husband's child?'

She smiled sadly and shook her head. If only he was . . . 'No,' she said evenly, swallowing the bitter taste of regret, 'Cameron didn't want children, Kevin, and I did. That's why the marriage broke up.'

'I'm sorry.'

She blinked and acknowledged this with a weak smile.

'So who is Oli's father then?' Suddenly Kevin brought his clenched fists down onto the table and spread out his palms, his face reddening. 'No, please don't answer that, Louise.

I'm sorry. My curiosity got the better of me there. It's none of my business.'

Her heartbeat quickened. Would he disapprove as her parents, and other people, had done? Would he understand the impulses that had driven her to take such drastic action to realise her dream of motherhood?

'I'd like it to be your business,' she said quickly and then, embarrassed at her boldness, felt her face flush. 'I want to tell you. I want you to know everything.'

He nodded and she went on, turning a fork over and over in her right hand as she spoke. 'His father is a sperm donor,' she said, looking him in the eye. 'A man I've never met. He lives in Glasgow. I've seen a picture of him, that's all. Once Oli reaches eighteen he can contact him if he wants but until then, they'll never meet.'

'So how . . .?' said Kevin, without breaking eye contact.

'Artificial insemination. That's how most Choice Mums go about it.' She held her breath and waited for his reaction.

'Why, that's incredibly brave of you, Louise. I take my hat off to you. Raising a child alone is no picnic.'

'Some people find it . . . what I did . . . unsettling,' she said and watched for his reaction. 'They think it's clinical and calculating and that children shouldn't be brought into the world without a father.'

Kevin shook his head. 'I don't see it like that at all. Isn't bringing a much-wanted child into the world with conscious thought and planning much better than the accidental, careless way so many are conceived?'

'I'm glad you think so,' she said, breathing out, relief spreading through her like warmth. She should not have doubted him.

'Oli has a much better chance in life than many children born to two parents.' He nodded thoughtfully and then went on, 'But why did you choose to go down that route? Didn't you think you'd meet someone else to have children with?'

'Not in time, Kevin. I was thirty-seven. Time was running out. I knew that if I didn't have a baby before the age of forty it would be too late for me. It wasn't how I imagined my life would turn out. I thought I would have a conventional family, like everyone else, but when I realised that wasn't going to happen, I chose to go it alone.'

'Good for you. I bet you're a wonderful mother.'

She blushed, uncertain if his praise was justified. 'I never wanted to be a trailblazer, you know. I just wanted to be an ordinary mum. But I try my best,' she smiled. 'Oli is loved so much. And lots of kids grow up without their fathers around, don't they? And he is just the best thing that's ever happened to me. It's because of him that I came back to Ballyfergus.'

Kevin reached over then and took her hand in his. He traced the fine shadowy veins on the back of her hand with his rope-roughened fingers. Then he looked steadily into her eyes. 'I think you should be proud of yourself, Louise. I don't know many women strong enough to do what you've done. And I don't think Oli will want for anything, materially or emotionally.'

Her heart flooded with happiness and Kevin squeezed her hand, then let it go. He raised his glass. 'I propose a toast.' Louise lifted her glass and he went on, 'To Oli McNeill. Because without him, Louise, you and I would never have met.'

As the days rolled into weeks, they spoke on the phone almost every day, and met often at lunchtime when they sometimes walked by the shore nibbling on sandwiches, while Kevin, an amateur ornithologist, told her about the Lough's bird population.

Only a few days ago they'd sighted the arrival of the first

light-bellied Brent geese of the season. She'd been amazed to learn that almost the entire world's population of these birds overwintered along the coast of Ireland. And that they endured one of the longest migrations in nature, travelling a staggering two thousand nine hundred miles from Ireland to their summer breeding grounds in Arctic Canada, via a gruelling flight up and over a one-and-a-half-mile-high ice cap.

'How could I have lived in Ballyfergus all these years and not known about these birds?' she asked.

'It's amazing what's around us in everyday life,' he said, squinting up at the sky. 'If we can only open our eyes to see.'

Other times they talked about her new home – she'd put a deposit down on a house almost identical in style to Sian and Andy's, though hers would be facing east and the waters of the Lough.

Louise had been to Kevin's compact, two-bedroom flat in a small development on Glenarm Road, ideally suited to a single man who very infrequently had his adult children to stay. It was bright and well-furnished in a pleasing, more homely style than she had anticipated. It was there that she'd met Kevin's daughter Aline, a serious, single-minded girl training to be a doctor at Queen's. Aline had been pleasant and friendly and, when Kevin was out of the room, the young woman had confided that her mother had a new partner and that she and her brother, Gavin, were keen to see Dad 'settled'. He needed someone to look after him, she said, though looking round the pristine apartment, Louise could see no evidence that this was true.

Every time she met Kevin and got to know him better, his personality peeling back like a banana skin, she saw more to like. She was falling in love with him and she saw no reason to resist. Apart, of course, from Oli.

Because of him, Kevin had not set foot in her home and the two had never met. Oli would always be her number one priority and she did not want him to know Kevin, only for him to disappear suddenly from his life should their relationship founder. But she also knew that their relationship had reached a juncture where she could no longer keep the two of them apart. Oli was utterly integral to her life, and Kevin was becoming so – she could no longer compartmentalise the two relationships.

So, after all her cautiousness, it was she, in the end, who suggested that all three of them meet in the park – a neutral venue where Oli was least likely to feel threatened.

The day came and Louise, dressed in jeans and a purple roll-neck jumper, watched her son arrange a row of thumb-sized green plastic soldiers on the arm of the sofa, each one frozen mid-battle, in disturbingly detailed action – gun raised to shoot; hands aloft in surrender; crouched down on one knee, taking aim; some even prostrate in death. They were a present from Dad. Louise never would have bought such non-PC toys for her son. She'd mentioned to Kevin her concern that the soldiers would encourage Oli to play aggressively and he'd laughed. Little boys, he said, would play war games whether you encouraged them or not.

'It's time to get ready, Oli.'

He looked up with a surprised expression on his face. 'For what?'

'We're going to the park, remember? To meet my friend.'

He screwed his face up. 'What friend?'

'Remember my friend Kevin that I told you about?'

He nodded. 'The one who draws pictures of houses and things.'

'That's right.'

'Ka-pooosh,' he said and flicked a soldier off the arm of

180

the sofa. 'He's dead.' He picked up the 'dead' soldier and examined him. 'Look, Mum, this one got shot.'

'Yes, I can see that, Oli. Now come on.'

'But you see 'evin at work, don't you?'

'That's right.'

'Why do you have to see him at the park as well?'

Louise took a breath before answering. 'Because he's a special friend. And I want to see him at other times, apart from when we're at work. Come on, let's get you ready.' She went into the hall and fetched his coat.

Oli looked at her and said stubbornly, 'But I want to finish this battle.'

'You can finish it when we get home. Come and put your coat on.' She held out his jacket.

He rubbed the soldier on the carpet and would not look at her. 'Come on, Oli,' she said irritably. 'We're going to be late.'

'I don't want to.'

'Well, I'm sorry,' said Louise, something inside her hardening a little. 'But we have to. The arrangements are all made.'

She bundled a reluctant Oli into his coat, realising how desperately she wanted Kevin and Oli to like each other.

She didn't expect her son to warm to Kevin straight away. After all, as far as Oli was concerned, Kevin was a complete stranger. She had realistic expectations – today, she hoped for little more than indifference on Oli's part. Though she was certain that, over time, he would grow to love Kevin.

But from Kevin she hoped for so much more. She wanted him to like Oli, love him even. Before she'd become a mother, and had relatively little contact with small children, she had assumed that they were all much the same – and that one's feelings towards other people's children, relatives excluded, were neutral and roughly equal. But now she knew this wasn't true.

Character was formed by a very young age and you either warmed to a child or you didn't. Louise found some children, like Oli's little friend Elliott from nursery back in Edinburgh, with his curly mop, long black lashes and winning smile, utterly irresistible. Other duller, shyer children, she found she could not connect with. And that initial impression, as with adults, did not alter much with time. You either liked someone – adult or child – or you didn't.

So, though she'd never expressed it in such terms to Kevin or to her sisters, today was a deal-breaker. And it was not going well.

She pushed the buggy into the wind along the long, flat Curran Road, towards the town centre, Oli lying with his hood up, his face pressed into the back of the buggy, resentful and stubborn. Walking briskly, she passed the caravan park on her left, then the papermill and rows of solid, terraced villas on her right, built at the height of Ballyfergus's Victorian maritime expansion. By the time Louise reached the junction of Circular Road and the abandoned cinema, the grey clouds had broken up and the sun came out. Louise slowed to a halt and opened the buttons on her jacket.

She looked down at Oli who was peeking curiously at the passing traffic. But his demeanour had not changed. As soon as he clocked her face looming over the buggy, he resumed his former position. Much as she was loath to allow Oli to dictate what they did and did not do, she recognised that it was a bad idea to persist with this plan if he was in a foul mood. He was well capable of keeping this up for several hours. Far from the bonding experience she dared to hope for, the meeting with Kevin would be a disaster. She pulled out her mobile phone and rang Kevin's flat. No answer. She tried his mobile. It tripped to the answering service.

She bit her lip and dithered about what to do. She couldn't stand Kevin up – she'd just have to plough ahead and hope for the best. She turned onto the Circular Road and ten minutes later she reached the rendezvous point in the park. Kevin was already there, dressed in jeans and a dark brown leather jacket, opened at the front. The hip-length jacket had a vintage look about it, in the styling and the stiffness of the leather. He had a plastic bag under his arm. Under the jacket he wore a fine wool navy crew-neck and a scarf, in shades of pale green and soft grey, was draped loosely around his neck. He looked gorgeous.

He walked towards her, his tanned face lit up with a smile. 'How are you, Louise?' he said, in that voice that made her go weak at the knees. He cast a cursory glance at Oli in the buggy, leant over the top of it and planted a kiss on her lips.

She blushed, a little perturbed that he had kissed her in Oli's presence, even though the child had his face so buried in the folds of the buggy he could not see. 'He wouldn't walk,' she said. Oli pulled his knees up to his chin and made a grunting sound.

'Sorry,' she added.

'You don't need to say sorry for anything.'

'I rang your mobile phone,' she said, finding that she was irrationally annoyed with Kevin for the fact that she'd been unable to contact him.

He patted the pockets of his heavy jacket. 'I guess I must've left it at the flat.'

'I was going to cancel.'

'Why?'

She gripped the handles of the buggy tighter and found

that she was cross with her son. 'Because as you can see Oli isn't in the mood for meeting new people. I was going to suggest that we re-arrange for another day.'

And then inexplicably she felt tears prick her eyes and Kevin came and stood beside her. He put a hand, warm and rough, over her closed fist. He nuzzled her hair, dishevelled by the wind, and whispered in her ear, 'Hey, honey, it's okay. Don't worry. Everything's going to be all right.'

He pulled away and looked into her eyes, his gaze so direct and so assured that all at once she believed him. She relaxed and smiled.

'Come on. Let's sit over here for a bit.' He led her over to a blue wooden bench with a view of the play area. She parked the buggy a fraction to the left and they both sat down. They chatted about work for a while and then he put his hand in his pocket and, rustling, pulled out three small purple bags and held one up for her to see. It was a small chocolate bar. Kevin nodded at the buggy and raised his dark eyebrows, seeking her permission to offer Oli a chocolate. She didn't have the heart to say that, in this mood, he wouldn't take it from her, let alone a complete stranger. But she nodded all the same.

'Would you like a chocolate bar, Louise?' Kevin said, loudly. 'It's shaped like a frog.'

She smiled and said, 'I don't mind if I do.' He placed one in her hand and winked.

'Are you going to have one too?' she said.

'Sure am,' he replied, opening the wrapper, 'and there's one for Oli too. I'll just leave it on the bench here for him and he can come and get it when he wants.'

They munched on the chocolate and talked about when the boat would be lifted out of the water for overwintering in a barn Kevin had rented from a local farmer.

'You should come down and see it. It's quite a spectacle. They hire a huge crane for the day to lift out all the big boats. Oli would enjoy it.'

'We might do that,' said Louise, watching the chocolate bar like a hawk.

Oli emerged some minutes later, unable to resist the bait Kevin had laid down for him. He snatched the bar like a pickpocket and scurried back to his buggy.

'What do you say, Oli?' said Louise sternly.

There was a pause, the crinkling of plastic and then a muffled, ''ank you.'

'You're welcome,' said Kevin and he winked at Louise again. He stuffed the chocolate wrapper in his pocket, stood up and pulled a simple small red and blue nylon kite from the bag. He unravelled a few feet of line and, without a word, walked onto the large grassy area in front of the bench. He threw the kite in the air and started to run, letting out cord as he went. It swooped and dived, like a fish caught on a line, and then suddenly it was airborne, its yellow tail whipping in the steady breeze. Kevin whooped and – once the kite was fluttering steadily above them in the sky – walked back to the bench slowly, grinning. 'Here, Oli, I need you to hold this,' he called out, without taking his eyes off the kite. And before Louise could say a word, Oli was out of the buggy and running across the grass.

'Okay, you hold it right there,' said Kevin standing behind Oli, his arms over the small boy's shoulders. He placed the winder in Oli's small hands. 'That's right. You hold it like this and pull if you want it to go up. That's right, just like that. And if it starts to fall, run . . . like now. Run! Run like I did.'

Oli scampered breathlessly, clumsily across the grass trying to watch his footing and the kite at the same time.

Louise put a hand over her mouth, willing the kite to stay in the air, and somehow it did. She removed her hand and smiled.

'That's it! Brilliant!' shouted Kevin. He and Oli were both some distance away from her now. She watched Oli's round face raised to the sun and to Kevin, the two of them chatting now at a level she could not hear, and a lump formed in her throat. She should never have doubted Kevin. He had Oli eating out of the palm of his hand. He'd raised two children of his own so, of course, he knew a trick or two. But experience aside, the warmth he displayed towards Oli seemed to be genuine.

If only Cameron could meet Oli too – she was sure he would love him. If only he'd given fatherhood a chance, she was confident he would've grown into it.

As she watched them now, Oli jumping up and down with excitement as the kite fell from the sky and Kevin picked it up and re-launched it, she thought how much they looked like father and son. And Louise realised then – with a clarity of thought that had eluded her until now – that she wanted a father for Oli, just as much as she wanted a partner for herself. The smile fell from her lips. It was a lot to ask of any man – and she had not been entirely truthful with herself, or with Kevin.

Later, when Oli had finished playing on the swings and the climbing frame and his legs were too tired for him to walk any further, Kevin said, 'Want to come to my house for tea, Oli?'

'What's for tea?'

'Bangers, beans and mash.'

'Yeah!' cried Oli, climbing into the buggy. Kevin gave him a 'high five' slap on the hand.

'Oh, I don't know,' interrupted Louise, thinking that she

wanted the day to end on a high, not the way it had started
– with Oli tired and grumpy.

'It'll be all right, Louise,' said Kevin, and he placed his
hand on her back and rubbed it in a soothing circular motion.
'Unless you've got something already planned for tea?'

She smiled. 'No,' she admitted, the idea of someone else
cooking, no matter how simple the fare, starting to appeal.

'Well, in that case, what are we waiting for? Come on. It's
only across the road. I'll give you a run home in the car
later.'

After they'd eaten, Kevin put on a DVD for Oli that he'd
borrowed from a neighbour. Then he and Louise stood side
by side in his small kitchen. He plunged his hands into the
washing-up basin, his sleeves rolled up, revealing thick, hairy
arms. Louise picked up a plate, dried it and set it on the
table. It was nice, working companionably together like this,
the way they would, she imagined, if they shared a home.

'Oli seemed to have a good time in the park,' observed
Kevin, rinsing a clutch of cutlery and depositing it noisily
on the red draining rack.

'Yes. He did, thanks to you.' Louise picked up a bunch of
knives and forks. 'I was losing patience with him.'

Kevin rinsed a saucepan and set it on the rack. 'Don't be
hard on yourself, Louise. When you're with him all the time
your reserves are bound to run low. And it's harder when
it's your own child. You're more emotionally involved.'

Louise finished drying the knives and forks in her hand
and placed them in the cutlery drawer. She swallowed. 'Kevin,
I realised something in the park today. Something that I
hadn't realised before.'

'What's that?' said Kevin, drying his hands on a towel.

Her heart beat against her chest. She could, of course, simply
not tell him. She could wait and see how things developed.

But it wasn't in her nature to hide anything. She didn't want to mislead – and then see Oli disappointed and Kevin hurt. She looked out the window at the tops of the leafless trees swaying in the breeze. 'That I want whoever wants me, to want Oli too.' She quickly brought her gaze to bear on him, to gauge his reaction.

He nodded slowly, thoughtfully.

'I'd hate for me to be happy and him not to be.' She paused, looked into his steady gaze and added, 'What I'm trying to say, I think, is that Oli and me come as a package.'

'Do you think I don't know that, Louise?' He dropped the towel on the table and came over to where she stood by the window. 'I knew that you were a single mother before I even met you.'

'I couldn't bear it if the man I loved didn't love Oli too.'

'The man you loved?' he said, his eyes glazed with hope.

This time it was her turn to nod. 'I want a partner. But I also want Oli to have a father, Kevin. And I think it's only fair for me to tell you that. Now, up front, before . . . before things get any more serious.'

He took her hand gently in his and stared down at it for some moments. And when he raised his eyes to meet hers they were full of an intensity she had not seen there before. 'I hear what you're saying, Louise. And I understand that you want the best for Oli. But this isn't something to be taken on lightly – by any man.'

She closed her eyes, wishing she hadn't spoken out. She had spoiled what they had. But how could she *not* speak out?

'That's why I want you to know, that I have thought about it. And I'm willing.'

She opened her eyes. 'You are?'

'I've done it before, so I know what I'm talking about,

Louise,' he said, looking at her hands again. 'It all depends of course on what happens between you and me. But if things work out,' he added, lifting his gaze to meet hers once more, 'then you don't need to worry about Oli.'

'Oh, Kevin,' she said. She touched the side of his rough, masculine face with her hand, and traced the line of his cheekbone. A white scar nestled at the base of his throat – his pulse throbbed under his skin. Their lips when they met were hungry with desire and she felt once more the way she had done with Cameron – and truly thought she never would again.

That night when she got home and Oli was in bed, Louise logged onto her computer to check her e-mails, her heart full of happiness and hope. She could not believe her good fortune in meeting Kevin, who was everything she could wish for in a partner and a father. She was playing it cool, taking it slowly – they had not consummated the relationship – but she could not believe her luck. Maybe dreams did come true, after all.

She scanned her inbox. There was an e-mail from Max, bless him, telling her all about his social life in London, the clubs and celebrity-studded parties – Graham worked in fashion and they got invited to all sorts of openings and launches. She smiled and decided to reply to it when she had more time. Then there was one from Friends Reunited. She had registered with the site a couple of years ago, but after an initial blaze of frenzied exchanges of e-mails with old school and university pals, she had fallen out of the way of it, in the same way she'd abandoned her Facebook page. She simply didn't have the time to devote to either and now that she was working that wasn't going to change. Still, curiosity got the better of her and she clicked on the e-mail, went into the website and read the message.

It was from Cameron. It was the first communication she'd had from him in three years. Her heart stood still, started again. She took a deep breath and began to read.

Louise, it said, *I know from Cindy that you are in Ballyfergus now. I want you to know that not a day goes by that I don't regret our divorce – and what led to it. I was a fool. I should never have let you go. Please forgive me. I love you still. Cameron.*

Louise sat stunned for many long minutes while all the implications of this succinct little message sank in, like so many poisoned daggers. Then she put her face in her hands and wept.

Chapter Ten

'So how are things with you, Gemma?' said Joanne. She was making sandwiches for Abbey's 'glamour' birthday party.

Gemma, balancing tip-toed on a small set of steps, was stringing bunting made from triangles of brightly coloured floral cloth across Joanne's kitchen wall – one of the few items from Sian's shop that Joanne considered tasteful enough to adorn her home. As usual Gemma wore her trademark black – today it was slim-fitting black Capri pants, faux leopard-skin ballet pumps and a black slash-neck top. She looked like she had lost a pound or two since the last time Joanne had checked. But then people often lost weight when they were in the throes of a love affair.

Three weeks had passed since Joanne had read Gemma's prescription and still her friend had not said a word to her about it. It was awful – all she could think about when she looked at Gemma was the fact that she was having sex with someone. And if truth be told, Joanne, on the routine treadmill of work and domesticity, was a little envious of Gemma's imagined, possibly illicit, love affair. She resented the fact that she was being denied the vicarious pleasure of being part of that romantic intrigue.

Gemma looked down and smiled, a little secretly thought Joanne. But then she was reading things into everything her friend did or said. 'Good, thanks.' Gemma stood, hands on hips, and admired her handiwork. 'What d'you think?'

'I think it looks great. Thanks,' said Joanne, brightly. She shoved eight sherbet-coloured candles into the pliable pink icing of a 'Barbie' cake, while Gemma ripped open a packet of pink balloons.

Maddy came into the room with a basket of nail polish in her arms. She wore skinny jeans and a long red and white striped T-shirt with a glittery 'I'm Gorgeous' emblazoned on the front. She and Roz had been roped in to help with the party – with the promise of a tenner each. 'Where do you want me to set up?'

'You'd better do it here. We don't want nail polish over the carpet. Roz can do the hair upstairs in the bathroom. I'll get you a cover for the table.'

Joanne rummaged under the sink for an oilcloth and spread it over one end of the table. 'Now don't let them out of here with bottles of nail polish,' she went on. 'They have to stay in the kitchen. And make sure their nails are dry before they go running about and rubbing it off on the furniture.'

Maddy rolled her dark eyes and adopted a bored-looking expression. 'I'm not that stupid, Mum.'

'No, of course you're not,' said Joanne with a smile, smoothing the wrinkles out of the cloth. 'Now set up there, will you? We'll have to do the food in the dining room.' If they had a larger house, of course, with a big family bathroom, rather than the tiny one upstairs, there would be room for Maddy to do nails in there . . .

Gemma took a break from the decorations. Her face was the same colour as the semi-inflated balloon in her hand. 'I'd better do the make-up in here too,' she said. 'If they spill eye-shadow or drop a lipstick you'll never get it out of the carpet.'

'You're right,' agreed Joanne, rubbing her chin. 'There's room at the other end of the table for you.'

Maddy laid out the bottles of nail polish in a neat row along with packets of nail stickers and stick-on 'diamonds' that Joanne had picked up for next to nothing in Superdrug on Main Street.

Abbey came running into the kitchen, and ricocheted around the room, bouncing off the walls like a ping-pong ball. She was nicely dressed, for a change, in new clothes Joanne had bought for the occasion in Primark – a pair of pink flared jeans, a pretty white blouse with short sleeves and gold ballerina pumps. 'Hey, calm down, will you?' laughed Joanne indulgently and Abbey stood in the middle of the room and jumped up and down, her fists clenched with excitement.

'But I'm soooo excited! What are you doing, Maddy?' She went over and fingered the bottles of varnish, knocking one of them onto the floor. Luckily it did not break. 'Are these for the party?'

'Yes, and hands off,' warned Maddy, picking the bottle off the floor. 'You'll have them all broken before we've even started.'

'Are Auntie Sian and Auntie Louise coming to my party?' said Abbey.

Joanne shook her head. 'No, darling. They both have to work this afternoon I'm afraid.'

Abbey went over to the breakfast bar and looked at the trays of food laid out – sandwiches and sausage rolls, biscuits and fairy cakes, all covered with cling film. 'Like Daddy?'

'Yes, like Daddy.' Joanne tried to deliver this impartially, as though Phil's absence did not annoy the hell out of her. Phil had said he would take this afternoon off to be at Abbey's party – and then last night he said he had an important meeting he couldn't get out of. She knew he was having a tough time this week – his car was off the road for repairs and he'd had to borrow hers to get to work, leaving her to manage without. Experience had taught her not to rely on him and she hadn't, hence Gemma's presence. What would she do without her? But still, his absence irked.

'But,' Joanne went on, anxious to allay Abbey's disappointment, 'Auntie Sian and Auntie Louise are coming round tomorrow for a big family get-together. As well as Grandma and Grandpa and Oli. And Daddy will be there of course because he doesn't work on Saturdays. We'll have a special family party.'

Abbey clapped her hands in glee and ran out of the room, nearly colliding with Roz on her way into the kitchen. She wore a floaty blue printed dress under a fine coral-coloured cardigan. On her legs were black leggings and on her fake-tanned feet, flat black pumps. She'd straightened the dark curly hair she'd inherited from her mother – and hated so much – so that it hung, lank and lifeless, to her shoulders.

'Oh, there you are, Roz,' said Joanne, cheerfully. 'Now I was thinking that you could do the hair in the bathroom, except for the coloured spray. If any of them want that, could you pop outside to do it?' She glanced out the window. Luckily, though overcast, it was a dry, mild October day. The trees had shed most of their leaves – the garden was thick with them, like giant crispy cornflakes on the grass. 'Looks like the weather's going to hold.'

Roz nodded. 'Sure.'

Joanne pointed to a hessian bag by the back door. It had 'Ballyfergus is a Plastic Bag Free Zone' written in green ink on the side – a gift from Sian. It was filled with combs and brushes and all manner of cheap and cheerful headbands, clips and slides, pretty barettes, bobbles and sparkly scrunchies. 'Everything you need's in there, Roz.'

Roz went over and started to rummage through the contents. 'This looks like fun! Hey, Maddy,' she said, holding up a canister of pink hair spray, 'how do you fancy going pink like Lady GaGa?'

Maddy laughed and Joanne turned to Gemma, who had just finished pinning two balloons above the kitchen window. 'Thank you. That looks fantastic.' She untied the apron around her waist, threw it on the kitchen counter and looked around with satisfaction. 'I think that's everything done now, isn't it?'

'Looks like it,' said Gemma.

'I've just got time to pop upstairs and freshen up. If the doorbell goes will you let them in? Thanks sweetheart.'

In the bedroom she powdered her face, re-applied lipstick and squirted a tiny bit of Agent Provocateur perfume, a present from Phil last Christmas, on her neck. As she was about to leave the room, the phone went. She picked the silver handset up and said, 'Hello,' fully expecting it to be either Phil or one of Abbey's little guests calling off.

So when the caller said, 'Hi, Joanne. It's me, Barry,' she hesitated.

'From Phil's work,' he added and it took Joanne a few seconds to register who it was. Barry McClure, nearing retirement and with a grown-up family, was Phil's boss – she'd met him several times over the years and liked him. He had a soft spot for Phil too. Years ago Phil had got into hot water about expenses – he'd been illegally claiming mileage for the journey to and from the office. The company had wanted to drag him over the coals but Barry had intervened and Phil had got off with a rap over the knuckles – and a repayment schedule for the erroneously claimed amount.

'Oh, hi, sorry, Barry,' she said warmly, walking over to the window and looking down onto the street below. Gemma had tied pink balloons to the cherry tree on the front lawn. She smiled. 'I'm just a bit distracted today. We're getting ready for Abbey's birthday party in a few minutes.'

'It's no wonder you're distracted,' said Barry darkly and Joanne frowned, thinking this an odd thing to say. 'Anyway,' he carried on, more upbeat, 'what age is Abbey?'

'Eight.'

He sucked air in and she could imagine him shaking his balding head. 'Where does the time go, Joanne? It seems like only yesterday, she was a babe in your arms.' Barry had met Abbey just once when she was nine months old, at a barbecue organised by one of Phil's colleagues – one of the rare social events she'd been to in connection with his work.

'I know,' Joanne smiled into the phone. The time *had* flown. Abbey's babyhood was a distant memory that she barely had time to reflect on. She should dig out Abbey's baby book after the party was over.

'Well, listen,' said Barry briskly, changing tone. 'You must be very busy. Don't let me keep you. I just wondered if I could have a word with Phil.'

'I'm afraid he's not here right now.' Why was Barry phoning Phil at home at three o'clock on a Friday afternoon? Didn't he know he was at work?

'Well, can you ask him to call me as soon as he gets in? I can't get him on his mobile. I need to speak with him urgently. I'll be here until six and he's got my mobile number. Tell him to call me at home if he doesn't catch me at the office. I'll be there all evening.'

'Okay,' said Joanne slowly, wondering what business crisis could demand such attention on a Friday night.

'I'm hopeful we might be able to sort something out for Phil.'

A ball of anxiety formed instantly in the pit of Joanne's stomach. She placed her hand on her belly and sat down on the edge of the bed. Somehow, in the space of a few seconds the phone call had turned from friendly, to menacing. Barry spoke as if Phil was in some sort of fix. As if Joanne ought to know what he was talking about. But why would she? Phil never spoke about his work. 'Sort something out,' repeated Joanne slowly, not wanting to give away the fact that she had no idea what Barry was on about. She was afraid that if he clocked her ignorance, he might clam up. It dawned on her then that, if Barry was talking to her about this issue – whatever it was – then, somehow, it must concern her.

'Well, technically he can be sacked for loss of his licence. But you'll know that already.'

'His driving licence?' said Joanne, stupidly, shaking her head, not really taking in the enormity of what Barry had just said.

'Well, yes, without it he can't drive and, without transport, he can't fulfil the terms of his employment. Human Resources want to throw the book at him.'

Joanne felt as if she'd just been punched in the chest. Her breath came in short gasps and her face flushed with humiliation. Phil had lost his driving licence. He was about to lose his job. And he hadn't told her? She bit her lip to stop herself crying out. No longer able to carry on with the pretence that she knew all about this nightmare, she was quiet.

Barry filled the silence, every word pounding her head like a sledgehammer until it throbbed. 'But I've spoken to a couple of the directors and I'm hopeful the board might agree to transfer Phil to a marketing desk job at Head Office until the disqualification expires. He'll have to take a pay cut – there'll be no bonuses – but it's only for three months. His lawyer must have pleaded his case very well to get it down

'Joanne?' came Gemma's voice from downstairs and Joanne stirred. She would have to make an appearance soon, pretend that nothing was wrong and try not to spoil Abbey's party with her misery. She stood up, went over to the window, wrapped her arms around herself, and looked out. Avril Dodds was coming up the drive with her daughter Jodie skipping alongside her like a spring lamb. But Joanne's attention wasn't on them – it was on the space where her car should've been. Phil had taken her car that morning, ostensibly for work. He had lied about going to work and he had lied about his car being in the garage for repairs – it must've been confiscated by his employers.

But more to the point what was he doing driving her car when he was disqualified? She put her hand over her mouth. What if he had an accident? Would she be responsible for letting him drive her car, even though she had not known of the disqualification? And if he was stopped by the police, what would happen? It was a serious offence – he could be arrested.

She wondered then what he had done to lose his licence? Was it something serious, like drunk, or dangerous, driving that had led to an immediate ban? Or was it, more probably, an accumulation of points – his attitude to driving was as irresponsible as his attitude to everything else in life. She knew he'd got at least six points on his licence – and probably more that he hadn't told her about.

The door of the room flew open and Joanne turned around. Holly burst in, her delicate, narrow face lit up with happiness. She wore a tiered skirt, each layer made from a different floral fabric and a pretty pale blue top with puff sleeves. 'What are you doing, Mum? Everyone's here. You need to come now!' She grinned, her cheeks flushed and her eyes, the same colour as the duck egg paint on the wall, flashed with excitement.

Joanne forced a smile onto her face – it took so much effort it was almost painful and she knew it would take every ounce of strength to keep it there all afternoon. 'I'm coming right now,' she said, and she followed Holly out of the room, her legs like lead and her heart numbed with disappointment. She was utterly worn out, never knowing what crisis was coming next, never trusting Phil, never relaxing, never being able to let go the reins of her family because she knew that he would never be there to pick them up. Well, this time he had gone too far. This time something had to be done.

Two hours later the party was nearly over. Joanne swept the debris off the dining room table into a black bin bag, while the children ran riot around the house. Only the finale to go and then everyone would go home and she would be left to face Phil and the mess that he had created. The paracetamol she'd taken earlier had eased her headache – she was so exhausted she felt like she could sleep for a week.

She hauled the bin bag into the kitchen, dodging screaming little girls in the hall, and set it by the back door to take out later. A job that, had her husband been a reliable man, had he cared, he would have done for her. She rinsed her hands under the kitchen tap. Gemma sat alone at the table tidying up the make-up.

'Are you all right, Joanne? You look tired.'

'No, I'm not all right.' Joanne slumped onto a chair opposite Gemma and quickly told her about the phone call in a quiet, neutral tone – too worn out for histrionics, too angry to cry.

Gemma listened without comment, then sighed and shook her head. 'I don't know why you won't listen to me, Joanne. You should leave him. No,' she said, pointing a tube of mascara at Joanne's chest, 'why should you leave? Kick him out. I wouldn't put up with that kind of behaviour.'

'Oh, I can't think of that right now. All I want is to get this mess sorted out.' Joanne ran her hands over her face and sighed heavily.

'He treats you like dirt, you do realise that, don't you? You let him walk all over you. I wouldn't put up with half the things you've put up with over the years.'

'You're not me,' said Joanne flatly. 'And he loves me.'

'Are you sure about that?'

Joanne was silent then considering this awful proposition. Perhaps Gemma was right. If Phil loved her, would he do the things he did? And if he couldn't, wouldn't, change perhaps their relationship was doomed.

Gemma's hand was on her arm then and Joanne looked tearfully into her friend's clear, certain gaze. 'I don't mean to speak harshly, Joanne,' she said softly. 'It's just that I care for you and want you to be happy.'

Joanne smiled wearily. 'I know.'

'And it seems to me,' continued Gemma, removing her hand, 'that being with Phil is making you miserable.'

Suddenly there was a cry from the front of the house. It was Maddy. 'Look, Abbey. Daddy's home. And look what he's got!'

Joanne's heart fluttered – thank God he and the car were safe home in one piece. She would hide both sets of car keys and make sure he never drove her car again. All the girls ran into the lounge and looked out the window. Even Gemma gravitated towards the front of the house to see what all the fuss was about. Joanne with a line of vision up the hall to the front door, watched proceedings from the kitchen, unable to bring herself to face Phil.

'It's a teddy bear,' squealed a little voice.

'The biggest one in the whole wide world,' screeched another.

'It's for me!' screamed Abbey, and she ran to the front door, flung it open and bolted outside, followed by a retinue of girls, frenzied with excitement.

'Oh, Joanne,' came Gemma's voice, soft with wonderment, from the end of the hall. 'Come and look. It really is the biggest teddy I've ever seen!'

But Joanne stayed where she was, watching warily from a distance, not sure how she would react to Phil when she saw him. Moments later, Abbey stumbled back into the house with a monstrous stuffed teddy bear in her arms. It was baby pink with a white face and belly and a fuchsia ribbon tied round its neck – and it was as tall as Abbey.

'Mum!' she cried, 'Mum! Come and see.' All her friends crowded around her, desperate to touch and hold the huge toy.

'Mum!' she hollered again and Joanne came up the hall slowly. 'Mum!'

'I see it, Abbey. There's no need to shout.'

'Daddy bought it for me.'

'I know.'

And then Phil, in a dark suit, was standing in the hall with Abbey wrapped round his left leg, grinning from ear to ear, delighted with himself and his dramatic entrance. The centre of attention – like Father Christmas. And Joanne, full of loathing, was unable to meet his eye. Noticing her foul expression, he scowled, then looked away.

Once the commotion had died down and the children dispersed Joanne went up to him and said, 'Phil, why don't you supervise the piñata while I clear up a bit in here and get the party bags ready?'

'Supervise the what?' he said as though this was news to him.

'The piñata,' she repeated dully, pointing towards the back

of the house. 'It's in the garden.' Earlier, while the girls had been busy eating their party food, she'd hung a cardboard piñata, in the shape of a purple butterfly, from a tree at the bottom of the garden. She had patiently explained the plans for the party, including this game, to Phil several times. But it was no wonder he had forgotten – she would've too, in his shoes.

He grunted and loosened his tie. She wondered for whose benefit he was wearing it. He hadn't, after all, been at work, had he?

'There are twelve strings attached to it,' she explained, instructing him like she would a child. 'Let the girls take turns pulling them. Only one is the magic string, the one that opens the piñata and releases the sweets I've put inside. Make sure they get shared out equally.'

Phil led the children through the kitchen in a marching column like the Pied Piper. Gemma looked up and smiled – Joanne ignored them. 'Follow me into the garden,' he commanded loudly, full of bonhomie, like he hadn't a care in the world. It was typical of him to leave all the hard work to others and then turn up to steal the glory at the last.

Parents started to arrive shortly afterwards and within half an hour all the guests had gone. Gemma gave Joanne a squeeze on the arm before she left with Roz. Maddy went up to her room and put on music. Phil hoovered up the remains of the party food, then disappeared upstairs. Joanne quietly put on a DVD for the girls in the lounge, tucked them up, both shattered, on the sofa and firmly closed the door. She climbed the stairs and found Phil in their bedroom.

He'd changed into jeans and a casual blue checked shirt. A crumpled white shirt lay on the floor. He was preening himself in the mirror, running his hand through his hair. The floral, powdery scent of the perfume she'd put on earlier mingled unpleasantly with Cool Water aftershave, fresh and clean smelling like the ocean. He had taken to wearing it recently, though Joanne thought it a 'young' fragrance and ill-suited to a man of his age. Like Phil and her, the two fragrances clashed.

'How'd the party go?' he asked. 'Looked like everybody had a good time.'

She regarded him impassively for a few moments wondering how he could stand there making small-talk – wasn't he worried sick about his job, like she was? When she did not reply, he pretended he hadn't noticed, looked at himself in the mirror again and said, 'I think Abbey liked the teddy bear, don't you?'

She shut the bedroom door and leant against it, her hand on the doorknob. 'Did you really think I wouldn't find out?'

His face coloured. He glanced at her but could not hold her gaze. He looked in the mirror, and started fiddling with the collar of his shirt. 'I've no idea what you're talking about, Joanne.'

'Liar.' She advanced on him until she was within touching distance. White anger bubbled up inside her – but somehow she managed to control it. She looked up into his face. 'I got a phone call today.'

He kept his eyes fixed determinedly on his reflection in the mirror, even though her face was only twelve inches from his. 'What phone call?' His hands, she noticed, were shaking, betraying his guilt. He hid them in the front pockets of his jeans.

'It's been going on for months and you never said a word.'

'Look, I don't know who you've been talking to,' he said, taking a step away from her and addressing some point on the wall, to the left of her shoulder, 'but—'

'This isn't a rumour, Phil. I heard it straight from the horse's mouth, so to speak.' She paused, watching the effect her words had on him, enjoying the fact that she was inflicting some discomfort, though nothing to match the anguish he'd put her through.

His face blanched. His brow furrowed in confusion. He opened his mouth to speak, then closed it.

'It's no good denying it, Phil. Barry McClure told me everything.'

He let out a long sigh, lowered his head, pulled his hands from his pockets and placed them on his hips. He lifted his head again and she saw a flicker of something – was it relief? – pass over his face. Then he pulled himself up to his full height and his features hardened.

'I can't believe you didn't tell me, Phil. You've lost your licence, for God's sake. You put your job on the line and you actually got in my car and drove it while banned. Are you absolutely out of your mind? Not to mention all the lies you told about your car being in for repairs – and pretending you had an important meeting this afternoon. You weren't even at work.'

'I did have an important meeting.'

'Yeah. Who with?'

He threaded a belt through the loops on his jeans. 'My lawyer.'

She snorted. 'You engaged a lawyer to defend you in court,' she said, spitting the words out in disgust, 'and you never thought to mention it to me?'

He glared at her, the muscles in his left cheek contracting involuntarily.

'How did you lose your licence? What did you do?' she demanded.

'Does it matter?'

She pursed her lips and folded her arms, waiting.

'All right. I got done for using my mobile earlier in the year. And a few months ago, I got a fixed penalty notice and three points for speeding. That took my total points to twelve. I got a summons to attend court.'

'Pathetic.'

He finished putting on the belt and buckled it. 'What did Barry McClure want?'

'He wants you to call him tonight,' she said sullenly. 'He said he might be able to offer you a desk job in Belfast for the duration of the ban.'

Phil's face lit up. 'Good old Barry!' he said and smiled. 'I still have a job, see. What are you so worried about? Everything's all right.'

'This isn't all right, Phil,' she said coldly. 'Whichever way you look at it, it isn't all right. You're going to have to take a pay cut for a start. And I'll have to do all the driving.'

'It's only for three months.'

'Three months of school runs and supermarket shops and driving the girls absolutely everywhere! And how will you get to work?'

'I'll use public transport.'

Joanne laughed bitterly. She couldn't imagine Phil on a smelly bus or crowded train, rubbing shoulders with the hoi polloi. 'Well, you needn't think I'm going to run you to the train station – or pick you up. And if you drive my car again, I'll report you to the police.'

His nostrils flared and he pointed a finger at her. 'Just keep your nose out of it, Joanne. This is my business, not yours. I'll sort it.'

She clenched her hands into fists by her sides, her nails digging into her flesh. 'For Christ's sake,' she yelled, at last letting the anger explode, 'would you stop saying that? Your business *is* my business. We're married to each other. We have three children together and all you can do is think about yourself!'

The tears bubbled over then. She sat down on her side of the bed and put her face in her hands and wept softly.

After a few moments he said a little sadly, standing over her, 'You want to know why I didn't tell you, Joanne? Because I knew you'd react like this.'

She looked up at him, her face composed, wet tears on her cheeks. 'How come I didn't see any letters?' she said as though he had not spoken. 'You've had hardly any mail for ages . . . in fact, only a few items these past few months.'

He looked at the carpet.

'What?' she said, realisation dawning slowly. She gasped. How could she not have twigged? 'You had your mail re-directed, didn't you?'

Still he would not answer but the uncomfortable expression on his face told her she'd hit the nail on the head. 'But why, Phil?'

He regarded her coldly for a few moments before he spoke. 'Why do you think?'

The level of his deception astounded her. She had not believed him capable of it. 'But what did you think was going to happen, Phil?' she said, softly, all anger spent. 'I was going to find out sooner or later.'

He rubbed his brow with his hand. 'I thought I might've got off. The lawyer put forward a convincing plea—'

'Yeah, I heard about that,' she said scornfully. 'You said your mother relied on you for transport, Phil. That's perjury!'

He ignored her and went on, 'The judge agreed to reduce the length of the ban to three months. The lawyer says I got off lightly.'

'But even if you had gotten off, can't you see that's not the point? Can't you see that the fact that you lied in court and hid all this from me – and went to such lengths to do so – is just not . . . not right?'

'I know,' he said and hung his head and she almost went over to him. But he lifted his head and added bitterly, his eyes hard like flint, 'But what's new? Nothing I do is ever right, Joanne. Is it?'

This she could not refute so she sat in silence staring at him, wondering how on earth they were going to manage.

He put his hands in his pockets and looked at the toes of his shoes. 'I think I should move out.'

'Don't be—' she began but he cut across her.

'No, I mean it this time, Joanne. It isn't working between you and me. It hasn't worked for some time and we keep limping along like some half-dead horse. And it's excruciating for everyone involved.'

She stood up, her arms hanging by her sides and said, incredulously, 'You're serious, aren't you?'

'Never more so in my life.'

She sat down again, numb. 'But you can't go, Phil,' she heard herself say, her voice disembodied, far away, like it belonged to someone else. She ought to have been furious, fighting, spitting, holding on to him but she felt detached and, oddly, shamefully relieved. 'It's Abbey's birthday lunch tomorrow. I promised her you'd be there.'

'I can't help that. I'll take her out another time – somewhere special, just the two of us.' He went over to the wardrobe and pulled out a large bag from the bottom of the wardrobe that he sometimes used on business trips and threw it on the bed. She watched him fill the case with clothes and found that she was, strangely, frozen to the spot.

'Where will you go?' she said.

'I'll stay with a friend.'

'Who?'

'Does it matter? You can get me on my mobile.'

He finished shoving things into the bag in a haphazard manner, closed it and zipped it up. He took a suit out of the wardrobe, put it inside a suit carrier and threw it over his shoulder. 'I'll get the rest of my clothes another time,' he said.

She nodded, believing in her heart that this was just a charade, that Phil would be back the very next day full of apologies and promises of new beginnings. But he'd never before actually packed a bag and left . . .

She stood up unsteadily. He picked up the bag and walked to the door. 'I'm sorry that I've been a disappointment to you, Joanne. Maybe I haven't been the best husband in the world, but you never let me forget it. A man can't live like that, being constantly undermined and nagged and made to feel incompetent and stupid in his own home. In front of his own children. The girls don't have any respect for me and they've learnt that from you.'

She opened her mouth to defend herself, then blushed because what he said was true – she avoided fighting in front of the children but that didn't stop her talking derisively about Phil when he wasn't there. She had not been a loyal wife. 'Please don't go, Phil,' she said at last, holding out a hand towards him. 'I'm sure if we sit down and talk about this, we can . . . we can work things out.'

'But why would you want to do that, Joanne?' he said matter-of-factly. 'You can't stand me.'

She shook her head. 'I'm sorry if I made you feel that way. But I don't hate you, Phil. I want to save our marriage and I . . . I still love you.'

'Well, I'm sorry, Joanne. But I don't love you.' And with that, he stepped into the hall, closing the door quietly in her face.

Chapter Eleven

Andy lay sprawled lifelessly on the sofa, in a T-shirt and cargo pants, his legs elevated on a beanbag, watching sport on TV. It was unlike him to be this inactive. 'Does Joanne really expect me to be there tomorrow? Kevin wants me to help him with the boat.'

'But it's Abbey's birthday celebration, Andy,' argued Sian, feeling aggrieved that they were even having this conversation. She shouldn't have to cajole him into going to an important family event like this. 'Everyone will expect you to be there, especially Abbey. You know how she loves you.'

Instead of bringing a smile to his lips, this made him look even more miserable. Sian frowned, perplexed. She hardly knew Andy these days, he was so changed from his former carefree self. Now he was edgy, preoccupied and unhappy. It had taken a lot of courage to face up to the fact that her relationship with Andy was falling apart. Since they'd moved into the house seven weeks ago she felt like she'd been walking on eggshells around him. When she tried to get him to talk about what was wrong, he'd somehow manage to change the subject. Funny how you could live with someone, even sleep with them, and talk about everything but the one thing that really mattered. But not tonight, she thought with steely determination – she was going to tackle him head on. She'd from six. I hear that the courts are accepting the exceptional hardship plea more and more, especially where some of the points result from speeding cameras. And of course the fact that Phil's mother relies on him for transport must've weighed heavily in his favour.'

Phil had engaged a lawyer. He'd gone to court. He'd told lies under oath about his mother – he hardly ever visited her in her sheltered flat in Carrickfergus, never mind ferried her about. Joanne pressed her forehead with the pad of her thumb and took a deep breath, trying to calm her frazzled nerves. She knew she ought to express her thanks to Barry for, yet again, saving Phil's skin. But she found her throat was constricted with rage. She could not speak.

Misinterpreting her silence as disappointment, Barry said, 'It's the best I can do under the circumstances, Joanne.'

Joanne swallowed and managed to reply in a small, worn-out voice, 'You . . . you've done more than enough, Barry. More than you should. Thank you.' The doorbell chimed and she forced some life into her voice. 'There's the bell, Barry. I have to go now.'

'Don't forget to tell Phil to call me, will you?'

'I won't.'

Joanne pressed the red button, ending the call, and dropped the handset on the cream bedspread. Then she sat on the bed staring at the blue-green wall, her face as implacable as stone, and listened to the squeals of excitement from downstairs. A day that had started with so much promise was ruined – she would forever associate Abbey's eighth birthday with her husband's deceit and betrayal. She had kidded herself that they were getting along better these days, that Phil had changed. Nothing had changed – nothing would ever change him. How did he think he could keep news of such enormity from her? News that would impact them all as a family?

given him space and time to sort out his feelings though, if truth be told, she'd been in no rush to press for answers, for fear she would not want to hear them. Now she was ready.

'Well, let's not talk about tomorrow now,' she said bravely, struggling to keep her voice, and emotions, on an even keel. 'Dinner's ready. Why don't we sit down and eat? I got us a nice bottle of wine – well, two actually.'

He followed her into the kitchen where the lights had been dimmed. The small nineteen-thirties table, salvaged from a skip, was laid with a vibrantly coloured tablecloth from a co-operative in Africa, matching napkins and candles in empty jam-jars. The room was warm and smelt of good food.

'What's the special occasion?' said Andy, when he saw the table, baulking a little or so it seemed to Sian.

She swallowed the lump of sadness in her throat, slipped on a pair of oven gloves and said, briskly, 'Nothing. Come on, sit down before it gets cold. It's mushroom goulash and rice and salad,' she continued, getting the food out and setting it on cork placemats. 'And I made a lemon tart for afters.'

He pulled the chair out, the legs making only a scuffing sound on the cork tiles. 'Thanks for doing all this, Sian. Where'd you get the time?'

'I left work a little early tonight. Bernie shut up shop for me. Pour us some wine, will you?' She nodded at the bottle sitting on the table.

Andy, looking uncomfortable, sat down on the edge of his seat and filled two glasses with white wine. He drummed his fingers on the tablecloth.

Sian shed the oven gloves, sat down and straight away knocked back most of the wine in her glass. 'Steady on,' he said, laughing, with his glass to his lips, 'or you'll be plastered in no time.'

Sian gave him a thin smile. She drank only on social occasions and rarely more than a few glasses. But suddenly, getting mindlessly drunk seemed tempting – anything to block out the fear and misery in her heart. She piled food on her plate and, while Andy was busy doing the same, nearly emptied her refilled glass. The wine, consumed so quickly, went straight to her head. Picking at the food, she felt her tensed muscles relax a little.

'This is absolutely delicious,' said Andy, tucking in enthusiastically.

Sian took another slug of wine and put her fork down, her appetite, small to begin with, suddenly gone.

'Is something wrong, Sian?' he asked, after a few moments of silence had passed between them.

She stared at him for some time and then said, glumly, 'Funny you should say that, Andy. I was going to ask you the very same thing.'

He wiped the corner of his mouth with a napkin. They both stared at each other for what seemed like an eternity until Sian said, 'What's going on between us, Andy?'

He shook his head, made as if to shrug his shoulders, and opened his mouth, no doubt to deliver some platitude, as he had done before, about how nothing was wrong, how relationships go through different stages and how it was unrealistic of her to expect intense emotional intimacy all the time.

'No,' she almost shouted, 'don't deny it. It started almost as soon as we moved into this house. Why don't you want to get married any more, Andy?'

'It's not that I don't want to. It's just . . .'

His voice trailed off, and he looked away. She waited for him to finish the sentence but instead he put his head in his hands and rubbed his face.

213

'It's just what, Andy?'

He laid his hands palm down on the tabletop, fingers splayed wide and stared at her. Their eyes locked together for what seemed like a very long time. 'It's just that I don't think you and I want the same things any more, Sian.'

Sian blinked and fought off the feeling of light-headedness, the rushing sensation that everything she held dear was slipping from her grasp. 'Of course we do, Andy,' she said, trying to bring him back from the brink of these treacherous thoughts. 'That's what makes us a great team. It's our shared values that make us strong. Values are something you believe in. Always.'

He was shaking his head before she'd even finished. 'Your values maybe, Sian. But not mine. Sometimes we change and what seemed right and certain before doesn't seem so clearcut any more.'

She really had no idea what he was talking about, but it terrified her all the same. She swallowed and pressed on, determined to get at the truth no matter what the cost. 'So you've changed, Andy?'

'Yes,' he said, choking with emotion.

She put a hand over his and squeezed it tight. 'In what way?' she asked gently, her voice a whisper.

'I don't want to marry you, Sian . . .'

She withdrew her hand and clasped it over her mouth. It was what she'd suspected all along. He no longer loved her. Her heartbeat fluttered erratically like the wings of a damaged butterfly.

The Adam's apple in his throat moved and his voice, when he spoke again was faint and strained. '. . . because you won't have my children.'

Her heartbeat stabilised again and she removed her hand from her mouth and placed it over her heart. He still loved her then. But what was this about children? Yes, it was true she didn't want children, but this is what they had both agreed on years ago. It was what they had both wanted.

'You won't, will you?' he said.

She sat stunned for a few moments, trying to take in the enormity of what he'd just said. 'You don't mean that,' she said with a desperate smile. 'Sure you don't?'

His expression when he spoke was full of pity. 'Yes, I do, Sian. I've tried to find the opportunity to raise the subject before—'

'No you haven't.' If he'd so much as mentioned this before, she would not have forgotten.

He cocked his head to one side and looked at the food congealing on his plate. His face was immobile with sorrow. 'Maybe I didn't try hard enough. But every time the subject of kids came up you were so resolute, so dismissive of any other choice but your own.'

Sian shook her head, trying to clear her head of confusion, as one of the cornerstones of her world shifted like sand beneath her feet. 'Are you saying that you *want* to have children? That you've changed your mind?'

'Yes.'

Panic took hold of Sian. If this was what he wanted, truly wanted, then she could not give it to him. She would lose him.

He reached over and took one of her hands in his. He pressed the centre of her palm with his thumb. 'I want to be a father. I'm going to be forty soon and if I leave it much longer it'll be too late for me. Too late to be an active father involved in my kid's life anyway.'

She pulled her hand out of his hot, firm grasp. She clasped her hands, cold as ice, in her lap, her mind racing. She must find a way to change his mind back again. 'Andy, you're having some sort of mid-life crisis. This isn't what you really want, believe me. Do you want to be responsible for adding to the population problem?'

'One child isn't going to make any difference.'

'But it would. If everyone said that then—'

'This is what I want, Sian,' he said cutting her off, though his voice was gentle. 'Please stop trying to tell me what's in my own heart.'

'Okay,' she said slowly, backing down in the face of his insistence. She raked through the scrambled thoughts in her brain for inspiration, for a way out. 'Maybe we could foster? No, adopt. A child from the third world. Yes,' she said as she warmed to the idea. 'We could give a home to a child that no one wants, that otherwise might even die.'

He shook his head. 'It's a noble idea, Sian. And I admire people who can love someone else's child. But I'm not sure I can. I want a child of my own. My flesh, my blood.'

She lowered her eyes, feeling cornered. Her options were running out. 'What's brought this on all of a sudden?' she said, buying herself time to think.

He leant back in the chair and let out a sigh. 'It hasn't been sudden. It started in July that day in the garden at Joanne's, when I was kicking a ball about with Oli. Something . . . something happened that day. I realised that I was going to die and I would leave no legacy behind. And I looked at Oli and thought, "I want a son – or a daughter – to live on after I'm gone".'

'That's not a reason to have a child.'

'But it is, Sian. It's the only reason. And I want to have that child with you, Sian.'

'But I couldn't have a baby,' she gasped, horrified. 'What about the shop? I couldn't give it up. And we couldn't afford childcare. How would we manage both our jobs?'

He shrugged off her objections. 'We just would. Other people do. Oh, Sian, can you imagine what it would be like to have our baby, our child, growing inside you?'

She shook her head – she had never envisaged such a scenario, not since early childhood anyway, and she could not do so now. She couldn't imagine anything more horrific. She blinked and fought back the tears, realising that his mind was made up. 'Oh, Andy, I love you with all my heart and I so want to make you happy. But I cannot give you a child.'

'Of course you can.'

Two cold tears slid down her cheeks. She wiped them away with the back of her hand. 'No, I can't . . . you see . . . you see I've made up my mind never to have children.'

'I know that and I understand why,' he said. 'And I respect your beliefs. But they don't have to be set in stone, Sian. They can change and it's good that they do. Because we don't have all the right answers, none of us do. We just muddle through as best we can.'

She shook her head, everything on the table blurred with tears. He did not, could not, understand. 'I can't change what I think, what I feel,' she said.

He came over and went down on one knee, as if proposing to her. He took one of her hands and held it sandwiched between his own, an excited grin on his face. 'Look, we can research the most ecological way to raise the baby. We can use washable nappies, feed it only home-made food, buy recycled equipment, use ecological products, whatever!' Then, noticing that she was not responding, he added, softly, 'I know this has come as a bit of a shock to you, Sian, but, honestly, it'll be fantastic. You just wait and see.'

She cringed and shook her head vehemently. She wouldn't give him hope when there was none. 'No.'

He dropped her hand in her lap. 'What do you mean, "no"?'

'I can't,' she whispered.

He got to his feet and stood over her, silent, for some moments. She could not bring herself to look up. 'You mean you don't want to, Sian,' he said sadly.

'If you loved me you wouldn't ask this of me.'

'If you loved me you would give me what I ask. I've never asked anything of you, Sian. Just this one thing.'

She wiped her eyes once more, looked up and his face came into focus. She saw that he was angry, his arms folded across his chest.

'I'm sorry, Andy. But it's the one thing that I can never give you.'

It had taken Louise three days to reply to the message from Cameron. And when she did, after many false starts, she settled on the shortest, most brusque message. *Yes, I'm happy and settled in Ballyfergus,* she wrote. *What do you want? Louise.*

His reply when it came was just as brief. *I always knew that things would work out for you. Can we talk? Please?*

She sat at the computer, listening to the rain outside pound the window like pellets from a farmer's gun, while her heart did somersaults and her stomach turned itself inside out. What could he possibly want from her? Forgiveness? She smiled crookedly. She wasn't sure she was ready to give him that. She wasn't sure she ever could.

. . . not a day goes by that I don't regret our divorce. I should never have let you go. The smile fell from her lips and she shivered though the radiators creaked with heat. Did he want her back? That was impossible, unless . . . unless he was prepared to take on Oli also. She imagined the two of them meeting for the first time, how Oli would win Cameron's heart with his smile and his cute ways. How could anyone not adore him?

218

But if she did let Cameron into her life once more, would he hurt her again? Quickly she switched the computer off, her heart pounding. His words rang in her ears. *I was a fool. Please forgive me. I love you still.* She jumped up from the table, took a step backwards, and wiped her sweating hands on the front of her sweater. She would ignore any further communications from him – she simply wouldn't read them. Her life here was happy and settled and full of promise – her face flushed with guilt when she thought of Kevin. And Cameron had ruined her life once before – she must not let him do it again.

Louise stood on Joanne's doorstep at lunchtime the next day, smartly dressed in a green jersey wrap dress and black patent boots. Oli was at her side, laden down with a large gift bag for Abbey that he'd insisted on carrying himself.

Joanne opened the door and Heidi shot outside and ran around the garden like a lunatic, frothing at the mouth in delight. She loped over to Louise and nuzzled her hand with her wet snout. Then she set off on a manic race across the neighbours' gardens and Oli giggled.

'Heidi! Will you come here?' shouted Joanne and under her breath muttered 'Bloody dog,' though there was no malice in it. She looked okay, if a bit tired in one of her trademark full skirts, heels and a turquoise roll-neck sweater. Eventually the dog came back and Oli ran over, knelt on the damp grass and threw his arms around her neck.

'Bad dog,' scolded Joanne and Oli looked up, hurt. 'She's not bad, Auntie Ow-an. She's just happy. Aren't you, Heidi?' He buried his face in the dog's black neck and Louise laughed. Joanne scowled and dog and child ran inside, leaving the gift bag abandoned on the ground.

Louise picked it up and handed Joanne a bunch of super-market flowers which she accepted mechanically, without looking at them. 'Are you okay?' said Louise.

'Yes, of course,' said Joanne brightly. 'Come on in. Lunch is nearly ready. Mum and Dad are here. And Sian too.'

After Louise had given Abbey her gifts, everyone squeezed round the kitchen table – five adults and four kids.

'Well this is cosy,' said their father and Joanne, rather unfairly Louise thought, shot him a withering look.

'Doesn't the table look nice?' said their mother, touching the streamers and the decorations with hesitant, groping fingers as if she could not see them. She picked up a party blower, held it between her dry, thin lips and blew. The paper crinkled into a long yellow tongue accompanied by a high-pitched hoot, like the sound of a bird calling to its mate. She giggled girlishly and Holly, Abbey and Oli followed suit, blowing the things into each other's faces, filling the room with hideous, ear-piercing shrieks.

'Now look what you've started,' said Sian, who had been very quiet up until this point. She looked particularly be-draggled, though that could be partly explained by the fact that she had cycled through the rain to be here, eschewing the offer of a lift from Louise.

'Girls! Girls! That's enough now,' said their grandfather laughing and the noise subsided.

Louise confiscated the red blower from Oli. 'You'll get it back after lunch. I promise,' she added as he folded his short arms across his chest and his lips turned down petulantly. She patted him on the knee. 'There's a good boy.'

'Isn't Phil here?' said Billy.

Joanne set a tray containing a side of roast beef at the head of the table, where Phil should have been. 'Playing golf.'

Maddy glanced at her mother, then looked down. 'Where was he last night and this morning?' she asked quietly.

Louise looked at Joanne's pinched expression, but her big

sister answered briskly. 'He was out late last night. And you were up so late this morning you missed him.'

'Mmm, that beef smells good,' said Christine.

'Did he have to play golf today? Of all days?' said Billy and he looked at Abbey, his meaning clear. Abbey, currently engaged in tickling Oli under the arm to produce shrieks of laughter, was oblivious to the conversation.

'Leave it, Dad,' said Joanne darkly, and then she added sweetly, 'Louise, can you serve the spuds and veg, please? Sian, can you pour the gravy into that jug over there? Thanks. Oh, and there's horseradish in the fridge.'

'Sure,' the sisters said in unison and got up from the table and made themselves busy. Louise moved round the table, dishing up roasties. Was there an atmosphere – or was she imagining it?

Joanne held the carving knife and fork aloft like she was about to stab someone. 'Right. Who's for beef before this gets cold?'

Once everyone was served and a quiet hum had settled round the table, Louise asked, 'Could Andy not make it then?'

'No, he had to help Kevin with his boat,' said Sian quietly. 'Something about preparing it for winter storage.'

'You should have brought this Kevin, Louise,' joked Billy, nudging his wife. 'Shouldn't she, Chrissie?'

'Well, there's plenty of food for one more, that's for sure,' said Christine. 'This is delicious.'

There were murmurs of assent and Joanne said, 'He was invited.' She looked at Louise to offer up an explanation for his absence.

Louise had not yet introduced Kevin to the family and today hadn't felt like the right occasion, not when her head was full of Cameron and her feelings so muddled. She blushed guiltily. 'Another time maybe.'

'I'm done!' announced Abbey, pairing her cutlery noisily on her plate. She jumped down from the table. 'Can I go?'

'Can I?' said Holly though there was still some beef and green beans on her plate.

Joanne looked over and sighed. 'Yeah, sure,' she said wearily. 'Off you go. I'll call you when dessert's ready.'

Oli wriggled out of his chair, his plate largely untouched. 'Yes, you can go too,' said Louise, deciding that now wasn't the time to wage a war over uneaten food. He padded out of the room in pursuit of his cousins.

Maddy pushed her chair out and stood up, her mobile phone glued to her hand. 'Mum, that was awesome. Do you mind if I pop over to Roz's for a minute?'

Joanne sighed. 'Oh, Maddy, can you at least wait until we've done the cake? And your grandparents are here.'

Billy said, 'Oh, don't mind us. You go and see your friend.'

Maddy smiled at her grandfather and pulled a face at her mother. 'Please, Mum? She's just texted me to say she's something *really* important to tell me.'

Joanne looked at the mobile in Maddy's hand. 'Can't she just text or phone?'

'Some things are too important. Some things you have to say face to face.'

Joanne gave Louise a wry smile no doubt wondering, as Louise was, what on earth fourteen-year-olds could have to discuss that was so important. 'Oh, okay. Give us ten minutes to digest our food, will you? I'll call you in when it's time for the cake. And you can go after that.'

'Thanks, Mum,' said Maddy and she slipped out of the room, already bashing away on the buttons on her mobile.

Sian pushed the vegetarian rissole that Joanne had supplied instead of the beef, around her plate. 'Aren't you going to eat that?' asked Christine.

Sian let her fork fall onto the plate with a clatter. 'No. I'm sorry, Joanne. I'm not hungry all of a sudden.'

Joanne, her chin resting on her hand, said indifferently, 'Oh, that's all right. I didn't make it specially. It was M&S. I'll put it in foil for you to take home if you like.'

'That'd be great,' said Sian without enthusiasm and the conversation petered out.

Louise looked from one glum-faced sister to the other and wondered what was wrong with everyone. She had an excuse for being miserable. She had Cameron on her mind.

'So,' said her mother, pleasantly, 'how *are* you and Kevin getting on, Louise?'

'Fine.'

'When are we going to meet him? You've been seeing him for quite a while now, haven't you?'

Louise shrugged. 'It's only been five weeks.'

Her mother nodded her head knowingly. 'Long enough.'

Everyone sat in silence looking at Louise, waiting for some sort of response. But what did she know? Only a few weeks ago she would've welcomed the contact from Cameron – part of her had never given up hope of a reconciliation. But that was before she'd met Kevin. When she thought of him her cheeks flushed with shame. She'd done nothing wrong, yet even thinking about her ex-husband felt like a betrayal. She felt words bubble up inside her throat. And when they came out, she was as surprised by them as everyone else. 'Cameron's been in touch. He sent me two messages through Friends Reunited. He says he wants to talk to me.'

'Really!' exclaimed Joanne, her green eyes suddenly alive with interest. She folded her legs and added, 'What did you tell him?'

'I haven't replied yet.'

Sian leant forward in her seat, her arms and legs crossed, like she was all tied up in a knot. 'What does he want to talk to you about?'

'I don't know. He said he regretted the divorce and what had led to it.' She swallowed, steeling herself to deliver the next sentence without breaking down. 'He said that he loved me. That he was a fool for letting me go.'

Her mother gasped and put her hand to her throat and said, 'How romantic.'

Joanne rolled her eyes at Sian. 'Well, I'd say it's pretty obvious what he wants,' she said. 'He wants to get back with you.'

'That isn't going to happen,' said Louise, without much conviction. She reminded herself that she had a new life now – and the promise of something lasting with Kevin.

'Well, I think you should talk to him,' said her mother, 'and see what he has to say. After all it wasn't him who wanted the divorce, it was you. I still think that if you hadn't been so rash, he might have come round to your way of thinking. And then you would've had your child and a husband.'

'Mum!' cried Louise, crossly. 'You have no idea what you're talking about. I wasn't rash. I waited all those years to find out that he didn't want children. Wasn't that long enough?'

Sian looked glumly at the floor and Billy interceded with, 'Well, he always struck me as a decent bloke, in many ways. I can't see the harm in talking to him, Louise.'

Sian pushed her plate away, the food hardly touched, as though it repelled her, and said coldly, 'Does Kevin know that Cameron's contacted you?'

Louise shook her head. 'We've only exchanged a few e-mails, that's all.' But she could not look Sian in the eye.

Her mother said, 'Well, all I can say is that in our day people stuck together and worked at their marriage. They didn't high-tail it at the first sign of trouble.'

Louise opened her mouth to defend herself but just then Maddy popped her head around the kitchen door. Everyone shifted in their seats as though they'd been caught doing something they shouldn't. 'Is that cake ready yet?'

'Just coming,' said Joanne rising eagerly from her seat with a plate in her hand.

Louise took a deep breath and tried to smile but righteous anger burned in her chest.

The cake was big, square and chocolate, and slathered with too much chocolate butter icing. Encrusted with eight pink candles and all manner of brightly coloured confectionery, it looked like the contents of a sweet shop had been tipped over it.

'That's rather a lot of sweets,' observed Louise wryly, standing beside Joanne at the table looking down at the eyesore.

'That's what happens when you let an eight- and a ten-year-old decorate a cake,' said Joanne, with no trace of humour in her voice.

Abbey sat at the table like a little princess, the cake in front of her. Her face glowed with happiness in the candlelight while they sang 'Happy Birthday' and Sian took photographs. Her mother stood behind Abbey, flanked by her father with his hand on his granddaughter's left shoulder. It struck Louise then how very odd it was for Phil to pass over his youngest daughter's birthday celebration for a game of golf. She knew he wasn't the most attentive father in the world, but still . . . She looked at Joanne's stony face, her glazed eyes staring into

225

the flames of the candles, her lips moving but no sound coming out. And Louise suddenly had the horrible feeling that something was desperately wrong . . .

The song ended, everyone cheered and Abbey blew the candles out. Joanne served the cake while Louise made coffee and Sian handed out napkins and small forks.

By the time Louise sat down at the table, her son had wolfed down his portion.

'Can I have more cake, Auntie Ow-an?' asked a chocolate-smeared Oli, holding out his plate towards his aunt like his little namesake, Oliver Twist.

Everyone roared with laughter and Joanne touched the top of his head and said, indulgently, 'Of course you can, my darling.'

'Hmm,' said Louise, clearing her throat. 'You didn't eat your lunch, Oli. You can't fill up on cake, you know.'

The radiant smile fell from Oli's face and he looked imploringly at his aunt.

Joanne dropped her fork on the plate with a clatter. 'Oh, for goodness' sake, Louise,' she snapped. 'It's a birthday party. A bit of sugar isn't going to do him any harm. You're far too strict about what he eats. It's because you've only him to worry about. In a normal family you wouldn't have the time to fuss so.'

Joanne's thoughtless words cut through Louise like a knife. How dare her sister say her little family wasn't normal? And in front of Oli! Anger welled up inside her and she fought desperately to hold back the tears.

'Auntie Lou, let him,' cried Maddy. 'He's so cute.'

Louise nodded, determined to reassure Oli who was staring at her, his bottom lip trembling. 'Yes, why not? Of course you can have another piece,' she said, hiding her rage. Joanne lopped a huge chunk off the cake and plonked it on

Oli's plate with a pointed stare at Louise. His face lit up like the sun and, in spite of her anger towards Joanne and the hurt in her heart, Louise forced a grimace of a smile.

Joanne sat in her lounge with everyone after lunch regretting her blunt words to Louise. They had just slipped out. She blamed it on stress and lack of sleep – she'd lain awake all night waiting for Phil to come home but he never did. She would apologise to Louise later but right now she had more important things to worry about.

The birthday cake sat in her stomach like a rock and the effort required to keep up appearances was exhausting – the smile on her face felt like it would crack and turn to dust any second. She put her hand over her mouth and yawned.

When Phil came back she was going to give him a piece of her mind. How could he have missed Abbey's birthday celebration? How could he be so cruel as to use an argument between them to punish a child? It was unforgivable. And he'd left it to her to explain his absence to Abbey, Joanne thought angrily, remembering the child's face flushed with disappointment, her bottom lip quivering as her blue eyes filled with tears. In the end she'd placated Abbey with the assurance that Daddy would do something *really* special with her, but her heart was filled with dread that he would never make good on the promise.

And now, as the conversation carried on around her, while she smiled and nodded and pretended to listen, creeping doubts began to worm their way into her consciousness. She had fully expected Phil to be home by now, his tail between his legs or, at the very least, ready to settle for a resentful truce between them. She drummed her nails on the arm of the sofa. Phil had been gone nearly twenty-four hours. Where was he? And where had he spent the night? Probably at Mark's, necking beer and watching football on TV, pretending that he didn't have a wife and three kids at home. He'd made his point.

Billy stretched his arms and stood up. 'I think we'd better make a move, Chrissie. You look tired.'

Joanne jumped to her feet, desperately hoping that Louise and Sian, sitting together on the sofa, would pick up on the cue and leave too. 'Thanks for coming,' she said. 'You made the day really special for Abbey.' She got her parents' coats and helped her mother on with hers. And then suddenly the front door burst open with an almighty crash. Everyone froze and Joanne's heart pounded. She put both her hands over her mouth to stop herself crying out.

It could only be Phil. Was he drunk? In a rage?

But it wasn't Phil. Maddy came running breathlessly into the room and Joanne's heart stopped racing. She removed her hands from her mouth and breathed easy. And then she noticed that her daughter was crying, her face streaked with tears.

'Maddy, what is it?'

Maddy, hysterical, gasped for breath, and clutched her mother by the sleeve. Her face was red and she was sweating furiously. Suddenly, her legs gave way and she crumpled to the ground, almost pulling her mother with her.

Joanne stumbled and her father said, 'Quick! Over here.' He put his arms round Maddy and hauled her over to the sofa. She sank down gratefully and sat there sobbing, her legs splayed out inelegantly.

Joanne sat down beside her daughter, placed her hand on her back and looked at the astonished faces around her. Everyone was on their feet except Christine who had sunk, ashen-faced, into the nearest chair.

'I'll get a glass of water,' said Louise and rushed out of the room.

Had Maddy and Roz fallen out? Had they had a fight? Maddy was prone to melodrama and over-reaction but Joanne had never seen her like this. Somehow neither scenario rang true. Had she been attacked? She scanned her daughter's clothing for evidence of an assault but there was none. Instinctively, somehow, she knew this was not the cause of her distress.

Sian passed Maddy a hankie and she pressed it to her eyes and wept.

'Take a deep breath, pet,' said her grandfather and his voice seemed to have a calming effect on the girl. She nodded, took several deep breaths and her sobbing eased. Heidi appeared, rested her head on Maddy's lap and the girl touched the top of the dog's head.

Joanne waited a few moments until Maddy's breathing had steadied and the weeping had stopped save for the occasional wretched gasp. Everyone was still and silent, the air filled with the sound of the children at play in the other room and Maddy's grief. Joanne massaged her daughter's slim hand – each nail painted a different colour – in her own. 'Maddy,' she voiced at last, 'what happened?'

Maddy gulped and nodded and took some seconds to answer and Joanne found that she was, inexplicably, dreading her reply.

'I saw Dad,' said Maddy and convulsed into tears again.

Joanne looked at the others, their faces furrowed with concern, and shook her head, perplexed as to why the sight of her father should upset her so. Then a terrible thought occurred to her and she snapped her head round to look at her daughter once more. Had Phil done something stupid? 'Maddy,' she said, her voice stern, more demanding than she had intended, 'is he all right? Is Dad okay?'

Maddy who was crying too hard to answer, simply nodded, and the tightness round Joanne's heart eased. She bowed her head for a moment, allowed that particular wave of worry to wash over her and said a silent prayer of thanks. She lifted her head, poised, ready to face the next breaker. 'Then what is it, Maddy? Why are you crying?'

'Because I saw him at Roz's.'

'So?' said Joanne, even as she said it, wondering why he was holed up there. Why had he gone to Gemma and not one of his own pals? Of course he'd known Gemma for years and years but, still, she was Joanne's friend, not his.

'Oh, Mum. You don't understand,' said Maddy, the tears suddenly drying up. She looked her mother straight in the eye, her sockets rimmed with black mascara, her expression full of pity. 'I don't know how to tell you this.'

Joanne sat very still and waited, her whole body tense with fear.

'He's with Gemma.'

Joanne nodded slowly, watching every muscle on Maddy's face, trying to read meaning into the unintelligible words coming out of her mouth.

'I mean he's *with* her. Like boyfriend and girlfriend. Roz says he stayed the night. It's disgusting.' And with that she began to sob once more.

Joanne's arm, suddenly a dead weight, fell to her side. She stood up slowly, the sound of her daughter's weeping subsiding like the tide. Heidi, sensing immediately that something was wrong, got up and stood mutely by Joanne's feet, looking up at her with knowing eyes.

She wished that she could make herself not believe it but of course, she knew it to be true. How could she not? The evidence was overwhelming. She had just chosen not to see it.

The contraceptive pills.

The fact that Phil always went out on a Tuesday night and often came home in the early hours – the same night Gemma's children stayed with their father.

The fact that almost every other weekend, he filled his Saturdays with golf followed by a late night out – the same weekends that Gemma was child-free.

And most telling of all, the constant urging from her best friend to leave her husband. The deliberate decision to fill the prescription for contraceptives at her pharmacy.

She had been so tolerant, so stupid. She had not wanted to know.

She heard voices around her, hushed whispers of concern. Someone called her name.

And then – blackness.

Chapter Twelve

'She says she doesn't want to go out,' said Sian's voice down the phone and Louise tutted. 'She says she's changed her mind.'

'Well, make her unchange it,' said Louise, standing in her small kitchen, watching the clock on the wall. Kevin was due to call any minute for her and Oli. They'd planned a trip to Glenarm forest. 'Sian, it's not good for her to sit about the house moping. I think it'd do her good to get out and let her hair down a bit.'

'Okay, I'll give it another go.'

'And tell her from me, that if she doesn't say yes,' said Louise, surprising herself with her bossiness, 'she'll have me to answer to.'

Funny how their roles had changed. Joanne had always been the domineering one in the family, but recent events had changed her. Her drive had evaporated overnight – she seemed a shadow of her former self and everyone was worried sick about her.

When Kevin arrived she waved him inside. 'Come in. Come in. Sorry we're not ready yet. I was on the phone to Sian about Joanne. Oli!' she called, 'Kevin's here.'

Oli came padding out of his room, went straight over to Kevin and held up a large orange and blue toy. 'This is Eagle. He's one of the goodies.'

'Is he?'

Oli took Kevin by the hand. 'Yes. I have all the Planet Protectors. Come and see.'

'Oh, Oli,' said Louise glancing at her watch, 'I don't think you've time to play. We're going to the forest, remember?'

Oli's head dropped onto his chest and Kevin, coming down to Oli's level, said, 'Why don't we take Eagle with us? I bet he'd love to see the forest.'

Oli's face lit up immediately. He let go of Kevin's hand and ran around the room squealing, holding the toy above his head. Louise caught him and wrestled him into his coat.

'So how's Joanne?' said Kevin.

Louise sighed unhappily.

'That bad, eh?' he said and raised his eyebrows knowingly.

'I'm trying to persuade Joanne to come on a night out with me and Sian. She keeps putting us off but I'm not having any of it.'

Kevin gave his head a little shake and said, 'Well, maybe she just needs time on her own to work things through.'

Louise considered this briefly, then said, 'I hear what you're saying but I'm worried she's going to get depressed. She hasn't been out since Phil left, except to work and the supermarket, and they don't count.' She sighed loudly then shook her head. 'Come on, Oli, time to go.' She held out her hand to him.

But he reached up, smiling, for Kevin's hand instead and Louise found the little act of trust brought tears to her eyes. And she thought immediately of Cameron and wondered if Oli met him, would he love him the way he seemed to love Kevin?

In the car Oli chatted away in the back seat. And unlike many other adults, Kevin, driving, did not ignore him but included him in their conversation. Louise tried to push her worries – Joanne and Cameron – to the back of her mind. They took the coast road from Ballyfergus to Glenarm hugging the shoreline, snaking round dramatic headlands and through the picturesque little settlements of Drains Bay and Ballygally. The sun defying the autumnal chill, bounced brightly off the rippling blue sea and filled the car with warmth. They passed the now boarded-up Drumnagreagh Hotel, high up on the hillside, where Joanne's wedding reception had been held years ago.

At last they drove up Glenarm's main street and through the impressive arched entrance to the forest. They parked the car, got out and followed the marked path westwards, into the dappled glow of the afternoon sun. The path was damp and soft underfoot, cushioned with red and brown and black leaves. A little stream gurgled briskly in the undergrowth. They found a hazelnut tree bearing hard, green nuts and a blackberry bush bereft of fruit. And while she listened to the crack of debris underfoot and inhaled the damp, pungent smell of the forest, Louise faced up to the uncomfortable sensation in her bones. She had to tell Kevin about Cameron. Not to, felt like a lie.

'I have something to tell you, Kevin,' she said at last watching Oli, a few yards ahead of them, poking the bracken with a stick. Immediately, she regretted the formal tone of her introduction.

She glanced over at Kevin. A little frown line appeared between his brows. 'What?'

'Oh, it's nothing really,' she said, colour rising to her cheeks. 'I made it sound like I was about to offload some big confession, didn't I? It's no big deal.'

He slowed, shoved his hands in the pockets of his jacket and looked at her with those piercing green eyes. 'That's all right. Go on.'

So she took a deep breath and told him about the messages from Cameron and what they had said. 'I didn't reply to the last one,' she added hastily, feeling like she was making a confession after all.

He nodded his head slowly and a small, unhappy smile came to his lips. He came to a complete halt and turned to face her. He swallowed, blinked and said, quietly, 'Well, I think you should, Louise.'

'You do?'

A muscle twitched in the corner of his mouth but still his smile held firm though there was no warmth in it. What did she expect? She'd just told him she was in contact with her ex-husband. How would she feel if roles were reversed?

'Because if the messages mean nothing to you,' he said, an uncharacteristic bitterness creeping into his otherwise mellow voice, 'then why are you telling me about them?' An awkward pause. 'It sounds to me as though you two might have some . . . some unfinished business to sort out. Would you say that's fair?'

'I . . . I think I'm confused. Hearing from Cameron after all this time, well, I just hadn't expected it. I wasn't prepared for it.' She stared into his sad eyes and felt like a complete cow. She had not meant to hurt Kevin. She had only meant to be honest with him. He bit his bottom lip, let out a long sigh and looked away.

'I thought that you and I might . . . well, I thought that we had a future, Louise . . .' His voice trailed off and he wiped his face with his hand.

'I thought so too,' said Louise, though her response lacked conviction. How could she commit herself wholly to Kevin when she was haunted by thoughts of another man? She told herself to get real. Her dreams of a happy life with Cameron and Oli were nothing more than fantasies. But she couldn't let go of them. They had sustained her for so long – in the lonely months and years before she'd met Kevin.

She reached out and touched his arm. 'I do care for you, Kevin. But I care for Cameron too. I guess I always will.'

'It's perfectly natural that after spending fifteen years together, you still think about your ex. And I dare say he has feelings for you too. But I care deeply for you, Louise. Don't ever forget that.' He started walking away from her towards Oli. 'Come on,' he said, rather brusquely, and turned up the collar of his coat. 'It's getting late. Time to go home.'

Louise followed him, her hands thrust deep into the pockets of her coat, confused and miserable.

'I'm tired,' said Oli when they'd caught up with him.

Louise looked down the long path ahead. 'Oh, Oli,' she sighed. 'We've ages to go yet.'

'It's all right. I can carry him,' said Kevin.

Oli, latching on quickly, raised his arms and cried, 'Up! Up!'

Without waiting for her approval, Kevin smiled at Oli, and scooped him onto his shoulders, like he weighed no more than a feather. And when he spoke to him, the hardness in his voice was replaced by tender warmth. 'Now, you've got to hold on to my hands. Like that. Yes, that's it. Good lad.'

They trudged back to the car park in awkward silence, save for Oli's chatter and the squelch of their boots on the mulch underfoot. In an instant everything had changed between them, the former ease replaced with awkward reserve. And she had caused it with her foolish declaration about something Kevin didn't even need to know about. All she'd done was exchange a few e-mails with Cameron. So why did it feel so much like a betrayal of Kevin?

When they reached the car, Kevin said, 'I have something

to tell you too.' He set Oli down on the ground and ruffled his hair. 'My work at Loughanlea is coming to an end, I'm afraid. I'm moving on to a big project in East Belfast. It's a big shopping, leisure and affordable housing complex between Tullycarnet and Ballybeen.'

'Oh,' was all she could say, her heart sinking. Had he planned to tell her this today? Or was it in retaliation for her disclosure about Cameron? 'Does that mean I won't see you at lunchtime any more?'

He shrugged, feigning nonchalance, but Louise could tell by his quick, almost brutal, movements that he was far from relaxed. 'Maybe the odd time,' he said, busying himself with unlocking the car and unbuttoning his jacket. 'I'll be around now and again but not as much and, in time, I'll move on full-time to the Tullycarnet project.'

She swallowed, utterly dismayed. She had come to rely on their frequent lunchtime trysts – they were the highlight of her day.

'But we will still see each other, won't we? At other times?'

He bit his bottom lip and was quiet for a few long moments and then he said quietly, looking at her over the top of the car, 'I want to, Louise.' She could hardly bear the way he regarded her with such disappointment in his eyes. 'But I . . . my wife, you know, she left me for someone,' he went on, his voice shaky with emotion. 'I don't ever want to go through that again. I don't think I could bear it.' He cleared his throat, opened the car door and added, evenly, 'I think you've a lot of hard thinking to do, Louise. And when you've done it, maybe we can talk. Meantime, maybe it's best if we cool it a little.'

At work the next day, Louise spent all morning thinking of Kevin and wondering what was wrong with her. Kevin was a wonderful guy, everyone loved him, even Oli. He was everything she could ever wish for in a man. But Cameron had said he loved her – *loved her still*. How could she turn her back on the promise inherent in those three words and all the happy memories of the life they had once shared? Didn't she owe it to him to give him a chance? Perhaps, as her mother had suggested, she had been too hasty in turning her back on her marriage.

A scheduled afternoon meeting was a welcome distraction, forcing Louise to set aside thoughts of Kevin and Cameron, and focus on something else. Amanda and Steve were there along with Finn, the recently recruited, unlikely-looking senior manager of the biking centre. In his late thirties, he had the figure of a whippet and a two-day-old beard. He wore a black T-shirt with the word *Evolution* written across it in white. Above the lettering, also in white, were the familiar sequential images showing, in outline, the evolution from ape to *Homo sapiens*. Except in the last image the human wasn't just standing erect, but mounted astride a mountain bike. Finn was passionate about mountain biking – and very well connected in the biking world.

'So Steve,' said Louise, 'you're going to look into taking a stand at next year's cycle show. Where is it again?'

'Earls Court, London. They claim to get twenty-five thousand biking enthusiasts through the door but I'll need to find out how many of them are mountain bikers.'

'Good thinking. And what about the World Cup rounds being held in the UK next year, Finn?' She consulted a bit of paper. 'In Dalby Forest, North Yorkshire and Fort William, Scotland. Anything we can do there?'

'They don't usually do an expo area as such,' said Finn.

'Do you want me to look at spectator numbers,' offered Amanda, 'and see if it's worthwhile us doing anything? Maybe even a leaflet?'

'Great idea.' Louise put down the piece of paper and said, 'Steve, how are things going on the viral marketing front?'

'I should have proposals from our shortlist of three companies to show you by the end of next week.'

'Good. That's a really important plank of our strategy. Finn, could you run your eye over those reports when they come in? Check to see if they've identified all the websites and forums you'd normally surf.'

'Sure thing.'

'Now, finally,' she said, pausing for effect, 'the Board want us to pitch for, and win, the right to host the downhill rounds of the biking World Cup in six years' time.'

Finn sucked air in through his teeth and whistled. 'Sweet.'

Louise smiled at him and said, 'It is. It sounds like a long way away but we've a lot of groundwork to do before then. Agnes is taking care of all the big stuff – household name sponsorship, partnership and public funding. It's our job to put this centre on the biking map. How are the plans for the launch going, Amanda? Maybe you could give us an update?'

Amanda stood up and delivered a brief outline of the plans for the official launch while Louise chewed the end of her pen. This was such an ambitious project – she was beginning to have doubts about whether they could actually pull it off.

'The date's going to be the sixth of January – new year, new start for Loughanlea,' said Amanda with a smile. 'We've got all the local great and the good signed up and the office of the Minister for Culture, Arts and Leisure's just confirmed his attendance. We shouldn't have any problem getting press coverage nearer the time – papers love this sort of thing. We're going to open the centre for free that day and Finn's arranged for some top riders to come and do demonstrations for us.'

Louise turned her attention to Finn, who had slumped in his chair with his legs splayed. On his feet were black 'Vans' trainers – everything about him was hip. 'Tell us about that, Finn. Have you had any luck with attracting some of the big names?'

'Yeah,' said Finn and he grinned from ear to ear. 'I got Ben McKinley and Jason Flood.' He opened his hands wide as if presenting a wondrous gift to them all.

'I'm sorry,' said Louise, 'I've no idea who these people are, Finn.'

He rolled his eyes. 'Just the Irish and British number ones, Louise. Just the top two dudes in the business.'

Louise smiled.

Her personal life might be falling apart but at least her professional one wasn't.

Sian found Andy downstairs at the kitchen table peering at the screen on the laptop. On the table was a pen and notepad with some numbers scribbled on it.

She put a hand on his shoulder and he tensed – or was she imagining it? 'What're you doing?'

'The British Open Surf Kayak Championship's being held in Portrush this week. I'm just trying to see if I can get a B&B for a couple of nights at the weekend,' he said, without taking his eyes off the screen. 'Might have left it a bit late though . . .' He scrolled down the page, picked up the pen and jotted down a number.

Sian's spirits lifted. It would do them both good to get away for a couple of days. Things had been strained between them since their conversation over dinner the week before. They hadn't had the opportunity to speak about it since or maybe the truth was, they hadn't wanted to talk about it. She certainly didn't – what was the point when you'd reached a complete impasse? But it was there, the proverbial elephant in the room, every way she turned.

'Have you ever seen surf kayaking?' said Andy. 'It's awesome.'

'Only on TV and YouTube clips. But I'm looking forward to seeing it for real.'

'Oh,' he said, and leant back in the chair so that her hand slid off his shoulder. He folded his arms across his chest and looked down at his lap. 'Did you want to come?' He sounded genuinely surprised. 'It's just that . . . well, I didn't think you would. I was thinking of going with a couple of guys from the centre. You know, for a bit of a lads' weekend.'

Sian's stomach turned over and she gripped the back of his chair. She put on a brave face, tried not to look devastated. 'But you never go away on your own. Not without me, I mean.' She hated the neediness in her voice, but it was true. They'd always done things together – from the very first day they'd met. Until recently. She'd thought the surfing trip to Donegal in September had been a one-off – apparently not.

He cleared his throat and did not look her in the eye. The words fell from his mouth like lead weights. 'I just thought it'd do us both good to spend some time apart. Give us a chance to think things over.'

'I see.' She let go of the chair and stepped back a little. Her knees were shaking, her chest tight with hurt. He did not want to be with her. He wanted to escape, literally. Was this how it started, the falling apart of a relationship? The slow unravelling of ties and bonds that bound one person to another. Was this how it had been for Joanne and Louise? She suddenly realised with awful clarity that he would leave her if she could not give him the child that he wanted. Not right now, not tomorrow, next week or even next month. But he would – eventually.

'Oh, no, you go with your mates,' she said lightly, 'and I'll . . . um . . . I'll stay here.'

'Are you sure? The boys wouldn't mind if you tagged along.' *Tagged along?* Like a stray dog? It was the most mean-spirited invitation she'd ever heard.

She shook her head, recoiled a little, folding into herself like a penknife closing. 'I can't anyway. Don't know what I was thinking. I have to work in the shop on Saturday. And I was going to invite Mum and Dad over for lunch on Sunday.'

'Well, if you're sure,' he said, but his eyes were already back on the computer screen.

She let her face fall then, her jaw slack with sorrow, no need to keep up the pretence. She went and got her coat from the peg at the back door and put it on. He didn't even notice. 'I'll see you later.'

'Okay,' he said distractedly. 'Remind me, where are you going again?'

Sian wiggled her right foot into a shoe and laced it up quickly. 'Out with Joanne and Louise. It's Louise's idea to try and cheer Joanne up.'

He looked at her and pressed his lips together. 'Can't say I envy you. You'll have your work cut out.'

Sian put on the other shoe. 'Yes, poor Joanne. I don't suppose it'll be much fun but, Louise is right, we ought to try.'

She pulled on a silver cycle helmet, snapped the clip securely under her chin and fished the keys for the bike lock out of her pocket. She walked to the back door. 'Andy,' she said and waited until he looked at her. 'You couldn't just get up and go off for the weekend like this,' she said, gesturing at the computer, 'if we had a baby.'

242

'If we had a baby,' he said, slicing her open with his words, 'I wouldn't go.'

Joanne stood in front of the bathroom mirror in a worn dressing gown, staring at the woman looking back at her, her face heavily made up, cheeks rouged and lips painted the colour of ripe mangoes. But all the slap in the world couldn't hide the gaunt features, the glazed and sunken eyes, the sallow skin. It would take more than cosmetics to cover up her misery.

The doll-like painted face was outlined by a halo of golden hair – she'd managed to tame the frizz into flattering curls. The result was passable at a glance, presentable even. Suddenly Joanne let out a wretched sob and put her hands on the sink to steady herself. She threw her head back and stared at the yellow patch on the ceiling where the roof had once leaked. She blinked ferociously, determined to hold back the tears, resolving not to let them spill over and spoil her carefully applied make-up.

She had not been out socially in two weeks, not since Phil left – and her sisters had gone to so much trouble to organise this night out just for her. She would not let them down. Their plan was to cheer her up. There was no hope of that, of course – the pain was too raw, too deep. But she knew she must face the world again. She could not stay in this house forever, venturing out only to run errands and go to work. And she could not ask for better company than her sisters, loyal and true. Because family stood by you – always, regardless, forever.

Not like best friends. Not like Gemma, whom she'd trusted both with her children and the deepest secrets of her heart. She had loved Gemma as a sister – and this was how she was repaid? She gripped the edge of the sink until her knuckles turned white and thought of Phil and Gemma and what they were doing right now. Curled up together on the sofa watching TV perhaps, giggling like teenagers, laughing at her trusting nature, her naivety, her idiotic blindness to what was going on right in front of her eyes. A knot of anger formed in her empty stomach – she'd hardly eaten since the night Phil left.

It was true that her marriage had been teetering on the brink of disaster for years but she and Phil had always come through it together. Their marriage hadn't been perfect by any means – it had its flaws, its cracks – but what relationship didn't? Gemma's devious talent had been to exploit those weaknesses, to inveigle her way into their marriage and Phil's heart. There were no words to describe how betrayed Joanne felt by Gemma's callous behaviour. It was worse than her husband's. Betrayal was in keeping with Phil's character – hadn't he proven time and again just how good he was at lying? And for this reason, she could not say, in all honesty, that his infidelity had come as a complete shock.

Her marriage had been the one thing that had made her feel superior to Gemma. She wasn't proud of that. And now Gemma had taken that from her and their relationship as friends was utterly destroyed. There was no going back, no possibility of forgiveness, no way to make this right between them. Or between her and Phil. Joanne crammed the make-up brushes, compacts, tubes and pencils back in the sponge bag, her hands trembling so much she could barely do up the zip.

She'd spoken to Phil four times since he'd left. He'd come while she was at work and cleared out the rest of his clothes, taken away some of his documents and bits and pieces from the garage. When he'd collected everything he wanted he sent her a text saying that he was done, he wouldn't be back. To prove it, he left his key hanging on a hook by the front door.

And then he'd phoned her.

'I'll continue paying the mortgage and the other bills – meantime,' he'd said down the phone as if he was doing her a huge favour. She imagined Gemma hovering in the background, or listening in on another phone.

'What do you mean "meantime", Phil?' she'd spat out, hating the venom in her voice.

'I'm not coming back, Joanne.' His arrogance was breathtaking.

'I don't want you back,' she'd hissed and she meant it.

He'd sighed irritably. 'I mean until we get a settlement worked out – preferably an amicable one. I suggest you get yourself a solicitor,' he finished, parroting what Joanne imagined were Gemma's words. Phil had never been a forward planner. He lived on impulse.

'Mum?' called Abbey's voice from somewhere downstairs.

Joanne sighed. 'I'm up here.' Could she get no peace?

A few moments later Abbey appeared in the entrance to the small bathroom. She was still wearing her school uniform of grey flared trousers and a red sweatshirt. 'Can I go over to Shannon and Ella's house to watch a DVD?' Her smile was broad, her face alive with excitement.

Which made it all the harder for Joanne to stand her ground. She took a tissue out of a box and pressed it to her lips, blotting her lipstick. 'No.' She gave Abbey what she hoped was a stern 'I'm-in-control-here' sort of look.

Immediately Abbey stuck out her bottom lip. 'Why not?' she said, playing the wide-eyed innocent.

'You know why not.' Abbey had been grounded for a week for taking the neighbour's dog, Harry, to the park without

245

permission – and sparking a street-wide manhunt during which the dinner had burnt to a frazzle in the oven.

Abbey's eyes narrowed. 'But that's not fair. I only went to the park because Harry wanted to. And then he didn't want to come home. And I'm getting all the blame.'

Joanne's resolve hardened. Abbey would never have dared pull such a stunt before Phil left.

'You're grounded and that's it, Abbey. No discussion.' Joanne threw the tissue in the bin.

'But that's not fair.' Abbey balled her fists by her sides.

'It is perfectly fair,' said Joanne, trying very hard to keep the irritation out of her voice. Abbey had a knack of getting under her skin in a way her other two daughters did not. 'Now go and put on your pyjamas please before Gran and Grandad come.'

'I won't! I won't! It's not fair!' cried Abbey, her face pink with rage. 'I hate you.' She stomped out of the room, went into her bedroom and slammed the door.

Joanne sighed and decided to leave the girl for now. Things would only escalate into a nasty slanging match. If Abbey's behaviour had been bad before Phil left, it was worse now, and she was always the one on the receiving end of her youngest child's rage. According to Maddy, Abbey was impeccably behaved when she was with her father. Which in itself was heartbreaking – was Abbey hoping that, by being the perfect daughter, her daddy would come home again?

Maddy appeared where Abbey had stood only moments before. She wore skinny black jeans and one of those extra long T-shirts that were fashionable at the moment. On top of this ensemble she wore a long grey boyfriend cardigan with the sleeves bunched up to her elbows. An assortment of bangles jangled on her wrist. 'Don't worry about Abbey. She'll be okay in a bit.'

'I hope so.'

'You look nice, Mum.'

'Thanks, pet,' said Joanne, clutching at the compliment like a life raft on the open sea. She felt so adrift, so fragile, so afraid. But she could not show that to Maddy who looked to her for strength and reassurance – and answers Joanne no longer had at the ready.

'Why can't I babysit? I've done it before.'

'Not on your own. Roz was always . . .' Joanne's voice trailed off. She glanced at Maddy who was leaning against the wall stubbing her toe on the skirting board. 'Do you miss her?'

'Uh-huh.'

Joanne took a deep breath. 'I appreciate you being loyal to me, Maddy, but it's not Roz's fault that this has happened. You shouldn't lose your best friend because of it.'

'You have.'

Joanne felt the tears well up in her eyes again and fought them back. 'Yes, well, you don't have to.' She sprayed her hair with lacquer and walked into the bedroom, her daughter following in her wake.

Maddy threw herself on top of the bed, lay on her stomach and watched Joanne haul a full-skirted purple dress out of the cupboard. She pulled a face.

'Isn't that a bit dressy, Mum? You're just going out to the Indian.'

Joanne held the dress up to her neck. It had three-quarter-length sleeves and a belt and wouldn't have looked out of place on *Mad Men*. It was dressy, glamorous and over-the-top for the occasion. And it was perfect. It would show the rest of the world that she was down, but not out.

'Maddy, my love, you have a lot to learn about clothes.'

'What d'ya mean?'

Joanne smiled at herself, trying not to remember that she'd worn this dress on her last wedding anniversary when Phil took her for a rare meal out. Ideally she'd like to ditch her entire wardrobe – and anything else that reminded her of her husband for that matter – but she had to be realistic. If she'd thought finances were tight before, they were only going to get tighter. Recycle, reduce, reuse – the mantra Holly had brought home from school – were her watchwords now. She threw the dress on the bed beside Maddy.

'Right now you're too busy following every fad that comes along, to develop a style of your own. But that'll come with maturity. And when it does you'll realise that you dress to please yourself and not other people.'

She reached into the wardrobe, avoided looking at the space where Phil's clothes used to be, and extracted a pair of satin purple peep-toes and a cropped royal blue cardigan.

'Anyway about Roz,' said Maddy. 'I kind of do have to fall out with her. She said that if you weren't such a narky old cow, Dad wouldn't have left.'

Joanne let out a long sigh – and counted to ten. 'Oh, Maddy, I bet she's only repeating what she's heard Gemma, or your father, say.' Maddy shrugged and Joanne sat down heavily on the bed beside her daughter, pushing the purple dress to one side. 'Look, you and Roz *have* to make up. Otherwise seeing your father is going to become very difficult, if not impossible. Holly and Abbey were happy to go over to Roz's house last week, weren't they?' she went on, trying to forget that the visit had stuck in her throat like a fishbone and she'd cried the whole day they were gone.

'That's because they're too young to understand what's going on.'

Joanne sighed and brushed the hair off Maddy's forehead.

It wasn't fair that her eldest, navigating the rocky road between childhood and womanhood, should also have to deal with her parents' break-up. 'Poor Maddy.'

Maddy frowned. 'This thing between Dad and Gemma. It might blow over.'

'I doubt it,' said Joanne glumly. 'And anyway, even if they did split up, I could never take your dad back. Not after what he's done. You do understand, don't you? I still have some self-respect left.'

When the three of them arrived at the restaurant, they were shown to a table at the back. Joanne chose to sit with her back to the door, as inconspicuous as possible, in spite of the dress and her earlier bravado. Sian and Louise had views of the restaurant and the door. The floor was laid in plush red carpet with tiny yellow dots on it and the walls papered with a rich red flock paper that had been up so long it'd come back in fashion. The tables were close together, the lights were dimmed and tealights flickered on every table, creating a warm, cosy atmosphere. Louise took charge by straight away ordering a bottle of white and Joanne had necked two glasses before they even ordered food.

Once the second bottle of wine was opened and the food was on its way, Joanne raised her glass and said, 'Thanks for bringing me out tonight. I think I needed it.'

Sian patted her on the knee under the table and Louise said, 'You look gorgeous by the way. Love the dress.' She was wearing an elegant, monochrome outfit: a black waterfall cardigan, over a white T-shirt and black trousers. It reminded Joanne too much of Gemma's pared-down style and she looked away. Sian was, as usual, much more casually dressed in crumpled jeans and a shirt, and her pretty face, bereft of make-up as usual, looked drawn.

Sian filled them in on the local gossip from the shop

– studiously avoiding the subject of Phil – while Joanne wondered if people were talking about her now. And then suddenly, out of the blue, Louise said, 'I e-mailed Cameron my phone number today.'

The waiter came at that moment with a mixed platter of starters – savoury pastries and chilli prawns. Joanne looked at the food and her stomach heaved.

Once he'd gone, Sian picked up a vegetable samosa and bit the corner off. 'But why, Louise? Surely you don't intend getting back together with him?'

Louise sighed and ran a hand through her hair. 'I don't know what I intend. Or even what I want. But Kevin was right. Cameron and I do have unfinished business.'

'What do you mean?' said Sian.

Louise cleared her throat, blushed, and said quietly, 'I . . . I still sometimes dream of us getting back together again. I know it's ridiculous,' she added hastily, her hand raised in the air, 'after getting divorced. But there you have it. That's the truth. It's pathetic, isn't it?'

'It's not pathetic at all,' said Sian into her glass, 'not if you love someone.' She paused and looked at Louise. 'But what about Kevin?'

Louise's eyes filled with tears and she stared silently at her plate. Joanne wondered how she'd react if Phil asked her to take him back . . . She thought Louise was making a mistake, but given the mess she'd made of her life, who was she to judge?

Sian finished the samosa and wiped her hands on a napkin. 'Well, all I'll say is this, Louise. If I had to choose between Kevin Quinn and Cameron Campbell, I know who I'd pick.' She gave Louise a hard look, then picked up another pastry. 'Aren't you two having anything to eat?'

Joanne had just managed to force down a prawn with the

help of a third glass of wine, when Louise said, 'Hey, look, there's Finn,' and she started waving frantically at a group of eight or so people, men and women, who'd just come into the restaurant.

'Who's Finn?' asked Sian while the group made their way to a long table at the other side of the room. Catching Louise's eye, one of the guys, quite good-looking in a scruffy kind of way, came over to their table, unwinding a long striped scarf from round his neck. His fringe of dark hair, slightly too long, was brushed carelessly to the side, curls of brown sweeping the collar of his jacket.

'Hi Finn, I want you to meet my sisters, Sian and Joanne. Finn McAvoy is in charge of the biking centre at Loughanlea.'

Finn flashed them both a nice smile, wide and warm, and shook their hands enthusiastically. He returned to his friends and Louise whispered, 'Great guy. And he's single. Split from his long-term girlfriend in April.'

Sian laughed. 'So what's stopping you?'

'Kevin and Cameron since you ask,' said Louise and she laughed too. 'No, seriously, he's not my type.'

When the laughter had died and everyone's glass had been topped up once more, Joanne gave them an update on the conversation she'd had with Phil about lawyers and amicable settlements.

'He doesn't muck about, does he?' said Louise, sharply. 'Sounds like he's got it all thought out.'

'You mean *she's* got it all thought out,' said Sian in a disparaging tone and Joanne loved them for their loyalty. 'Bet she's been planning this for months.'

'The thing is,' said Joanne, not wanting to dwell on the subject of how long she'd been duped, 'I have to be practical about all this. What worries me is what that settlement's going to look like. Whatever way you look at it, I'm going to be worse off, especially now that Phil's deskbound for the next few months and not earning as much.'

'Stupid idiot,' growled Louise.

'And I was struggling to make ends meet as it was.'

'What'll you do?' said Sian.

'Cut back wherever I can. And,' she said, taking a deep breath, 'go back to work full-time. They still haven't filled that vacancy for a full-time pharmacist and Derek Carmichael said it was mine if I wanted it. It could be a long time before an opportunity like that comes up again – so I said yes.'

'Good for you!' said Sian. 'When do you start?'

'End November.'

'It'll be tough, though,' said Louise, 'going full-time. You'll need to be very organised.'

'I suppose I should be grateful,' said Joanne bravely, 'and I don't mind going full-time. It'll not be easy but I'll manage. It's just that I won't get the school holidays off any more.'

She picked up a clean table knife and turned it over in her hands. She pressed her thumb against the blunt blade. 'In the end, it's the children who suffer, isn't it? The younger ones'll have to go into after-school and holiday clubs and I don't know what I'll do about Maddy. She needs someone around just to keep . . .' Her voice died and a sob caught in her throat.

'Oh, Joanne,' said Louise's soft voice.

Joanne felt a hand on her back, gently caressing. She swallowed the sob and dabbed her left eye which threatened to leak and spoil her make-up. 'It's okay,' she sniffed. 'I'm all right. I know there's plenty of families where both parents work full-time and the kids go into childcare but it's different when you've done it from when they were tiny and didn't know any better. It'll be such a shock to my kids. I used to love the freedom they had in the summer, playing out in the street all day long.'

'Maybe you can pay someone to be in the house?' said Louise hopefully.

Joanne tilted her head to one side and threw the knife on the table more forcefully than she intended. 'It's finding someone reliable, Louise. That's the thing.'

They all sat glumly with nothing to say while the waiter cleared the unfinished starters away and brought another bottle of wine. Joanne went to the toilet and when she came back, Louise brightened. 'Why don't we all do a spa day? The Marine are doing a special offer. It'd cheer you up, Joanne, and Mum could come too. We could have facials.'

Sian nodded her agreement and Joanne laughed. 'So long as it's not like that one I had last year. Do you remember? The girls got me a voucher for Christmas.' She brushed imaginary crumbs off the jacquard tablecloth, surprised that she was actually enjoying herself. 'Anyway, I'm lying on this heated bed thing with a blanket over me and there's eastern music playing and the smell of scented oil fills the air. And the therapist's rubbing all these lotions and potions on my face and a steamer thing's pumping out moist air on my face. It's all fabulous and relaxing and then, all of a sudden, she stops what she's doing, flicks on this bright overhead light. And guess what?'

'What?' asked Louise, her eyes wide in anticipation.

'She starts squeezing your blackheads,' said Sian.

Joanne waved her hand at Sian and, laughing, took a swig of wine. 'You've heard that before!'

'She did what!' cried Louise, in between bouts of loud laughter, her hand splayed across her upper chest.

Joanne's delivery was intentionally deadpan, eliciting shrieks of laughter from her small, but appreciative, audience. 'Squeezed my blackheads. Honest.'

'Yuk!' Louise pulled a disgusted face. 'What did you do?'

Joanne grinned. 'I let her. It was actually quite therapeutic having someone do them for you. Sort of like coming clean about something we all do in secret and never talk about.'

'Oh, Joanne,' said Sian, giggling, 'that's gross.'

Louise wiped away tears of mirth and the main courses appeared as if out of nowhere – lamb curry for Joanne and Louise, vegetable biryani for Sian, naan bread and yellow rice. Far too much food. The others got tucked in while Joanne placed a tiny morsel of the lamb, hot and sweet, in her mouth.

'Here,' said Sian, holding out a heaving plate. 'Have some naan bread. It's Peshawari, your favourite.'

Joanne shook her head. And then something very odd happened. Sian and Louise both froze, all traces of good humour falling from their faces like masks. They exchanged a horrified glance. Louise dropped the spoon she was holding into the metal serving dish with a loud clatter. 'What?' demanded Joanne, swallowing the food in her mouth, her fingers closing round a napkin like a vice.

'What the hell,' said Louise, looking at Sian, 'are *they* doing here?'

And then both Louise and Sian looked straight at Joanne and there was silence, save for the murmur of conversation coming from the other diners and the distant clunk of metal on metal from the kitchen.

She knew what she would see before she even turned her head. But she had to look all the same.

Phil was standing just inside the door, his chest thrust out cockily, his hands shoved deep into the pockets of beige trousers. He was wearing a navy, crew neck jumper over a checked shirt, the set her parents had bought him last Christmas out of their meagre pensions. Seeing it on him now, made Joanne suddenly, irrationally angry. His parents had never so much as bought her a box of Quality Street. Gemma was standing beside him, simpering, with her arm around his waist looking at him like the sun shone out of his arse. She wore skinny black jeans and black riding boots and a bright red, chunky jumper.

'Of all the nights,' groaned Sian, 'and all the places. Why did they have to come here?'

The waiter pointed at two tables near the front of the restaurant, asking them to choose. They had not seen the sisters, too busy playing lovebirds to notice. A sharp jagging pain pierced Joanne's skull just above her right temple. The room felt suddenly too warm, the air too thin. She took a deep breath, tried to steady her shaking knees under the folds of her dress. Sweat oiled her palms – she wiped them on the napkin. She wished she could disappear.

'Let's hurry up and leave,' whispered Sian.

Joanne turned her head slowly to look at her sisters, both half out out of their chairs already, and something inside her snapped. She furrowed her brow, forcing her brain to function through the pain of the headache. Why should she run for cover? Why should she let Gemma and Phil dictate everything? She suddenly realised that if she didn't do something now to regain control, she would forever feel like a victim. She would spend the rest of her life shamed and cowed by what they had done to her.

'I'll pay the bill,' hissed Louise, in a voice not meant for Joanne to hear. 'You get the coats, Sian.'

'We're not leaving,' said Joanne, her voice steady and icy. 'We've hardly touched our main courses. And here's still half a bottle of wine to drink, if I'm not mistaken.' She lifted the green bottle out of the ice bucket and tipped wine into her glass – her hand was shaking so badly much of it slopped onto the pristine white tablecloth. Sian and Louise exchanged terrified glances and sat down again.

'Joanne,' hissed Sian, 'don't you think we should just go?'

'I think somebody should go. But not us.' She must've been drunk because, as she pushed her chair back, and got unsteadily to her feet, the nerves melted away. She felt removed from the scene as though she were an observer watching a performance, and not the main actor. A sense of calm, righteous anger, complex and sour like the tamarind in the curry, washed over her. She pushed the sleeves of her cardigan up, the way her daughter had done earlier, and touched the buckle of her belt. Then she took precisely twelve strides towards the door and came to a halt right in front of Phil and Gemma.

'Joanne!' cried Phil, like he'd seen a ghost. He took a step back, away from her.

Joanne had not seen Gemma since the day of Abbey's party. She stared at Joanne boldly with eyes the colour of a stagnant pond in high summer, and gave her head a little toss. Her face was unsmiling, but it contained no hint of remorse. A thousand images of their friendship flashed before Joanne's eyes like a film in fast forward. And from these jumbled images emerged memories, as crystal clear as the Aegean Sea, in which they'd once bathed together on holiday.

Joanne washing up after lunch, while a bronzed, bikini-clad Gemma lay under the blazing sun, ostensibly supervising the children in the pool. Joanne sweating over a hot stove in the searing Mediterranean heat because they couldn't afford to eat out every day while Gemma maintained, laughingly, that she'd poison everyone with her cooking – *and we wouldn't want that, would we?* And at home, the many days and nights Joanne had minded the children for her after

Jimmy left, sometimes with hardly a word of thanks. The countless times she had told Joanne, tearfully, that she couldn't afford to give the girls a birthday, or a Christmas, present because she was short of cash. How sorry Joanne had felt for her then, somehow overlooking the fact that Gemma always had money for nicer clothes than she, good bottles of wine (not the half-price supermarket offers Joanne bought), going out and holidays. Joanne would've gone without, and sometimes did, to make sure she treated Gemma's children like her own niece and nephew.

How had she not seen Gemma for what she was?

Joanne pulled herself up to her full height, glad that she'd worn a high pair of heels, and said, as regally as she could manage, 'I'm here on a night out with my sisters and I'd very much appreciate it if you went elsewhere.'

Phil's gaze snaked across the room to where Sian and Louise sat. Gemma didn't even blink. 'Don't be ridiculous, Joanne,' she said sharply, looking down her nose, leaving Phil with his mouth open, half-formed words on his lips. 'You can't tell us where we can and cannot eat.'

Joanne folded her arms. 'That's rich coming from you. You never had any problem telling me what to do, Gemma. How many times did you tell me to leave Phil?' Her voice rose. 'Eh? Pretending that you had my and the girls' best interests at heart. When all you wanted was to get your scheming claws into him.' She gave Phil a derisory, long stare from head to toe. To give him credit, he looked a little cowed.

'You didn't want him, Joanne. Don't you turn this around and make it sound like I stole him,' said Gemma, her voice rising in response to Joanne's. 'You were clinging on to your marriage for all the wrong reasons because you hadn't the courage to end it.'

Joanne, ignoring the truth of this, shook her head and

said bitterly, 'You were always one of life's takers, Gemma. You even had to take my husband.'

'For your information, I didn't *take* him,' shouted Gemma, jabbing at the air in front of Joanne's chest with a pointed index finger. Her nails were painted red to match the jumper. 'He pursued me. Not the other way around. And it wasn't until he came to me the night of Abbey's party and said that he'd left you that I finally gave in.'

'My going had nothing to do with Gemma,' said Phil quietly. 'You know our marriage was over long before I walked out the door.'

'You're a liar, Gemma,' said Joanne loudly, ignoring Phil. A sudden hush descended on the room and every head turned in their direction. The young waiter, serving wine to a young, dewy-eyed couple at the table right beside Joanne, froze.

'How dare you!' cried Gemma, her face by now an impressive shade of puce, like the inside of the exotic pomegranate Joanne had once bought at the supermarket and nobody liked.

'I know about the contraceptive pills,' said Joanne, her voice flat like a calm sea. 'You've been on them for four months.'

This momentarily silenced Gemma. She blinked like a goldfish. Joanne was aware of the presence of Louise and Sian standing right behind, her loyal guard. The knowledge gave her strength.

'Which means you've been sleeping with him for at least that long. Unless you shagged your way round half of Ballyfergus before ensnaring my husband.'

'Jesus Christ,' erupted Phil, through gritted teeth. 'Do you have to air all our linen in public like this?' He glanced furtively around the room. 'I think we should discuss this another time, Joanne,' he hissed. 'Or, preferably, not at all.'

Joanne followed his gaze, embarrassed that everyone in the room was hanging on their every word – but gratified too. It clearly bothered Phil more than it did her – perhaps because her self-esteem was so low, it could fall no further. And of course he was the one who had something to hide, not her. 'It's not my dirty linen, Phil,' she said in a theatrical stage-loud voice. 'I've done nothing wrong. You're the one who's been shagging my best friend behind my back for the past four months. You're the one who walked out on your daughter's birthday, leaving me to console an eight-year-old who cries for her daddy every night.'

'I'm not listening to any more of this,' said Gemma, trying to sound outraged but not quite pulling it off. It was difficult to play hard done by when you'd been caught telling a pack of lies. She put her hand on his arm. 'Let's go, Phil.'

And then Phil made a mistake. 'You're hysterical, Joanne,' he said in disgust. 'You don't know what you're saying. You should go home, get yourself a strong cup of coffee and sober up.'

'I'm not hysterical, Phil,' she said calmly, as a surge of adrenaline coursed through her veins like a drug. Her heart beat so violently she was certain that if she put a hand to her breast she would feel it pounding against her ribs. Her peripheral vision faded out – all she could see was the sneer on Phil's face, and Gemma's nervous glance flitting around the room. She heard her breath come in short gasps and above it, Gemma's low voice urging Phil to leave. Joanne stood on the balls of her feet, poised for action. And then she remembered what she had seen sitting on the table right beside her.

In one fluid, elegant movement she leant over and scooped up the water jug full to the brim with water and ice and lemon slices. The jug was heavy, but it felt like a feather in her hand, her muscles primed for action. The young woman at the table, anticipating what would happen next, gasped and put her hand over her mouth.

'This,' said Joanne, looking at the glass pitcher in her right hand, 'this is hysterical.'

She swung the pitcher backwards, then brought it swinging forward like a piston, and splashed the contents into Phil's face. The water went everywhere, drenching Gemma too. Cubes of ice and lemony half-moons fell to the floor, on the doormat and the plush carpet. Gemma gasped, grabbed Phil by the arm and hauled the door open, spouting expletives.

'For the record,' called Joanne, as they stumbled outside, and a slow smile spread across her face. 'You're welcome to him, Gemma. I've never met two people who deserve each other more.'

Then the door to the restaurant creaked slowly shut and Joanne stood there, stunned, her ears full of a rushing sound like wind. And as the noise inside her head died away, and the madness that had possessed her evaporated, she became aware of a dreadful silence all around her. She bowed her head, her anger spent, as embarrassment crept over her like a chill. For those few brief moments the tables had turned – for the first time since Phil walked out she was no longer a victim.

Now, she felt like an idiot. Instead of maintaining her dignity she had resorted to what amounted to a physical assault. She should not have sunk that low. Especially in such a public place. In front of all these strangers. She set the jug back on the table in front of the stunned young lovers and said, quietly, 'Sorry about that.'

'Ouch,' came a lone male voice from a table to her left.

She lifted her head and glanced over. It was Finn, watching her with a big grin on his face, revealing even, white teeth. Then he lifted his right hand, gave her a military salute and started clapping, loud and slow. She felt the tension ease – her face broke into a grateful smile.

And then suddenly the whole place erupted in cheers and whistles and Joanne lifted her chin and, blushing, led a rather shell-shocked Louise and Sian back to their table.

Sian stuttered an apology to the waiter. 'I . . . I'm sorry. My sister . . . I mean, we don't normally do this sort of thing. I'll pay for . . . for any damage.'

'Don't worry about it, She-ann,' he said. 'It is only water, is it not? No harm done. Now, why don't you sit down and enjoy the rest of your meal?' They all took their seats once more and Sian said, squeezing her sister's hand, 'You were absolutely magnificent, Joanne. Wasn't she, Louise?'

'Awesome. Like Boudicca. The great Celtic warrior queen.'

Joanne's lips formed into a victorious smile and her regrets melted away. What she had done was neither ladylike nor dignified, but Phil and Gemma deserved it. 'You know what? I might have some of that Peshawari after all.' She grabbed a piece of the bread and crammed it hungrily in her mouth. 'Maybe I shouldn't have done that,' she said, her mouth full. 'But do you know what? It felt good to just . . . do something. In fact, it felt bloody brilliant!'

Louise and Sian exchanged glances and laughed. And then the waiter came over with a bottle of sparkling wine and three glasses on a tray and held it out to Joanne. 'With the compliments of the gentleman at table number five.' He nodded at Finn on the other side of the room.

Joanne looked over at him, her cheeks stuffed with bread like a hamster. Finn met her gaze, winked once and ever so imperceptibly raised his glass to her. And then, with a look of quiet amusement on his face, he returned to the conversation he was having with the woman on his right. Joanne turned back to the table, her feelings an unsettling mix of exhilaration and embarrassment. She swallowed the dry bread with difficulty.

Her sisters exchanged a meaningful glance while the waiter poured the wine and Louise said, teasing, 'Guess who's got the hots for you, then?'

'Don't be daft.' Joanne allowed herself a small smile born from the fact that her shattered self-esteem had been partially restored, 'I think he just likes a good floor show.'

'Well, you'll not see better than that anywhere in Ballyfergus,' said Sian. 'You were absolutely amazing!' She lifted a glass of bubbly and said, 'Good on you, Joanne.'

Louise followed suit and Joanne blushed uncomfortably, the euphoria seeping away almost as quickly as it had arisen. When the toast was over, Louise, sensing Joanne's changing mood, said, 'You do realise that you're better off without him, don't you, Joanne?'

'I don't know if I'll ever feel like that,' she answered truthfully. 'I'd never take him back. But right now I just feel . . . alone.' She reached for the bubbly. 'And angry. The girls . . . well, they're broken-hearted, aren't they? I wasn't lying when I said that Abbey cries for Phil every night. Holly's gone all quiet and introverted, and Maddy hardly leaves the house. She's lost her best friend.' Joanne looked into the glass, watching the bubbles rise to the surface and burst, in much the same way her dream of a happy family life had imploded. But she still couldn't bring herself to admit, even to her beloved sisters, that it had imploded long before Phil walked out.

She looked into the two anxious faces staring at her. 'You

mustn't worry, you know. I'll be all right. Nothing else for it, is there?' she said, and sourness crept into her voice. 'But coming to terms with what those two have done to me – and the girls – is going to take a very long time.'

Chapter Thirteen

Sian stood in the doorway to Louise's small kitchen wearing an old pair of Louise's sweatpants and socks – her things were on a radiator drying. She was here out of desperation, because she did not know who else to turn to, aware that if she didn't do something her world was going to fall apart. The night before Andy left for Portrush he'd turned his back on her in bed and told her he was too tired – a first. And as she'd lain there in the dark, silent tears seeping into the pillow, she knew they couldn't go on like this – something had to be done.

Louise, in jeans and a Kelly green sweater, made tea, her hair tied back in a ponytail and her face bare of her usual make-up.

'So have you seen Kevin lately?' said Sian, too terrified to tackle the reason she'd cycled over here uninvited on this filthy, wet night.

Louise handed Sian a mug and sighed. 'No. I think he's really annoyed with me – and a bit hurt.'

'Well, you can see why, can't you?' said Sian, leading the way into the cosy lounge where she sank down on the carpet in front of the single armchair and crossed her legs. She sipped gingerly from the mug and tried to stop her hands from shaking. 'The two of you are getting along like a house on fire and then your ex-husband sends you a few e-mails and, all of a sudden, you're at sixes and sevens.'

Louise set her mug on a side table and stretched herself out along the cream leather sofa, and stared at the ceiling.

'Louise, what are you playing at? I thought you liked Kevin.'

'I do. I like him very much.'

There was a silence and Sian asked, 'Has Cameron phoned you?'

Louise shook her head and rested her forearm on her forehead.

'Why does that not surprise me?' said Sian. 'Cameron could always talk a good game. Delivery was his problem.'

'I don't remember him like that at all,' said Louise quietly.

'What about the time he promised Andy and his mates tickets for the rugby international in Edinburgh? They travelled all the way over and when they got there, there were no tickets. They ended up watching the match in a pub.'

'There was a mix-up with the tickets. That wasn't Cameron's fault.'

'It never is,' said Sian quietly.

'Cameron was always helping people. Just sometimes he committed to more than he could manage, that's all. And we had good times. Great times together,' said Louise stubbornly. 'Anyway,' she changed the subject, 'you didn't come here to talk about Cameron, did you?'

Sian set the mug down on the floor because her hand was shaking so violently she could no longer hold it. She looked at the pile of paperwork on the table, the computer humming away quietly in the background and felt that she'd made a mistake. 'I shouldn't have come. I'm sorry. I guess you were trying to get some work done?'

Louise glanced at the table, laden with documents, and shook her head. 'I must be the only saddo with nothing better to do on a Saturday night than work.'

Sian looked at her feet, encased in fluffy pink socks, unlike anything she had in her wardrobe. 'No sadder than me stuck at home on my own.'

Louise sat up and took a sip of tea. 'How come? Where's Andy?'

Sian explained where Andy was and shared the fact that she hadn't been asked along. Misery settled on her like a blanket.

Louise set her mug down and leant forward, her arms circling her knees. 'But you and Andy always do things together.'

Sian nodded, unable to speak for the tightness in her throat.

'What's going on, Sian? Don't tell me you and Andy had a fight. You never fight.'

Sian nodded. 'It's worse than that,' she said miserably, the words finally tumbling out against her will. 'He wants to have a baby.'

Louise opened her mouth in astonishment then threw back her head, revealing the ribbed roof of her mouth. She clapped her hands and laughed delightedly like this was the best news she'd heard in months. Then she got up and went over to Sian, crouching down beside her and giving her a big hug. 'That's fantastic, Sian. We always said Andy would make a great dad, didn't we? And you'll make a great mum. Have you started trying? You should be taking folic acid, you know.'

Sian let out a deep, irritated sigh. 'Louise, you're not listening,' she said crossly looking into her sister's eyes, and struggling to retain her composure. She wanted to cry. Louise

– and Joanne – never listened to her, not properly. 'I said he wants to have a baby. I didn't say I did.'

The smile melted off Louise's face. She got to her feet and stood with her arms dangling by her sides looking, first perplexed, then cross. 'And this is what you've fallen out over? Are you crazy, woman?' she cried, her words pelting down on Sian's head like hailstones. 'The man you love wants to have a baby with you. What could be more perfect than that?'

She shouldn't, in hindsight, have expected Louise to understand. What was Sian's nightmare – her husband wanting her to have his child – was Louise's dream come true. She shouldn't have come.

'Just because your life's ambition was to be a mother, it doesn't mean it's mine,' said Sian, pulling her knees up and resting her chin on them.

Louise went over to the sofa and threw herself down on it with a loud, exasperated grunt. She opened her mouth to speak then closed it again. At last she said, 'Please don't tell me this is all about you wanting to minimise your impact on the environment.'

'I just want things between me and Andy to stay the way they are,' Sian said, stubbornly.

'But they can't,' said Louise with sudden softness in her voice and eyes. 'Not now that Andy wants something different from you. Unless one of you gives in, you're going to end up down the same road as me and Cameron. Don't let that happen. Please.'

Sian lifted her chin off her knees, her heart pounding against her ribcage. The thought of breaking up with Andy was unthinkable. She felt, suddenly, hot and fevered. Louise was right. Was this how it would end between her and Andy? 'You think that I should be the one to give in,' she said.

'It's not my place to say that,' said Louise, suddenly buttoning up. 'You know I'm biased.'

Sian sniffed, fighting back tears. How could she give him what he wanted? It was impossible. 'Having a child is the very worst thing anybody can do for the environment. Categorically. Full stop,' she said, starting off a little shakily. But as she went on, reiterating an argument as familiar to her as the sound of her own breathing, her voice steadied. As if the repetition of the logic could make it as solid and unassailable as a castle wall. 'And the very best thing you can do is not procreate. The government spends all this money on promoting energy-saving light-bulbs and telling you to insulate your loft and lag your hot water tank and use public transport and compost your potato peelings – and a million other things that go absolutely nowhere close to meeting the vast resources a single human being uses in his or her lifetime. Especially in the Western world.'

She paused, and Louise said, with a grim expression on her face, 'Sian. That is a very extreme view.'

'I don't think it is. It's just before its time. The reason nobody wants to talk about the subject in this country is that we're not ready to hear it. And that's because our wealth cushions us from the effects of global over-population. People in the third world don't have that luxury – they're the ones starving to death.'

Louise's face reddened. 'What you don't understand is that having children is, for most people, the thing that gives meaning to their lives. If you take that away, then what's the point of it all?' She set her mug on the table and gave Sian a hard stare. 'Anyway, we're talking about one baby. Can't you find a way to compromise? Andy's not asking you to have a football team. What's so bad about having just one child?'

Sian looked at the floor and clenched her jaw, trying to control the muscles in her face that were starting to do things she couldn't stop. She believed in everything she said, she really did, but that wasn't what was holding her back. Much as she believed passionately in saving the world, she believed in Andy more. A compromise along the lines Louise suggested wasn't outside the realms of possibility – *if* the environment was the only thing that worried her.

But that wasn't her only concern, not by a long shot. She closed her eyes.

When she opened them again, Louise was kneeling on the floor in front of her. 'Sian, love, what is it? What are you afraid of?'

Sian opened her mouth to speak. But she could not. All she could do was remember. The day of Abbey's birth.

With their parents on holiday when Joanne went into premature labour and Phil nowhere to be found – he was away on business up north and, surprise, surprise, couldn't be contacted by phone – it had fallen to Sian to accompany her sister to hospital. The labour had lasted hours. Joanne was exhausted, panicked, and on the verge of hysteria when they finally decided to cut her open and pull the baby out. Sian, nauseous with fear, didn't want to witness the caesarean but Joanne, terrified, clung to her and she was forced to accompany her sister into the operating room.

Sian closed her eyes. She could still feel the claustrophobia of that hot, sterile room and see Joanne's hair plastered to her face with sweat. She could smell her sister's blood and her desperation as she dug her nails into Sian's wrist so hard the marks were visible for days after. And she remembered her own fear – the sweat on her brow, the prayers for deliverance falling silently from her lips, the terror of not knowing if her sister would survive. When the doctor had finally held up the tiny alien-looking baby, slippery with vernix and blood, Sian had fainted.

'What is it, Sian?' Louise was staring at her, her brow furrowed with concern, a hand placed lightly on her sister's forearm.

'I've never met anyone with an honest good word to say about giving birth,' said Sian, exercising at last some control over her shaking limbs – and her vocal cords. 'Women wax lyrical about their newborns and gloss over the birth itself with talk of how the baby "makes it all worth it".'

Louise nodded in agreement, like Churchill the dog on the TV ads. 'That's true,' she said enthusiastically, and she actually smiled. 'That is what it's like. Once you have that baby in your arms you forget everything.'

Sian opened her mouth to speak, closed it again. How could she tell Louise the truth? She would not understand. No one would. People would think her strange, weird. For her fears were absurd, utterly irrational . . . and yet she could not conquer them. She had tried for decades.

Louise frowned. 'Sian,' she said gently. 'Please.' Her fingers tightened round her sister's arm. 'Let me help you.'

Sian pulled her knees close to her chest like a shield. 'I can't,' she said looking at the floor.

Louise's hand slipped away. 'Yes, you can,' she said quietly. 'Take your time. We've got all night.'

It took Sian a few long moments to compose herself and she made a few false starts, her thoughts and fears so jumbled in her own mind that she did not know how to express them. In the end it was the thought of losing Andy – and the realisation that she had to do something to stop that happening – that made her blurt it out.

'I'm afraid to have a baby.'

270

'Because of the effect on the planet?' said Louise slowly, patiently, trying very hard to keep the cynicism that was so evident in her face, out of her voice.

'You don't understand.' Sian paused, and felt her face colouring. And suddenly her breath came in short, tight gasps. She put her head between her knees and fought the panic. She inhaled quickly, counted out the breaths – one, two, three, four – and after some moments, with Louise's hand on her shoulder, she gained control once more. She would not let this thing beat her, she would not let it control her life, not any more. She lifted her head, and told Louise what she had never told anyone. 'I'm afraid of giving birth. Of actually delivering a baby. The whole process. It . . . it terrifies me.' And then the tears came, relief flooding through her like a burst dam. She had not realised what a burden her secret had become.

'Oh,' said Louise and she sat down on her bottom beside Sian. There was a long pause and then she added, 'Why, that's incredible. I had no idea.' She shook her head and took a few moments to collect her thoughts. 'But, Sian, can't you see how crazy that is? Giving birth is the most natural thing in the world.'

Sian's face turned red with embarrassment and she swiped at the tears on her cheek. 'I shouldn't have told you. You don't understand. You'll never understand.'

She jumped up and walked over to the radiator and scooped up her things, hot from its heat, in her arms. And despite her best efforts not to, she started to sob, her shoulders heaving with despair. After all these years, she had shared her secret only to be met with derision.

Louise came up behind her and placed a hand on her shoulder. 'Sian, please. I'm sorry. I am trying to understand. I really am. Come on, sit down.' She took the clothes out of her sister's arms and led her over to the sofa. She went and got them each a glass of white wine and shoved one into Sian's hand. 'Drink. It'll do you good.'

Sian obeyed, downing half the glass in a few gulps. The effect was almost instantaneous – immediately she felt less hysterical. When she'd composed herself, tears clinging to her cheeks like winter rain, she said, 'I know it's not rational, and it doesn't make sense. But that's the way I feel. Everything about pregnancy and childbirth disgusts me. I know it's ridiculous but I can't help it. There's a name for it. I looked it up on Google. Tokophobia.'

'Toko-what?' Louise's mouth hung open.

'Tokophobia. A morbid fear of childbirth. It's a recognised condition.'

Louise gave a little laugh and crossed her legs. 'But it's perfectly natural to be afraid,' she said gently, leaning back, nursing her glass. 'Everyone is to some extent.'

Sian shook her head and inched forwards until she was sitting on the edge of the sofa. She held the glass in her right hand and gesticulated with her left, in an attempt to convey to Louise the intensity of her feelings. 'This is much more than normal anxiety. I'm completely and utterly repulsed by pregnancy and childbirth. I'm more afraid of it than anything.'

Louise's brow furrowed like a ploughed field. 'Oh, Sian. You're over-reacting. You really are. It's not that bad.'

'Maybe not for you, Louise. But I'm not you. And this is how I feel. It's not that I don't want a baby. I just can't get past the idea that I would have to carry it inside me.' She pulled a face, her stomach heaving with nausea at the idea. 'And that I would have to give birth to it.'

Louise was quiet for a long time and then she said, 'What exactly is it that you're afraid of?'

'Everything. It's all so medieval and barbaric – I can't believe that with all our modern medicine women still have to go through such a horrendous experience. It's just repulsive. I can't bear the idea of the pain, the ripped muscles, stitches, all that blood . . . Ugh!' She shivered involuntarily. Then she looked warily at Louise who had uncrossed her legs and was leaning forward slightly, the almost empty wine glass now wedged between her knees. She looked like she was trying very hard to understand which gave Sian the courage to go on. 'I've never told anyone how I feel before because I know people won't understand. They'll think I'm weird. Because either hardly anyone else feels like this or no one wants to admit that they do. I tried to talk Andy into adopting instead but he says he wants his own child.' She paused, took a deep breath and added, the words primitive and biblical-sounding, 'He wants a child that's his own flesh and blood.'

Louise became suddenly animated. 'Oh, Sian. You're not weird. It's just a . . . a phobia like you said. An irrational fear. Like being pathologically afraid of . . .' She waved her right hand above her head, grasping words out of the air. 'Of spiders, or the dark. Or enclosed spaces. There must be some treatment. Hypnotherapy. Or something.'

Sian shrugged hopelessly. 'From what I've read, the medical profession has no time for people like me. They just think women should get on with giving birth without making a fuss.'

Louise's response was forthright. 'I'm quite sure that's not true. I'm sure there are some doctors and midwives who'll understand. It's just a question of finding them.'

'You think so?' Her sister's optimism gave her some hope. It wasn't that Sian didn't want to overcome her fear – there was nothing she desired more – she just wasn't sure it was possible.

'Absolutely. And talking about it is the first step, Sian. Which is what you're doing now.' Louise shifted in her seat, emptied her glass, and her voice dropped an octave. 'How long have you felt like this, Sian?'

Sian blinked, remembering back to that time when she was a little girl . . .

Louise waited.

Sian's voice came out no louder than a whisper. 'In S2 biology class we were shown this video of a woman giving birth. It was just one horrific bloody mess. I watched it through my hands. And I've spent the rest of my life wishing I hadn't. It didn't help that Mum never talked about it, except in hushed whispers we were never meant to hear . . .' She coughed to clear her throat and went on, 'I've been petrified ever since. Abbey's birth was just the nail in the coffin. I had a notion, once, that a caesarean would be better than giving birth naturally. I thought it would be less gory because I could be sedated and I wouldn't feel as much pain. But having seen it – well, that kind of blew that theory out of the water.' Sian set the empty glass down on the side table and leant back, her head resting on the sofa. She closed her eyes.

'Sian,' said Louise.

'What?'

'Have you discussed this with Andy?'

Sian opened her eyes and looked at Louise. She shook her head. Exhaustion washed over her like a wave. 'He thinks I won't have a baby because of the environmental impact,' she said and closed her eyes.

'You're going to have to tell him, Sian. If he knew what was behind your refusal to have a baby, he'd understand. I'm sure of it. And you're going to need his support if you want to overcome this phobia. You do want to overcome it, don't you?'

Sian nodded. 'More than anything.'

Louise patted her sister on the knee and said brightly, 'That's good. And I'm going to help you, Sian. This family has seen two relationships go down the pan already. And, if I can help it, you and Andy aren't going the same way. Not over something like this.'

Sian forced a weak smile. 'You know, telling you this . . . it's so difficult . . . But I feel like there might be hope for me at last. I've struggled with this for so long . . . you've no idea . . .'

'You poor thing,' said Louise compassionately. 'And you've every reason to hope, Sian. You've admitted you've a problem and that's the first step.'

Sian's eyelids fluttered and she stifled a yawn. With Louise in charge she felt like the little sister yet again, but this time she was grateful rather than resentful. She knew that this was one problem she could not solve on her own. Ignoring it and hoping it would go away – her strategy for the last twenty odd years – had not worked. It was time to do something different. 'I feel so tired. The wine . . . it's made me sleepy.' She yawned again. 'I'm sorry. I don't know what's wrong with me. I feel completely exhausted.'

'I'm not surprised, carrying all that worry around with you. It would exhaust anyone.' Louise squeezed Sian's knee lightly. 'Look, why don't you stay the night? You can sleep in with me. You're in no fit state to be cycling home to an empty house. And I'd be much happier if you stayed.'

Sian nodded. She didn't think she had the energy to cycle to the end of the street, never mind all the way out to Loughanlea. 'Thanks.'

Downstairs a car door slammed and Sian hauled herself to her feet. Feeling suddenly cold, as well as tired, she wrapped her arms around herself. 'Goodnight then.'

Louise gave her a warm hug, holding her close for a few moments. She rubbed Sian's back with the flat of her hand. 'Everything's going to be all right,' she whispered in her ear and released her.

'I hope so, Louise,' said Sian quietly. She hugged her sister briefly before going to bed, crawling under the duvet fully clothed. When she closed her eyes, she fell instantly asleep.

Louise flopped down on the sofa and glanced at the clock on the mantelpiece. It was ten-thirty – too late to phone Joanne and discuss this latest, extraordinary family crisis.

She had always considered Sian to be strong, brave, independent and firm in her values and beliefs even in the face of scepticism and ridicule. And for that she had admired her, envied her even, because she herself had always been full of self-doubt. But it turned out that Sian was just as emotionally flawed and vulnerable as she was. Worse even. It made Louise feel wretched to think that Sian had wrestled with this largely unfounded fear all her adult life and that she was close to jeopardising her relationship with Andy because of it. Looking back on the events of the last two decades, she tried to recall signs of Sian's phobia but could remember nothing.

Louise yawned and ran a hand over her forehead. The encounter had tired her out, left her feeling as exhausted as her sister appeared. It had taken all her powers of concentration to try to understand and empathise with a condition that she had never even heard of before tonight. No one looked forward to giving birth – it was unpleasant and painful, no doubt about that – but to have such a morbid phobia was bizarre. And to allow it to rule your life and threaten your happiness was madness. But the bottom line was, whatever she thought didn't really matter.

Sian had a serious problem. And Louise would do what-ever she could to help her sister.

A sudden noise downstairs caught Louise's attention. She sat up ramrod straight and strained to listen. She heard footsteps on the stairs – stairs that led only to her flat, and nowhere else – and froze. Thinking fast, she got up and padded silently over to the end of the dim hall, her heart fluttering against her ribs, her breath shallow. She ran her gaze quickly over the locks and bolts on the door. Each one had been carefully secured after Sian's arrival. She told herself to calm down. She tried not to think about the day she'd woken up in her Edinburgh flat to find she had been burgled.

Tap-tap-tap came the sharp sound of bare knuckles on the solid wooden door.

Louise did not move. Think, she told herself. Who could it possibly be at this hour? A member of her family perhaps? No, that wasn't likely. Phil? He had no reason to come here – she had not seen him, apart from that night in the Indian restaurant, since he'd walked out on Joanne and the kids.

Tap-tap-tap. The noise was quiet, insistent, as though the person on the other side of the door knew she was there, knew they did not have to knock any louder for her to hear. If it wasn't Phil . . . she could think of no one else.

Apart from Kevin.

This thought calmed her frazzled nerves and galvanised her into action. She crept across the carpet, silent as a cat, and pushed the small shiny disc over the peephole to one side. She closed her right eye and pressed her left one to the fisheye lens embedded in the door. A man was standing on the doorstep, close to the door, his face turned to the right as though he might be listening for sounds from within. But it was not Kevin. A small sound escaped her, she jumped back and placed her hands over her face, her breath hot and damp on her palms.

Her heart pounded in her breast and this time it had good cause. She glanced frantically around the small space, looking for an exit, an escape, an answer as to what she ought to do. But there was no way out, no place to go, only her standing alone in the narrow hallway and him on the other side of the thick wooden door.

Tap-tap-tap came the sound once more and she knew she had no choice – she would have to open the door. With shaking hands, she reached for the bolt at the top. Screech-clink-snap went the bolts and locks while the cogs in her brain clunked slowly into place. What was he doing here? What did he want? How had he found her? The last to go was the security chain – she slid it out of the slide catch and let it fall with a tinny rattle against the door. Then she paused, ran a hand down the front of her top, turned the snib on the Yale lock and opened the door.

'Cameron,' she said, with her hand still on the knob. 'What are you doing here?'

He gave her one of his crooked smiles, his grey eyes looking up at her from beneath dark brown eyebrows, the shadow of black whiskers on his chin lending him a rakish air. He wore jeans and a casual khaki jacket with the collar turned up – spots of dark rain peppered his broad shoulders. The years had done him no disservice – if anything, he had improved with age. The fine lines on his face had deepened with age and his short dark hair, greying at the temples now, lent him a mature, worldly air.

'What is this place?' he said, piercing her with his steel-grey gaze, the corners of his eyes creasing with humour. 'Fort Knox?'

'It's home,' she said flatly, looking away, remembering suddenly that she was wearing no make-up, and her hair was in need of a wash.

'You look well,' he said, without a trace of irony, and she blushed out of embarrassment. This was not how she would've chosen to meet Cameron, not here, not like this. He was as handsome as ever and she looked a complete mess. He looked over her shoulder into the flat. Instinctively, she positioned herself in the middle of the doorway.

'Look, Cameron, I'm sorry. I don't mean to be rude but you can't just turn up at my house like this, unannounced, in the middle of the night. You scared the living daylights out of me.'

'I'm sorry,' he said, bringing his gaze back to her face, and smiling pleasantly. 'My flight was delayed. I didn't intend to be so late.'

She folded her arms. 'Are you over here on business?'

He shook his head and leant against the wall outside the door, the tough cotton fabric of his jacket rasping against the grey harl. 'I came over to see you.'

Her pulse quickened. 'To see me?'

'Yes. I told you I wanted to talk to you, didn't I?'

She nodded. 'But I thought you meant on the phone or by e-mail. I sent you my number. But you never called.' She shook her head. There were so many questions she wanted to ask, not only about this visit, but about his life as well. What had he been doing these last few years? Where did he live? Did he have a partner? Had he re-married? Was he happy? But instead she settled for something more immediate that was troubling her. 'How did you find me?'

'Your mother. I called from Edinburgh airport and she

gave me your address. I thought she might have let you know I was on my way.'

Louise glanced over her shoulder at the black answering machine sitting on the small hall table. The light was flashing, indicating a new message. Her mother must've called when she'd been bathing Oli – she hadn't heard the phone ring.

'I meant what I said in my e-mail, Louise.'

The words were etched in her memory. *I . . . regret our divorce. I should never have let you go. I love you still.* She stared at him, her tongue at once thick and dry, unable to speak. She realised then that she had never stopped loving him, that she never would.

'Is everything all right?' asked Sian's muffled voice and Louise started. She turned abruptly to see her sister just a few feet away, blinking, her hair standing up in tufts. 'I heard voices,' she said, moving slowly towards the door. 'And I was . . . Cameron! Is that you?'

'Hello Sian.' He gave her a thin, awkward smile and looked at his feet.

'What are you . . .?' Sian came and stood beside Louise and gave her a concerned look. 'Is everything all right?'

Louise moistened her lips and said, 'Yes, everything's fine. Really. Cameron was just going.'

'Yeah,' he said and looked out into the night. 'It's late. Maybe I shouldn't have called round tonight. I just so wanted to see you,' he added, bringing his gaze back to Louise. 'Look, we need to talk. Properly,' he said earnestly, with a sideways glance at Sian as though he resented her presence. 'I'm staying at The Marine Hotel and flying back Monday night. Can I see you tomorrow, Louise? Please.'

She nodded dumbly. How could she refuse? She didn't want to refuse.

'I'll pick you up about twelve? Maybe we could have lunch?'

'I'd like to but . . . Sian,' she said, looking at her sister imploringly. 'Could you look after Oli?'

'Oh, yes, Oli. I mind his name now,' said Cameron, as though he'd only just remembered that the child existed.

Sian scuffed her toe on the carpet. 'Okay.'

'How is the wee fella?' said Cameron. 'He must be, what, four by now?'

'Three,' said Sian.

'He's good,' said Louise, a smile at last cracking her face. 'Brilliant, in fact.'

'That's . . . hmm . . . great. Well, I'll see you tomorrow then. Bye Sian.'

'Bye,' said Louise and Sian, wide awake now, stared coldly at Cameron's retreating back.

When he'd disappeared down the stairs, Louise shut the door and leant her back against it, the palms of her sweaty hands pressed against the painted wood. She closed her eyes, her head giddy with uncertainty and promise. Cameron had come all this way to see her, to talk to her. Was he going to ask her to come back to him? And if he did, what would she say? Seeing him had come as a shock, as did the longing she felt now deep inside. And yet, there was worry in her heart too – anxiety that Cameron's presence threatened the new and happy life she had established here. A life in which she had thought Kevin would play a major part . . .

'What on earth is he doing here?' said Sian's voice, interrupting her thoughts. 'And what does he want?'

Louise opened her eyes and listened to the sound of a car starting and driving off, as Sian's questions fell around her like confetti. When the sound of the car had entirely died out, she said, 'I don't know.'

Sian took a sharp intake of breath and put her hands on her cheeks. 'Oh, Louise,' she said, her voice hushed with disappointment, 'I am so afraid that you are going to get hurt.'

Chapter Fourteen

On Sunday morning Joanne struggled into the kitchen with the weekly shop to find Maddy standing in a dressing gown with her arms folded across her chest. 'The lock on the bathroom door's not working.'

'What do you mean it's not working?' sighed Joanne as she heaved the bags onto the table, still strewn with breakfast things.

'When you turn the knob it just goes round and round and the metal bar – the one that slides into the door frame – doesn't come out.'

'Okay,' said Joanne, through gritted teeth, 'let's have a look.'

She marched upstairs and fiddled with the broken lock to no avail. 'I can't fix it now.' She plucked at her bottom lip with her right hand, thinking. 'I'll have to get a handyman in to do it. Or maybe Grandad could take a look.'

'When? When could he fix it?'

'Oh, I don't know, do I? Sometime this week perhaps. Or maybe next weekend.'

'But what am I supposed to do until then?' cried Maddy. 'Holly and Abbey kept running in and out the whole time I was in the bath and they wouldn't stop it even when I told them to.'

'I'll have a word with them.'

'But, Mum! What about when I have to . . . you know, go to . . .' she lowered her voice, 'the toilet.'

'Be thankful you don't have a brother,' said Joanne, a little callously and headed down the stairs.

'I'll get Dad to come and fix it,' Maddy called after her.

Joanne stopped in her tracks and looked up, one hand on the banister. 'Don't you dare do that. He doesn't live here any more, Maddy. And I don't want him in my house.'

Maddy let out a great rush of air and stomped across the hall towards her room. When she got to the doorway she turned and faced her mother. 'I hate this house,' she yelled. 'Nothing ever works properly. And I hate my life. And it's all your fault. If you hadn't nagged Dad so much he never would've run off with Gemma.' And with that, she slammed the door shut so hard it vibrated in the frame.

Joanne let the words bounce off her like hailstones, hard and painful on impact but of no lasting substance. Or so she told herself. She knew she had to cut Maddy some slack but she was fed up of being the punch-bag for her daughter's frustrations. The sound of muffled, gut-wrenching sobs seeped from behind the door – wearily Joanne climbed back up the stairs.

'Maddy,' she said, when she'd managed to get her to stop crying and the two of them sat side by side on the single bed. 'I know this has been hard for you.'

Maddy looked away. 'You've no idea, Mum. Your parents never separated, did they?'

'No,' said Joanne carefully, stroking the pink satin duvet cover, 'but I understand how difficult this must be for you. Especially because of Roz.'

Maddy started to cry again, this time silently. 'She said she wasn't my friend any more,' she sniffed. 'She told everyone at school not to talk to me. And now everyone's ignoring me, when she's around anyway.'

Joanne raised an eyebrow. 'Everyone?'

'Everyone that matters,' said Maddy sullenly.

'A bit like her mother then,' observed Joanne.

Maddy wrinkled up her face. 'What?'

'Not much of a friend in the end, was she?'

Maddy shrugged, unconsoled.

Joanne pulled her daughter to her and kissed the top of her greasy, unwashed hair. 'I'll tell you what, Maddy, why don't you invite a group of girls over for a sleepover? I'll farm Holly and Abbey out for the night and you can have the place to yourselves – apart from me, of course. You can get the latest rom-com DVD and popcorn and ice cream in – what do you say?'

Maddy's face lit up. 'Okay.' Her face fell again. 'But what about Roz?'

'Invite her too. I guarantee she'll not come – not when she has to face me – but that way she can't complain that she's been excluded.'

Maddy nodded her head slowly, warming to the idea. 'Do you think it'll work, Mum? I mean, do you think it'll get the others back on my side?'

'I'm sure of it,' said Joanne and she summoned up the most reassuring smile she could manage, wishing that her problems were so easily solved.

Downstairs, she unpacked the groceries, while Heidi circled her expectantly. Joanne went to stuff packaging in the bin only to find it full to bursting and cursed under her breath. The fifty-litre bin had seemed like a good idea at the time – but not now that she was the one that had to empty it. She dragged the heavy bag of rubbish outside and, sweating, threw it in the bin. On the way along the path, she nearly tripped over Abbey's bike, where it had lain since the chain had come off two days ago.

This single mother lark was everything she had imagined it would be. Lonely, frustrating and hard bloody work. And with no one to do the things that a man about the house would do, even one as useless as Phil, the house was falling apart, or so it seemed. Dad, bless him, had helpfully given her one of his old DIY books called *Essential Repairs Around the Home.* He'd meant well, but every time she glanced at it, wedged in beside the bread bin and the side of the fridge, she wanted to cry.

She fitted a new bin liner and let the lid slam shut with a loud clang. She finished emptying the shopping bags and then cried, 'I don't believe it!' She looked forlornly at the blocks of butter and cheese and cartons of orange juice strewn across the counter. She'd forgotten to buy a chicken for lunch. The thought of getting in the car and going back to the supermarket was more than she could bear. She sat down at the table, put her head in her hands, and allowed herself a few silent tears of pity.

And she thought of Gemma – the person she would've phoned right now if she hadn't been the architect of her misery. She had thought their friendship invincible and eternal. A friendship that would ride out storms and stand the test of time. She had assumed that they would be there for each other when they both sailed into their golden years, two white-haired old dears marvelling over trials overcome, children grown and married, grandchildren and great-grandchildren. She had lost the best friend she'd ever had. And that brought fresh tears to her eyes.

'What's wrong, Mummy?' said Holly's voice and Joanne quickly wiped her face and looked up.

'Nothing.'

'Please stop crying, Mummy.'

'I'm not crying,' smiled Joanne.

'Yes, you are. You're always crying,' said Holly.

'Oh, sweetheart. Come here.' Joanne gestured to her daughter to come closer and hauled her onto her knee where she sat awkwardly, her face solemn, her eyes watchful and wary, long legs dangling only inches from the floor. 'I'm crying because I forgot to buy a chicken at the supermarket,' said Joanne. 'And now we have nothing for lunch.'

'Oh,' said Holly and her face brightened. 'I forgot to tell you. When you were out Auntie Sian called and asked us over to her house for lunch.'

'She did? Wonderful!' Relief flooded through Joanne and she smiled and this time it was genuine. Good old Sian. She had saved the day – and Joanne's sanity. For she wasn't quite ready to face Sundays alone with only the girls for company. 'Well, that's brilliant news.'

Holly shrugged and looking a little sheepish, bunched up her slender shoulders. 'Mum?' she said quietly, her nail-bitten hands sandwiched between her legs.

'What?'

Holly fiddled with the hem of her top, avoiding eye contact. 'When's Dad coming home?'

'He's not, darling.'

Holly looked into her mother's eyes, horrified. 'What? Not ever?'

Joanne swallowed, holding back the emotion like a dam. 'No, I don't think so.'

Holly's eyes filled with tears. 'But I miss him.'

Joanne stroked her daughter's cheek with the back of her hand. Her freckles, coaxed out by the summer sun, were fading now. 'I know.' Perhaps Phil had been a better

287

dad than she'd given him credit for. 'But you'll still see him every week. It's not like he's gone completely.'

'It's not the same.' Holly looked up into her mother's eyes. 'If you both said you were sorry for shouting at each other, and made up, he might come home, mightn't he?'

Joanne shook her head.

'But that's what you tell me to do when I fall out with one of my friends. It works, most of the time anyway. And,' she added, crossly, 'you won't even try.'

Joanne sighed. How could she expect a ten-year-old to understand the complexities of a relationship that were, largely, beyond her own comprehension? She saw every day the damage the separation was doing to her daughters. And she hated Phil for that.

'Holly,' she said, at last, 'your dad and I have tried to make up, lots of times. In the past. But sometimes you just can't be friends with someone and you have to accept that.'

Holly narrowed her eyes. 'It's because of Gemma, isn't it? It's because he likes her more than you.'

Joanne bit her lip and considered this. 'Yes.'

Holly's face coloured and she pressed her lips together, the way she did when she was mad. 'Then I hate her.'

To her shame Joanne said, 'So do I.'

'And I hate you,' cried Holly, and she ran out of the room before her mother could respond.

Joanne sighed. How long were the girls going to carry on blaming her? She knew exactly how they felt – insecure, vulnerable, afraid. She hated it and she hated feeling so powerless. Sudden anger welled up inside her and she marched outside to the garage. She assembled a selection of tools, and clutching them in her hands, marched back into the house and up the stairs. When she burst open the bathroom door she found a startled Maddy standing in front of the mirror putting on her make-up. She said in astonishment, 'Mum, what're you doing?'

Joanne dropped the tools on the bathroom floor with a clatter. 'I'm fixing the lock.'

Maddy frowned. 'But I thought you said Grandad would have to do it. Or a handyman.'

Joanne, slightly out of breath, laughed as she unscrewed the brass finger plate around the door handle and the cover fell off, revealing a mosaic of screws and springs. 'Haven't you heard of girls doing it for themselves, Maddy?'

'Huh?'

'I've decided. Instead of waiting around for a man to do things for me – even one as sweet as your Grandad – I'm going to do them for myself. After all,' she added, with a wry smile at Maddy, 'if a man can fix it, it can't be that difficult, can it?'

When Joanne arrived at Sian's with the girls later, her parents were already there looking smart in their Sunday best and the house was full of the smell of cooking. Oli sat between them watching CBeebies. As soon as he saw Abbey and Holly, he scrabbled off the sofa squealing with excitement and the three of them disappeared upstairs.

Joanne greeted her parents and set a plate of shop-bought brownies on the kitchen counter, feeling like she should have made more of an effort with her clothes. She'd not bothered to change out of her jeans – but then neither had Sian. Her rust-coloured needle cords had a worn patch on the left knee and she wore a crumpled cream blouse that looked like it could do with an introduction to an iron. 'Something smells good,' said Joanne, glancing round the kitchen. Two jars of sprouting beans sat by the kitchen taps, jostling for space with a plastic tub for compost scraps.

'Veggie lasagne,' said Sian. 'Thanks for the brownies by the way.'

'Can I go on your computer, Auntie Sian?' said Maddy, barefoot in black opaque tights, a short, frayed denim skirt and a ludicrously overpriced, red Jack Wills hoodie – a present for her birthday in May and her most prized possession. 'I just want to check MSN and Facebook.'

'Sure, you know where it is,' said Sian. Maddy gave her an affectionate peck on the cheek and disappeared upstairs.

'I fixed the bathroom lock today,' said Joanne beaming with pride. 'Plus the broken chain on Abbey's bike and the wonky bedside lamp in Maddy's room.'

'Well done. What's got into you?'

Joanne picked a slice of courgette from a bowl of salad. 'I was just fed up feeling like a victim. And I know it probably sounds ridiculous but it felt like a sort of turning point for me. Like I was back in control and not waiting around for other people to come and sort things out for me.'

'It doesn't sound ridiculous at all. I'm glad you're feeling more positive about things.'

There was a short pause while Sian checked things in the oven and when she straightened up, she said, 'Well, wait till you hear the latest news. Louise is meeting Cameron at The Marine Hotel – that's why Oli's here.'

Joanne's mouth fell open and Sian pressed a glass of white wine into her hand. 'Here, take this and I'll tell you all about it.'

They went and sat with their parents and Sian quickly filled them in on the events of the night before, giving them a blow-by-blow account of Cameron's surprise appearance.

When she'd heard the full story, and recovered from her astonishment, Joanne said, 'I hope she knows what she's doing.

After all the heartache he's caused her . . .' She left the sentence unfinished and shook her head sadly.

'Well, I think it'd be nice if there was a reconciliation,' said Christine. 'I always liked Cameron.'

'We all did, Mum,' said Sian quietly, 'but he hurt her. I don't want to see that happen again.'

'None of us do, pet,' said her father, sitting with a glass of beer in his hand, looking rather sombre. 'But what can you do? If she loves him . . .'

'He could have changed,' said Christine hopefully.

'And she could do worse,' said Billy. 'After all, better the devil you know. And that child needs a father.'

'Dad!' protested Sian. 'In case you don't recall, Cameron never wanted to be a father. That's why they split in the first place. What makes you think he's suddenly changed his mind? He's not interested in Oli. He couldn't even remember his name or how old he was.'

'Doesn't alter the fact that the child needs a father,' said Billy stubbornly and this time his comment was met with silence.

'No, he doesn't *need* a father,' said Joanne, who had been quiet for some time, and everyone looked at her in surprise. She looked at her hands, her nails in need of a good manicure, and went on, 'It would be nice if he had one, but I think he'll manage just as well without. Ideally, every child would grow up in a traditional family with two parents but how many kids have that luxury nowadays? Look at mine,' she said grimly. 'And how can Oli miss something he's never had? His mum will always put him first – look what she sacrificed to have him – and he's surrounded by people who love him. I can't see much wrong with that.'

Her mother tutted her disagreement.

'Well,' said Joanne in response, 'let me put it this way, who do you think is happier just now? Oli or my daughters?'

No one replied and Joanne carried on, staring into her drink. 'I've done a lot of thinking over the past few weeks. And it's true, I was very critical of Louise but I think now that perhaps I was wrong to judge her the way I did. She's capable of giving Oli everything he needs to grow up happy and well-balanced. I've struggled for years, none of them very happy, to keep my family together and it's blown up in my face. I know it's only a matter of time before Phil lets the girls down. In fact, he's already done it.'

'How's that?' asked her father, with a glum face.

'Well, you know how I decided to take that pharmacy job?'

Everyone nodded.

'I asked Phil if he could have the girls for part of the Christmas holidays – they get more than two weeks off you know – and now he says he can't take the time off work. Wait till I tell Holly and Abbey that they're going to have to go to Holiday Club,' she said grimly. Holiday Club was an extension of after-school care.

'And what about Maddy?' said Sian. 'What's she going to do?'

Joanne shook her head.

'I know,' said Sian all of a sudden. 'Why doesn't she come and work in the shop? Bernie's going away and I could use the help. She could do mornings for me, right through till two. She'd be doing me a favour and you'd know where she was – for part of the day, anyway.'

'That'd be fantastic!' said Joanne, feeling her worry evaporate.

Sian smiled and then said, 'Don't beat yourself up about

what's happened, Joanne. It's not your fault. And from what I can see the girls seem to be coping just fine.'

Joanne's reply was instinctive. 'No, they're not. Holly asked me this morning when Phil was coming home. And Maddy told me that she hated me and it was all my fault he'd left. Oh, and Abbey thinks that too.'

Billy shook his head sadly. 'Dear, oh, dear.'

'That's what I mean about Oli,' Joanne went on. 'He's never going to have to face that disappointment, is he?'

'He might have other problems to contend with,' said Sian darkly.

Billy frowned. 'Like what?'

'Like a step-father who doesn't seem all that interested in him.'

Christine let out a deep sigh and everyone turned to look at her. She opened her mouth to speak then closed it, her lips pursed together like she was holding something in.

'What, Mum?' said Joanne.

She sighed heavily again, and shook her head. 'I sometimes wonder where your father and I went wrong.'

'What does that mean?' said Sian and she shared a look with Joanne.

'A grandson born out of wedlock. One daughter divorced, another one separated, and one,' she said, staring pointedly at Sian, 'living in sin.'

Billy, shifting in his seat, looked uncomfortable but he did not contradict his wife – he always avoided confrontation with her.

'I can't believe how old-fashioned you are,' said Joanne, suddenly cross. 'We're all good daughters. And we have good jobs, pay our taxes, look after ourselves – and Louise and I have four gorgeous children between us. And I, for one, am not separated through choice. You should be proud of us, not ashamed.'

Billy raised his hand. 'Ah, now. To be fair, your mother didn't say she was ashamed of you.'

'Disappointed then,' said Sian, with her arms folded protectively across her chest.

'Not even that,' said Billy sadly and then he addressed his wife as much as his daughters. 'Maybe we are old-fashioned. It's just that, well, the world we grew up in was a simpler place, wasn't it? People got married and stayed married and no respectable, unmarried woman got herself pregnant and kept the child.' He looked at the palms of his hands as though searching for the truth there. 'When you were little girls all I wanted was to see you all married one day with good husbands and healthy kids.'

'And living happily ever after. It sounds like a fairytale,' said Sian, cynically.

Christine blinked, her pale blue eyes watery. 'I think what your dad's trying to say is that we never dreamt you girls would have such hard choices to make in life. But we support you in them. We wouldn't want any of you to stay in an unhappy relationship. Or see Louise without Oli. So I suppose this is the modern world and we just have to get used to it.'

'This is Cameron, Oli,' said Louise, holding her son firmly by the shoulders in front of her as if he might slip from her grasp like a slippery fish. They were standing in her little lounge dressed to go out. Louise had slept little the night before and come to no conclusions regarding Cameron, bar one – it was essential that he meet Oli.

'Oh,' said Cameron and his face coloured a little. Then he seemed to regain his composure. 'Well, hello there, little man,' he said, without coming down to the child's level. 'How are you?' And he held out his hand to Oli as if he were a little businessman.

Oli turned his face into his mother's skirt and said, 'I want to stay here.'

Cameron, standing there with his hand outstretched, cleared his throat and plunged his hand back into his pocket.

'He's a bit out of sorts—' she started to explain but Cameron cut across her.

'He can't really come with us. I thought your sister said she'd mind him.' He looked at Oli and frowned.

'Of course he's not coming with us,' said Louise, a little irritably. Did he credit her with no sense? 'I'm going to take him over to Sian's now. I just thought it'd be nice if you two met first.'

'Yes, good idea. I just assumed that you'd have dropped him off already. My mistake.' He consulted his watch and added, 'Shall we get going? I was thinking we might go to The Londonderry Arms in Carnlough. We can go in my hire car.'

'No,' said Louise instinctively, her hand caressing the back of Oli's head. Cameron looked at her. They'd first visited Carnlough and 'The Derry' as newly-weds and had returned many times afterwards on visits home. The suggestion that they return there now, as estranged spouses, seemed wholly inappropriate to Louise.

'Let's stay closer to home. I know,' she said, thinking on her feet, 'why don't I go and drop Oli at Sian's? We can meet in the bar at The Marine Hotel in what?' she consulted her watch, 'twenty minutes?'

'Oh, okay,' he said, looking disappointed. 'But we can still have lunch, right?'

'I'm not hungry. You can eat if you want to. The bar food at The Marine is pretty good.' How on earth did he possibly think she would be able to eat? Her stomach was tied up in knots.

'Bye Oli,' said Cameron but, to Louise's chagrin, the child ignored him.

She let them both out of the flat, put Oli in the car and drove him to Sian's. Crisp, dry leaves skittered across the road in the breeze and broken clouds, some heavy with the promise of rain, scuttled across a pale blue sky. Louise scowled. The meeting between Cameron and Oli hadn't gone as well as she would've liked – but Oli was always shy of new people. She felt certain that if he and Cameron spent some time together, they would become firm friends. Just like Oli and Kevin.

In the back seat Oli played with a toy Kevin had given him – a tiny plastic Superman, which had come free in a cereal box. A thoughtful, rather than a showy gift – that was Kevin all over. Just like the little chocolate bar he'd given Oli the first day he met him. Had Cameron known he was going to meet Oli today, no doubt he would've given him a small gift too . . .

Her heartbeat quickened and sweat pricked the back of her neck – she uncoiled the scarf from around her neck and threw it onto the passenger seat. She felt desperately guilty about Kevin, as though this meeting with Cameron was somehow clandestine. But she'd been honest with Kevin, hadn't she? She tried to convince herself that she'd done nothing wrong. Except that she had hurt him and she'd never intended to do that. Would he ever forgive her?

And guilt wasn't the only reason she felt uncomfortable. What was she doing meeting up with her ex-husband at

The Marine Hotel, him carrying on as if they were on a date? Had she forgotten that they'd spent the last year of their marriage fighting, driven apart by conflicting values and ambitions? Why was she letting him into her life again without any idea where this was going?

Cameron was waiting for her at the bar, on a tall stool. The place was relatively quiet, as she had known it would be, some of the tables taken by people eating bar lunches. The pleasant hum of conversation provided background noise. While he ordered her a drink, Louise took a proper look at her ex-husband. He was dressed much the same as the night before, except she could see the collar of a clean white shirt sticking up under his jacket. This morning he was freshly shaved and the daylight revealed a healthy tanned complexion acquired, if past history was anything to go by, on the golf course.

In profile, he had a small bump on the bridge of his nose and his forehead sloped back slightly from a strong brow. Exactly as she remembered it. How intimately she had once known every line and contour of that face – and how she had loved it. She looked away and reminded herself sternly that she was here for answers.

When they'd got their drinks Louise said, coldly, 'Cameron, what do you want from me?'

'Why don't we take a seat over there?' he said, gesturing to a table in the corner. 'Where we can talk properly?'

They sat down and he said, immediately, 'Do you mind if I order something to eat?' but he was already gesturing the barman over. 'Please have something too.'

'No thanks.'

He ordered himself fish and chips to go with his pint of Guinness. He clasped his hands together and rested his forearms on the table, the stout, black as peat, sitting on the

297

table in front of him. Louise stared at her glass of Sauvignon Blanc, too nauseated by nerves to drink it.

'So,' he said staring at the table. He hesitated momentarily and looked at her, the little pause paving the way for the conversation he'd come all this way to have. 'It sounds as though you're quite settled here.'

'I am. I love my job and being near my family.'

He put the pint glass to his lips, just as he'd been instructed to by her father who had tutored him in the art of drinking Guinness, and took a long, slow drink of the stout. When he put the glass down, one-third was gone, leaving a trail of lacy white froth on the sides. Cameron wiped his mouth with the back of his hand. 'But you haven't bought anywhere yet, have you?'

She frowned. 'No, not yet. But I've put down a deposit on the house at Loughanlea, the development where Sian lives. I'm looking forward to moving in come the spring.'

He nodded and knit his brows together as if this information perplexed him. 'Just a deposit,' he said. And then, moving on swiftly, 'I bought a house in Nile Grove a few months ago.'

Morningside. One of Edinburgh's most desirable addresses. She knew the area well because they had often visited the Dominion Cinema on Newbattle Terrace and sometimes browsed in the shops on Morningside Road.

'It's in the conservation area of the village,' he said, using the slightly affected local euphemism for the city suburb. Morningside may once have been a village but now it was entirely consumed by the great Edinburgh urban sprawl.

'Nice.'

'Yeah, it is. It's a six-bed Victorian on three floors with gardens front and back. It's got a huge conservatory the length of the building at the back. And three reception rooms. Bay windows and balconies, all that old architectural stuff you like so much.'

'You must be doing well,' she observed, ignoring his last comment. She put the glass to her lips and took a sip of wine, trying not to look impressed. A house of that size in Morningside would cost a fortune. How had Cameron, a manager with a telecoms company, gone from a modest flat in Stockbridge to a Morningside mansion in four short years?

'One of my mum's unmarried sisters left me money in her will,' he said, answering her question. 'Do you remember my Aunt Gladys?'

Louise nodded. She recalled Cameron's spinster aunt from their wedding day – a sprightly, white-haired lady in her seventies who clearly doted on her nephew. 'I'm sorry she died.'

Cameron accepted her sympathy with a slight nod of the head. 'I spent some of the inheritance on the property,' he said and added, casting the next sentence out like a fishing line with a hook on the end, 'It's a big house for just one person.'

Louise swallowed. He was right. The house he described, and which she could clearly picture, was a family home, not somewhere a single, guy-about-town would choose to live. With that kind of money at his disposal, Cameron could've bought a luxury penthouse flat near the city centre. So why had he purchased it?

'You never remarried?' she said.

He shook his head.

'And you don't have a girlfriend? A partner?'

'No.' He stared at the pint glass and turned it round three times, as though examining it from every angle. There was a long pause. Had she embarrassed him with questions that were too personal, that she had no right to ask? The noise of the diners nearby only served to highlight the silence between them.

Louise, suddenly self-conscious, looked away. 'I'm sorry,' she said, looking at her hands, 'I shouldn't have asked you that. It's none of my business.'

'No, I'm glad you did,' he said and stared at her, his pupils wide in the relative darkness of the bar. He opened his mouth.

And then the barman appeared with the food. He set the plate down with some cutlery and disappeared.

Cameron was still staring at her, apparently oblivious to the meal in front of him. 'I want to be honest with you, Louise. It was kind of fun being single again but the novelty soon wore off. Everyone I know is married now, and most of them have families. I've dated several women since we split up. Even moved in with one for six months. They were all great,' he said, and he looked up and to the right and paused momentarily. 'But,' he said bringing his gaze back to her, 'none of them worked out. After a while I realised that the reason I couldn't build a successful relationship was because none of them could hold a candle to you. I was always comparing them to you, you see, and they always came up short. It took me a long time to admit to myself that I was still in love with you, Louise.'

She sat utterly motionless, her breath coming in short, shallow gasps, while the noise around her seemed to recede like a tide. She was mesmerised by the earnest expression on his face and the words on his lips, words that any woman in the world would have been thrilled to hear.

Cameron shifted in his seat. His broad, athletic shoulders strained the yoke of the white shirt. He rested his chin on his clasped hands, his elbows on the table. 'I've thought about you every day for the last four years.' He paused, cleared his throat. 'I bought the house for you. And our children.'

'Our children?' she said, dull with shock. 'Since when have you wanted children?'

'Yes, I know that'll come as a surprise to you. It came as a surprise to me too.' He looked at her from under his eyebrows and his face broke into a wide, warm grin.

Louise did not know how to take this news. Her emotions fluctuated wildly and they were not good ones – bitterness, disbelief, anger. Memories of the precise moment when she knew their marriage was over flooded her mind – memories she would rather forget.

Like lots of men, Cameron had played the commitment dance. They'd lived together for four years before they got married and, looking back, the road to the altar had been a long and tortuous one. She recalled, with some pain, that he had probably never asked her to marry him. It had been a mutual decision they'd arrived at after several booze-filled discussions, of which she could not remember much except the fact that she had got what she wanted – in the end. Perhaps his reluctance to commit had been part of the attraction. Once married, she ignored his derisive comments about 'rugrats' and overweight mothers and how he pitied and despised gaunt-eyed, new parents walking their brats in the park, their social lives blighted forever. She had ignored all this because she knew that when they had *their* baby, it would be different.

But the years rolled on and there was no baby, only excuses – they were too young (what was the hurry?); he couldn't compromise his chance of promotion; her job was too busy; how on earth would they ever fit a child into their hectic lives? Then there was all the (expensive) travelling he wanted to do – Thailand, a safari in Kenya, the Florida Keys, South America. Adventures he kept pointing out that they could not afford, or undertake, if they had a screaming kid in tow. Oh yes, they had some great adventures – but no baby.

The signs were all there, right from day one, but she was so in love, so determined to have him and mould him into the father of her children, that she had closed her eyes to the warnings. But over the years her frustration grew and they drifted further and further apart. At last, at her insistence, he agreed to go for marriage counselling.

And it was there, sitting in the drab, brown office of a therapist with a beard and patches on the elbows of his tweed jacket, that she finally heard the truth. The words Cameron could say to a complete stranger, but in all their years of marriage, could not bring himself to say to her face.

'I don't want to have children. I don't want to be a father.'

She tuned back in to what Cameron was saying, his face alive with excitement and possibility. 'I've changed, Louise, my priorities have changed. I guess I was immature back then. It's taken me a while to grow up. But I know what I want now. I want a wife and a family and all the noise and mess that goes with it – and a dog, a Golden Labrador!' He smiled then, broadly. 'All the things you want too.'

He was right. It was what she'd wanted years ago – it was what she wanted still. And he had it all worked out. But there was only one thing wrong – it was years too late. And she was forty-one now – her chances of having more children were in no way guaranteed. 'Let me get this straight, you want us to pick up the pieces where we left off and carry on?'

'Yes. I don't see any good reason why not.'

'But what about Oli? Have you forgotten about him?'

302

'Of course not, Oli will be part of our family. But we'll have other children too, Louise. It's not too late for either of us. Maybe a boy and a girl. I know I messed up, Louise, big time. And I know you might find it hard to forgive me, but please give me another chance to show you that I can be a good husband – and a good father.'

She was momentarily speechless. If all this was true, then Cameron was utterly transformed from the man she had divorced. 'I was angry with you, Cameron, and I guess a part of me still is. But once I had Oli, and I realised what you were missing out on, I mostly felt sorry for you.'

He reached out and took her hand in his. His firm, hot grip sent a bolt of electricity down her spine. 'I'm asking you to marry me, Louise. Again. If you'll have me.'

Louise could hear her own heartbeat pounding in her ears. He was offering her everything she'd ever dreamt of. A beautiful home, the big family she had always wanted, a comfortable life, even a dog! And the chance to put back together a marriage that she'd been forced to leave, but never wanted to. She thought of her marriage vows – *for richer, for poorer, in sickness and in health, till death us do part* – and realised that here was a chance to make it right again. The divorce had legally dissolved her marriage. But, in her heart, she felt as though part of her would always belong to Cameron.

He squeezed her hand. 'I've money set aside to put the children through private school. I'd make sure they had the best of everything. And Oli would have a dad,' he said. 'I would adopt him, of course. Give him a proper family.'

Something about this last comment jarred and she could not let it go unremarked upon. She had fought so hard to prove that her little family, whilst unconventional, was as legitimate as the next. 'We are a proper family,' she heard herself saying and she gently removed her hand from his hot grasp. 'Me and Oli. And we're doing just fine, the two of us.'

He patted the back of her hand where it lay on the table. Her fourth finger was bare – it had taken months for the imprint of her wedding band and engagement ring to completely fade. And it had taken much longer for her to get used to the idea that she was no longer married.

'Of course you are,' he said. 'And I think you've managed brilliantly on your own.' He gave her a warm smile. 'But wouldn't it be nice to share the burden of parenthood? And every kid wants a mum and dad, don't they?'

He had touched a raw nerve. It was one of the things she feared most about Oli getting older – realising everyone else had a dad and he didn't. And hating her for it. She broke eye contact and stared into the fire. She loved Cameron but she harboured resentment towards him. It had hardened round her heart like play dough left out uncovered for too long. She must not let that get in the way of what was best – for her and Oli.

'What do you say, Louise?'

'I wish . . . I wish you'd thought like this before. It would've saved me – both of us, I imagine – a lot of heartache.'

'I know. And I'm sorry.'

'It wasn't the way I wanted it to happen,' she said quickly, lest he misunderstand her meaning, 'but I'm glad I had Oli. He's the best thing that ever happened to me.'

Cameron nodded and looked at the food on his plate. 'I ought to eat this,' he said, 'before this gets very much colder.'

He took a swig of Guinness and picked up his knife and fork. Louise said, 'You're asking me to move back to Edinburgh?'

'Uh-huh,' he mumbled, his mouth full. He covered it with his hand.

Of course he was. Cameron would never settle in Northern Ireland – he'd made no secret of the fact, when they were dating, that he thought the place provincial and backward. Still it was worth a try, just to be sure. 'Would you ever consider coming here to live? In Ballyfergus?'

He made a little noise in the base of his throat. He glanced about the room as if collecting visual information and said, 'Are you serious?' Then he went on without waiting for her answer. 'Ballyfergus is a lovely wee town, Louise, don't get me wrong, but wouldn't you rather live in one of the most stunning cities in the world?'

'I did,' she said, thinking of the break-in, 'but it wasn't all champagne and roses. I actually prefer Ballyfergus.'

'Well, you were raised here, Louise. Of course it's going to feel like home. But it feels . . . alien to me. I'm sorry, I could never see myself living here.'

Cameron was the one responsible for this mess. Through his immaturity – which he'd readily admitted to – he'd caused the break-up of their marriage. And now that he'd come round to her opinion, he thought nothing of asking her to drop everything and high-tail it back to Edinburgh.

She sat in silence for a few moments trying to analyse her confused feelings. Part of her wanted desperately to accept Cameron's offer. She had never stopped loving him, in spite of everything that had happened. He'd offered to adopt Oli and give her the children that she wanted, but would never have if she remained single. It was hard enough raising one child alone, she would not have others, not as a single parent. She could picture her future now – her, Cameron, Oli, and siblings yet to be born – living in the big house in Morningside full of toys and dog hairs and laughter and sun streaming in the tall period windows. And she smiled inside when she saw herself mistress of this busy, happy home.

And yet, accepting his offer, tempting though it was, would mean giving up so much. She clasped her hands under the table.

She'd worked hard to build an independent life here for herself and Oli. Only now was it all coming together. She'd finally found her feet at work, Oli was settled both at nursery and with Klaudia, and she'd set her heart on her new home. She already knew exactly what colour she was going to paint Oli's bedroom and where she was going to display her collection of Art Deco pottery, currently in storage.

She loved being part of her sisters' lives and, of course, there was Kevin whom she had come to love. Not a mad, passionate, grand affair kind of love but a gentle kind of love based on mutual respect, kindness and shared interests. The problem was, it was too early to say if they had a future together, if they would be compatible as man and wife. Whereas she knew Cameron better than she knew anyone else.

And she still longed to be married, to have a husband and for her son to have a father.

'I can't just drop everything, Cameron. Oli and I, well, we're very happy here.'

Cameron set down his knife and fork. 'And I can make you just as happy in Edinburgh, Louise, happier even. I know I can. Don't you remember how good we were together – in every way?' She blushed and looked away. The physical attraction had been an important part of their relationship and their lust for each other had never waned even after years of marriage. Sometimes, it was the physical intimacy she missed the most. Her life of self-imposed celibacy was only bearable because she had Oli. But she did not want to live like this forever.

'I know you can't move back overnight,' Cameron went on. 'I appreciate that it'll take a few months to get things sorted.'

She thought of her son – how upset he would be at leaving Klaudia and nursery. Not to mention his aunts, cousins and Uncle Andy. And what about his grandparents? Moving close to them had been at the core of her grand plan. It seemed so unbearably cruel to bring Oli into the heart of his extended family, to expose him to their loving warmth, only to wrest him from it again. And not only would she be letting her employers down, she would be letting down Sian, who she had promised to help, too. And there was Joanne, struggling to cope with her new status as a single mum and desperately in need of a helping hand also.

She realised a long time had passed in silence and she focused once more on Cameron. He gave her a hard stare and the softness had gone out of his eyes. They were cold like the flat grey sea in the Lough on a cloudy, windless day. 'There's someone else, isn't there?'

She looked away. 'No.' Silence. 'Possibly.'

'What does that mean?' he said. His left hand, that lay on the table, curled into a fist.

She looked into his face. His eyes had narrowed slightly, and his brow was furrowed. She remembered how Cameron liked to get his own way. 'I have met someone,' she said. 'We've gone out a few times. And he's met Oli.'

Cameron nodded slowly, and unclenched his fist. 'I see,' he said slowly. 'But has he asked you to marry him?'

Louise smiled and gave a half-hearted laugh. 'Of course not. I've known him less than two months.'

His fist unclenched and he nodded knowingly, as if this information, if not exactly pleasing, was satisfying.

'Louise,' he said. He leant forward and lowered his voice. 'I'm flying back to Scotland tomorrow and I need to have your answer by then.'

Chapter Fifteen

The taxi dropped the girls off and Joanne ran out to it, parked beneath a lamppost outside her house, before it could drive off. She took a deep breath. If Louise could have lunch and a civilised conversation with her ex-husband, then so could she. It was time to put emotions aside and find some way to get along for the girls' sake. And for her own – she felt like her anger was eroding her soul, turning her into a nasty, bitter person she did not recognise and did not like.

Phil, a dark shadow in the front passenger seat, rolled down the window.

'I was wondering if I could have a word, please,' she said. She could hardly bring herself to speak civilly to him – invariably every time they saw each other it degenerated into a fight.

'What about?' His face was creased up in a frown, his eyes narrow and unreadable in the darkness. The taxi driver stared straight ahead and tapped his fingers on the steering wheel.

'Holidays and things,' she said pulling her cardigan around her against the November chill. 'Look, why don't you come inside for a minute? We can't talk properly out here.'

He stared straight ahead for a few moments, then sighed loudly. 'Okay, all right. I'll be right in once I've settled up here.'

In the hallway Holly was waiting with Abbey at her side. 'Is Daddy coming in?' she said, her little face full of hope.

The expectation in her face was too much to bear. Joanne had to look away. 'Yes, darling. But only because we need to discuss some practical things.'

Holly giggled nervously, Abbey copied her and they both shared a knowing look. Joanne sighed and gave them a hard stare. She did not want them getting their hopes up, reading too much into the simple fact that Phil was in the house for the first time in weeks. And the fact that she had swapped her grey sweatpants for jeans and touched up her make-up. But she'd done this only because she did not want him to see her as a loser.

'Like what?' said Maddy's wary voice from behind and Joanne turned round to find her standing in the doorway.

'Well, mostly holidays.'

'I don't want to go to that after-school club ever again,' said Holly, throwing herself down on the sofa with her arms crossed, her face thunderous. In preparation for starting her new job, Joanne had booked the girls in for a trial run one day after school and it had not gone well. 'It was horrible!'

'Me neither!' cried Abbey, flopping down beside her elder sister.

'Well, I can't promise either of you that,' said Joanne, evenly. 'But your dad and I will do our best to—'

'To what?' said Phil and Joanne turned around. He was standing behind Maddy, whose jaw was taut with tension, no doubt waiting for her parents to launch into a slanging match at any moment. Joanne blushed with shame and resolved to keep this encounter civilised, no matter what the cost.

Phil wore his usual going-out clothes of smart trousers, shirt and V-neck jumper, under an open golf jacket. He looked

310

well, if a little thin and pale. There was a time, she thought sadly, when she would've remarked on his appearance, perhaps encouraged him to take a multi-vitamin. But his health was now no concern of hers.

Suddenly a flash of black fur appeared from nowhere and launched itself at Phil. It was Heidi, slobbering and panting and wagging her tail like something demented. She raised her muzzle to his face, trying to 'kiss' him on the lips as she liked to do but he was too tall. 'Get down, you daft dog,' he said, pushing her down. He ruffled the top of her long flat head.

'She's missed you, Dad,' squealed Holly. 'See Mum. Look how much Heidi's missed Dad.'

Joanne forced a faint smile while Heidi continued to yap and lick and entwine herself around Phil's legs. Eventually she calmed down and flopped on the floor in the lounge.

Joanne looked at Phil. 'I was just saying that we were going to try and sort out our holidays a bit better so that the girls don't have to go into Holiday Club as often.'

'It's not my fault I can't take them at Christmas,' he said defensively, 'I haven't got enough holidays left.'

Joanne smiled pleasantly, and it felt like her face would crack. 'I understand that can't be helped,' she said and a little air went out of him. His shoulders lowered an inch and he said, 'Oh.'

'Maddy,' she said, seizing the initiative, 'could you put a DVD on for the girls please? Your dad and I are going to talk in the kitchen.'

Maddy folded her arms and gave her mother a hard stare. Joanne touched her lightly on the arm. 'We're just going to talk. I promise.'

In the kitchen, she opened the fridge and took out a bottle of white wine.

'Look, Joanne,' said Phil, standing behind a chair with his hands on the back. He looked nervous. 'I don't really see what there is to talk about. Can't we sort this out through our lawyers?'

Joanne peeled off the metal foil covering the cork. 'I don't think we need lawyers to arrange a few holiday dates.'

He frowned. 'But I thought we had access arrangements sorted out. The girls come to me every Wednesday night and one night every other weekend. Hey,' he said and he raised his right hand, the palm presented to her like a shield. His voice, when he went on, was slightly panicked. 'I hope you're not wanting to change the arrangements because if you are—'

'I'm not,' she said, interrupting and he stopped abruptly. He'd completely missed the point – she was talking about holidays, not weekly arrangements. She knew what he was getting himself in a flap about. Right now he and Gemma had Tuesday nights and every other weekend to themselves. He was worried that she might upset this cosy apple cart. It was pathetic. He was pathetic. She found the corkscrew made from recycled metal that Sian had given them as an anniversary present a few years ago. She pushed the tip of the spiral into the cork, twisted it as far as it would go, then placed the bottle between her knees and pulled hard, blood pulsing in her neck with the effort.

'Do you want me to—' he said, half-heartedly.

'No. I can manage.' To her relief, the cork slid out smoothly and noiselessly. Just another new skill on her growing list.

She set two glasses on the table and poured herself some wine. 'Want one?'

'No,' he said and glanced at his watch.

'Suit yourself.' She sat down at the table and placed the bottle in front of her.

'I really need to be going. I'm meeting the guys for a beer and a game of pool.'

She smiled at this, wondering if he was indeed meeting his mates or using it as a cover to cheat on Gemma.

He looked at her warily. 'What's so funny?'

'Nothing.' She took a slug of wine.

'So what did you want to talk to me about?'

'Come on. Sit down, Phil. I'm not going to bite.'

He glanced at his watch again, let out a long sigh and pulled out the chair opposite her. He sat down and looked at the bottle of wine. 'I might have a glass, after all.'

'Help yourself.'

He filled the glass. 'Thanks.' He took a drink and there was a silence. He cleared his throat and looked at the table. 'I'm sorry things didn't work out between us, Joanne.'

She stared at him, astonished. It was the first time he'd displayed the slightest hint of remorse.

'But I couldn't take any more, Joanne. To live like that . . . being constantly belittled, made to feel like I was incompetent at everything, the constant nagging. And the way you used to speak to me in front of the girls . . . Gemma, well, she listens to me – she makes me feel like I matter.'

She paused, because there was some truth in what he said. But, remembering that the best form of defence was attack, she took a deep breath. 'Now just a minute. I never—'

'Gemma told me, Joanne. She told me how you did nothing but complain about me all the time.'

Joanne felt her face colour. 'She did, did she? What else did she share with you, Phil? Things that I told her in confidence? Things that shouldn't be shared with anyone, least of all you.'

He sighed, raised his hand. 'I didn't need Gemma to tell

me that you despised me. I could feel it every time I came into a room.'

Joanne sighed sadly and took a drink of wine. 'It wasn't the best marriage, was it?'

'No,' he said and looked at the table, tracing the grain in the wood with his index finger. 'But maybe I didn't handle things very well, walking out like that.'

'That's not what hurt me the most, Phil. It was the fact that you walked straight into the arms of my best friend. Can you not understand why I'm so angry at you both?'

He nodded.

Joanne felt another wave of hurt rise inside her. 'The two of you were having an affair behind my back, Phil. For months. Have you any idea how much that hurt me?' she went on, her voice beginning to crack. 'How betrayed I felt?'

'I do and I'm sorry. That was wrong. I should've left before I got involved with Gemma. But it happened and I do love her, Joanne. I can't change that.'

Tears pricked Joanne's eyes and she looked away, fighting bravely to keep them in check. She would not cry, she would not let him see how deeply she had been wounded. He was infatuated with Gemma. She could tell by the dreamy look that crossed his face when he mentioned her name. She was jealous – envious that she could not inspire the same devotion, torn up by the thought that Gemma was better than her in every way. And she realised that he was utterly lost to her. 'There's not much I can say to that, is there?'

There was a long silence and then he changed the subject, for which she was grateful. 'Maddy and Roz seem to have patched things up.'

Joanne sniffed. 'I know.'

'Gemma suggested that they go to the cinema together,' he said, proudly. 'It seemed to do the trick.'

Joanne swallowed the bitter lump in her throat. Phil gave Gemma too much credit for her mediation skills. The thaw had started at the sleepover when Roz, to Joanne and Maddy's surprise, had turned up. But what was the point of challenging him? Phil was too infatuated to listen.

'It means Maddy can share Roz's room when she comes to stay,' he went on, 'which is great because the three of them in the spare room is a bit of a squeeze.'

Joanne held her glass up to the light and stared at the pale, straw-coloured liquid, trying to block out what Phil was saying. She had no interest in his and Gemma's domestic arrangements. 'It's only supermarket plonk,' she said. 'It's half price at the minute. But not bad.'

He drank some and said, quietly, 'You didn't ask me in to talk about the wine.'

'That's right.'

A pause.

'Joanne, you know I'm not coming back?'

'What?' she said, slightly startled, and put a hand over her heart. 'Do you think that's why I asked you in tonight? To try and persuade you to come back?' She paused to collect her thoughts and quell the rage his assumption induced. 'Oh, don't flatter yourself, Phil,' she said and laughed carelessly. 'I'm seeing someone. I'm surprised the girls haven't mentioned it.'

She paused to let this sink in. Phil looked a little startled. It was a lie of course, but she suddenly realised that it *could* be true. She was ready to do what had only a few days ago seemed unthinkable – start dating. Why not? She was sick of the way she'd let Phil and Gemma become the focus of her life. The way she'd allowed her life to stagnate while they set up home and a new life together. Why shouldn't she have a new life too?

315

'Look,' she said, more confrontational than she'd planned. 'I asked you in because it's time you and I, both of us, stopped acting like prats and started acting like two grown-ups. We have three daughters between us and we owe it to them to try and get along.'

'You want us to be friends?' He sounded as sceptical as she felt.

'You and I can never be friends,' she said icily. 'But I don't see why we can't behave like two civilised people, especially around the girls. It's affecting them, you know. And it's setting a pretty poor example too.'

'I agree with you,' he said glumly, twirling the delicate stem of the wine glass between his big finger and thumb.

'So I think we should try to be polite to one another – even if we don't mean it.'

'Okay.'

There was a silence then, during which Joanne tried to calm her frazzled nerves. Phil really did think he was God's gift. Did he think she was so desperate that she'd actually take him back? The pathetic thing was that a few weeks ago, when she was at her lowest ebb, she probably would've. And she was ashamed of herself for being so weak. Because now, staring at her ex across the table, she saw his handsome features in a different light. Everything he had ever done was selfish. She thought of the endless worry he had caused throughout her marriage and she knew she was better off without him.

True, she had found it difficult at first, managing every-thing on her own – and it would be tougher still once she started working full-time. But she was determined to make it work. The girls would have to pull their weight around the house a bit more but that was no bad thing – they had become rather spoilt by her lifting and laying for them all the time. In short, she was confident she could manage – in fact, she could manage very well. So long as Phil kept paying the bills. And while she was financially dependent on him, she would continue to worry about him. If he lost his job, he wouldn't be able to make the payments.

'How's the desk job going?'

'Oh, so-so,' he shrugged. 'Just hanging in there. Come the middle of January I'm back on the road.'

This was good news. Once he had a car again he would be able to take the girls places and it would mean bonuses again – so no excuse not to meet his commitments.

He took another drink of wine and glanced at his watch. Putting the hurt aside, Joanne reminded herself why she had asked for this meeting, and got down to business.

'We need to have a chat about how we're going to cover the school holidays,' she said, pulling a wall planner from the pile of paper that lived permanently at the end of the table.

'I thought you said the girls were going into Holiday Club over the Christmas holidays,' he said defensively.

'They are. But we need to plan out the entire school year, Phil, not just crisis manage each holiday that comes up.' She spread the chart out in front of Phil and picked up a pencil one of the girls had left lying about. She pointed to the dates highlighted in yellow. 'These here are the school holidays – Christmas is coming up next, obviously. Then,' she said, moving the pencil to another column, 'February half-term, Easter and summer, not to mention all the bank holidays and in-service days in between. They get a lot of time off school.'

'Don't they just,' said Phil, looking a bit concerned.

'Yes. And we need to be sitting down twice a year and planning out how we're going to cover all the holidays so that we both know when we need to take time off work.'

He sat with his hands between his legs, staring at the chart. 'Sounds reasonable.'

'That's what I meant when I said we needed to be more proactive. Once I start working full-time my holidays won't be as generous – I won't for example get the summer off like I used to.'

'You won't?' he gasped.

'I've had a look at all the dates,' she said, and pulled a large piece of lined paper with handwritten calculations on it from the pile. 'And fiddled about with some figures.' She pushed the paper towards Phil, pointed at a number and said, 'Taking off weekends, there are two hundred and sixty working days in the year. The girls attend school for one hundred and ninety of them. Allowing for ten statutory holidays – St Patrick's Day and the like—'

'Spare me the maths lesson, Joanne,' he interrupted rudely. He put his head in his hands. 'Just tell me what your point is, will you?'

She counted to ten. She had spent hours on this, mulling it over, playing about with figures while she was pretty sure Phil hadn't given it a moment's thought. Why should he? She had always sorted out everything and this was no exception. She threw the pencil on the table. It rolled to the edge and fell to the floor with a slap.

'It means, Phil,' she said slowly, as if talking to an idiot, 'that there are sixty days in the year when the girls are off school and need childcare arrangements.'

'So?'

'I propose that we split them between us, thirty days each.' She rummaged for yet another piece of paper, this time with two photocopied lists of dates on it, one column headed up with her name, one headed up with Phil's. She showed it to him. 'This copy is for you. I've gone through the year and divvied the dates up as fairly and sensibly as I could. It's only a suggestion, of course, but it'll give us somewhere to start.'

He pulled the list towards him, scanned it for a few moments and then looked at her in astonishment. 'I get six weeks' holiday a year,' he said, 'plus bank holidays.'

'So do I,' she said coldly, sensing that she would not like where this conversation was going.

'Your proposal means that every single holiday I have off work I'd have to have the girls. Apart from a few bank holidays. Is that right?'

She nodded, feigning surprise that he should be questioning it, though she knew exactly what he was thinking. When would he be able to jet off on holiday with Gemma, unencumbered by kids? If Gemma was here, she'd be spitting feathers. 'So?'

'But that . . . that's—'

'Don't say it's not fair, Phil.'

He ran his hand through his hair and picked up the list of dates. 'But it isn't! I need to have a proper break from work – a couple of weeks without work or the kids.'

She shook her head, frowned and looked at the sheet of calculations once more as though perplexed, though she knew exactly what was written there. 'What do you propose then, Phil? Surely you're not suggesting that I take them for a fortnight while you swan off on holiday? I can't. I'll be working. And taking your argument to its logical conclusion, when do I get my two weeks off work without kids?'

He threw the list on the table. 'They'll just have to go into Holiday Club or your parents can look after them.' His voice was petulant, like a thwarted child.

'My parents are too old and the girls hate Holiday Club.' She leant forward a little, just managing to keep her anger in check and rather enjoying his discomfiture. She picked up the list of dates, held it up and stabbed it with her finger. 'This is what you signed up to when you became a parent, Phil.' She pointed at the back door. 'And when you walked out that door.'

She laid the sheet in front of him again and carefully flattened it with her hand, feeling strangely in control. Then she leant calmly back in her chair and folded her arms.

He shifted uncomfortably in his seat, picked up the list, folded it in four and slipped it into his pocket. 'I can't agree to this now. I'll need to give it some thought.' Discuss it with Gemma, more like.

'Fair enough. Just don't leave it too long – Christmas will be on us before we know it. And then the February break.'

Her first Christmas as a single parent and she was dreading it. How could she create a festive, happy atmosphere for the girls when their family was torn asunder?

'I want a divorce,' he said suddenly.

The words cut through her like a brutal north wind, her breath catching in her throat. This should not have come as a shock. She had been waiting for it, steeling herself for the moment when he would say those very words. It was only a matter of time before Gemma started agitating for legitimate status. And yet, when she lifted the wine glass to moisten lips suddenly too parched to speak, she found that her hand was shaking. She took a long drink and set the glass down. Her first instinct was to make this as difficult and awkward for Phil as possible. To inflict on him some of the suffering she had endured.

But then she thought of Maddy's pale, worried face and she knew she could not do that. She owed it to her girls to be reasonable at least, to try to retain whatever shred of harmony remained between her and Phil. She took a deep breath.

'Okay. On what basis?'

She could almost hear his sigh of relief. 'If you petition for divorce, I'm prepared to admit to unreasonable behaviour.' No doubt Gemma had set him up to do this. She would not be pleased at all if she didn't get her way. But Joanne was in no mood to compromise, not on this.

'No.'

'What?' He looked astonished.

'I'll petition for divorce so long as you admit to adultery and Gemma is named as the co-respondent.'

He paused for a few moments, looking dumbfounded. 'Is that really necessary?' He tried to laugh. 'I mean, do we have to let the world know our business?'

'They know it anyway, Phil. And it's the truth, isn't it? I don't mind agreeing to a divorce, Phil, but I'll not tell lies about the reasons for it.'

'Joanne, let's be reasonable about this,' he smiled.

'Take it or leave it, Phil.'

He glared at her, his fists clenched on the table.

She leant forward once more, held his gaze and lowered her voice. 'It's either that or you wait two years – five if I don't consent.' She did not mean it. She would not withhold her consent, partly because she had a sudden urge to rid herself of him, partly because it wasn't in her to be that mean. But she enjoyed watching him squirm. She thought she deserved that much.

The left corner of his mouth turned up but it wasn't a smile. 'You have been doing your homework.'

She cocked her head to the right and thought of how much he suddenly seemed to know about divorce proceedings. 'Well, looks like I'm not the only one.'

He stood and zipped his jacket up. And as he stormed out of the kitchen and slammed the back door behind him, she wondered how she was going to tell her children that their parents were getting divorced.

On Saturday afternoon, while her parents entertained the children indoors, Louise toiled happily in their back garden with Joanne – sweeping leaves, weeding and generally tidying up. Although there was little heat in the December sun, the day was clear and the wind light. Both women were well wrapped up in old jeans, fleeces and scarves and Louise, raking damp mouldy leaves into a pile in the middle of the lawn while Joanne scooped them into a bin bag, was glad to be out in the fresh air.

Joanne glanced at the house, squinting in the sun, already low in the sky. 'Listen, we haven't much time to talk. What are we going to do about Sian?'

Louise drew the rake slowly across the surface of the lawn and sighed. 'I don't know. Six weeks have passed since she told me and nothing's happened. She won't tell Andy and she won't get help.'

Joanne shook her head. 'I know. I can't seem to get through to her either.'

'I have to say it's the strangest thing I've ever heard,' said Louise. 'It's perfectly normal to be a bit apprehensive about giving birth and I'm sure there aren't many women who actually look forward to it. But this morbid fear . . . to the point where it prevents you getting pregnant. Well that's another thing.' She turned the rake on its end and picked moss off the prongs with her gloved hand.

She thought for a moment, staring at the house. Inside the kitchen she could see her mother moving about slowly. Sian had insisted they did not tell their parents about her phobia. 'I think it's quite understandable though, when you think about it. Women go through this pretty gruesome, bloody experience every day and people, including other women, sort of play it down.' She turned her gaze on Joanne. 'If men had to do it, the human race would cease to exist.'

Joanne smiled. 'You're right there.' She stood up, placed her hand in the small of her back and arched her spine.

Louise threw a handful of moss on the pile of leaves. 'The question is, what can we do to help her?'

Joanne touched the side of her nose with a gloved hand, looking rather pleased with herself. 'Well, after trying and failing to get Sian to seek help herself I talked to Doctor McCrory on her behalf. He's actually very understanding and he's agreed to have a chat with her along with one of the community midwives who's had some experience in dealing with the condition before.'

'Why that's wonderful. Does he think he can help?'

Joanne probed the leaf pile with the toe of her old walking shoe. 'Doctor McCrory said she might benefit from hypno-therapy to help her overcome her phobia. He seemed quite positive about the outcome. Like anything, he said, facing up to the fear, admitting it, is the first step. If Sian's willing to undergo some therapy, he thinks she could benefit enormously.'

'Have you told Sian?'

'Not yet. I'll ring her tonight.'

'She might be cross with you for talking to the doctor.'

Joanne shrugged and was quiet for a few moments as she stared across the garden, her cheeks pink with the cold. 'The doctor said something else too,' she said, sounding slightly ominous.

Louise leant on the rake and prepared herself for bad news. 'What?'

Joanne looked into her face. 'Women who have tokophobia have an increased risk of post-natal depression.'

Louise chewed her bottom lip, trying not to worry. 'Well, that is something you and I can help with, Joanne. We both know how hard it is coping with a new baby, no matter how well prepared you think you are.'

There was a silence and then Joanne said, 'It must've been especially hard for you, being on your own. I had Mum and Sian and Phil, for what he was worth. You didn't have anyone.'

Louise tensed. If this was going to be another dig at her, she was ready for it. 'Oh, I wouldn't say that,' she said airily, playing down just how difficult it had been in the first six months after Oli's birth. She had long since found that she belonged to the only category of mother not allowed, under any circumstances, to moan about how difficult motherhood was. 'I had Cindy and Max.' She scraped the rake across the grass and said, 'Come on. It's getting cold. Let's get the rest of these leaves bagged up.'

Joanne bent her knees to scoop up a bundle of leaves and stuffed them in the bag. 'But still, it must've been hard.'

Louise, raking vigorously, glanced at her, feeling as though she was under some sort of scrutiny. And when Joanne opened her mouth to speak, Louise was prepared for criticism. But instead, her sister said something entirely unexpected.

'I owe you an apology, Louise.'

'What for?' asked Louise, perplexed.

Joanne looked at the palms of her woollen gloves, soggy and stained. 'For judging you. For not being as supportive as I should have been about Oli and your right to have him. Before Phil walked out I had pretty conservative views on marriage and how children should be conceived and raised. I believed that there was one right way to do it – but now, well now, I'm not so sure.' She looked at Louise. 'I think you're doing a fantastic job with Oli and from what I can see he doesn't miss having a father in his life one little bit.'

Louise felt her face colour and vindication, warm like the rays of the sun, spread through her. Her family's approval meant so much. Joanne had never taken much care to hide her views about Louise's decision to have Oli by herself. And now she had made a complete U-turn.

Louise, astounded, said simply, 'Thank you, Joanne. I appreciate that more than you know.'

Joanne cleared her throat and pushed back a stray lock of hair. 'While we're on the subject, there's something I've always wanted to ask you, Louise. About the baby thing.'

Louise threw down the rake and scooped up a pile of leaves. She put them in the bag. 'What's that?'

'If you wanted a baby so much, why didn't you just get pregnant without telling Cameron? Lots of women do that, I think. It kind of resolves the issue in a way because once the baby comes, the father just has to get on with it. And most men grow into fatherhood quite happily. Sometimes they just need a little push along the way.'

Louise's hands stilled momentarily. The wind picked up suddenly and a leaf, curled like a feather, somersaulted across the damp, earthy grass. 'Was it like that between Phil and you?'

A silence. Then a quiet admission, 'I think there was a wee bit of that going on. We weren't actually trying for a baby when I got pregnant, you see. We were a bit sloppy about contraception. But Phil was happy about it when it happened.'

Louise considered this for some moments. She did not

approve of the dishonesty inherent in this approach – and she thought it explained a lot about Phil's attitude to his family responsibilities. She picked up the last few remaining leaves, put them in the bag, pressing down with her hands, and stood up. 'I couldn't do that. It was important to me that my baby's father wanted him. What you're suggesting amounts to tricking a man into fatherhood, and I never wanted to be responsible for doing that.'

Joanne shrugged and tied string round the top of the bag. 'It's nothing new. It's been going on since time began.'

Louise stared at her sister in astonishment as she dragged the bag across the grass towards the garden gate. She'd had the audacity to judge Louise yet she was the one with the decidedly dubious moral code. Louise followed her, still holding the rake in her hand.

'Please don't take this the wrong way,' said Joanne, 'I am truly trying to understand. But what I don't get is this – Cameron says he doesn't want children so you go and conceive a child using donor sperm. Which means Oli doesn't have a father at all.'

'He does.'

'Well, yes. But only in the strictest biological sense.'

'He can meet him when he's eighteen if he wants to,' said Louise, leaning her back against the fence for support. They were in the shade now and it was very cold. 'And, although his father isn't currently a part of his life, he did want him. He *wanted* to father children or he never would've become a donor, would he?'

Joanne pulled a face, clearly confounded by her arguments. 'But why didn't you ask someone you knew – like Max? He might have loved to be a father and it's unlikely that he ever will be. He could've been involved in Oli's life from the outset. And it's, well, it just seems so much nicer than using a complete stranger's sperm.'

'You don't just go round asking people at random to father your child,' said Louise crossly because Joanne wasn't making a very good job of hiding her distaste. 'Max never expressed an interest in being a father. He was over the moon when I asked him to be Oli's godfather, yes. But once Graham came on the scene, he completely lost interest. I'm not sure that would've been any different had Oli been his child. He would've let Oli down and I think that's a whole lot worse than not knowing your father in the first place.' She paused and rubbed the bridge of her nose with her finger. 'And that's another advantage of using a donor – he has no legal rights to children created using his sperm.'

Joanne led the way to the shed at the bottom of the garden where tools they'd used earlier lay discarded on the grass. Picking up a pair of secateurs and a small trowel she said, 'But I thought you said Oli could contact his father when he was eighteen.'

'He can,' said Louise, 'but that doesn't mean he has any *rights* with regard to Oli. He's no say in how he's raised and he's no right of contact.'

Joanne sucked in air through her teeth noisily. 'And yet Cameron did come round to the idea of fatherhood. Eventually.'

Louise sighed, opened the shed door and went inside. The air was damp and musty and smelt of old wood. She put away the tools in her arms along with the rake. Joanne handed her the rest. 'But I didn't know that at the time, did I, Joanne? What was I supposed to do? Hang on in there waiting for him to change his mind? I loved Cameron, I really did, but having a family was as important to me as he was. Is.' Tears unexpectedly pricked her eyes.

Joanne touched Louise lightly on the arm and said gently, 'That part I do understand. It was the same for me.'

'Time was running out for me,' said Louise, the words tripping out quickly, one on top of the other. 'I didn't even know if I *could* conceive. If I'd left it any later, and had fertility problems, I might never have had a child. I just wish . . .' A ball of emotion, sorrow she thought, was lodged in her chest, making it hard to breathe, hard to speak.

Joanne stood in silence, her foot wedging the door open, giving Louise time to compose herself.

'I just wish,' she went on more calmly, 'that Cameron had got his act together earlier.'

There was a pause and Joanne said, 'So what are you going to do about him?'

Cameron had reluctantly gone back to Scotland without an answer from Louise because she found, in the end, that she could not give him one. She wanted to say yes but something she couldn't quite put her finger on was holding her back. She'd parried his barrage of e-mails, texts and phone calls ever since then with the reply that she needed more time.

'I don't know,' she said miserably.

'You can't go on like this, Louise. He asked you at the end of October, for heaven's sake. You can't keep him hanging on like that. You're going to have to give him an answer.'

'I know,' Louise sighed. 'It's just . . . Oh, I don't know. He wants me to move back to Edinburgh.'

'That's asking a lot,' said Joanne quietly.

'I know that he's no friends or contacts in Ballyfergus but I can't help thinking that if he loved me, he would at least try to make a go of it here? It's not like he's got a huge extended family in Edinburgh. He hardly sees his parents.' They'd retired to a cottage in Angus and he only saw them a few times a year. He didn't have a particularly close relationship with them and Louise had always found them cold and distant – they were unlikely to turn into warm, doting grandparents overnight. Cameron's sister lived in France and his younger brother down in Cheshire.

Joanne nodded thoughtfully. 'Whereas you and Oli have all of us here.'

'Exactly.' There was a silence and Louise stared at the workbench, now dusty with lack of use. 'What do you think I should do?' she asked, fully expecting Joanne to come down in favour of rejecting Cameron's offer. But for the second time that day, her sister surprised her.

'I think you should listen to your heart, Louise,' she said, softly. 'And the only person who knows what your heart is saying, is you.'

Joanne's green eyes filled with tears then and Louise, sensing something wrong, reached out and held her hand.

'What is it?'

Joanne stepped inside the small shed, and the door slammed behind them, pressing them together in the confined space. Their breath steamed in the frigid air.

Joanne took a deep breath and her eyes filled with tears. 'There's something I haven't told you. Phil asked me for a divorce, Louise.'

Louise formed her lips into an 'O' shape but made no sound.

'He told me few weeks ago but I just couldn't bring myself to talk about it until now.'

'Oh, sweetheart,' said Louise, remembering how bitter and hurt she'd felt in the aftermath of her divorce. 'What did he say?'

Joanne sniffed and touched the corner of her right eye with the tip of her index finger, in an attempt to prevent a tear spilling out. 'He said he was sorry.'

'For what exactly? His apology list must be as long as Santa's present list.' This raised a half-hearted smile from Joanne. Louise handed her a hankie she'd found in the back pocket of her trousers. 'It's clean. Just a bit crumpled.'

'Thanks.' Joanne dabbed her eyes. 'He apologised for walking out the way he did. And for getting involved with Gemma while we were still living together under the same roof.'

Louise snorted, unable to hide her disgust, but she tried to say something positive. 'Well, at least he had the guts to admit that what he did was wrong.'

Joanne attempted a smile but, before it was fully formed, it disappeared. 'He told me that he loves her.' She blinked rapidly like she was staring into bright headlights, trying hard to retain her composure.

Knowing that there was nothing she could say that could take away this hurt Louise was silent. It was a while before Joanne spoke again.

'I guess that's it then,' she said with finality, having regained control of her voice. 'At least I know exactly where I stand. And, you're right, it felt good to hear Phil apologise. I didn't realise how much I needed that.'

'Well, it sounds as though you cleared the air a bit. Your very own truth and reconciliation commission,' said Louise, trying to inject some humour into a decidedly downbeat conversation.

This time it was Joanne's turn to smile, though a little sadly. 'Well, we might have had the truth but I don't know about the reconciliation. He ended up storming out.'

'Why?'

Joanne folded her arms. 'Because I told him I would only give him a divorce if he admitted adultery and Gemma was named in the petition.'

'Bloody good for you!' cried Louise and she gave her sister a gentle punch on the arm.

'And I told him he would have to use his entire annual holiday entitlement to look after the girls.'

'How come?'

'It's what I'll be doing,' said Joanne a little defensively. 'Why shouldn't he?'

Louise puffed up her cheeks and blew out air. 'One of the very few perks of being separated – or divorced,' she said, 'is that you should be able to take time off work occasionally and not have the children at the same time. What do other parents who both work full-time do?'

Joanne cocked her head to one side and mumbled, 'I guess their kids go into childcare or holiday club.'

'Well, can't yours? Just for a week or two during the summer to give you a proper break?'

Joanne shook her head vehemently. 'They hate it.'

Louise paused for a moment to consider this, then put her gloved hands on her sister's shoulders. 'This is going to sound rather blunt, Joanne. But I'm afraid the girls are just going to have to get used to it. You need time off work to spend on your own, doing what you want. You can't spend every single day of your annual leave with the girls. You'll burn out. And so will Phil.'

Joanne sighed and blinked. 'I just want things to be the same for them as they were before Phil left. Or as close to it as possible.'

'I think even Abbey's old enough to understand that that's

not possible,' said Louise, quietly. 'Things are never going to be the same, Joanne. And the sooner you all start getting used to that, the better.'

And Louise as it turned out was right. Because that very evening, after she'd returned home and sent the younger girls up to bed, something happened that changed the direction of Joanne's life.

Maddy took the call and came into the kitchen where Joanne was ironing and thrust the phone at her mother. 'It's for you, Mum,' she shouted above the noise of the music blaring from the radio.

Joanne mouthed 'Who?' and Maddy screwed up her face and shrugged her shoulders.

Joanne set down the iron – water leaked out one of the holes onto the hot plate and fizzed angrily. She turned off the radio, took the phone and said 'Hi, Joanne here.'

'Joanne, it's Finn,' said a male voice. 'Finn McAvoy. Louise introduced us briefly a while back in the Indian restaurant.'

He paused. Joanne nodded stupidly and a flush of embarrassment crept up her neck and into her face. That was an evening she would rather forget. What must he think of her? And, more to the point, why on earth was he phoning her?

'Oh, yes, Finn. I . . . eh . . . I do remember you,' she said, turning her back on Maddy who was listening with interest. 'How are you?'

'Cool. What're you up to?'

'Ironing,' said Joanne realising too late that his question wasn't meant literally. It was his way of saying 'How are you?' She cringed and put a hand over her mouth.

'Well, I was just wondering if you'd like to come out for dinner with me?'

Joanne's hand fell away and she opened her mouth in

astonishment. She'd just been asked out on a date by a man she hardly knew – albeit a rather cute one. Her first date in how many years?

'Joanne? Are you still there?'

'Yes. Sorry. I'm still here.' She laughed and took a deep breath. 'And I would love to go for dinner with you.'

Chapter Sixteen

Sian stared out the shop window decorated with paper snowflakes she'd made herself, and clutched the telephone handset to her chest. The orange glow from the street lamp reflected on the wet pavement – the rain was relentless. She would most certainly get wet going home tonight.

All day, every time a customer came into the shop a cold blast of air, blown south from the frozen wastes of Siberia, gusted in sending shivers down her arms, in spite of the woollen thermals she wore under her clothes. Though she tried to keep the heating in the shop to a minimum, perhaps it was time to turn it up a notch or two. Then she remembered that she'd heard a climate-change expert on the radio the other day explaining that the unseasonably cold weather was possibly caused by global warming. She decided she could endure the discomfort after all.

Sian looked at the phone in her hand, the tips of her fingers pink with cold. She knew the number off by heart, she'd attempted to dial it so many times. All she had to do was press six digits and speak to Doctor McCrory. And once she'd made the appointment she would tell Andy. That was what she'd promised herself. Simple.

The only problem was that Sian had been telling herself this for some time. And now it was the middle of December and, in spite of making all sorts of promises to Joanne and Louise, she had neither called Doctor McCrory nor told Andy.

Sian took a deep breath and inhaled the musky-sweet scent of the patchouli oil she'd placed in an oil burner earlier in an attempt to calm her nerves. She thought it was worth a try but in her heart, she knew it would take more than an aromatherapy oil to counter her abject terror.

Fear paralysed her, literally. Every time she picked up the phone with the intention of making the call and arranging an appointment, her fingers froze, the connection between her brain and the digits cut off by the more powerful impulses from her petrified heart. The very idea of expressing her innermost fears to a doctor and a midwife made her feel sick. It had taken every ounce of Sian's courage to tell Louise and then Joanne. She wasn't sure she could do it again – not to strangers. And yet she knew that she must find the courage because the consequences of not seeking help, of not telling Andy, were absolutely unthinkable. She believed that if she didn't do something soon – either agree to give Andy the child he wanted or tell him the truth – he would leave her.

But fear held her back. She feared he would not understand, that he would treat her concerns dismissively. But she was even more terrified that he would be angry – and he would have just cause. She had moved in with him and got engaged without telling him about this phobia. And she had not been honest about her reasons for not wanting children.

Joanne and Louise had tried very hard to empathise, to understand, but she could tell by the solutions they offered, that neither of them had a clue.

It seemed so straightforward to them. Joanne had even laid it out in a simple three-stage plan – get help, tell Andy, have a baby – counting the steps off on her fingers. Louise had even offered to tell Andy herself – a suggestion that she quickly retracted when she saw how distressed Sian became at the idea. And it was kind of Joanne to seek medical help on her behalf, but really, she didn't need her sisters to tell her what she needed to do. Hadn't she thought about taking the very same steps – the first two anyway – every day since she'd met Andy?

The problem was that each step seemed like climbing Everest to Sian. In theory not impossible, but something that she knew she could never do. The task seemed utterly overwhelming, entirely beyond her capabilities. She had tried, but somehow she could not find the strength within herself.

Sian yawned and covered her mouth though there was no one there to see. She had not slept well since telling Louise, her sleep punctuated by vivid dreams of bloody births and blue-faced infants slippery as newborn lambs. Dreams disturbing enough to wake her and dreams that she could not, of course, share with Andy. And so most evenings she lay wide awake in the dead of night with Andy breathing peacefully beside her, feeling more lonely and isolated than she had ever felt before while fear tightened its grip on her chest, making her breath come in panting, shallow gasps.

And sometimes in the day when she was alone she imagined holding a tiny, milky-sweet baby in her arms. *Her* baby, swaddled in spotless white, pure as the driven snow. And when she allowed herself to imagine it, she thought that she might quite like to be a mother after all. But then the fantasy would come crashing down in the face of reality. The only way she was ever going to hold her own baby was if she gave birth to it – and how on earth could she ever do that?

Sian glanced at her watch. It was nearly four o'clock and

no one had entered the shop in the last fifteen minutes. There would be no more customers today.

And then just at that precise moment, the door flew open and a man stepped inside accompanied by a blast of bitter air that threatened to rip the brightly coloured paper chains from the ceiling. It took Sian a few moments to register that it was Andy. She dropped the phone, fumbled with it like an inept juggler and just managed to catch it before it fell crashing to the floor. She felt her face redden. Hastily, as if the phone could betray her secret, she set it on the counter.

Andy shut the door behind him and pulled down his hood. He was dressed in black waterproof trousers, Gore-Tex hiking boots, and a red and black North Face mountain jacket. Water dripped from his hair down his forehead, pale now that his summer tan had faded.

'What are you doing here?' asked Sian and Andy's face immediately clouded.

'Nice to see you too,' he said sarcastically.

'I . . . I didn't mean it like that,' said Sian, pushing the handset further away across the counter. 'I'm just surprised to see you here, that's all.' Her heart thudded against the wall of her chest so hard she thought it must be audible.

Mollified somewhat by her answer, the heat went out of Andy's voice. 'We couldn't get out in this weather. We caught up on admin, did a bit of planning and cleaned out one of the stores but in the end Davy said just to go home.'

He stood by the door shaking the raindrops off his hair while Sian remembered a time when he would not have come into the shop without walking straight over and kissing her full on the lips, customers present or not. And now the shop was empty and he stood ten feet away, staring at her like a stranger.

'I tried to call you earlier,' said Andy. 'But I couldn't get through.'

'That's not my fault,' said Sian, looking guiltily at the phone.

The muscles on Andy's jaw tightened and flexed like a mooring rope. He stared at her and the atmosphere in the shop went from cold to decidedly icy. 'You know what, Sian, I didn't say it was. I don't know what's going on with you.' He glared at her and shook his head. 'Anyway, I came to offer you a lift home. Connor's waiting outside.'

'I don't need a lift.'

'Have you seen the weather, Sian?'

'It's only a bit of rain,' she said stubbornly, ignoring the sound of the wind howling round the building.

'Are you mad? The wind's gale force and it's coming in unpredictable gusts. You could get blown off your bike. If I had to do a risk assessment I wouldn't let anyone walk in that weather, never mind get on a bike.'

She knew the ride home would be hellish but she didn't care. She deserved to be punished for failing Andy, for failing herself. Her head felt like it might explode. 'Andy, stop fussing, will you?' she snapped.

He clenched fists into a ball and said, 'Is that any way to talk to me, Sian? To the man you claim to love?'

'But I . . . I . . .'

He shook his head. 'I've had enough, Sian. I don't know what the hell is going on with you but I'm moving out. Tonight.'

'What?' said Sian, and the blood drained from her head. She leant against the nearby counter. 'What do you mean, "moving out"?'

'Just for a bit. Until we both get our heads clear. Because you've stopped talking to me, Sian, and I don't know what the hell's going on.' He ran a hand through his wet hair and lowered his voice. 'I think we both need a bit of time away from each other. Just to think. I know I do. I'm sorry. But I can't live like this.'

He left the shop without another word. The door closed behind him, the chimes on the back tinkling against the wooden frame like broken glass.

Sian walked over to the door, and placed her hand on the pane. It felt like ice. She pressed her face against the window and watched Andy's figure receding along the pavement. Connor's car was parked a few yards along, where the double yellow lines ended. His hazard lights were blinking rhythmically. Andy opened the car door and, even from inside the shop, she could hear the thud of the loud music that Connor played all the time. Andy got in, the door slammed shut and the car drove off. Sian slid the bolt in the lock and turned the old-fashioned sign hanging in the window to 'Closed'.

Her hand slid off the glass and hung by her side. Her heart ached with heaviness, her limbs felt like dead weights. That was it then. The start of the end. Tears bled silently from her eyes. She'd seen it coming and she'd been powerless to stop it. And it was her fault. She'd pushed Andy away because if she'd let him get too close he would've somehow guessed her secret.

But if she didn't tell him, he might never come back. She wiped the tears from her eyes.

She had to get help. Now! Before Andy was gone for good. She picked up the handset, cradled it momentarily in her hands and then put it in the base unit as gingerly as if it were a bomb. Mental and physical exhaustion washed over her, leaving her light-headed. She would not phone Doctor McCrory tonight. Perhaps tomorrow when she was feeling stronger. She brightened a little at this thought. Yes, tomorrow morning would be a better time – she was after all a morning person. How silly of her to have forgotten. She went over to the till and emptied the change into coin bags from the bank. She would just have to ensure that, unlike every other day, she didn't let the morning slide past her in a haze of self-driven busyness. Her productivity over the past weeks had been astounding – she would rather do anything, even tackle her tax return, than face up to the thing that was, slowly, eroding her relationship with Andy.

She promised herself that it would be different tomorrow. This time, she told herself – while a knot of terror formed in her stomach and her shaking hands sent shiny twenty-piece coins scooting across the floor – this time she would do it. She had to. She had no choice.

She scrabbled around on the floor collecting the silver coins and placed the whole lot in a safe in the storeroom. Back in the shop, she checked that the till drawer was open, protruding like a grey, toothless lower jaw. She angled the till so that the drawer was visible from the street, reinforcing the lie that she displayed on a prominent card in the window – 'No cash held on premises overnight'. She was so good at telling lies. She blew out the candle under the oil burner and switched off the lava lamp in the window.

In the storeroom she struggled into her outdoor things, securing the straps on her wrists and on the ankles of her waterproof trousers. She knew that the wind-blown rain would soon penetrate her defences, cold rivulets seeping up her wrists and soaking the sleeves of her thermals, wool layer and fleece. But what did it matter? She didn't care if she got cold or wet. She didn't care what happened to her any more. Without Andy what did anything matter?

A silent sob escaped her – crossly she pulled herself together. All was not lost. Andy had only moved out for a bit – it wasn't permanent. She could still win him back. If she could just get the help she needed, and then tell him everything . . . all would be okay, wouldn't it? She swallowed and resolved, this time, to follow through. It would be a good idea to get an early night – she would need all her reserves of energy for tomorrow.

Sian went out the door at the back of the storeroom, securing the locks with shaking hands. She collected her bike from under the old lean-to in the yard, while the wind howled around her head like a banshee, driving wave after wave of rain into her face and chest. She opened the gate that led onto the lane at the back of the High Street, checked the lights were working, secured her helmet, and swung her leg over the crossbar.

Out on the Shore Road the wind blew erratically not just from the north but from all directions, literally taking her breath away. She bent her head into it, welcoming the stinging rain on her cheeks – anything to take her mind off the pain in her heart. The driving rain blurred her vision. It had already penetrated her gloves and her fingers were numb with the cold. She concentrated on forcing her weary legs to push – right, left, right, left – as the bike made painfully slow progress towards home. And every few minutes a vehement gust of wind, so powerful it nearly plucked her off the bike, would blast across the road. Andy had been right, the conditions were terrible, but she was an experienced cyclist and there was only a mile to go. She took a deep breath, narrowed her eyes against the driving rain until they were little more than slits, and put her back into it.

And as she pedalled, the awful truth hit her. Andy had left her. Tears came once more and her earlier resolve crumbled like the pages of an old book. Who was she trying to kid? She would not phone Doctor McCrory tomorrow. Because when she tried to formulate what she would say to him, her mind came up blank. She could not visualise herself in a consulting room with the kindly old doctor and a midwife she didn't know, telling them her deepest fears. And because she knew she could not do this, she could not win Andy back.

A car driving too fast for the conditions whizzed past, showering her with spray from head to toe, though she was too wet now for it to make any difference. Up ahead, its tail-lights blinked in the dark as it slowed for the approaching sharp right-hand bend, just shy of the entrance to Loughanlea.

If she didn't tell Andy, if she didn't find some way to overcome this problem, Andy would never come home. He'd find someone else. Someone who could give him what he wanted. Tears of self-pity mixed with rain washed down her cheeks.

The lights of a car shone from behind. The screeching wind had almost drowned out the engine noise. She was nearly on the bend in the road now, still creeping along slowly up the slight incline. To her left was a grass verge, maybe three feet deep, bordered by an old stone wall that followed the curve of the bend. A big black and white sign up ahead indicated the direction and sharpness of the turn.

The car could not overtake because of the bend but she could sense the driver's impatience. She glanced over her shoulder. The car was too close for safety, too close in the event of an accident. Sian muttered crossly to herself and looked ahead, concentrating on keeping a steady, confident course a couple of feet out from the edge of the road.

Maybe she should let Joanne make the appointment on her behalf, as she'd offered to do on several occasions. If someone went with her to see the doctor maybe it wouldn't be quite so bad, maybe she would be able to cope. But even if she managed that – and it was a big but – she'd still have to tell Andy.

And then suddenly, the beam from the car's headlights moved towards the centre of the road and she heard the sudden rev of an engine behind her. The car was trying to overtake her! She sensed rather than saw the hulking mass of a steel bonnet nudge her alongside, forcing her too close to the verge. Her eyes were glued to the ground ahead, searching for the small holes and loose stones that lurked at the edge of every road – and could so easily send the razor-thin tyres of a road bike like hers into a skid.

At that precise moment, up ahead, the bright yellow lights of another vehicle blinked around the bend, momentarily blinding Sian. Seconds later a white Transit van came hurtling round the corner. It headed straight for the car now parallel to Sian. The car's vivid red paintwork gleamed like freshly drawn blood in the van's headlights. The driver of the van opened his mouth, his knuckles white on the wheel. He cried out a silent warning, his face frozen in shock. As for the driver in the car, Sian anticipated his actions.

Panicked, the driver took his foot off the accelerator, snatched the steering wheel in an anti-clockwise direction to avoid the van, and the car lurched abruptly to the left. Some part of the car, Sian didn't know what, clipped the back wheel of the bicycle. She made no attempt to regain control of the bike, or even stay on it. She let go of the handlebars and, as she felt the bike skid away beneath her, threw herself to the left, onto the grass verge. She heard the screech of brakes and the scraping sound of metal – her bike being dragged under the wheels of the car. She hit the verge hard, rolled, and smacked her head on the stone wall.

And that was the last thing she remembered.

On the way home from work in the car, Louise was briefly held up by an accident on the Shore Road. She tapped the steering wheel with her fingertips, ready to burst with frustration and anguish, while the rain pounded against the windscreen and the wind rocked the car.

The day had gone well – all the plans were in place for the official launch of Loughanlea. Louise was in the main office with Steve and Amanda sharing a box of cream éclairs from the bakery, when the phone rang, changing everything.

It was Cameron. He was in Northern Ireland and he wanted to see her tonight. Was she free for dinner? Of course, she'd said yes.

And now she sat in the car, listening to the wail of an ambulance siren heading off into the distance taking some poor soul to Antrim Hospital, thinking about what she would say to him. Her emotions, and views, had fluctuated wildly over the last weeks but lately she'd begun to think she might have reached a decision.

For all the drawbacks to Cameron's proposal – chief of which was that she would have to leave Ballyfergus and uproot Oli yet again – she couldn't help but be seduced by the idea of marriage and the romantic notion that Cameron had bought the big house in Morningside just for her and her son. And, of course, the rest of the family they were going to make together – if they were lucky enough to be blessed with more children. And she couldn't help but be impressed by the way that he'd pursued her, flying over to Ballyfergus, not on one, but two occasions. If proof were needed of the seriousness of his intentions then that, as far as Louise was concerned, was it.

Of course she had doubts. Would they get along? The last two years of their marriage had not been good, she reminded herself, but she put that firmly down to conflict over the issue of having a baby. Now that they both wanted the same thing, they would get along like a house on fire – wouldn't they?

Oli would lose regular contact with his extended family, which was a bitter blow, but he would be gaining a dad. Through this marriage she would be making restitution for the one thing she had denied him. She would just have to work hard at making friends and integrating into the local Morningside community, replacing the regular contact they had with family, with friends instead. And she would encourage her family to visit Edinburgh anytime they liked. With all those bedrooms, there would certainly be enough room.

She would miss her work and her colleagues but, she reminded herself, it was only a job – there would be plenty of opportunities in Edinburgh. On the financial front, she'd lose her deposit on the house at Loughanlea but it was only money. It was harder to let go of the dream she had of living there, picturing herself and Oli moving about those rooms, living so close to the sea, happy and content. She tried not to be sentimental about Loughanlea but something about the place – not just the house, but the marina, the Lough, and the wildlife – pulled at her heartstrings in an elemental way. The house was only a building, she told herself, just four walls and a roof, bricks and mortar.

A home was something different, a place built out of love, shared values, common goals – and didn't she and Cameron want the same thing now? With these ingredients present, you could make anywhere home. And that's what she would do in Morningside.

As for Kevin, she tried very hard not to think of him and what might have been. Because when she did a well of sadness, inexplicably heart-wrenching, filled her soul. If they'd known each other for longer . . . but they hadn't and Cameron was here, with his offer of marriage, and she was afraid that if she said no, she might live to regret it.

Yes, if she tried very hard, she could make it work.

And she still loved Cameron. She pictured him as he'd appeared that night standing on her doorstep in the rain – the way his eyes crinkled round the edges when he smiled, the Scottish accent she'd fallen for, the rough shadow on his chin she'd wanted to reach out and touch just to check that he was real. He'd disappointed her, yes, but she was the one who'd cast him aside in the single-minded pursuit of mother-hood. Not many people got a second chance – and Louise wasn't going to throw away the opportunity to put back together a marriage that, with hindsight, she had been too quick to dissolve.

Yes, she thought she had reached a decision. But instead of being filled with a sense of certainty and calm, she was as jittery as Oli on a sugar high.

Oli ran forcefully into her arms when she got to the nursery, the way he did every time she collected him. He held up his grubby little face to be kissed, lips pouted, his nose caked with snot. Louise bent down and kissed his wet lips, hoping that whatever bug his immune system was currently fighting, she didn't catch it too. Then she scooped him up in her arms, held him tight till he squealed and whispered into his neck, 'I'm doing this for you, Oli.'

The next couple of hours were spent with Oli. Louise made his tea while he played with a pirate ship on the floor of his room. Then she sat with him at the table while he ate macaroni cheese and broccoli, painstakingly, nibble by nibble.

He was eating too slowly, distracted by the toggle on the zip of his fleece; the sound of the wind, still fierce but dying now, outside; the moulded plastic handle of his 'Bob the Builder' spoon, the only implement with which he would eat these days. Then his attention was caught by a mask he'd made in nursery a few days ago. He held it up to his face, said, 'Woo-woo,' and giggled.

'What sort of a noise is that?' smiled Louise, loading the spoon Oli had discarded on the table, with gloopy macaroni and a small spear of broccoli.

'It's a scary noise. I'm a monster!' he shrieked.

'And what a scary monster you are!' She laughed, gently peeled the mask off his face and added, 'Here, eat this.'

He opened his mouth obediently, took the soft food off the fork and gummed it around his mouth. And then Louise asked him something that she really shouldn't have, not until she was absolutely certain it was going to happen.

'How would you like to go back to Edinburgh to live?'

He looked at her blankly.

'Where we used to live – but in a different house. A big house with lots of rooms to play in and a big garden. Where Elliott lives.'

His face lit up. 'Will Elliott be there?'

'Not in the big house.' And not at nursery either she thought, or when it came to it, school – they would be in a different catchment area for nursery and she knew Elliott's parents had no plans, nor the means, to send their child to private school. 'But he could come and play at our house anytime you like – and you could go to his.'

Oli smiled broadly. 'Yes, I'd like that,' he said.

'If we went to live in this big house in Edinburgh someone else would come to live with us too.'

'Abbey!'

'No, not Abbey.' His face fell and she went on, 'A nice man that Mummy . . . likes very much.'

'Kevin!' he grinned and her heart sank. Oli hadn't seen Kevin since that day in Glenarm forest and yet he remembered him . . .

'No, not Kevin. His name is Cameron. You met him here, remember?'

Oli shook his head. 'Why can't Abbey come?'

Louise sighed, realising that the child had no concept of what 'moving to Edinburgh' meant. It was unfair of her to ask his opinion. 'Abbey can come and visit,' she said and Oli accepted this – as he accepted every word that came out of her mouth as the absolute, God-given truth.

After he refused to eat any more, Louise tidied up the kitchen, bathed him and read him a bedtime story. And all the while, as she splashed him in the bath and as he chattered about what Santa was going to bring him for Christmas, she reflected upon the fact that she had gone to all this trouble to relocate only to have to uproot and go back to where she started.

She finished reading, closed the book and lay down on the bed beside Oli. Joanne would not approve but Louise knew that this was the quickest route to get him to sleep. She stroked his head, his hair still soft as down, and held his little body against her own, his limbs hot and sturdy. Oli clutched his teddy, eyelids drooping as she whispered sweet words of endearment in his left ear. And soon he was asleep.

When she opened the door to him, Cameron was slightly breathless as though he'd just run up the stairs. 'Louise, it's great to see you,' he grinned, running his eyes over her simple outfit of a black dress and boots.

Her stomach flipped over like a pancake. She stood aside and gestured for him to enter.

He stepped over the threshold and went to plant a kiss on her lips but, at the very last moment, for some reason she didn't even know herself, she turned her head and the kiss landed rather awkwardly on her cheek. His smile faltered a moment. 'Are you ready?' he said, recovering quickly.

'Just about.' Louise slipped on a thick black wool peacoat, buttoned it and added a warm red scarf. Amanda, who'd agreed to babysit at short notice and was still in her work clothes, bless her, appeared at the end of the hall, her neat figure silhouetted by the Christmas tree lights. She knew who Cameron was and why he was here and she looked as if she was dying of curiosity. Brief introductions were made, but it was clear Cameron didn't want to linger. Louise gave Amanda parting instructions and they left.

It was Louise's idea that they go back to The Marine Hotel. For some reason she liked the idea of being close to home, on familiar ground. Cameron insisted they eat in the formal dining room, decked out in classy gold and silver Christmas decorations, rather than the more relaxed bar. Once they were settled in the stylish room and all the usual prelimi-naries were out of the way – drinks served and food ordered – Cameron got down to brass tacks. 'You know why I'm here, Louise,' he said, grasping the stem of his white wine glass between the index and middle fingers of his right hand, his digits like blades on a pair of scissors. He repositioned the white glass above the point of his knife, a centimetre from its original location.

She nodded. She opened her mouth to say something but it died in her throat. She wanted to pick up her wine glass and take a long drink, but she knew her shaking hands would not comply. Instead, she pushed the elaborate Christmas cracker, its festive cheer so incongruous with their conversation, to one side.

'Why didn't you reply to my recent e-mails? I thought . . . well, I didn't know what to think. It's been six weeks, Louise.' He tugged irritably at the collar of his shirt.

Louise fingered her throat, her nails catching on the fine gold chain and lozenge-shaped pendant Cameron had given her for their sixth wedding anniversary – for some reason she'd held on to it. 'I told you why. I just needed some time to think clearly . . .'

'I was planning on coming over,' he said, following his own train of thought, as though she had not spoken, 'when another business trip came up at short notice and I just thought, well, it's fate bringing me to you.' He smiled.

Something jarred inside Louise's head. 'What do you mean *another* business trip?' She was under the impression that this visit, and the last one, had been made specially to see her.

'What does it matter?' he said, brushing her concerns aside, and staring straight into her eyes. 'I'm here now, aren't I?' He placed his hand over hers like a cold blanket.

She glanced at the back of his strong hand, dark and sinewy against her pale skin. Little shivers went up her arm. 'Well, yes, but . . .' Her voice trailed off and she frowned, confused. She was almost certain that he'd said he'd come specifically to see her the last time. He'd certainly left her with that strong impression . . .

'You were saying,' he said softly, removing his hand. 'About needing time?'

She shook her head casting the doubts off like bothersome insects. Perhaps she had gotten it wrong after all. 'I needed time to make up my mind, Cameron.'

He touched the foot of the glass lightly with the tip of the knife, so lightly it did not make a sound. 'And have you? Made up your mind, I mean.'

'I think so,' she said seriously, crossing the index and middle finger on her left hand, concealed under the table.

He fixed her then with those grey eyes as deep and dark as pools and his Adam's apple bobbed in his throat. His smile was gone now replaced by a tight and focused expression she had only rarely seen on his face – once, when he didn't get a long-coveted promotion at work and another time, when he was waiting on the results of tests for suspected cancer.

'Well,' he said, after some time had passed and she had not spoken, 'what's it to be, Louise? Will you marry me? Again.' He allowed himself a brief, one-sided smile.

'I think,' she said and struggled to find just the right words, 'we could make it work.' Every muscle in his face relaxed. 'But we've a lot of issues to sort out first,' she added hastily, lest he make the mistake of taking this as an unqualified acceptance.

'Oh, Louise!' he cried and she glanced nervously at the other diners. But no one appeared to have noticed their little drama unfolding. He grabbed her hand again. 'You don't know how much it means to hear you say that. These last weeks have been just awful, not knowing . . . how I've longed to hear you say those words! They mean as much to me as they did the first time round. We're going to have a great life together, Louise.' He beamed happily, his sweaty hand gripping hers like he was afraid she might disappear suddenly.

'And Oli,' she said, not able to help herself. Oli was so much a part of her, completely and inextricably tied up with her identity and everything she did. Why did he keep forgetting about him?

Cameron let her hand go and made a waving gesture. 'Yes, yes, of course. Oli too. Now,' he said glancing over his shoulder and raising a hand to attract the attention of a waiter, 'let's get some champagne!'

'We haven't got anything to celebrate yet, Cameron.' Louise slid her hand off the table and felt her face redden. She felt like a killjoy but the success of this marriage would be all in the detail. She didn't want to rush in, to be swayed by grand gestures and euphoria, while neglecting the things that mattered. Like they had done the first time round.

His hand fell from the air like a lead weight. 'What do you mean?'

'In principle I accept but—'

He interrupted sharply, sounding offended. 'It's not a job interview, Louise. I'm asking you to be my wife.'

'And I want to be, Cameron. I still love you. I never stopped. And I do want to give us another chance.' His features softened, reassured by these words. She toyed with the dessert spoon on the table, trying to make her words as smooth and reassuring as the contours of the metal. 'But,' she went on, 'I don't want to make the same mistake we made last time.'

'I don't understand you, Louise,' he said crossly, staring at the spoon in her hand as though affronted by it. 'Here I am asking you to be my wife and all you can do is talk about past mistakes.'

She stared at her upside down reflection in the bowl of the spoon. 'You never did understand me,' she said flatly and they both froze and looked at each other. 'I'm sorry. This isn't how I—' she said and stopped without finishing the sentence. She set the spoon down. 'I shouldn't have said that.'

He rubbed his hand over his mouth and down his chin. 'Look, let's start again, shall we?'

She nodded.

'What were you saying about not making the same mistakes?'

She took a deep breath. 'The mistake we made last time was that we weren't honest with each other about what we wanted from the marriage. I always wanted children and you didn't. Yet we both failed to communicate that to each other at the outset.'

'But that's not a problem any more,' he said with a disarming smile. 'We're both agreed that we want children together.'

She resisted the urge to concur and let herself be swept away by his confidence. 'But that decision is just one part of a bigger puzzle, Cameron. We have to make sure all the other pieces fit together too. I'm used to my independence now and making my own decisions.'

'If you want independence, why are you considering marriage?' he said a little too tetchily.

She sighed, frustrated. 'I'm just trying to explain to you . . . how I've changed. We need to be sure that we're agreed on the big questions before we take this any further. What, for example, about the issue of me going back to work should we have other children?'

He shrugged. 'You can do what you like.'

'And what about practicalities? For example, should I complete on the house at Loughanlea and then try and sell it – or write off the deposit? And when should I hand in my resignation?'

'You always were a detail person, Louise,' he said a touch patronisingly.

She cocked her head to one side and gave him a hard stare.

He looked a little sheepish. 'Look, all I'm saying is these

353

things – well, they're all minor details. They'll get sorted. You don't need to worry about them.'

Hit by sudden inspiration she said, 'What if we can't have children together, Cameron? What then? That's hardly a minor detail, is it?'

This seemed to blindside him. He leant back in the chair and folded his arms, considering this with a frown on his face. 'I hadn't thought about that. But that's not likely to happen, is it?'

It suddenly occurred to Louise that, though they had been together for fifteen years and had several accidents with contraception, she had never fallen pregnant. 'It's more common than you think. Ten per cent of men in Britain are infertile and, in half of all infertile couples seeking IVF it's the man who has the problem, not the woman.' She had learnt this and a whole lot more in her pursuit of motherhood. She paused to let her words sink in and then added gently, 'If we couldn't have children, Cameron, it's unlikely it would be because of me.' Though Oli was the living proof of her fertility, he'd been conceived four years ago – she did not share with Cameron that there were no guarantees she would be able to conceive in the future.

Her phone went off, the ring tone bleating like a lamb. 'Sorry,' she said, pulled it out of her handbag and looked at the caller's number. 'It's just Joanne.' She pressed the red button and slipped the phone back in her bag. 'And if having children is important to you, and you did turn out to be infertile, you need to consider the alternatives. For example, would you be happy to consider having a child using donor sperm?'

He pulled a face, shook his head and shivered. 'Ugh! I don't like the idea of that,' he said and Louise's blood ran cold.

The waitress came then, carrying two starters of chicken liver pâté with chutney and melba toast. She set them down, poured water and disappeared. The smell of the liver hit Louise's nostrils, nearly making her retch.

'This looks good,' said Cameron and when she, stony-faced, did not reply added, 'Look, Louise, I just know that's not going to happen to me – to us.' He picked up his knife and rested the end of the handle on the table. 'And if it does, well we deal with it. But let's not worry about things that haven't even happened yet, eh?' He gave her a reassuring smile. 'Come on, tuck in,' he said, picked up a piece of the thin, curling toast and spread it with pâté.

Louise stared at her plate and all she could see was Oli, with his perfect button nose, the dimple on his left cheek, the way his whole face lit up when he smiled. The happiness in his laughter and in his heart, the innocence that she would defend with her life. He was the best thing that had ever happened to her. She would always put him first.

The phone rang again. 'For God's sake,' she said under her breath, and pulled it out. It was Joanne again. Whatever was so important would have to wait. She chucked the phone in her bag and turned her attention back to Cameron, who balanced a dollop of chutney on top of the pâté and took a bite.

'Oli was conceived using donor sperm, Cameron. Had you forgotten?' she said coldly.

He nearly choked. He put his hand over his mouth, finished chewing the pâté and toast and washed it down with a swig of water. 'I didn't mean to cast any . . . er . . . to . . . I mean I wasn't talking about Oli. I was talking about a theoretical situation and how I would personally feel about it. It's not my place to pass judgement on what you did, Louise. I can understand why you were driven to take such drastic

355

measures, I really can. And I don't blame you at all. All I'm saying is that I'm not sure that it's a route I—'

But Louise had stopped listening. Oli a drastic measure? Her little darling, her bubba, the light of her life?

When Cameron finally stopped talking she said, 'If you find the idea of having a child using donor sperm so repulsive, then I presume you would find it hard to love a child conceived that way?'

Cameron, backed into a corner, fumbled with the napkin, put it to his brow and dabbed the beads of sweat that had formed there like drops of dew. His face went red. 'I'm not saying that. I'm just saying that the natural instinct to love your own would be missing. But I'm quite sure I could learn to care for a child that wasn't my own.'

'Like Oli.'

'Yes, like Oli. Didn't I say I would adopt him? And I'll do my very best to give him a happy home.'

But Oli deserved so much more than that. He deserved to be loved. A sudden image came to mind of Oli, perched on Kevin's shoulders that day in Glenarm forest, laughing, his dark curls burnished red in the autumn sunlight. Two people on the same wavelength, connected, the warmth of genuine affection radiating between them.

She pushed her plate into the middle of the table. 'You didn't even want to meet Oli, did you, Cameron?'

He raised the palms of his hands in the air. 'Now that's not true. I did meet him, didn't I?'

'For all of three minutes. Hardly long enough to get to know him.'

'Well, I haven't had time to spend any longer with him, have I?'

'You never asked to. It didn't even cross your mind, did it?' The meeting had only happened because Louise had engineered it. She thought back to the brief encounter in her flat, when all Cameron had done was exchange superficial pleasantries, look at his watch and ask if Oli was going to Sian's. He'd shown no interest in him – none at all. 'What if you don't get on, Cameron? What if he doesn't like you?'

'He probably won't,' said Cameron and this struck Louise as the most perceptive thing he had said so far this evening. She had a funny feeling they would not hit it off – and yet Oli had taken to Kevin like a long lost friend . . .

'He'll not like having to share you, will he?' said Cameron, 'I mean he's been used to it just being you and him. I dare say he's a bit spoilt. But he'll get used to the idea.'

'My son isn't spoilt, Cameron,' she said coldly. She should've smelt a rat when she'd found out where Cameron was staying – in a hotel in central Belfast which, she recalled now, he used when he came over here with work. If he'd come to Northern Ireland to see her, why was he staying there and not in Ballyfergus? Because both this trip and the one before had been about business, not about her and Oli. They were just afterthoughts. If he'd really wanted her, he would've been on a plane over long before now.

She got to her feet, the napkin that had lain on her lap crushed in her fist. She set it gently on the table, and stood looking down at Cameron for a long time, motionless as a statue. She could hear her breathing, shallow and fast as a million thought waves jostled through her brain. At last they all coalesced into one crystal thought. 'I think I very nearly made a stupid mistake.'

'Louise, sit down please. People are looking.' Cameron glanced nervously at a table of diners on the other side of the room.

'Couldn't you get anyone else to marry you?'

'What are you talking about?' he snapped, angry now that

she would not comply and sensing at last that what he wanted was slipping from his grasp.

She shook her head, everything suddenly as crisp and clear as the sky on a frosty winter's morning. 'I believe you when you say you want a wife and a family, Cameron.'

He nodded his head vigorously. 'I do.'

'Not me, Cameron. *A* wife. I don't think that necessarily has to be me, does it? And Oli certainly isn't part of your happy family dream, is he?'

'Oh, for heaven's sake, Louise. I said I would adopt the child. What more do you want?'

'I want,' she said, and her eyes filled with tears and her throat constricted making her voice a hoarse whisper. 'I want my son to be loved. Treasured. Adored. Cherished.' She paused, gained command of her vocal cords and continued more assuredly, 'And I don't think you're capable of putting a child before yourself, and certainly not one who isn't your own flesh and blood. I thought you'd come here because you'd changed and I was ready to believe in you. But you haven't changed at all. You're not here to make amends, to put things right. You're not even here because you love me.'

'That's not true. I do love you,' he said, his eyes sparking with rage because he saw now that he was not going to get what he came for.

'Not as much as you love yourself, Cameron. You're here for your own selfish reasons, because you want a family and you need someone to give you what you want. And you thought I would be a pushover. You thought that I'd be so grateful to you for adopting Oli, that I'd fall into your arms. Well, let me tell you something.' Her voice strengthened with anger and rose above the quiet hum of conversation. 'Oli and I deserve a whole lot better than the scraps off your table, Cameron Campbell.'

He stood up, held out an arm towards her like an olive branch, his hand upturned and said, 'Louise, please don't do this. If you send me away you'll regret it.'

She hooked her bag over her shoulder and pushed the chair out of her way. She put her hand to her throat, remembering suddenly the necklace that burned against her skin like the anger burned in her heart. She clasped her fingers around the fine gold chain and yanked it brutally from her neck. The pendant fell onto the tablecloth with a dull thud. She threw the chain at his face. Instinctively, he flinched but the chain fell short of its intended target.

'What's that for?' he said, staring at the thin snake of gold coiled on the table where it had fallen.

'You don't even remember, do you?' she said softly. 'You gave me that on our sixth wedding anniversary. In Barbados.' She turned and walked away.

And the last thing she heard was Cameron's voice, confirming just how lucky an escape she'd had. 'You're making a mistake, Louise. I'm warning you, I won't come looking for you again.' She continued unsteadily towards the exit, her heels sinking into the plush carpet, his voice rising with every step so that, when he delivered his parting shot, the words were audible to everyone in the room.

'I mean, who else is going to adopt your bastard?'

By the time Louise got out of the restaurant and made her way to the ladies' toilets, her face was wet with tears and her body was shaking with rage. How dare he? How dare he call Oli such a disgusting, obscene word? How dare he label him like that? There was nothing illegitimate about her son. It was such a nasty, dirty, seedy concept and it had nothing to do with the beautiful child she had conceived and borne through love. The love of one parent, yes, but enough love to sustain him all his days.

She stood in front of a bank of spotless white porcelain sinks with shiny chrome taps that looked like they had never been used. The room was filled with the scent of fresh white lilies that stood in an elegant vase at the end of the room, and the sound of piped piano music. She fished a tissue out of her bag, started to cry and then pulled herself together.

What had she been thinking, entertaining the idea of going back to Cameron in the first place? She'd been driven by the desire to give Oli a dad and some sort of twisted notion of loyalty, about somehow owing it to Cameron and to herself to give the marriage another go.

She'd been trying too hard, she realised suddenly. In spite of all her careful planning and mental preparation, she had never quite convinced herself that single-parenthood was the right and proper way to bring a child into the world. It had always smacked of failure and desperation, despite trying so very hard to convince herself otherwise. Cameron had offered her the traditional family that for so long had been her dream. He had offered to adopt Oli and so eliminate the only flaw in her otherwise happy family. She thought that she could resurrect a family out of the ashes of her first marriage, that she could somehow patch it all up and pretend that it was something it wasn't. It was time to let go of that dream and face up to a new reality.

There were more non-traditional families in the UK than there were traditional ones with both parents living under the same roof. Oli would always be a little bit different because of the way he had been conceived and there was nothing she could do to change that. But there were plenty of single mothers raising children who had never known their fathers. And, she reminded herself, the stability of a home was what mattered, not the number of people in it.

Studies had shown that children like Oli, with a highly motivated, educated and financially secure mother, did better long term than children from broken homes. You cannot, after all, miss what you've never had. It was time she started believing the research and stopped apologising for what she had done.

Chapter Seventeen

'The nurse tells me you'll get out tomorrow,' said Andy softly, perched on the side of Sian's hospital bed, where she was lying propped up by several pillows. They were alone in a small ward of four beds, the other three currently, and very temporarily, empty. The other patient, who'd been there when Sian arrived the night before, had been discharged that morning. The ward would fill up over the weekend the nurses warned, but by then Sian would be long gone. She was grateful for the privacy but all she wanted to do was go home. Sian hated hospitals – the chemical stink, the suspect hygiene, the oppressive heat.

Her bed was in the corner beside a window with a view of a car park. A shaft of weak afternoon sun, the calm after the storm, filtered through the glass and formed a golden rectangle on the blue hospital blanket.

'That's right,' she said, gingerly moving her right hand into the sun. Every muscle in her body ached, every movement took extraordinary effort. And because of this she was acutely aware, in a way she had never been before, of how much she ordinarily took her body for granted. An earlier trip to the loo had taken her a full twenty minutes and left her utterly exhausted.

Andy picked up a battered pink teddy bear with a bandage improvised out of toilet paper over its right eye, and smiled.

'It's from Abbey,' said Sian. 'Joanne brought it over this morning. Along with this pair of pyjamas.' Sian slowly tilted her chin to look down at Joanne's cotton pyjamas, covered in pink and blue and grey polka dots. The top was slightly too narrow for her frame, the button across her chest straining, and the sleeves a tad too short. This only added to the unreal, dreamlike quality of her perception. Because only now was reality starting to hit home.

'Sweet,' said Andy, and put the teddy back.

Sian nodded in agreement, and immediately regretted it. A pain shot up her neck and into her skull. She winced. The nurses had her on a cocktail of painkillers but even that wasn't enough to completely dull the pain. Her left arm, broken in two places, was plastered from wrist to shoulder and she had stitches on her leg where something had penetrated the fabric of her trousers and gouged a hole in her leg. According to the doctor she'd been lucky – the helmet she'd been wearing had saved her life. But she'd sustained nasty cuts and bruises all down the left side of her face and body and it hurt like hell, especially the grazed open skin on her left cheek. All superficial of course and time would heal.

'Are your mum and dad coming this afternoon?'

'No, I told them not to bother. It's a long drive and I'll be home tomorrow. I asked Mum to come and see me then. I think this place, and seeing me like this, would upset her.' Sian had examined her facial injuries in the mirror earlier, and it was not a pretty sight.

'I think you're wise,' said Andy.

'Joanne and Louise said they might pop in tonight to see me. If I'm still awake.'

She yawned, overcome with fatigue even though she'd slept most of the morning. Her brain was foggy with the effort of trying to piece together exactly what had happened – and cope with the trauma her body had endured. She closed her eyes and images of the night before, disjointed and jerky like camera footage taken in a warzone, flashed across her consciousness. A red car bonnet, glossy with rain, the sound of her panting breath and the howling wind, the wet road ahead and blinding lights . . . the sensation of flying through the air and then . . . nothing. She'd woken up in the ambulance, disorientated and so full of adrenaline she'd felt no pain until several hours later.

And now she was just glad to be alive. And filled with an overwhelming sense of gratitude that she had been allowed this chance to put her life straight. Her fears about childbirth were no less real than before, but now she felt angry with herself for allowing them to control her the way she had.

She opened her eyes. She knew she had to tell him, if their relationship stood any chance of survival. She knew she had to and she wanted to. But still, she could not find the words. She opened her mouth but nothing came out.

'What is it, love?' Andy leant closer as if it was her voice that was broken and not her resolve.

Instead of a confession she said, 'My bike?'

He shook his head. 'You won't be riding it again. Tell you what,' he went on, his voice brightening, 'how about I buy you a brand new one? One of those specialized mountain bikes you've always wanted?'

'Can't my old one be repaired?'

'It's a write-off, Sian,' he said gently, and then his handsome face, so rarely angry, darkened with rage. 'That bloody stupid woman drove right over it.'

'It was a woman, then. In the red car?' said Sian in surprise.

'Her name's Rawson. Joanne knows her vaguely – says she

has two kids at the same school as Holly and Abbey. Apparently she was on her way home from work and she was running late to pick up her children from their grandmother's out at The Glynn. She says she didn't see the bend up ahead, forgot it was there. Stupid cow.' He shook his head in disgust.

The woman had made an error of judgement in trying to overtake on a bend, no doubt about that, but Sian did not share Andy's anger towards her, because she felt she bore some of the blame too. If she had not been thinking about personal problems she never would have allowed herself to end up in such a vulnerable position on the road. 'Did you speak to her?'

'No. The police told me. They said she was pretty badly shaken up. She bloody well should be. She could've killed you. And the van driver.'

'Is he okay?'

Andy sighed. 'Yeah, he's fine as far as I know. She didn't hit him. The only thing that got hit was your bike. You could press charges you know.'

If she didn't tell him now, when would she? This was the moment right here, right now. She felt it in her heart. She must find the courage somehow to face up to this problem before it completely ruined everything. She could so easily have been killed – but she hadn't. The accident had been a warning, a wake-up call, to let her know that life was precious and wonderful and she was a fool for squandering her and Andy's happiness. She'd been given a second chance. No one could do this for her. The fingers on her right hand closed around the blanket like a vice.

'Sian,' said Andy's voice. 'Did you hear what I said? You should sue for damages.'

Sian shook her head very gently and relaxed her hand. 'No, I won't do that.'

'Why not? Look at the mess you're in. You're entitled to compensation for your injuries and the bike and time off work.'

'Oh, the shop! I'd forgotten all about it.' Sian struggled to sit up.

'Shush. Lie still. It's okay,' said Andy and he placed a firm but gentle hand on her undamaged shoulder. 'The shop is fine. I spoke to Bernie this morning and she said she can hold the fort for a few weeks until you're back on your feet. Maddy'll help out too.'

She relaxed, letting her body sink into the comfort of the pillows once more, and tried to let go of that particular worry. The shop wasn't, after all, what was wrong with her life. She closed her eyes and lay quietly for some moments listening to the sounds around her – the exchange of voices down the corridor, the tacky sound of rubber soles on the lino in the hall, the ceaseless hum of machinery. The heat was overpowering – her palms sweated against the blanket. People thought her strong and independent and capable. But she wasn't. She was a coward. She criticised other people for their failings, their weak will when it came to making the lifestyle changes necessary to save the environment. But she was the weakest of them all. She could not find courage, not even for the man she loved.

She felt a touch, light as a feather, on the back of her hand and opened her eyes. Andy swallowed and looked at the small, greyish bruise on the back of her hand, where a line had been inserted the night before and only removed that morning. He gasped suddenly and then she realised that he was crying. 'I thought I'd lost you, Sian. As soon as I got that phone call from the hospital, I knew you'd come off your bike.'

The sight of him in such distress brought tears to Sian's eyes.

'You could've died, Sian,' he said, his voice breaking.

She tried to hoist herself into a sitting position, desperate to comfort him, but his weight had her trapped beneath the covers. She struggled for a few moments then collapsed back onto the pillows.

'It's my fault this happened,' said Andy, and he sniffed. 'I should've insisted you come with me or get the train home. I should have just gone round the back of the shop and taken your bike, whether you liked it or not. And then this never would've happened.'

She squeezed his hand. She would not let him take the flak for her foolishness. 'No, you absolutely must not blame yourself, Andy. You tried. It was my stupidity, my stubbornness that led to this. I should've listened to you about the weather.' He let this pass unremarked and Sian continued, paving her way towards the truth, 'And I am partly responsible for what happened last night. I should've taken evasive action as soon as I realised that the car wasn't going to back off. If I'd been thinking straight I would've pulled over and let it pass.' Her voice wobbled and she took a few moments to bring it under control. 'I was in no fit state to be in charge of a bike.'

'Because you were upset?'

She looked at him. 'That's right.' Her voice was a whisper.

Andy let go of her hand. 'I was a prat. I shouldn't have walked out on you like that.'

'I don't blame you. I was . . . I was . . .' she began and could go no further, her throat constricted with fear and the muscles round her heart tightening like a laced corset. She wept freely. She closed her eyes but it made no difference – the tears seeped uninhibited from beneath her lids.

Andy found her fingers and entwined them with his. He lifted the back of her hand to his face and, through her tears, she saw him tenderly press it to his lips. 'Sian, darling, what is it? What's wrong with us?'

This brought forth a fresh wave of tears. 'There's nothing wrong with us,' she managed to blurt out between great sobs. 'It's me. There's something wrong with me.'

She cried uncontrollably then for a long time, gut-wrenching sobs that left her shaking and short of breath. Andy pressed the palm of her hand against his cheek and whispered, his voice a lullaby, 'Shush, my darling. Please don't cry, baby.'

When the sobs had at last eased and she looked into his ashen face she saw it was rigid with alarm. She stared into Andy's dark brown eyes, the pupils wide with fear, and her love for him – her inability to see him suffer – finally forced her to put aside her own fear. It took every ounce of energy she had left to force the words out, her determination at last winning out. 'I . . . I have a problem, Andy. A sort of mental problem.'

He nodded once, the expression on his face as solemn as an undertaker's.

'It's a phobia.' She paused to force air into her lungs which suddenly seemed too small, too tight. Her pulse raced, the skin on her neck began to tingle and she could feel the beads of sweat on her brow. She thought that having confessed twice before, it would be easier the third time. But she had been wrong.

When he saw she could not go on Andy squeezed her hand gently and said, 'What are you afraid of?'

She would not let this fear rule her life any more. She would overcome it. She would win. And so she mustered up every last bit of courage to finally spit out what had dwelt in her heart, like a cancer eating away at her from the inside, for so long. 'Of giving birth. Of having a baby.'

Her breath became shallower, the room was suddenly

spinning and the tingling sensation spread from her neck to her face and torso. She closed her eyes and all the while she could hear Andy's voice as though he were far away at the end of a tunnel, whispering soothing words of comfort. 'It's going to be all right, baby. It's going to be all right.'

And then, when she thought she could bear it no more, when she thought that the shallow breath she had just taken might be her last, her heartbeat slowed, her chest muscles relaxed and the tingling sensation slowly died away.

Andy sat in complete silence for a long time with a glum expression on his face and when he said, 'Well, that explains a lot, Sian,' she burst into tears once more.

'Come here.' He shuffled further up the bed, leant over and held her gently, awkwardly, against his chest, enveloping her in his arms. He pressed his lips against her forehead, greasy with sweat, and smoothed her lank hair with his hand. 'Sometimes I don't know what to do with you, Sian, you do know that, don't you?' and she managed a brief, sad smile.

Later, after he'd held her and the tears had dried, she told him everything.

'I wish you'd said, Sian. Long before now. I wish you'd given me the chance to help you.'

'I'm sorry.' Sian reached out and touched his chin. 'I just couldn't. I was so worried that you would hate me.'

He tutted. 'Why would I hate you for being afraid of something?' he asked, sounding hurt.

She lowered her eyes. 'Because I wasn't honest with you. I told you that I didn't want children and it's true that I don't have strong maternal feelings, not like Louise. And I've spent a lot of years telling myself that I didn't want a baby. But it's not that I don't want a child. Not really,' she blurted out, 'I just don't want to give birth to it.'

There was a long silence during which Sian could almost

369

hear the cogs turning in Andy's brain. She looked away, her face burning with shame for all the years she had kept her miserable little secret so close to her chest, letting it poison their relationship like a love letter from an old flame. She only hoped and prayed it wasn't too late. That Andy could find it in his heart to forgive her for what she had done. And what she was. A coward.

'So,' he said at last, 'all that stuff about the environment, it was just a smokescreen?'

'No, not at all. I do care about the earth and I think people should limit the number of children they have,' she said in a quiet voice, still unable to meet his eye. She fingered the blanket, half moons of dirt still under her nails from last night. 'But that's not why I can't give you the child you want.'

Andy put his hand up and gently lifted her chin until she was forced to look at him. His eyes were glazed like the road last night, wet with rain. 'You said you can't, Sian. But the real question is, do you *want* to?'

She nodded as the tears flowed again. 'I think we'd make a beautiful baby together, Andy. And I want to give you that child because I know that it means so much to you. I'm just sorry that I can't do it. And I should've told you that a long time ago. But I was afraid that if you knew you'd finish with me. And I couldn't bear that, Andy.'

He looked at her sadly and shook his head. 'Surely you know me better than that, Sian?' He paused, cleared his throat and then, clearly irritated, said, 'I just wish you could hear yourself, Sian.'

She sniffed, startled by his abrupt tone. 'What do you mean?'

'Don't you want to overcome this phobia?'

What a silly question. Couldn't he see what this phobia

was doing to her – and them? She would give anything to be free of it. 'Of course I do.'

'Then stop talking as if you can't,' he said and his gaze, hard and unflinching, took her aback. 'Because by talking like that, you're programming yourself for failure. And it doesn't have to be like that. You can change the way you think. The way you feel about this.'

She swallowed, his criticism stinging like the graze on her cheek. She blushed, feeling patronised, her pride hurt. But what he said made sense. She had lived with this phobia for so long that it was part of her make-up, her character. Unless she started thinking differently, she would never be free of it. 'Do you really think it's possible for me to change?'

'I know so,' he said, his voice softening. 'And the first thing we're going to do is get you some professional help, right?' He smiled at her then, the way he used to before things had gone wrong between them.

And she smiled back. Maybe, just maybe, with Andy on board, together they could find a way to overcome her phobia. Because if he believed it possible, then there might be hope after all. 'Okay. Will you come with me?'

'Sian, darling,' he said, his voice deep and throaty, 'I would go to the ends of the earth with you and back again.'

Louise, at her desk in the office, glanced at her watch. It was nearly twelve o'clock. Sian had been home for three days and Andy had gone back to work. Louise felt so guilty for not answering her phone the night of the accident – she'd put Cameron first when her family needed her most. Thankfully, she would not make that mistake twice. She'd not heard from Cameron since and she knew she never would again.

She put on her coat and scarf, told the others where she was going and headed over to the marina. It was a lovely winter day, her breath fogging in the crisp, cold air, the trees bereft of every leaf. It had rained in the night and the board-walk was still damp, the pale December sun too weak to dry it. The water in the marina was calm, quietly lapping against the hulls of the few boats still left in the water.

She looked over at the spot where Kevin's boat used to be and came to a halt, standing there with her hands in her coat pockets, remembering. The craft had been taken out of the water two months ago, but she could still visualise every detail of the yacht and the day when they'd sat aboard, the wind whipping her hair, and eaten salmon sandwiches – their first date. She'd imagined then that they might have a life together but she'd spoilt it all by chasing after a fantasy that had turned out to be a delusion.

Out on the Lough, the sea shimmered like a sequinned dress and a flock of light-bellied Brent geese flew overhead, their black necks as straight as rulers, tender pale underbellies exposed, the air filled with their guttural call. Soon this would be the view from her own front window – and she would have Sian as a neighbour. A shiver ran down Louise's spine when she thought of what had happened to her sister. Her face had swollen so badly that Louise had hardly recognised her. But thank God she was on the mend and thank God she had finally found the courage to tell Andy about her phobia.

Together Sian and Andy were so strong – if any couple could overcome this problem, they could. The first step had already been taken – Sian had booked an appointment to see Doctor McCrory next week. Louise would have all her fingers and toes crossed that day. Today, once they'd eaten a quick lunch, she thought she'd offer to wash Sian's hair – an impossible task for her to do on her own given the cast on her arm.

Louise went into the sandwich shop that had recently opened up on the waterfront. She ordered two takeaway sandwiches and two cups of tomato and basil soup from a cheery woman with cheeks like a baby's bottom. And while she waited for the order, she wondered if Kevin had met someone else. She couldn't expect him to hang around waiting for her, while she went off chasing dreams of happy-ever-after with a man she had divorced for very good reason.

She had been a fool. Cameron wasn't half the man Kevin was. She missed him and she hadn't realised quite how much until now. She thought of the courage Sian had displayed in telling Andy her deepest fear and wondered if she had the courage to call Kevin and tell him . . . tell him what? That she'd made a mistake – that he was the one she loved, after all? She wasn't sure she could. After that awful experience with Cameron at The Marine Hotel, she'd lost her confidence.

She paid for the order and walked slowly in the direction of Sian's house, her head bowed, staring at the wooden boards beneath her feet. The recent encounter with her ex-husband had left her jaded, doubting her own judgement and common sense. Perhaps what she needed, she told herself sensibly – while her heart told her something different – was a period of calm, of reflection. Not a man. A time to gather her thoughts and adjust to the realities that had suddenly become clear to her. It was time to stop chasing dreams and finally learn to be at peace with the choice she had made and the family she had created.

When she got to Sian's pale blue front door, she rang the bell and, without waiting for an answer, stepped inside. She picked her way around the clutter in the hall – muddy boots, a bike helmet, a battered rucksack, a frayed fluorescent running jacket and a battered asymmetrical kayak oar propped up against the wall. She set the brown paper bag of food on the floor, took off her coat and scarf and hung them up.

'Sian, it's me,' she hollered, picked up the bag and walked towards the kitchen. 'I've brought lunch.'

And then suddenly a male figure on the sofa, whom she had not, at first, noticed, stood up.

She put her hand to her throat, startled. Then she saw who it was and her stomach flipped.

'Hi Louise,' said Kevin Quinn, in a deep voice, smooth as velvet. He was casually dressed in a long-sleeved navy shirt, open at the collar, and dark jeans. His shoes had been left at the door. Papers were strewn over the coffee table and he held a slim silver pen in his right hand.

'I . . . you . . . you gave me a surprise.' She put a hand on her belly. 'I wasn't expecting you to be here. Where's Sian?'

He raised his green eyes to the ceiling. 'Upstairs.'

'Is she all right?' She moved towards the stairs and looked up anxiously.

'Absolutely fine,' he said reassuringly. 'She went up to get the laptop. We were just planning the agenda for the next Friends of the Lough meeting.'

'But she's supposed to be taking it easy! The doctors said she must rest.'

Kevin shrugged and gave her a wry smile, his eyes sparkling with humour. Although only a little older than Cameron, he seemed so much more centred and so much wiser. Happiness, born of contentment with life, radiated from him in a way she had never seen in Cameron. 'Since when has your sister ever done what she was told?'

'Good point.' Louise smiled then, and said, 'It's good to see you, Kevin.'

'You too.' He stared at her until she had to look away.

'I've missed . . . having lunch together,' she said.

374

He nodded in agreement and opened his mouth to speak when Sian's voice said rather artificially, 'Oh, I wasn't expecting you today, Louise.' Louise turned to see Sian limp gingerly down the stairs, a silver laptop tucked under her good arm. She wore an old grey T-shirt of Andy's and a brown over-sized man's cardigan draped over her shoulders. The plaster on her arm was decorated with scribbles and pink hearts – evidently the girls had been to work on it. The left side of her face was crusted with dark, bloody scabs and her hair had never looked more in need of a wash. Poor Sian – she looked awful and yet . . . she seemed happy, in spite of her painful injuries and battered appearance.

'Weren't you? But I said I would pop over yesterday.'

Sian came and stood between them and turned to face Louise so that her back was towards Kevin. She gave Louise an exaggerated, conspiratorial wink and Louise felt the colour rise to her cheeks. 'Ahem,' said Louise, and narrowed her eyes. 'I thought you were supposed to be resting.' Not playing match-maker.

'No time for that,' said Sian, shuffling over to the coffee table and opening the laptop. She knelt down slowly on one knee, pressed a few buttons and the screen came to life. 'Have you heard the latest?'

'What?'

'They're planning to store gas under the Lough in seven massive salt caverns.'

'Blimey.'

'And we,' she said, pausing to search for something on the computer, 'need to ensure that the wildlife is protected. There,' she said, turning the laptop towards Kevin, 'there's the e-mail I was telling you about.' Kevin bent over to peer at the screen, his hands on his thighs.

Louise, feeling like a gate-crasher, said, 'Should I go?'

'No,' said Sian with a cross frown, rising unsteadily to her feet, 'don't be ridiculous.'

Louise held up the bag. 'I brought lunch. But only enough for two, I'm afraid.'

'Not to worry,' said Sian, 'I've enough food to feed an army. People keep bringing me stuff. Come on, let's see what's in the fridge. Kevin, you wouldn't put on the kettle and make us all some tea, would you?'

'Yes, Ma'am.' Kevin got to his feet, brought his heels together, though they made no sound, and saluted Sian's back. Louise giggled.

'Stop taking the piss, Kevin,' said Sian good-naturedly, hobbling over to the kitchen, 'and make yourself useful, will you?' It was good to see Sian in such high, happy spirits.

He chuckled to himself, then did what he was told. They cobbled together a lunch of bits and pieces – Louise's contribution plus cheese and crackers, fruit and home-made chocolate cake from one of Sian's regular customers.

'I didn't know you were involved with Friends of the Lough,' said Louise when they were seated round the table, eating and drinking tea.

'I wasn't,' he said, taking a bite of a sandwich, chewing and swallowing quickly. 'Until she,' he went on with a nod in Sian's direction, 'decided otherwise.'

'You make it sound like I strong-armed you!' protested Sian.

'I'm only joking,' said Kevin and he turned to Louise and said seriously, 'I was glad to get involved. I love this Lough and the wildlife that it sustains. There are a lot of competing demands – the harbour, sailors, wildlife, the marina and now this gas storage proposal – and our job is to help them work in harmony to keep this Lough special.'

Sian raised her cup of tea. 'Hear, hear to that!'

Louise laughed and said, 'Well, I admire you both, I really do.' She couldn't help but compare Kevin's altruistic motives to Cameron's purely selfish ones. And it made her wonder, also, if it was time she looked beyond the narrow confines of her work and home and got involved in the wider community. These last few years, she'd thought only of Oli and herself. 'I'd love to stay and hear more but I have to get back to work.' She'd do Sian's hair tomorrow.

She quickly tidied away some of the lunch things, then gave Sian a peck on the cheek. Kevin said, 'I'll walk you over.'

'What about the agenda?' Louise glanced over at the papers on the coffee table.

Kevin looked at Sian. 'Oh, I think we're just about done, aren't we?'

Sian nodded her head. 'Definitely.'

'So how are things?' asked Kevin, once they were outside. He'd put on his leather flying jacket, the one Louise loved so much, a bright green striped scarf and black leather gloves. In her work heels she was only a couple of inches shorter than him. The golden rays of the lowering sun shone in his eyes, making them gleam like polished emeralds.

She shoved her hands in her pockets and tried not to stare. 'Good. You know. Busy.'

They walked in the direction of the marina, keeping a careful distance from each other. 'I stopped by earlier and had a look at the house,' he said.

'You did?' That was nice of him – to take an interest. Perhaps he still cared for her after all . . .

'Well, I said I'd keep an eye on it. It's coming on well,' he said, watching her as they walked. 'The chipboard floor's down and they've started on the plasterboard walls. I think you'll be in by the beginning of March.'

Louise nodded. They came to the marina, took a left and

started walking inland towards her office building, the sun casting two truncated charcoal shadows on the boardwalk behind them. 'Yeah, that's what I've been told. I'm looking forward to having a place of my own. The flat's all right but it doesn't quite feel like home. Whereas, this . . .' She paused, turned around to face the sea once more, pulled her hands from her pockets and raised both palms in the air. 'This feels like home already. I can't wait to move in. Neither can Oli.'

'I think he'll like it down here. You should get a telescope so he can bird-watch from the house. He seems to have a real affinity with nature.'

'Do you think so?' asked Louise, surprised and slightly resentful that she had not recognised this characteristic in her own son before.

'Oh yeah. Much more so than my two when they were that age. Have you noticed the way he's captivated by the tiniest bug or leaf?'

'Yeah,' said Louise thoughtfully. 'He is, isn't he?' Now that she thought about it, Oli could spend hours watching a spider or playing with a pile of dirt in her parents' garden. She had assumed all children were the same. The problem was, without a sibling to draw comparisons against, she had not realised this behaviour was exceptional. Soon Oli would have a garden of his own and he could watch bugs all day long if he wanted. She could picture him already running around outside in the summer in little khaki shorts and a fisherman's sun hat. She would install a climbing frame and maybe a swing.

'Louise,' said Kevin and something in the tone of his voice made her stop and turn to face him. He looked deep into her eyes and the pleasant expression on his face evaporated. 'How did things go with Cameron? Sian said that he came over to see you again last week.'

Where to start? Louise looked away, and sighed loudly.

'That bad?'

She smiled and said bitterly, 'Let's just say that divorcing him was the best move I've ever made. I thought he'd changed but I was wrong. I won't be seeing him ever again.'

'You sound very . . . adamant.'

'I am. He called Oli a "bastard", Kevin,' she unintentionally blurted out, tears springing suddenly to her eyes.

His face hardened. 'Stupid idiot,' he said.

Louise flicked the tears away with her hand. 'I'm sorry.' Her fingers were pink-tipped with cold.

Kevin slipped his right glove off and enveloped her fingers in his warm hand. 'You're freezing. Here.' He took off the other glove and held them both between his knees. Then he pressed her hands together as if in prayer and rubbed them briskly, their heads bent together, foggy breath mingling in the air. His touch was sure and capable – it made the hairs on the back of her neck stand up. After a short while, the circulation came back and the tips of her fingers returned to a normal hue.

'There, that's better isn't it?' He slipped his gloves back on.

He grinned and she nodded. 'Thank you.' The simple, caring act spoke volumes to Louise and the physical contact reminded her how sterile her life had become. She shoved her hands back into her pockets. Every waking minute of her day was filled with either work or Oli or the humdrum practicalities of living. But all the busyness in the world could not disguise the fact that she was lonely.

'Come on, let's get you back to the office.' He started to move away.

'Kevin,' she said, rooted to the spot. She would be late for work now but she didn't care. She could not let this moment, this opportunity, pass.

He turned, the sun behind him, bathing his fine frame in a gentle golden glow. 'What?'

'I'm sorry I never called.' She paused as a woman with a dog passed and nodded a greeting.

He looked at her searchingly. 'I figured you needed a bit of time.'

'That's right,' she said, grateful that he had spared her the censure she so rightly deserved. She took a deep breath. 'Do you think that we could maybe pick up where we left off?'

He took a step towards her. His smile was warm and eager. 'There's nothing I'd like more. You know, I really believe you and I were made to be together, Louise.'

She blushed. 'There's just something I want you to know.'

'What's that?'

'I don't expect you to be a father to Oli.'

He frowned and cocked his head. 'Okay,' he said slowly and then observed, 'That's an odd thing to say.'

She screwed up her face and tried to explain. 'It's just, well, I very nearly made the mistake of getting back with Cameron just because he offered to adopt Oli.'

Kevin's eyebrows, dark and thick, went up a millimetre.

'And I know that might sound odd considering I chose to have Oli on my own, but I was so desperate for him to have the one thing I couldn't give him – a dad – that I nearly made the biggest mistake of my life in taking him back.'

Kevin nodded but said nothing, his eyes squinting in concentration.

'And there was the pressure from my family. They've been very supportive, and they love Oli and they're good to him. I can't fault them for that. But they've also been judgemental too – my parents in particular. I guess I want their complete approval,' she said, and she could not get the words, bitter and full of hurt, out fast enough, 'but no matter what I do

I'm never going to get it because I can't change the way Oli came into this world.' She closed her mouth, her sealed lips like a dam over bitter words.

'Oh, Louise,' said Kevin. He came close and cupped her face in his gloved hands. The leather was cold and smooth against her skin. His eyes scanned her face. 'I raised two children with the help of a partner and it was the hardest thing I've ever done. Choosing to raise a child on your own is one of the bravest things anyone can do. *Especially* when the people you love don't approve. You should be proud of yourself, not racked with guilt. And if your parents can't accept what you've done then that's their problem, not yours.'

Tears filled her eyes. 'But it hurts.'

'I know, pet,' he said, the term of endearment slipping off his tongue so naturally it made Louise's heart momentarily soar. 'But you can't take responsibility for the way they feel. Or change them. You'll always fail. You have to accept that, however much you disagree with them, they have the right to their opinions the same way you have the right to yours. And then you just have to let it go.'

'It's hard,' she sniffed and he took his hands from her face. 'I just so badly want them to say they're proud of what I've done.'

'I'm sure they are proud of you,' he said, his gaze steady. 'I think the fact that they've welcomed Oli into their lives speaks volumes, even though your lifestyle choice goes against what I imagine are deeply held values.' He smiled and tried to lighten the tone of the conversation. 'Anyway, what does it matter what other people think when you know you're right?'

Louise was silent and looked at the white water marks on the toes of her black boots from the rain the day before. Out on the water, the Brent geese called to each other, their plaintive 'rhut, rhut' distinctive above the hoots and whoops of the other birds. Overhead a seagull, the scavenger of the sea, screeched then swooped down, its wings flapping like sails, to feast on a discarded sandwich crust. And suddenly, standing there by the marina, the water lapping quietly under the boardwalk and the warmless sun on her face, she felt a sudden urge to bare her soul to him. To articulate what she had never shared with anyone else.

She focused on a leafless tree in the distance, still as a photograph. 'Because having Oli the way I did was never the way I wanted to have children.' She swallowed. 'It was always a second best option and a poor one at that. And I've spent the last four years trying to convince myself, as much as anyone else, that that isn't the case. That I can do as good a job as any couple. But in my heart I know I can't. I can't properly make up for the fact that he doesn't have a father.'

There. She'd said it. For four years she'd kept up the façade that she was a hundred per cent positive about her choice to become a single mother. She'd made Oli the centre of her life, read every parenting manual she could get her hands on, and taken a career break to devote herself full-time to the business of parenting – and all to prove that she could do it on her own. But she was plagued with doubts.

Kevin sighed. 'That's tough.'

She nodded sadly and looked into his eyes, as green as the sea. 'It was such a difficult choice to make. I had to accept the end of my marriage and, well . . .' She paused for a moment's reflection. 'I guess what I'm trying to say is that while Oil has brought me great joy, there's a part of me that still mourns what might have been. The husband and the big family – I won't have another baby on my own.'

'Well, you never know what the future holds, Louise.' He paused and stared at her for a few moments, a little furrow between his eyebrows. 'And not many people are lucky enough to have the perfect family, if such a thing exists. Look at me. I had a good wife and two lovely kids but we married too young – we couldn't make it work. And look at your sister, Joanne. Don't waste your life yearning after a model of perfection that rarely exists in reality.' He paused for a moment, staring off into the distance, and then brought his attention fully back to Louise. 'All any of us can do is muddle through the best we can. Nobody, and no marriage, is perfect and there are many different – and equally successful – formulas for a happy family. You have to put your disappointment aside and let go of the idea that you've failed Oli. Because believe me he will pick up on it. He will absorb your disappointment and start to feel that there *is* something inferior about his family.'

This thought struck fear into her heart. She thought that she'd done a pretty good job of hiding her true emotions on the subject from Oli, frequently reinforcing the idea that families came in many shapes and sizes, like pieces of Lego.

But maybe she was kidding herself. Maybe Oli understood far more than she gave him credit for. Had he already detected her underlying disappointment? The danger, which she saw straight away, was that he might somehow interpret this as disappointment in him.

'I think you're right. That is how I've felt, how I've let other people make me feel. And it's got to end right now.'

She had to get over the idea that her little family was somehow second-rate. And there and then she decided. Instead of grieving for what she and Oli did not have, she would be thankful for her many blessings – her health and that of Oli, financial security, the love of her family and friends and, of course, Kevin. She would do it, for her own sake and for Oli's. And with this resolution came a sense of purpose and a gladness that had been absent in her heart for a very long time. Because it wasn't just other people who had been judging her harshly – she had been judging herself.

'Oh, Kevin,' she said, as slow tears of happiness ran down her cheeks. 'I love you.'

'And I love you too, Louise.'

Chapter Eighteen

Sian stood barefoot on the beach at Ballygally, the cool sand damp between her toes, the folds of her simple pale blue cotton dress flapping in the wind. The sea, whipped up by the fresh breeze, rippled like the frosting on top of the cake Louise and Joanne, between them, had baked for this, her wedding day.

Opposite her stood Andy, tanned and relaxed-looking in a cream linen shirt and long khaki linen trousers. Since they'd walked onto the beach together he had not taken his eyes off her and now he stood with the hot June sun on his face, smiling.

'Welcome, family and friends,' began the Humanist celebrant, a warm personable woman called Kate, who stood between them facing the small crowd, the three of them forming a triangle. She wore a trouser suit of cream cotton and flat sandals and held a small black book open in her hands. 'We are here on this glorious day, in this special place, to celebrate the love that Sian and Andy have for each other, and to recognise and witness their decision to journey forward in this life as marriage partners. The greatest gift bestowed upon us is the gift of love freely given between two people . . .'

Sian let the words she and Andy had chosen together wash

over her like the gentle tide. She could barely believe that they were, at last, getting married. And it was perfect, exactly as she had imagined it. Just her and Andy on the gently shelving beach, the fairytale towers of the Ballygally Castle Hotel and the pretty green scenery of the Antrim coastline – the perfect backdrop to their magical day.

And the handful of guests – their closest family and dearest friends – who stood a few metres away, witnesses to the most important day in Sian's life.

She took Andy's hand. Between the forefinger and thumb of his other hand he held a plain wedding band made from recycled gold. It glinted in the sun. The smile had fallen from his face now, his expression so serious Sian held her breath.

'I accept you just as you are today,' he said, looking down as he slipped the shiny band onto her ring finger. He grasped both hands in his and looked into her eyes and he was smiling now. She began to breathe again and he went on, his voice soft but steady. 'I give you my promise that from this day forward we will walk together, side by side, through all the years and in all that life may bring us. With this ring, I give you my heart. I have no greater gift to give you.'

She repeated the words – slipped a matching ring on his finger – and Kate said a few more words Sian barely registered, her heart so full of joy it pounded in her ears like the sound of the sea. Andy pulled her gently towards him and they kissed. And then a cheer went up and someone threw rice – a symbol of fertility – over them. They turned to face the small crowd, hand in hand, united at last, bound together forever. And Sian closed her eyes and thanked the Gods for her great fortune.

Later, Louise moved happily around the small kitchen in her new home putting the finishing touches to a wedding buffet lunch. Sian had given strict instructions that she wanted a simple, relaxed affair and her family had done their best to honour her wishes. They'd followed the dress code – everyday casual – and the only extravagances were the champagne and the rich fruit cake, decorated with a silver horseshoe and a little bunch of fake pink flowers.

Louise wore a simple linen shift with bare arms and, on her feet, flat slip-on sandals. The patio doors off the kitchen were open onto the garden, where the breeze coming off the Lough tempered the hot sun, and the children ran amok. She'd been told not to let anyone walk on the newly turfed lawn for six weeks, but she didn't care about the lawn half as much as she cared about everyone's happiness on her little sister's wedding day.

She remembered her own, lavish wedding crammed full of distant relatives and friends of Cameron's family – people she hardly knew and some of whom she never saw again. How much nicer this wedding was – a special, thoughtful day with the focus entirely on Sian and Andy with only the people who really mattered as guests. Outside, Andy's mother and his sister nursed glasses of pink champagne.

On the lawn, Abbey and Holly were teaching Oli how to skip. He was dressed in shorts and a T-shirt, pretty much the way she'd imagined that day when she'd stood by the marina, the cold pinching her cheeks, and told Kevin the secrets of her heart. Unable to get the timing right and his body movements still clumsily uncoordinated, Oli ended up tangled in the rope, which sent the girls into fits of hysterics.

The men sat on the patio, around the wooden table she'd just bought from B&Q, watching the children and drinking beer while she, Joanne, Sian and Christine buzzed about happily in the kitchen. There was a time when the feminist in Louise would've baulked at such an arrangement, but she now regarded the natural segregation of the sexes that occurred on social occasions as one of life's pleasant curiosities. She loved being in mixed company but there was an intimacy about women-only conversations that she loved just as much.

'That ceremony was lovely, Sian,' said her mother who was taking beetroot out of a jar into a small glass dish. All of a sudden, she set down the jar and the fork and searched in the pockets of her checked blue and yellow daydress until she found a clean hankie. She dabbed at her eyes as a fresh wave of tears overcame her. She did not look like a woman who'd just attended her daughter's wedding – on her feet she wore sensible flat beige sandals. All her previous objections to the Humanist ceremony – Was it legal? What would all the relatives think about not being invited? Weren't casual clothes inappropriate for a wedding? Why weren't they having a formal wedding breakfast afterwards? – seemed to have melted away. And it was no wonder – the service was the most moving one Louise had ever witnessed.

Joanne, buttering slices of home-baked wheaten bread, stood beside her mother in a pink gingham sundress that revealed tender, pale skin that had yet to catch the rays of the sun. She set down the butter knife and put her arm around her mother and squeezed her shoulders. Her long blonde hair fell about her shoulders like a shawl. 'Come on, Mum,' she said brightly. 'No tears now. You promised. This is a happy occasion.'

'I know,' sniffed her mother, turning to Sian. 'You were just so lovely standing there on the beach with Andy. It was so romantic.'

Sian blushed. 'It was perfect, wasn't it?' she said, looking out the patio doors at her husband, who threw his head back just then and laughed. 'Exactly the way I always wanted. Just us, in nature, and the people we love around us.' She paused for a moment and added, thoughtfully, nibbling the end of a carrot, 'Though we very nearly didn't get this far.'

She looked at Joanne and Louise and continued, 'And it's down to you two that we did. I can't thank you enough for everything you've done to help me. Having a baby doesn't seem outside the realms of possibility now. And only a few months ago I never would've believed that possible.'

'Oh, pet,' said her mother who was now fully up to speed on Sian's phobia. And she dabbed at her eyes some more.

'Are you still seeing that hypnotherapist Doctor McCrory referred you to?' probed Joanne gently.

Louise unwrapped a package of feta cheese, the sound of laughter filtering in from outside. She chopped it into cubes and added it to a bowl of cubed cucumber.

Sian wandered over to the patio doors, still barefoot, her legs slim and tanned but not, Louise noticed with a smile, hairless. She looked out on the garden where Andy was now playing a game of chase with Oli and his two younger cousins. Maddy was hunched on one of the folding wooden chairs that had come with the table, texting. 'Not for much longer,' she said and she slid her foot over the tiles where the sun, beating in, had warmed them, like she was dipping her toe in a pond. 'You know it's incredible what that woman has done for me. I must get her a nice thank you present . . .'

'Do you think you're completely cured, then?' said Joanne, freezing for a moment with the bread basket in both hands. She glanced quickly over at Louise who held her breath.

Sian turned to face them and thought for a moment. She raised her eyebrows and rocked her hips from side to side as if warming up for a run. 'I wouldn't say I'm completely cured but I don't feel nearly as terrified as I did before. I feel nervous about the idea of giving birth obviously but I also feel confident that it's something I can do. Whereas before, as you know, I never would've even contemplated it.'

Joanne and Louise smiled at each other.

'Well, thank God it's working for you, love,' said Christine. 'That's all that matters.'

'So, do you think you and Andy might start trying for a baby now that you're married?' ventured Louise, tossing tiny plum tomatoes into the bowl with the feta cheese and cucumber. She rinsed her hands under the tap and wiped them on a towel.

A slow, secret smile spread across Sian's face. 'We've started already.'

Joanne clasped her hands together and squealed, 'Oh Sian, that is just wonderful news.'

Louise went over and gave Sian a big hug. 'It'll be the best thing that ever happened to you, Sian. You just wait and see. Once you hold your baby in your arms . . .' She shook her head and smiled, her eyes brimming with tears.

'Do you mean you could be pregnant already?' said Christine, staring at Sian's stomach. The heat in the kitchen had made her pink lipstick seep into the fine lines around her mouth.

'Yes,' said Sian and when Louise let out a little gasp, she added with a smile, 'though I'm pretty sure I'm not.'

'Couldn't you wait till after the wedding?' tutted Christine.

'Stop doing that, Mum,' said Louise quietly and there was a sudden hush. All eyes turned to Louise.

'What?' said Christine.

'Criticising.'

Their mother blinked behind her glasses. 'I'm not criticising. I'm only saying.'

'You're making it pretty clear what you think, Mum,' said Louise. Recalling the conversation she'd had with Kevin on the subject, she took a deep breath. And despite her tummy doing flips that would've made a gymnast proud, she pressed on, 'Sometimes, though, it's better to keep opinions to yourself, don't you think?'

Her mother stuck out her lower jaw and said, 'I don't know what you mean.'

'The world's changed, Mum. People live together, and they have babies out of wedlock all the time and some like me have them without a father even being on the scene.'

Her mother's gaze slid away, a sort of resentful look on her face.

'I know you and Dad don't approve of the way I had Oli and I don't suppose you ever will. But it would be better if you tried to keep your feelings to yourself, no matter how difficult that is.' She smiled. 'You know that old saying, if you can't say something nice, don't say anything at all?'

Her mother's shoulders stiffened and she ran her tongue round the inside of her lips. 'Well, I'm sorry. I wasn't aware that I was doing that.'

Louise forced a smile, trying to make her point without offending her mother. 'You do it all the time, Mum. And the strange thing is, you'd think you, of all people, would be more understanding, because of the fact that you did something unconventional in marrying Dad. Nobody thought it was a good idea at the time but you didn't let that stop you, did you? You married him even when everybody disapproved.'

Her mother lifted her chin. 'And if I had to do it over again, I wouldn't change a thing. I'd still marry your father. But that doesn't mean it was easy. Your father and I paid a hefty price. He got a phone call the night before the wedding saying that he'd get a bullet through the head if he married me – a Taig.'

Louise, who'd heard the story before, said, 'Oh, Mum.'

'Of course it came to nothing,' her mother carried on, 'it was just an empty threat. But a lot of my friends dropped me after I got married. And my parents never forgave me.' Her voice went all wobbly. 'But I never wanted you girls, or my grandchildren, to be different. To be judged. Being unconventional can be a hard and lonely road.' And just as quickly she regained her composure. She went over to the sink, picked up the dishcloth and wiped round the sink while Louise stood there like a statue.

And suddenly Louise realised that was why her mother had been so opposed to her decision to have Oli. And to the idea of Sian being pregnant before she was married. And it was why, also, she strongly disapproved of Joanne's impending divorce.

'I'm sorry that you and Dad had to go through that. But we live in a different world, Mum, than the one you grew up in. Nobody cares about that sort of thing any more, well not much anyway.'

Her mother stopped what she was doing and looked at Louise. 'Well, I hope you're right, is all I can say.'

Louise lowered her head, looked at her mother from under her eyebrows, and said, 'Do you think you could stop judging everyone?'

'I'll certainly try, pet,' she said and looked a little flustered. She put a hand to her breast, the rings on her wedding finger tight like elastic, and looked at the others. 'I didn't mean to hurt you, any of you. I didn't realise—'

'We know you didn't.' Louise went over and gave her mother a brief hug. She felt soft and small, and she smelt of talcum powder and the Chanel perfume Louise had bought her for Christmas. 'Let's not talk about it any more,' whispered Louise and she patted the loose, freckled skin on her mother's arm.

The others, who had been watching, busied themselves while Louise drizzled balsamic vinegar and olive oil on the feta salad. Having finally tackled her mother head on, she felt oddly elated. As if she had successfully cauterised a stubborn, open wound that had been bothering her for a long time.

Mum cleared her throat and said brightly, 'Well, tell us all about your honeymoon in Donegal, Sian. What have you planned?' The mood in the room lightened immediately and everyone chatted away merrily for a few minutes.

Then Oli came barrelling in with an orange plastic water gun in his hand. 'I can't get it to work, Mummy. It's broken.' His bottom lip protruded and he looked as if he might burst into tears at any moment. 'Can you fix it?'

'Oh, Oli, love, I can't right now,' she said, ripping basil leaves and scattering them in the bowl. 'I'm busy.'

Just then Kevin strolled in from the garden, his hands in the pockets of his blue shorts. His brown deck shoes were well-worn and his white shirt was open at the neck. His legs were thick with dark hairs and the scar on his throat from an emergency tracheotomy many years ago, was white against his tanned skin. For a moment Louise imagined how different her life would be now had that operation, performed by a Boys' Brigade leader on a camping trip, failed. A wave of gratitude washed over her and she lifted her face and stared out at the blue sky, a kind of melancholy joy in her heart. She was just so thankful to have found Kevin after all those years of uncertainty.

'What is it, son?' said Kevin and Louise smiled at him.

The first time Louise had heard Kevin address Oli by this term, it had plucked at her heartstrings. She'd forgotten momentarily that the salutation was often used locally as a term of endearment for a boy, in much the same way a Yorkshireman might use 'lass' to address a young girl. But though it was not meant literally, it was evidence of the close bond that had developed between Kevin and her son.

Kevin hunkered down in the small space in the middle of the kitchen while Oli explained the problem. Kevin rubbed his chin and said, 'Looks like your mum's busy right now. Do you want me to have a look?'

Oli nodded solemnly and placed the gun in Kevin's outstretched palms. He followed Kevin through the patio doors, where they both sat down on the step and examined the gun, Oli's face cupped in his hands in concentration. The girls, in sweetie colours, were practising handstands on the grass. 'The trigger's jammed.' Kevin turned the gun over. 'Let's just see if we can . . . mmm. I might need to adjust that screw. Louise,' he called over his shoulder, 'do you have a screwdriver?'

Louise lifted plastic beakers out of a cupboard. 'There's a set out in the shed,' she hollered. The screwdrivers had been a housewarming gift from Dad and were still in their box, unused.

Oli came inside and announced, 'I'm going to look at the birdies.' He ran over to the far side of the room, where the window faced onto the glittering sea. He climbed onto a plastic stool set up in front of the brand new telescope Kevin had given him for his birthday last month. 'Kevin says there's ferns.' He pressed his eye to the eyepiece and his tongue, pink like cold ham, peaked out the corner of his mouth.

'He means terns,' said Louise and smiled. She set the beakers on the breakfast bar and filled a jug with orange squash. 'Oli,' she called, 'what's your favourite type of tern?'

He looked over. 'The 'andwich one. Cos you can eat them,' he said and giggled.

Everyone laughed and Christine remarked, nesting a dish

of olives on the breakfast bar between a quiche and the bread basket, 'I have to say when Kevin gave that telescope to him, I thought it a strange birthday present for a child, but Oli's really taken to it, hasn't he?'

'Yeah,' said Louise, marvelling at how well Kevin understood Oli. But Kevin had been wrong about one thing – it was possible to have the perfect life. At work, the official opening of Loughanlea had gone like clockwork, Finn calling in all sorts of personal favours to attract the big names in mountain biking. They'd got great media coverage and early responses to the Scottish advertising campaign were encouraging. She'd moved into her wonderful new home, Oli was happy and secure and sleeping in his own bed at night.

And Kevin loved her.

'I think the telescope's fabulous,' said Sian. 'The only problem is that Andy wants one now! He reckons he can put it in the spare room.'

'Won't be room for it once the baby comes!' said Joanne brightly and Louise crossed her fingers and prayed that God would give Sian and Andy the child they wanted.

Sian blushed and deflected the attention from herself with, 'Well, what about you and Finn, Joanne? How are things going?'

But before Joanne had time to answer, Louise winked at Sian and said, 'They'll be the next ones getting married.'

Joanne, brushing crumbs off the breadboard into the bin, blushed like a schoolgirl. 'Steady on, Louise,' she laughed, 'it's early days.' She slid the breadboard back in its place, on its side, between the wall and the toaster with a resounding thud.

'I don't know about that. You've been seeing him since before Christmas. What's that? Nearly six months?'

'Is it? You're keeping better track than I am,' said Joanne, brushing imaginary crumbs off her dress.

395

'Well, you obviously like him a great deal,' said Louise, quite determined to tease more information out of her reluctant sister.

Joanne leant against the kitchen counter, her hands behind her back, her frame as dainty as a girl's and stared dreamily out the door at the sky. 'I do. I like him very much.'

'And how are things between you and Phil these days?' said Sian, slipping her hands into a pair of oven gloves.

Joanne's face darkened and she looked at her toes. Nails the colour of red Smarties peeped out of her mules. 'I try not to think about him if I can help it.'

'I'm sorry,' said Sian, 'I didn't mean to, you know, spoil the moment.'

Joanne brightened and gave Sian a thin-lipped smile. 'No, it's all right. Really. I can't pretend he doesn't exist, can I? I just find it hard to believe sometimes that I spent all those years married to him and putting up with . . . well, it's water under the bridge. He's almost like a stranger to me now.'

'And did you get the summer holidays sorted out?' asked Louise, lifting a glass jug down from the shelf above the cooker.

Joanne wrinkled her nose. 'Yeah, Holly and Abbey are going to go into Holiday Club for three weeks while Maddy works in the shop. That way Phil and I both get a bit of a break without the kids. Finn's talking about taking me away somewhere romantic.'

Sian tipped a tray of cocktail sausages for the children, slippy with grease, into a shallow, round dish. 'Lucky you!'

Louise poured thick, syrupy Ribena into the jug and winked at her sister.

'And the divorce?' ventured their mother.

Joanne shrugged and set a stack of plates on the breakfast bar, every inch of which was now covered. 'Finally going ahead.

Phil e-mailed me last week to tell me that he would admit to adultery and that Gemma would be named as co-respondent. It's maybe a bit vindictive but I wasn't going to let the two of them get away with anything less.'

'Damn right,' said Louise, topping the jug up with water.

'Well,' said Joanne, dusting her hands together as though brushing off all traces of Phil, 'as far as I'm concerned it can't come soon enough. I just want to get on with my new life with Finn.'

'Speak of the devil,' said Sian as Finn walked through the door, barefoot with a pair of reflective sports sunglasses perched on his head and a clutch of empty lager bottles in his hands. He'd ridden over from his flat in Carrickfergus on his bike for the meal and he wore cycling shorts and a tight Lycra T-shirt over his lithe body. It was hard not to stare at his toned, fit silhouette. Joanne made no effort not to.

'Hey, what's up? You guys talking 'bout me?'

'Well, yes, actually,' said Sian and she winked at Joanne. 'We were just wondering how long it would take you to come in here looking for more beer.'

He laughed, went over and nuzzled Joanne's hair.

Christine, who looked a bit affronted at this public display of intimacy, moved away and made herself useful tidying dishes at the sink. Louise smiled happily to herself, both amused by her mother's prudishness and overjoyed to see Joanne happy after so much heartache.

'Hi gorgeous,' said Finn.

'Hi handsome.' Joanne looked up into his face, and a beautiful smile that started in her eyes, lit up her features.

'Missed you,' he said and grinned.

'Me too.'

Finn held up four empty beer bottles. 'Any chance of a refill?'

'Cheeky beggar,' laughed Joanne and she poked him in the ribs. 'You only came in to get more beer. Not to see me!'

He chuckled and pulled her close and kissed the top of her head. 'I came in to see you too, babe. Honest.'

She pushed him away playfully and Louise said, 'There's plenty more beer in there, Finn.' She pointed at the fridge. 'Just help yourself.'

'Alrighty.' Finn got the beers, planted a kiss on Joanne's faintly blushing cheek and ambled outside again just as Maddy brushed past on her way inside.

She was wearing a short white denim skirt and a long pink T-shirt. Her legs were the same orange colour they had been all winter.

'So, Maddy, what do you think of your mum and Finn?' asked Louise.

Maddy shrugged, indifferent, and picked a cube of cucumber out of the salad. 'He's okay.' Then she thought for a moment, nibbling the edge of the cucumber like a hamster and added, 'Actually he's quite cool. He likes the Kings of Leon.'

Louise raised her eyebrows at Joanne. From what she could remember of being a teenager, that sounded like a pretty positive assessment.

'When are we going to eat?' asked Maddy, surveying the spread of food, her interest in Finn forgotten. 'I'm absolutely starving.'

'I think we all are, pet,' said Christine and Maddy went over and put her arm around her little grandma's shoulder. 'I must be shrinking,' chuckled Christine, 'or else you're growing!' and they all laughed.

Louise stood on the step just outside the patio door and called, 'Food's ready, everyone!'

The children made a stampede for the kitchen followed

more slowly by the adults. Dad brought up the rear and laid a hand on Louise's arm as he passed her. 'Thanks for doing all this for Sian and Andy. Your mum wanted to, but . . . well, we're past it now aren't we?'

Louise placed a hand on his forearm and squeezed it.

After they'd eaten, Louise brought out the wedding cake and laid it proudly on the table for everyone to see. It was a little lop-sided and the icing was starting to melt in the heat but she knew Sian and Andy wouldn't mind for it had been made with love. They stood at the end of the table with the cake in front of them, holding hands and laughing like two teenagers. Everyone crowded round and Oli cried, 'Let's sing Happy Birthday!'

They all laughed and Billy ruffled Oli's hair. 'It's not a birthday cake, son. It's a wedding cake.'

'No candles?' said Oli, his mouth open in astonishment.

Louise opened her mouth to speak but Sian, seeing Oli's devastated expression, spoke first. 'Oli's right. We do need candles. Louise, have you got some?'

Louise scurried off and came back a few moments later with some mismatched candles – they were all she could find – and a box of matches. Sian stuck a handful into the cake, lit them and Billy called out, 'Congratulations to Sian and Andy.'

Everyone cheered and Sian said, 'Let's all blow out the candles together, shall we?' and that's what they did.

The children blew air and spit all over the cake. The last flame went out and a tiny plume of black smoke rose from the charred wick. Sian, with Andy's hand over hers, pressed the knife into the soft icing and everyone cheered.

Later, when everyone had gone and the day was drawing to a close Louise slipped on a cotton cardigan and she, Kevin and Oli took a walk along to the marina, less than a hundred yards from the house. It was packed with dinghies, boats and yachts in all shapes and sizes and there, out at the end of the farthest right pier, was *Jenny-B*.

They strolled out to take a look at her and all was shipshape. Kevin stood behind Louise on the wooden wharf and she raised her face westward to catch the dying rays of the sun and sighed happily. Oli, on his knees, examined a spider's web he'd found stretched between the metal pile and the rope securing *Jenny-B*.

'I'm going to rename her,' said Kevin, resting his chin on Louise's shoulder.

'But isn't it bad luck to rename a boat?'

He laughed into the back of her neck, his breath hot and damp. 'Only if you don't do the renaming ceremony right. You have to appease Neptune and then the Gods of the winds – Boreas, Zephyrus, Eurus and Notus. The Gods of the North, West, East and South winds respectively.'

'And how do you go about doing that?' said Louise.

'With champagne.'

'What? You pour it into the sea?' said Louise, arching her back against him.

'That's right.'

'You're having me on.'

'No, honest. You pour champagne in the sea for Neptune and chuck it in the air for the four Gods of the winds. And there's an incantation you have to repeat while doing all this. It's a very serious business.'

Louise shook her head sceptically. 'Anyway, why do you want to rename her? *Jenny-B*'s a lovely name.'

'Because,' he said and his hand slipped round her waist and rested on her belly, which was only now starting to swell with new life, 'I want to name her after you, my darling.'

Louise opened her eyes.

'I want to call her *Lady Louise.*'

'*Lady Louise,*' she repeated and smiled. She placed her hand over his. 'I'd like that.'

She leant against him and they stood there wordlessly, listening to the peaceful sounds of the marina, the call of the terns, and Oli mumbling quietly to himself at their feet. And Louise knew then that this moment, this happiness, was what she had waited for all her life.

Read on for an exclusive reading guide to *Promise of Happiness*

Reading Group Questions

1. The title of the book *Promise of Happiness* reflects an important topic of today's society – what do you think is the author's message here in terms of where true happiness lies, and what other examples does she use to explore this theory?

2. Louise chooses Artificial Insemination to have her child. Explore the opinions of Louise's father, Joanne and Sian on this choice and how they develop and change throughout the book. Who do you identify most with?

3. When Louise arrives back in her home town, she receives varying levels of support from her family. Do you think there is a generational gap in terms of the disapproval that she finds?

4. How important is the father figure – is it better for a child to have an unreliable father like Phil, or no father at all? What are the repercussions that both Louise and Joanne's children experience throughout the novel as a result of their father figure, or lack of?

5. Did you feel that Joanne was at all to blame for the

breakdown of her marriage? Should she have given Phil any more attention and paid attention to his movements away from home?

6. Sian struggles with her fear of childbirth. Do you feel that phobias are something that can be treated? Looking forward, we see the seeds for Sian's recovery but is it something that you feel she could truly overcome?

7. Discuss the relationship between the sisters. What role do they provide for each other, and how does this change?

8. Louise had always hoped she would stay at home to support Oli until he was at the primary school age. Joanne, on the other hand, has always had to be a working mother. Which option do you think the book favours, and what are the pros and cons of both positions?

9. There is a strong eco theme in the novel which is particularly portrayed in the character of Sian. Discuss the pressures of over-population on the world – do you think it's irresponsible to have children?

10. The novel discusses the role of parenting primarily from a woman's point of view. Consider the differing sympathies in the portrayal of Andy and Kevin compared to Phil and Cameron. In what ways does the author identify with both sides of their stories?

Read on for an interview with Erin Kaye

In Conversation with Erin Kaye

1. *If you were stranded on a desert island, which book would you take with you?* *Jonathan Livingston Seagull* by Richard Bach – a celebration of everything wonderful about the human spirit. (Assuming this is like *Desert Island Discs* and I have the Bible, complete works of Shakespeare and the Encyclopaedia Britannica as well?)

2. *Where does your inspiration come from?* My childhood in Larne, where I grew up, for setting. And increasingly North Berwick, where I now live. Once I have my core idea or theme for a book, I then look around me for sub plots and details like occupations, character quirks etc. I love gossip and hearsay and local newspapers – all great inspiration.

3. *Have you always wanted to become a writer?* I came to writing fairly late at the age of thirty. As a child I had no burning ambition and left school not knowing what I wanted to do. I read Geography at Uni and went into banking because I wanted a secure, well-paid job.

4. *What's the strangest job you've ever had?* Writing. You sit alone in a room for months on end churning out a

story you've made up, in the hope that people will want to read it and someone will pay you for it!

5. *When you're not writing, what are your favourite things to do?* Spending time with my family and friends and doing active things like walking and swimming and water sports. And I'm quite a keen cook.

6. *What is a typical working day like for you? Have you ever had writer's block? If so, how did you cope with it?* My working hours are determined by school hours (I have two boys aged 11 and 8). I walk the dog first and settle down at my desk about 9.45 a.m. I usually spend 45 mins catching up on emails and admin, then work until 3ish with a short break for lunch. Once I'm in full flow with a book and a deadline's looming I also work nights and weekends and holidays. I don't usually get writer's block once I've got a synopsis written – I just get on with it and write every day, even though it's sometimes poor and gets scrapped later. I worry more about coming up with ideas for novels and can panic a bit when they don't come. Best to relax and not worry about it and they come when they're ready.

7. *Do you have any secret ambitions?* I'd like to learn to do one new thing every year. This year it was kayaking. Next year sailing.

8. *What can't you live without?* The internet and online shopping.

9. *When you were a child, what did you want to be when you grew up?* Rich. I thought financial security was the key to happiness. It's not – but it helps.

10. **Which five people, living or dead, would you invite to a dinner party?** My siblings (four actually). We live on three different continents and the last time we were all together was a quarter of a century ago.